Praise for *The Last Valley*

"*[The] Last Valley is a great read! I could not put it down. The main character is a hero and man of integrity! Imagine those two things together. Exactly what our world needs today... someone who loves Jesus and lives his beliefs, especially in the face of the world falling apart around him. Literally!*"

—David Garison, Minister
Spring, Texas

Samantha,
Thank you for all
the driving you did for
me. Hope you enjoy this
tale!

MT 6³³

Claire bit her lip for a moment, then asked, "Could we really be the only people left alive?"

The Last Valley – Book 1

Ashes to Ashes

by Samuel Ben White

First edition, January 2016

ISBN-13: 978-1523379682

ISBN-10: 1523379685

www.garisonfitch.com

For David & Gina Garison, who have lived in and fought for the last valley and showed the rest of us what victory looks like—both here and in the victory to come.

"What the?" several of us asked in unison as the ground shook beneath us.

Just one shake, strong enough to make us each grab for the nearest thing that might hold us upright—in my case, a tree.

Then nothing.

We all looked up. Since it was the ground that shook, looking up might seem to an outsider like a strange thing to do. We were back in the canyon, on the space once known as the Selkirk Campground, in the narrow valley below Boreas Pass. It wasn't a place that was given to the shakes under normal circumstances, but many of us had been in the canyon before when jet fighters out of The Springs had used the narrow mountain pass for training runs. Those always made the ground tremble and the air roar. This hadn't seemed at all like one of those events, but neither did it seem like anything else we had ever felt in that canyon before. So we looked up, perhaps for a new kind of jet.

It was my sister, Claire, who first spoke, "I didn't hear anything."

Several voices responded in query, to which she pointed out, "No plane, no boom like an explosion. Just the ground jumping."

We all commented in varying degrees of assent.

I looked at my wrist and then mentioned, "Huh. My watch stopped." I tapped it and nothing changed. Not having a functioning watch all of a sudden, I couldn't check the time, but I was pretty sure the battery shouldn't have died that early. So I checked my phone and, just as several other people nearby were discovering, learned that my phone was operating as well as the watch—which is to say: not at all.

Then, everyone who hadn't been checking their phones began to do so, only to find that they were all inoperable. Some of them turned on, but none of them could pick up a signal. We had heard of such things from our parents, of course, but none of us had ever experienced a true dead zone like that. We began discussing the matter as we moved closer to each other, wondering if it were a matter of a nearby tower being knocked out by whatever had made the ground jump. A couple in the party disabused that idea, pointing out that their phones weren't tower-dependent. In fact, none of our phones were, we soon realized. And we represented at least three different carriers.

Something had knocked out all the phone service in the valley.

"My watch is fine," said Aunt Jenny, holding it up for us all to see. It was just a plain old digital watch, the kind one could get for next to nothing at any store in town. I wasn't actually related to Jenny Malone, but everyone who knew her called her Aunt Jenny because that was how she had been introduced to us by one of her many relations. She tended to send Christmas cards to everyone (I and my sister would receive separate ones, for instance) and they were always signed "Aunt Jenny".

"Mine, too," said Mister Glass, a white-haired neighbor who was working with us. His watch was a slightly-more-expensive model than what Aunt Jenny wore, but no more technologically advanced.

"So all the phones and smart watches are gone," someone— I think it was my little sister—commented. "Grampa always said this day would come," she added with a rueful laugh.

Out of curiosity, I went over and started the pick-up truck, commenting unnecessarily over the noise of the ancient (and often persnickety) engine, "Truck works."

It was late in the afternoon, so there were no lights to be seen anywhere—though, back in the canyon like that, it was unlikely we would have seen any lights even in the middle of the night. We hadn't been playing any kind of music—owing to a general disagreement earlier about what kind to play—and all the tools we had been using were shovels, rakes and axes. As if in continuation of my pick-up experiment, Mister Glass fired up one of the chain-saws—brought along but unused to that point in the day. It took three pulls to start it, but that was neither better nor worse than usual, for it had been known to take as many as five on cold mornings.

In short, we had only two clues that something was amiss: a one-time shaking of the earth and absent electronics.

And then the sky began to go dark.

Chapter One

I came home forever.
~Charles Lamb

My father had always dreamed of going to college but, other than a few night and on-line courses here and there, he never made it. There was always something that kept him from it, including some of his own choices.

It was his dream, then, that all his kids go to college. My brother was already there and my sister and I, though still in high school, had been applying to colleges since at least our sophomore years. In my case, it was sort of against my will.

It wasn't that I had anything against college, I just didn't have any use for it, yet. Maybe because it had always been impressed on me that I *should* go, it had come to be something to resent. Maybe I'm just a contrarian.

So I would mention to my father every now and then that I might like to join the military after high school. I wasn't really interested in the military, but I was more interested in it than in college. I had an uncle that had been in the Air Force and a cousin who had joined the Marines a couple years before and both of those branches seemed like passable options to me. I didn't really know much about the Army—other than movies—and figured I was too much of a land-lubber to even consider the Navy. My father had no more against the military than I had against college, but he was so set on college for his kids that the only way he would hear of me joining the military would be for me to get a degree first, then enter as an officer.

I sometimes thought my father would have let me take up a life of crime or politics, just so long as I went to college first. I said as much once and he laughed like it was a good joke, but I think he considered it for a moment. In consequence of my father's desire and in no way part of mine, I was registered to start college at the University of Northern Colorado in about three weeks. I had even been to freshman orientation and, while I didn't hate it, I still had no desire to go to college other than that I had read that girls outnumbered guys there at a rate of about 60-40. And the girls I had seen at freshman orientation had driven my interest up a little bit. But only a little bit, for I also realized that, being a freshman, I had little chance with all those girls because there had been junior and senior men waiting at the doors with rings in their pockets and pre-nups in hand. To meet a girl, then, I was going to have to wait a year or two and wait for a new herd to be brought in.

G.K. Chesteron once wrote "There are two ways of getting home; and one of them is just to stay there." That was what I wanted to do. I didn't mind travel and I don't think I was afraid of the outside world in any way, but what I wanted to do more than anything was just stay home and work the ranch. Shoot, it had occurred to me more than once, "how about I stay home and run the ranch and my father go off to college?" It seemed like that would have made both of us happy. I think he gave it some thought when I mentioned it to him, but he still wanted me to go, while I was young, before anything could get in the way.

In consequence, I was registered for college—having been accepted to the University of Northern Colorado in Greeley without problem as I had always carried pretty good grades—and there I was going to study animal husbandry. (It was also my thought to try to "walk-on" to the baseball team, but I hadn't mentioned that to my father for fear he would consider it a distraction from "our" overall goal.) With any luck, I figured to graduate in four to five years then come back and run the ranch. It wasn't that I thought I already knew it all, but despite his lack of college education I figured my father **did** and that spending those college years learning from him would be every bit as productive as going off to college.

Still, there were advantages to going to college that even I saw. Besides the off-chance that I might procure an education, there were those girls. Lots of girls. Where we lived, there was an extremely limited selection of girls. And, other than my sister, every girl I knew in the valley had one overriding factor in common: a complete disinterest in me. UNC had several thousand girls, so surely they wouldn't all be disinterested in me. So if nothing else, I

10

figured college could help me find a wife. If a degree got thrown in, so much the better.

Five years before, we had experienced the culmination of the worst drought in the state's history. The scientists said it had something to with a confluence of Pacific weather patterns unlike any ever seen before; the less scientific blamed each other; but those of us who were living through it just knew it was dry. As a ranch, we had to sell off almost all our stock, just to stay alive. On a personal level, we learned to conserve water like never before—which is saying something, for ours has always been an area that, even in wetter years, could experience a tightening of the available water just about every summer.

My great-grandfather had been one of the pioneers of water conservation in our area of the mountains, building the maximum legal amount of holding tanks and installing water-conscious plumbing in all our buildings. I used to hear stories about how he had hated the early "low-flow" toilets and had invented on his own one that both conserved water and actually disposed of waste. He patented the design and later sold it for a considerable amount of money, money which kept the ranch going in some lean years and still provided us a little bit of income decades on.

Still, that five-year drought had been something else. We were all reduced to taking extremely short showers, and only on every third day. My sister was embarrassed to go to school on non-shower days, but she eventually came to realize that all the other students were in the same dry boat. Over time, we all came around to the idea that our school just, literally, stunk. We tried to think of ways to use that to our advantage in sports, but most of the towns we played were just as dry, sweaty and smelly as we were.

Four years ago, or one year after the worst drought in state history peaked, came the forest fires. The winter snowfall had been a little—just a little—better than the previous year, and the spring had some rains like we hadn't had in a couple years, but with the rains came lightning. Lightning and dry trees were not a good combination and, of course, we didn't have the water reserves to fight the fires. In any year, our state would have at least one forest fire somewhere, in bad years there would be five or six. That year, there were twenty-four fires *at one time* during a stretch in August and, statewide, more than a hundred forest fires in total. Everyone from the politicians to the environmentalists railed against it all and pointed fingers, but there was just little that could be done except get out of the way. Many people just left the state entirely—some by choice, some because their homes or businesses were destroyed and some because they just saw no future in staying. So many people departed that we actually lost a congressional seat.

The news was saying that the state lost over a fourth of all its forested lands to fire, but my brother and father both quoted sources who said the number was closer to a third. And there was not a single forest in the state that had not been touched.

I could believe either number, for fires had ravaged our lands and all the forests I could see. If someone had told me that half the forests had been burned or even three-quarters, I would have believed them, for all the forests I could see were burned, some—like the one right behind our house—gone entirely.

North and west of our property there had been a little valley below Boreas Pass that had once been filled with mining camps. The gold and silver had played out, but the beauty of the valley had attracted campers over the years so the state had built a couple "primitive" campgrounds, the kind without running water or electricity, just picnic tables and a marked off spot where you could park an RV or pitch a tent. Between the campgrounds, people had built weekend homes—some of pretty fair size and others that were no more than a place to put a bed and maybe a fridge. Some of them were very nice, but some of them did not meet any known building codes and would not have survived an inspection.

The campgrounds and better than ninety percent of the houses in the area we called the Selkirk (after the Selkirk Campground) had been destroyed by fire. The insurance companies, I heard, weren't inclined to pay people to rebuild in the valley, so only a couple families even tried. The building was slow because resources were stiff all over the state and running new water and sewer lines to some out-of-the-way valley was not on the priority list. As a consequence, the valley stayed empty even after the drought and fires ended.

The year after the fires, the winter snow was the best we had seen in ten years. This made the ski areas happy and brought in tourists who had skipped the area the last few years, but panicked the rest of us because we began to anticipate the spring thaw.

It was worse than we had imagined. Worse than I had imagined, anyway. I think my father had pegged it pretty well.

Those Pacific weather patterns had made some sort of adjustment that led to great skiing … and voluminous spring rains. A decade before, such a winter and following rains would have been met with cheers of joy and even popping champagne. Back in those days, however, we had trees and undergrowth that could absorb the water and slow its travel downhill. That spring, we had burned-out hillsides, dead trees that looked like charcoal, and nothing at all to stop the water. Soon, we had nothing but flowing mud. I happened to be looking one day as it appeared that a square mile of Mt. Volsh just slid off and went downhill with the water. The Tarryall was clogged for several days and a small lake formed, but then the water broke through and more mud went downstream.

The houses that had survived the fires were wiped out by the mud slides. Every one of them. I'm not sure how bad it was in the rest of the state, but every single one of those houses up in the Selkirk area that had survived the fires was washed away by the mud. One, we never even found again, though we had all seen it standing proud after the fire. After the mud, there wasn't even a spot on the mountain where the foundation had been. Somewhere downstream, I imagined, there were enough house parts to build a whole new town, if a fellow could gather them.

We had saved all but one of the buildings of our ranch, losing only an old barn that had been kept for no reason other than that it looked rather picturesque sitting near the Tarryall. It had made it through more than a hundred years of ranch life, and all the fires, but when the mud came through, it took our barn on a ride that ended about three miles downstream, out on the plains east of town. The fires had crept close to our main ranch buildings, and the mud had pushed up to the edge of the house where I grew up, but overall we had come out pretty well.

My father tried to get a lease to run some horses on the Selkirk lands, as the grass had come back over the mud pretty quickly, but the courts couldn't decide who owned it. Still, some of us—my family, some others from around the valley—started going up into the Selkirk and cleaning things up. Officially, we were up there (and the authorities were letting us be up there) so that we could replant some trees to try and fight future mud slides and reclaim the Tarryall, but I think we were up there—I was, anyway—because it was such a lonely spot. Even on days when there were fifty people up in the valley, planting trees and laying out sod and running heavy equipment, it seemed like we were the only fifty people in the world. No high wires, no sound from nearby roads (for large sections of the Boreas Pass road had been reduced to a barely-passable track and the state's plans to repair it lagged somewhere behind the plumbing issues of a few paragraphs back). Just us.

In two years' time, we had made a lot of progress. It didn't look like it used to back in there, and probably never would in our lifetimes, we figured, but there was definite and visible progress. Thousands of tiny pine and aspen trees had been set out—many donated by people from all over the west, but many purchased out of the savings of us locals. Grass seed had been sprinkled liberally about and, as mentioned, some sod had been placed in areas where we thought it would do the most good. When most of the sod held after the first winter's snow and following spring rains, we felt like we had a handle on how to do it for the next summer.

On evenings and weekends, the summer after the worst of the fires, a fair crowd of valley locals could be found on the Selkirk or back up on the Elkhorn (across the valley) or in a dozen other spots about the South Park, planting trees and taking care of the land. Thanks to stories in the national media, we even had people driving up from the flatlands or even other states to help us. It was hard work and, often, the only accommodations we could provide was a place to pitch a tent, but people loved to come. A fellow down by Salida tried to make some money off a project he called "The Great American Re-Planting" or something like that, but I think he

14

got run out of town. There may have been some people somewhere who made a profit off the mess—maybe the people who sold the trees and sod—but I never got an idea they were overcharging us and didn't begrudge them their capitalism.

It became something of an extended picnic for many of us. We'd bring sandwiches and even grills and sometimes, after the work was done, we'd get up a volleyball game in one of the rare flat spaces or even (don't tell the authorities) sit around a campfire while someone played the guitar. Maybe it was this overwhelming spirit of conviviality that kept me from wanting to attend college in the fall. No, that's probably not it. But it was a contributing factor. I was already figuring the projects I wanted to undertake when home the next summer … and secretly hoping something would keep me from college in the fall so I could just stay and work right through.

Before the wrong impression is given, or given too strongly, I should point out that it wasn't as if the entire valley full of people were donating all their spare time to the repopulating of our burned forests. Many people gave much time, but for most people it was an evening now and then, or maybe one Saturday a month. I was probably the only person out there six and seven days a week—after doing my chores at the ranch.

Nor should you get the idea that I was some idealistically hardworking young man out to reclaim the mountains for posterity. I wanted to do some good, and I've generally always been a hard worker, but I think I was out there because—as stated earlier—I saw it to be my last summer. Soon, college and life and everything else were going to crowd me out of the valley where I had grown up. As stated: I planned to come back. But in my mind I knew that even if I did make it back, and even if I took over the ranch from my father, it was going to be at least four years in the future, and possibly longer because I knew my brother had been in college for four years and still had one to go. I think I felt like, deep down in my soul somewhere, I had to get as much done *that summer* as I could, before the chance passed me by.

In consequence, I was given a modicum of respect and deference by most everyone else who worked on the area around Selkirk due to my experience in the matters at hand. As an eighteen-year-old, it was intoxicating to have my opinions valued like that, which was another reason why I was out there so often, though I probably wouldn't have admitted it to anyone even if asked. Still, there was something about having grown people—in some cases relatives and in other cases just grown-ups I had known all my life—coming to me with questions about how to do some thing or another or where we should plant or how we should plow. To say I was getting a big head would not be inaccurate but I must have kept it just enough in check that they hadn't run me off the work crews and did, indeed, still come to me for my thoughts.

I wasn't just someone whose knowledge was the result of luck, either. Even before the recent horrible drought, our family's land had been through some weather. Over the generations, we had learned how to take care of our resources pretty well, surviving and sometimes thriving through dry, wet, snowy, cold and—even though most of our lands were above ten thousand feet—even some hot summer days. The reason we hadn't lost everything to either the drought or the fires was the lessons learned about terracing, water run-off, fire breaks and a hundred other little tips we had passed down from generation to generation. Those things had been ingrained in myself and my siblings as early as we could walk around, following our father over the ranch. I wouldn't have been surprised to learn that he had been teaching those things to us when he carried us, or even when we were still in the womb.

They say it had all started with the founder of our family line and the man who had first run the ranch I grew up on. A cowboy from Texas, he had drifted north until settling in the mountains as just another hired hand on a small ranch. Over the years, he had not only taken control of the ranch, but improved it— both financially and environmentally. People who knew him said he was a Bible-reading man and while he liked turning a profit, also considered it his sacred duty to take care of the land and turn over to his children a better place than what he had found. The years had gone by—pretty slowly, some said—but each successive generation had tried to follow that lead.

So maybe I was up there every weekend and most evenings taking care of land that wasn't mine because to do so was borne into me.

Chapter Two

I don't know
Where I'm a-gonna go
When the volcano blows.
~Jimmy Buffet

On those occasions when we went anywhere—like down into Texas to visit our distant cousins or, once, to Tennessee—when we told people we were from Como, Colorado, they would inevitably ask, "Where's that?"

My mother's standard answer, which I came to adapt and use as my own, was, "Make an equal-sided triangle of Denver and Colorado Springs and Como would be the third point, to the west." Maybe that wasn't exactly accurate, but it got people close enough that they could find our little town on a map. If they could find the town, we'd just tell them we were a mile west of that little dot, snuggled up against the hills. Como was, officially, 9796 feet above sea level and our ranch was about four hundred feet higher than that. The ranch house, anyway, though some portions of our ranch were a little lower than the town. And some portions of our ranch were almost to the eleven thousand foot mark.

It was a pretty place, with pine trees and aspens and rolling hills and all surrounded by mountains. People had been running cattle and horses on the land for three centuries—that we knew of for sure—and the Utes and Cheyenne had lived on the land for centuries before that. Before them? Who knew? I would wager that whoever they were, they picked the spot for its beauty—beyond any considerations like defensibility or the like. It had plenty of water—if you used it wisely—but much of it was in underground aquifers, so the Indians probably hadn't tapped into it.

To the south of our ranch a few miles, there were some natural salt flats, which might have also been a draw for the region. Those saltwater flats were also the reason for one of the area's nicknames: The Bayou Salado. Not exactly French, and not exact Spanish, the best translation would be "Saltwater Swamp". Still, in the days when salt was what enabled people to ship meat by rail, it was those salt flats that kept a lot of the people in our valley employed. Eventually, easier ways to mine and transport salt, as well as refrigerated cars for transporting meat, put the salt works out of business. Yet, two hundred years later, there were locals who called the valley the Bayou Salado who neither knew what it meant or even where the salt works had been located.

The wind had started picking up shortly after the ground jumped, but I don't think we really noticed it—I didn't, anyway—until the sky started to go dark. No one panicked, as sudden storms had blown in before on everyone who lived in the mountains. All of us, even those people from the flatlands who were just up and helping for the weekend, had a story or two about being out in the mountains on a sunny day when a storm had rolled in so quickly and so fiercely that you were out of breath and soaked before even having a chance to comment.

This didn't look like one of our normal summer squalls, though. This was a wall of black descending on us like something out of the dust bowl era. Claire happened to spot it first, mumbled something unintelligible but alarming, and pointed. We all turned and several other sounds, many of them intelligible but better left unprinted, escaped our lips.

We were above ten thousand feet and the black, roiling wall that rushed toward us was that tall again, it appeared. Some said later it was a grey wall, but the sun had just begun a-westering and backlit the whole thing, making it appear black to me. Whatever color, it soon bathed us all in its dark shadow, and then it bathed us in darkness itself. A darkness you could literally taste, for it coated our tongues and nostrils and, it seemed to me, rapidly filled the lungs.

It was ash.

Those of us who lived in the mountains during the fires had experienced ash before. I could remember being outside, playing catch with my brother by the light over the door of the barn, while a wildfire blazed twenty miles away and the flakes of ash in the cone of light looked like snow. When it first happened, we were all a little wary of breathing it in, but after a while we stopped caring, though some people wore those paper masks like you see at hospitals. My mother thought we should all do that, but even she only wore hers for about two days before ditching it.

The wall that crossed the great divide and descended upon us in the Selkirk that day was ash, but it only took us seconds to realize it was not from any run of the mill wildfire. Someone muttered something like, "They must've nuked Denver!" but even I knew the wall was coming from the wrong direction for that. And it wasn't hot ash, it was cold, as if it had been carried to great altitude before coming our way.

The day was warm, though, so the thought of fall-out occurred to us all, making us flinch from the flakes as if they were hot. There were forty-something people in our work crew that day and most started making for the vehicles, holding hands with others so as not to get separated in the quickening darkness. Some swooned, many screamed, and we all showed varying levels of panic—from continued screaming, to being rooted in place, to (as in my case) running for the vehicles without thought to anyone else. I was interrupted from my selfishness by almost running over my sister. I helped her into our pickup truck's cab, then started looking around to see who else I needed to help.

The problem was: I couldn't see much of anything.

Holding my arm over my mouth and nose, as if that might help when early evidence said it didn't, I stumbled around for a bit before becoming disoriented and, blessedly, running into my own truck. With the last of my senses about to depart, I scrambled to the door and climbed in, thinking only of myself. Claire—who was already inside the truck—screamed, but when I told her it was me, she threw her arms around me and began to sob, asking plaintively, "What is it, Josh? Is the whole mountain on fire?"

"I don't know," I replied, barely able to get the words out with my breath coming as it was in ragged gasps. I couldn't tell if the air were really that bad or just looked bad, but my lungs were taking their cues more from my eyes than my brain or the air itself and, so, were *feeling* clogged.

I knew there were other people out there and part of my brain said I ought to try and find them, but I was frozen in the cab.

The other half of my mind wanted to blame it on my sister and a need to take care of her, a part of me said I was just chicken, but I honestly think it was the rational part of my brain that said wandering around in that mess was nothing more than suicide. So I held onto my sister as the dark thickened around us and the truck rocked in the wind.

I tried listening for other voices, but I could hear nothing over the moan of the wind. It wasn't the loudest wind I had ever experienced, but it was constant and—pretty soon—my brain had shut off almost all auditory perception. I zeroed in on the sound of Claire's breathing, realizing she had stopped crying but still clung tightly to me. I thought about making some crack about how she was cutting off the circulation in my chest, but realized I was holding just as tightly to her.

"Do you think this hit Mom and Dad?" she asked. They had gone into town for a date night and weren't expected back until late. I pulled out my phone, hoping it had come back to life, but it was still just a very light paperweight. Claire looked at hers and found the same result.

"I would imagine so," I said in reply to her query. They were twenty something miles away or so, and in a different part of the valley, so it was possible the wall of ash had missed them, though I was pretty sure they would have seen it from where they were. That made me pause, for I figured their first concern was for Claire and I, though maybe they wouldn't be too worried, not knowing what it was that was hitting us or how strong it was. I hoped they wouldn't try to come and find us until it had passed for there was no way they could safely drive to us. I hadn't tried to drive Claire and I out of there because I had no confidence in being able to see the road—which wasn't a great road under the best of circumstances, as I could well attest after having knocked the oil pan off the truck earlier in the summer on a perfectly clear day.

We sat there expecting the wall of dust and ash to pass on over in a matter of minutes, but it didn't. When a good fifteen minutes had passed and I noticed the fine layer of ash forming inside the truck, I grabbed some facial tissues and told Claire to hold one over her mouth and nose. I did the same while digging around under the seat and finding an old sweatshirt I had shoved down there one morning when it had been cold enough at the start of the day to merit wearing one. Drawing my knife, I cut off the sleeves, then split them open and beckoned Claire to follow my lead and tie the cloth on like a bandana. It was stuffy, but I felt like it provided us a little protection. It probably looked ridiculous, but in the limited light it was hard to tell.

Our next priority was going to be water, but I wasn't too worried. There was most of a case of bottled water in the back of the truck and I was counting on grabbing us each a bottle as soon as the wind let up. If it didn't soon, I told myself, I could hold onto the side of the truck and feel my way to a couple bottles and then back to the cab.

Of course, once that thought was in my mind, the thirstier I became. When it didn't seem like the wind was letting up—even though it was only a few minutes since the thought entered my head—I turned to Claire and said, shouting above the moan of the wind, "I'm going to get us some water!"

"Don't leave—" she implored.

"There's some in the back of the truck. I'll hold onto the side the whole time."

"Tap."

"No, bottled."

I could hear the smile in her voice as she said, "Tap on the side of the truck so I can hear you and know where you are."

"Um, sure," I nodded. Then, I surprised myself for it was something I had never said before, "Say a prayer."

She nodded and watched fearfully as I opened the driver's door and slid carefully into the wind.

I shut the door to keep as much of the ash away from Claire as possible and slapped at the side of the truck as I made my way toward the back. I knew I needed to only travel five feet at most, but with the high winds and the ash and all, it seemed like a mile at least. I reached over the side of the truck bed and felt the case of water. Tapping a couple more times, I leaned in and picked up the whole case. I couldn't tap as I made my way back to the front, but I kept one elbow pressed against the truck so that I could tell where it was. I felt the indentation of the door handle sooner than I expected and held the case of water against my hip with one hand as I opened the door with the other. I slid the case into the seat, followed it, then shut the door.

I turned on the dome light just long enough to assure us both that we were together in the cab, then turned it back off. "Have some water," I said, though I could hear her opening one already. I put the rest of the case in the back of the cab, a space that the manufacturer claimed was for two passengers but was too tight for human consumption.

"I guess we should be sparing," she mumbled. "Just in case."

"Yeah, you're right," I replied. I had a large serving in my mouth but realized the wisdom of her words and took my time swallowing it. Meanwhile, I quickly screwed the cap back on.

Chapter Three

All the brothers were valiant,
And all the sisters virtuous.
~Inscription on the tomb of the Duchess of Newcastle

Our family were all big readers. My mother, she loved to read autobiographies about famous and infamous people. If some famous personage were mentioned in school and I didn't know who the teacher was talking about, I could ask Mom and she usually knew. She usually knew more about the famous person than the teacher did, and could impart way more info than I was interested in. Of course, things being how they became, I wished I had listened better. Not that having listened better would help us in our post-ash world, but having my mother's words in my brain would have been a comfort.

My father liked to read, but it was more of the "short-reading" variety. He subscribed to every on-line or print horse journal known to man, many about cattle even when we weren't running any, and read them all straight through. Especially good or intriguing articles, he would pass on to us kids. I think I was the only one who ever read his recommendations, though Claire might have skimmed them on occasion. I don't think this either irritated or surprised Dad, for he knew which of his progeny was planning on being involved in ranch life and which were not.

Rusty liked to read, but maybe not as much as the rest of us. As a boy, Rusty had been a big fan of comic books. As he grew into the teenage years, he became fascinated by the adventure stories of the twentieth century. He loved what were once known as "pulps" and kid-friendly stories like "The Hardy Boys". He had a few he had picked up in actual book form, and an on-line collection that was pretty extensive. He liked going on-line with other aficionados and discussing the ins and outs of characters that only a few people had even heard of. When I was razzing him once, he told me it was the twentieth century's version of the old Greek myths. He would tell me some of the stories, in brief form, and I could enjoy the telling, but when it came to reading them the bug never bit me.

Claire liked to read, though it had to be under perfect circumstance: in her room, curled up on the bed, light just right. Then, she would read anything, providing no one else in the family were reading anything like it. I once knew her to read an entire volume about cooking without gluten just because she knew no one in our family was allergic to gluten.

Clair was seventeen years old that summer. Middling height, thin figure, shoulder-length hair somewhere between brown and blonde, brown eyes, but my friends said she had a pretty face. She was my sister and I loved her, but I wouldn't have said she was pretty. I wouldn't have said she was ugly, either. She was my sister. (I had a cousin that made it to the finals in the state beauty pageant but it was hard for me to think of her as pretty since we were related.)

Claire and I had always spent a lot of time together. A year younger than me, she had followed me everywhere as a child—whether I wanted her to or not. I had eventually gotten used to her, for the most part, and had even come to enjoy her company most of the time. We squabbled now and then, but overall got along pretty well. Once in school, we had our separate friends and mostly went different directions, but we still got along pretty well. People always said we looked like brother and sister (same general features of hair and eyes) and we sometimes got compliments for not acting like siblings, which I took as a reference to the fact that we weren't the kind who picked on each other.

Who Claire didn't get along with was our mother. Mom was a throwback woman in many ways, and some say it was after her that I took, at least in so far as we were both happiest at home. Mom wore dresses or skirts at all times and loved to cook and homemake. She would have fit in well in a previous century when women stayed home and had other women over for teas. Mom actually did that. She volunteered with the PTA and led a women's Bible study at church and kept a garden and—like me—didn't seem to mind if she never left the valley. I had tried to learn how to cook and, while I could read the directions, I had no flair for it. I couldn't sew, but I was something of a homebody. I didn't just stay in the house—was rarely in the house for anything other than sleep, in fact—but neither did I travel far afield. I could almost always be found on the ranch, or riding our horses on nearby property.

Claire was not really a tomboy, but she loved wearing jeans and shorts and only wore a skirt for very rare, very special, occasions. Claire would take it in her mind to cook once in a while, and did quite well at it, but it wasn't a passion for her. She hung out with other girls her age, but still liked to get out there with her two older brothers and throw the football or baseball around.

And Claire couldn't wait to get out of the valley. She was going to go to college and then she was going to set the world on fire. Or just live in a house on the beach somewhere, or maybe even write software out of a loft in the city. Maybe she was going to do all those things. Whatever she did, though, it was going to be away from the house where we had grown up and, more specifically, away from Mom.

I know Claire loved our mother, but they were just one of those mother-daughter pairs who were always going to be at odds. If Mom said "red", Claire said "blue". If Mom wanted to go left, Claire wanted to go right. If Mom said, "Yes," Claire said, "Why?" Dad had tried to intervene over the years and had even sent them to counseling, but to no avail. Mom and Claire were oil and water. Myself, Dad and Rusty could only watch and, occasionally, try to defuse the bombs.

And this had been only the second day all summer that she had come up to the Selkirk to help out. Her thing was horses and she spent most of her spare time helping our father with the horses. When she talked about going away and leaving the ranch for good, I had no trouble believing she could leave us behind, but I wondered if she could leave the horses. She was an excellent rider and knew as much about horse-care as anyone on the ranch, but she was so determined to leave that I half expected her to find some way to take at least one horse with her even if she went to a college that was downtown in some major city.

You can only live in panic so long. Eventually, you have a nervous breakdown or you wear out. Claire and I just wore out. It had been about six o'clock in the evening when the wall of ash descended on us and minute after minute, then hour after hour, of sitting in a darkened pick-up truck, clinging to your sibling for dear life, while outside the wind moans and nothing is visible takes its toll. Throw in that we were already tired from an afternoon of work and, somewhere in there, we fell asleep. Or my brain shut off, which was a lot like sleep.

I remember having the momentary thought that I probably wouldn't wake up. I pictured the ash covering the truck until every crack was full and the air was used up. I fell asleep picturing our parents crying one day as they got word from the Forestry Service or someone like that, saying that a pick-up with the remains of their two youngest was found buried under a mountain of ash. I look back now and am a little surprised that I fell asleep under those conditions, but at the time there just wasn't anything else to do.

"Josh," a voice whispered in my ear. I hoped it was my mother, waking me up in my own bed, the events of the day before just a dream.

"Josh," repeated Claire, a little more loudly. "I can see."

"Hmm?" I asked, trying to wake up and realizing just how uncomfortable sleeping upright in a pick-up truck can be. I finally got my eyes to open and realized Claire was right: we could see, if dimly.

The wind was still blowing a hefty breeze, but the cloud of ash had dispersed enough that we could actually see a little of what was outside. It was a weird light, though, and it took me a few more moments before I realized that what I could see was because the moon had broken through a gap in the clouds—whether clouds of water vapor or of ash I couldn't tell at that moment in time.

As my brain came into focus with my eyes, I realized that part of why we could see—even by the light of a not-full moon—was because the moonlight was reflecting off the light-gray coat of ash that covered everything. It wasn't quite like moonlight on snow, but it was a little brighter than if it had just been shining on the dirt. "Wonder what time it is?" I mumbled.

"Middle of the night, looks like," Claire responded. "We must have slept several hours."

"I'm just glad to wake up," I told her. She cast me a strange look, but didn't ask me to explain.

"Think we can drive home now?"

"Maybe. I can see the road, anyway. Wonder if we ought to check and see if everyone made it to safety, though?"

Claire looked like she was about to say something in response to that, then pursed her lips and nodded, saying, "You're right." She pulled a flashlight out of the glove box and checked to make sure it worked. She started to reach for the door, then gave me an ironic smile as she gestured with the flashlight, "Why didn't we remember this earlier?"

"Just geniuses, I guess," I replied with a shrug.

The wind was blowing, yet not really high like it had been when I had gone after the bottled water. Still, as soon as we were outside and next to each other, Claire took my hand as she swept the area with the flashlight in her other hand. If memory served, the last time she had held my hand for anything other than a family prayer was when we were both pre-school age and Mom had made us hold hands while we crossed the street. It was a strange sensation and not particularly comforting to me, but maybe it was to her. Just as I thought that, she gave my hand a reassuring squeeze, then let go.

The ash beneath our feet stirred up with each step, making us cough even though the makeshift bandanas were still in place, and then making us go slower so as not to stir so much up. It wasn't deep—perhaps no more than a half-inch to an inch in most places—but it was pervasive. The wind kept ash in the air, but another glance up at the moon showed me that we were in a sort of trough where "new ash" (like new snow) didn't seem to be falling. The ash in the air seemed to have just been stirred up from the ground or been blown off the ridge that hung above us to the west. To the north and south, on either side of the gash in the sky, it looked like the ash still roiled.

We walked nervously over to where the flashlight showed us a lump under the ash. Claire held back a step but curiosity forced me to close the distance and kneel down, even though the shape beneath the ash was pretty clear. I reached out gingerly and brushed the ash away, hoping I would startle whoever it was awake.

The body was cold beneath the ash.

"Can you tell who it is?" Claire asked, coming a half-step closer.

"Annie Meyers," I replied, then wishing I had a way to cover her face back up with a blanket, or the ash. A muffled sob escaped Claire's lips.

"If we had … " Claire mumbled.

"Yeah. *If* we had known, and *if* we could have found her, and *if* we could have brought her into the truck—"

"You don't care that she's—she's dead?"

"Of course I care. And I will spend the rest of my life telling myself I should have seen her and picked her up but I'll also spend my life knowing there's nothing I can do to change the past."

"Why are you so cold?"

I stood up and responded angrily, "Cold? Claire, look around you. There are at least three other lumps in the ash about the same size as this one was. I'm not cold, I'm … I'm scared to death!" I was a little surprised at my ability to say it out loud, but once having said it, I knew it was true.

She came over and, putting an arm around me, offered, "Maybe someone else made it to a vehicle." I nodded and we began to gently step towards the nearest vehicle, an old van owned by Mister Glass.

I pounded on the side of the van and was both startled and relieved to hear a response. The side door of the van slid open and Mister Glass stuck his ash-covered and bespectacled face out into the wind. "Josh? And Claire. How have you survived this long?"

"We were in our truck," I replied. Claire shined the light into van as I asked, "Did anyone else make it through with you?"

"There are five of us," Mister Glass replied, stepping outside and looking up in apparent surprise at the moon. "I think the others are asleep, but I haven't slept a *wink*. Anyone else make it?"

"We don't know, yet. We know that, um, Mrs. Meyers didn't."

Mister Glass swore lowly, then said, "I got a couple lights. Let's see if we can find anyone else."

Howard Glass was a semi-retired electrician from Kansas who had come to the mountains with his wife a decade before. She had died of cancer a couple years after they arrived. He always talked about going back to Kansas, but he also talked about how much he loved the mountains. When he lost his house to one of the fires, we all figured that would be his signal to head back to the flatlands. Instead, he had lived in a trailer while rebuilding and spent many weekends helping with one of the valley's replanting projects. He still spoke fondly of Kansas, but never mentioned going back there anymore.

Mister Glass picked up one flashlight from the floor of the van, gave his other to Aunt Jenny, and then we began to walk to the other vehicles that had been parked along the road. We spread out a little, but stayed within sight of each other's lights. Personally, I kept a hand on Claire's shoulder, telling myself it was for her comfort and safety but knowing it was mostly for my own peace of mind.

The other lumps were just that: lumps, which was an extreme relief. It seemed that everyone from our work party except Annie Meyers had made it into a vehicle. While some people were still having trouble breathing, they were all still alive. As word went around, people began to point fingers in regards to Annie Meyers. Why hadn't anyone helped her to a car? Why hadn't anyone looked for her?

"Wait," Claire interrupted. "How did Annie get here?" Several people grumbled in reply, but Claire stood firm and asked, "All of the rest of us scrambled for the vehicle we came in, right? Who did Annie ride with to get here?"

At varying speeds, we all came to the idea that Claire's question was a good one. We didn't immediately have an answer until someone declared, "The Roxons!" As several people, me included, said something interrogative as to what the speaker meant, he (Freddy Wilson) said, "The Roxons were working with us earlier today. Were they still here when the storm hit or had they already left?"

Everyone spoke but no one could remember when the Roxon brothers left, whether Annie might have come with them, or whether she was friendly enough to have ridden with them in the first place. A couple people said they thought they had heard a car moving along the dirt road in the early moments of the storm, but they weren't for certain and other people were sure they *hadn't* heard a vehicle. Someone said, loudly, that it would be just like the Roxon brothers to run off and leave poor Annie to die as they took care of their own skin. Others argued that the Roxons wouldn't have done that. I stayed silent, remembering how my own moment of selfish panic had only been thwarted by the happy accident of my sister beating me to the truck. I said a prayer of thanks in my mind that I had found her, for if I hadn't, she might have suffered Annie Meyers' fate.

Someone said something about how it must be one whale of a forest fire, to be interrupted by Danica Frowley, who said in a tone that brooked no argument, "This is volcanic" as she rubbed (apparently) ash between her fingers.

Someone objected, "We don't have volcanoes around here!"

Danica happened to be looking at me as she said, "I didn't say it was around here. It could have come from a hundred miles away, or a thousand. But no forest fire is going to produce this amount of ash—look at the places we've been working these last couple years. Somewhere, maybe Capulin down in New Mexico or Krakatoa in Hawaii or one of the Alaskan volcanoes or— somewhere, a volcano blew."

"This came from the west," Mister Glass pointed out. "Does that mean it was Alaska?"

"There are volcanoes all along the Pacific rim," Danica told him. Danica Frowley was a banker from nearby Fairplay who loved to hike in the woods. In her mid-thirties and fairly attractive with her flawless dark skin and lithe frame, I had heard more than one person wonder why she had never married. I had gotten to know her a little on these weekend work parties, but not well enough to have any sort of answer for that question. I had a guess that she was married to her work, but that might have just been nothing more than a guess. "And just because we saw the ash coming from the west doesn't mean the volcano is in that direction. Did you see how high that wall of ash was? I think it came from the west, too, but at that altitude, the winds can blow differently than—" She shook her head and said, "That's neither here nor there. I can't tell you where the volcano is, but I can tell you this much ash has to be volcanic."

Since she seemed to know what she was talking about, and as none of us had any better ideas (and agreed with her assessment that this level of ash was beyond any of the fires we had seen in past years), we all turned to her as our authority. "How bad?" Claire asked, receiving nods of agreement from many of us.

Danica thought a moment, then replied, "Depends on where this happened. If we're right and this came from the west—probably from the Pacific Rim—if it can blow up there and hit us with ash here … then I would think we've got to be talking a death toll in the millions." As we all mouthed the words—twenty-plus of us standing around her—Danica continued, "Seattle, San Francisco, if they were closer to the blast they might be leveled now. And if this set off the San Andreas … "

Aunt Jenny looked at her watch and said, "We felt that first quake at about five-fifty, our time. It was probably, what? Better part of an hour before the wall of ash hit. Then, it was almost five hours before the ash let up enough for us to get out of the vehicles. Does that tell us anything?"

Danica answered, "I have a cousin who's a geologist. It might mean something to him. I have no idea how far or fast a wall of ash like that could travel. And if there's a weak spot in the earth's crust, that might not be the only volcano—others could open up or it might just be the one. Either way, I don't think this is a good thing."

"Well," I said, speaking for the first time in a while and finding the nerve to do so I knew not where, "It seems to me that the thing for us to do now is try to get back to town or to our homes. See if there's power there and if anyone's hurt."

Several people agreed, but someone asked, "What about Annie? Do we just leave her here?"

"Somebody help me get her into the back of my truck. I can take her at least as far as Como."

"And then what?" Claire objected. "Put her in the barn until someone claims her?"

32

"It's either that or leave her out here," I replied. Did I mention that, as brother and sister, we were often very skilled at pushing each other's buttons? In the past, we had just been better at keeping it off public display. Of course, we had never had one of these discussions over a dead body before, either.

Claire, in an overly-logical voice I had come to hate over the years, said, "We can either take her into town and bury her or fire up the front end loader over there and bury her now. Either way, the salient point is that she's *dead*." That last word was said with pointed irony that deserves its own special typeface.

"We'll take her in the truck," I pronounced somewhat imperiously. "She was Catholic. We can take her to the Catholic Church in Como. Probably people gathering there right now, trying to figure out what to do next."

Claire clearly wanted to object, but she didn't interfere when a couple ladies wrapped Annie Meyers in an old blanket and then myself and Freddy loaded her into the back of the pick-up truck. It suddenly registered on me that I was going to be driving around with a dead body in the back of the truck and I wasn't crazy about the idea but I wasn't going to tell my sister that. What I said to her was, "Come on. Sooner we can get to the church, the sooner we can get her out of the truck."

Claire said nothing in response, but got into the cab and slammed the door.

I was relieved when the engine fired up, though I had no reason to think it wouldn't. I turned on the headlights, but that actually reduced the visibility due to the ash still in the air. I turned off the headlights and switched on the fog lamps and that helped some. I looked in my rearview and saw several other vehicles turning on their lights. I was glad I had parked with the truck pointing down canyon as I watched people behind me do three point turns on the narrow dirt road.

"Why aren't we moving?" Claire asked, none too happily.

"Just making sure everyone can get their wheels going," I replied as I slipped our truck into drive.

As we moved out slowly, Claire surprised me by saying, "I'm sorry I argued back there, Josh. I just—I just—I don't know. I just get a feeling way down in my stomach that Annie's not the only one who died here this evening and, well, maybe if I can deny she did, maybe no one else did, either."

"Yeah. I understand." I looked over at my sister in the glow of the dash-lights before us and headlights behind us and asked, "You think Miss Frowley's right? Millions dead?"

"Dear God, I hope not," my sister replied quietly.

At the mouth of the valley, where it opened out onto the larger South Park Valley near the site of what had been the town of Peabody back in the gold rush days, there was less ash. As if the valley we had been in were a large pipe that had blown the ash away from its entrance. But then, as we passed onto the grounds where once had stood the other mining town of Hamilton, the ash started getting thicker. By the edge of Como—itself once a prominent mining town but by this time a burg with an official population of less than fifty people—the ash was six inches deep and, like snow, drifted higher in some places. I was only going about five miles an hour—at the beginning due to visibility but then because the traction was so miserable. I had driven that old truck in snow storms and on ice, but driving on that ash was the least in control I had ever felt in a vehicle. Only a mile down the road and I could already feel the ache in my shoulders from the tense way in which I gripped the wheel.

And then someone started honking their horn and flashing their lights behind us. I came to a stop, panicking for a moment as it seemed like we were just going to keep sliding indefinitely, and then got out. Mister Glass had been right behind me in that old conversion van of his and he was getting out as well. We had started out from the Selkirk with six vehicles in our caravan and now there were only five. "What happened to Miss Frowley and her bunch?" I asked, as if Mister Glass could somehow know more than I did under the circumstance. Rather than snap back pithily, he just shrugged and we started working our way down the line.

At the last car, driven by Freddy, we were told, "I just looked up and Miss Frowley wasn't behind me. I didn't see her go off the side or anything." Freddy was getting out of the car as he said this and began walking back down along the road.

Mister Glass had had the presence of mind to grab one of his flashlights and began to sweep the road and the ditches to either side. We had only gone a couple hundred yards when we found Miss Frowley and the three people with her gathered around her car, the hood up. As we came up closer she said, "I tried honking, but I wasn't sure if anyone had heard me."

"What happened?" Freddy asked her.

"Just died on me. I can't get it started back up."

Freddy motioned for her to get into the car, then said, "Try again."

The car made a chugging noise, but wouldn't engage. Freddy opened up the air intake, took out the filter, and looked at it in the light of Glass's flashlight. "Full of ash," Freddy commented, banging the filter against the engine block. Putting it back in place, he motioned for Danica to start the car again. She did, and it came on, but still sounded sluggish.

"This is going to be a problem," Freddy commented sardonically, to be punctuated by the sound of one of the cars ahead of us honking wildly. As we three set out at a run, Miss Frowley's passengers jumped in her car and followed us.

The third car in the caravan had been driven by Wlllard Guthrie, who was now standing beside his car and peering under the hood. "Just died. Acts like it's not getting gas."

"It's not getting air," Freddy told him, and us. "And who knows? The gas line may be clogging up, too." He looked around and said, "There's a good chance none of us are going to make it very far this night."

"Well, let's go while we can," Mister Glass said, then we could hear his van dying from where we were. At that moment, Danica pulled up even with the convoy only to have her car die again.

"We're not that far from town," Freddy told us. "We might be better off hoofin' the rest of the way before our engines suck in so much soot they ain't never runnin' again."

We hesitated, but as the fourth car in the caravan chugged to a stop, we realized he was right. I ran up to the truck—which was still running though it sounded to me to be somewhat uneven—and told Claire as I shut off the engine, "Come on. We're going to walk the rest of the way into town."

"Why?"

"The ash is choking out the motors. Come on. We'll, um, we'll come back for Annie."

Claire cast a glance toward the bed of the truck, then got out and, as before, took my hand. In a soft voice, she said, "Mom and Dad are out in this."

"I know," was all I could think to say in reply. Then, "Maybe not. They're probably in the restaurant, waiting for a chance to get out and come home. They'll probably just stay there until this is over."

Como, under its best conditions, didn't show a lot of lights at night. That night, there were none. I could see the vague shapes of houses—some of which I knew to have been occupied earlier in the day—but there were no lights emanating from them. Of course, it *was* the middle of the night, but even so there were usually a few porch lights on and a couple security lights hanging over driveways. On that night, there was nothing.

After everyone had gathered up whatever water or drinks they could carry, we made our way across the open space, each being careful to not let much space get between ourselves and the people fore and aft. Somehow, I was leading the way again, with Claire walking beside me and still holding my hand. Twenty-three people fanned out behind us, with Mister Glass taking up the drag position and making sure no one fell behind. It probably felt like he was riding drag like in the old west as each step we took kicked up a plume of ash. In the back like that, he must have been getting the worst of it. I thought briefly of my earlier estimate that forty-something people had been working on the reclamation project and realized that number had been a bit high. I asked myself if I had overestimated. I worked back through my mind and the only other workers I could come up with who weren't in our little parade were Annie Meyers and the Roxon brothers.

The first house we came to was a weekend place owned by a family named Williams who lived in Denver. A pretty big house with two stories and a detached garage big enough to hold three cars, it sat empty most of the year as the Williams family only came out a couple weekends a month at most. Our group huddled in the cover of their carport as myself and a couple others banged on the doors and windows. No one replied and flashlights shown through windows showed no signs of occupancy.

Someone suggested we break in and get out of the ash, but the rest of us were reluctant to do so. I know the idea had crossed my mind, but it seemed like a rather extreme step to take. At least so soon.

"There's no sense in us all traipsin' all over everywhere," Freddy said. "Why don't me and Josh go from house to house 'til—"

"Josh is not getting out of my sight," Claire objected forcefully. Several others said they would rather we all stayed together. Eventually, that became the consensus and, so, we all looked wistfully at the relative peace of the Williams' carport, then set out once again single-file. Freddy led off this time but I was right behind him, with Claire beside me. Mister Glass was still walking drag.

There was no one at the little cabin owned by one R.M. Reynolds and a glance through the windows showed it to be empty not just of people but of furniture. This surprised us at first but, as we talked about it on the way to the next house, no one remembered seeing R.M. or his wife in more than a year. No one remembered hearing any stories about them giving it up after the fire, but—like the Williams family—the Reynolds family had never lived in Como full-time and, so, were not well known, other than by sight.

When we found the Spencer house—a large, two-story home owned by a retired couple who actually lived in Como—to be silent, we got worried. Aunt Jenny was sure she had seen them at the post office that morning and suggested we break in and see if maybe they were inside somewhere. We debated this for a few minutes before Aunt Jenny actually took the initiative and broke the glass on the back door. She was about to go in first but Freddy pushed by her and went in, calling out, "Monica? Peter? Anyone here?"

We had all piled into the kitchen and bottom floor, figuring we might as well get out of the blowing ash while we could, while Freddy and Aunt Jenny took the flashlights and went upstairs. We had barely all gotten inside when we heard Aunt Jenny scream. Letting go of Claire's hand, I rushed up the stairs, a surprisingly spry Mister Glass right behind me and most everyone else behind him. We found Aunt Jenny standing in the hallway and pointing into what had been the master bedroom.

Just then, Freddy came out of the bedroom holding a pill bottle and saying, "Looks like they done themselves in."

Danica pushed past the rest of us and was soon saying, "Monica's still alive."

I had made my way to the bedroom by then and found both Monica and Peter Spencer laid out comfortably on the bed. Peaceful, they looked. Danica was holding Monica's arm and gently patting her wrist and then face as she said, "Monica? Monica wake up."

The elderly woman stirred slightly, then seemed surprised when she caught sight of Danica. She pointed with her left hand and said, "It's the end of the world." I looked at where she was pointing and thought she might have been gesturing toward the TV, but I wasn't sure. There was also a bookshelf in that general direction so maybe she meant something there. Then she closed her eyes and her breath got slower and slower as more people peeked in, then it stopped entirely.

Aunt Jenny had calmed down by then and, looking at the bottle Freddy had found on the night stand, said, "Tranquilizers, I think."

I suddenly (and, again, from what source I knew not) took the initiative and started hustling everyone out of the bedroom, saying, "Let's all just settle down here until daylight. It should only be a few more hours away."

"What about the Spencers?" someone asked.

"They're not going anywhere," I replied. "In the morning we can look into burying them but, for now, let's just enjoy a few hours of relatively ash-free air."

Some were in favor of pressing on and trying to find out if anyone else were alive in town, but eventually it was decided that there was nothing we could do about t one way or another so we might as well just relax. So we shut the Spencers up in their room and spread out through the house. Claire and I wound up next to each other on a love-seat that folded out like a recliner. There, she cuddled up next to me, something she had never done in either of our memories. She might have cuddled with Dad now and then while we watched TV, but I think on any previous night if I had tried to cuddle with her she would have taken it as a joke, said something like, "Yuck!" and slugged me. That night, though, she whispered (for there were others in the room), "I'm really scared, Josh. What if Mrs. Spencer was right and this is the end of the world?"

"Yeah," was all I could think to say in response.

"I'm not ready for the world to end."

"I can't imagine anyone would be. I doubt that Annie Meyers was."

I don't think anyone was really sleepy, for I heard low conversations going on for quite a while. Or, maybe they were sleepy but afraid to go to sleep. What if the sun didn't come out? What if the ash we were seeing outside wasn't just being blown off the ground but was still continuing to fall from somewhere? What if the volcano erupted again—or what if Danica were right and there was some weak spot in the crust where several volcanos were about to break through?

Claire and I had a conversation that night such as we had never had before, at least that I remembered. In whispered voices we talked about everything—from big topics like religion and faith, to mundane memories about growing up on the ranch. I think I knew at the time that we were discussing such things not because we cared about them—though we cared a bit about them, I suppose—but because we didn't want to stop and think about what was really going on. About why we weren't out there, checking every house in town or walking up the road to our own house a mile away. About why we weren't carrying Annie Meyers up to the Catholic Church like we had talked about.

As brothers and sisters go, I think Annie and I had always been fairly close. We rarely fought, and it had never come to blows. We did a lot of things together: working in the forest, playing catch, we had even double dated a couple times. But I realized that night that we never really talked. For my part, I think I just assumed I already knew everything there was to know about Claire. Probably assumed the reverse, as well. So I reclined there on that couch and listened to my sister like never before and talked like never before and was actually feeling pretty good about the moment in time … because I was doing all I could to avoid the moment in time and I think Claire was, too.

I wondered how many people had the same thought that I did: maybe Annie Meyers was lucky. Choking to death on ash didn't sound like a great way to go, but at least she was gone. What if the rest of us were looking at days or even weeks of a slow death? Who wouldn't prefer a quick one?

Still, its human nature to fight, and I could also feel that welling up inside of me. The urge to battle whatever this was, to save our horses, to save our ranch, to save my sister. In my teenage mind the Spencers were old—though, in reality, they may have only been in their late sixties—and, so, I rationalized that maybe their choice made sense to them. It didn't to me, though. I had many years ahead of me, or had thought so when I got up that Saturday morning, and I wasn't prepared to be short-changed just yet. I saw it as being up to me to find Mom and Dad and get them home, to find a way to contact Rusty, and—above all—to stay alive. To see better days. I was eighteen and naïve enough to think that this was an opportunity, a chance to show myself and the world—mostly the world—what Josh Overstreet was made of. I didn't know what other people were thinking as we huddled in the Spencers' house, even Claire had become silent, but I was picturing myself leading everyone out of this mess, of firing up that front end loader and pushing back the ash. Maybe I even saw into the future as I saw Claire married and having kids and they talked about how Uncle Josh had saved the day as they played with my own kids.

Amongst such ridiculous thoughts, I eventually fell into a light and fitful sleep.

Chapter Four

The world is weary of the past,
Oh, might it die or rest at last!
~Percy Byshe Shelley

The ranch where I grew up had been a l but founded by the first of our family line. Born with a different name none of us remembered, he had taken the name of Overstreet as a young man and drifted west from Texas. Catching up with a horse rancher from Colorado, he had eventually taken over the ranch upon the man's death, and then bought up the remaining interest from the man's family members. It wasn't as nefarious as it might sound, for the man's daughter lived on the ranch in her later years, a great friend of my forebear.

The original affair had just been a small ranch, headquartered a mile west of Como, on maybe a hundred and fifty acres. Over the decades, my family had bought up land here, sold some there, traded here and yon, and eventually come up with a ranch of about ten thousand acres, if you counted the few acres we owned up near Lake Jefferson and some more by Hartsel. How the Jefferson parcel came to be in our possession I never heard, but it was hard to get to so we never had any luck with selling it. For all my life there had been talk of maybe building a little cabin up there, a place we could get away to, like the city folk get away from Denver by coming to Como. During my life, we had tented up on that property a few times, but that was as close as we ever got to putting up a structure.

The hill behind our ranch house, which was a foothill to the mountain we called Little Baldy (which was, itself, a foothill to the mountain known as Silverheels, named for a famous dancehall girl of the 1800s who figured into my family line in an unexpected way), used to look considerably different. All my growing up years, that hill behind the house had been covered with a thick stand of pines and aspens, a wonderful forest for a boy to grow up in. I and my brother built forts and camped out and even ran our own zip line once (that had been a lot of fun, right up until the broken cheekbone).

After the fires had swept through, denuding that hillside even though our house was saved, it was like my world had changed. Everything I found security in seemed gone. So maybe that's why I was mentally, sort of, kind of, almost prepared for the cloud of ash.

My sleep was broken by the sound of someone stumbling through the living room where so many of us were. I looked up through foggy eyes with a foggier brain and saw a slatternly figure silhouetted against the front window. When he detected movement, I heard him say, "It don't look right."

I gently got up, hoping to let Claire sleep, and came over to the window. Looking out, I could see what Freddy meant.

Above the mountains that lined the east side of our wide valley, I could barely discern a line of sunlight. It wasn't breaking over the mountains as I had been used to seeing each morning of my life. It was just a faint line that edged the space between the mountains and what I guessed to be a sky-borne dome of ash. As the sun rose, the day grew a little lighter but the sky itself grew darker as the sun moved behind the ash.

The ash cloud surrounded us, as if there were just a little slash through it that started behind us on the Selkirk and extended in a narrow path across the valley. I had stepped out on the Spencers' porch by then and could see that the ash was thick to the north, towards Jefferson, and to the south, as well. It was only where we were that a gash a couple miles wide allowed something like blue sky to be seen above us.

I sensed Claire beside me before she even said anything, and then it was, "How far do you think this stretches?"

"No idea," I mumbled in return. It was cool out there, the wind still pushing on our backs as it came out of Boreas Pass.

We were startled from our reverie by seeing a group of people coming towards us. I recognized each of them, for they were residents of Como. They walked warily, until they saw who we were. Walter "Wally" Preston was somewhat in the lead and asked, "Josh? Claire? Where'd you come from?"

"We were back up on the Selkirk when it hit. Whatever it was that hit," I replied.

"I was watching the ball game," Wally told us. In answer to the question that was bound to be next, he said, "No weather warning or anything. Just felt this bump like something big had smacked into my house, then the power went out. I was outside, checking to see if something had smacked into the power pole or something when that wall of ash came over the mountains. I expect you all saw it."

"Very clearly," Claire told him.

Wally Preston was a middle-aged, heavy-set man who worked for the county and was considered the mayor of Como, mainly by default as we didn't actually have one. He was almost always seen in work coveralls, even on his day off. Oddly, though, they were always clean. As a kid, I used to marvel that Wally Preston could drive a skip-loader or shovel a ditch and still come out clean. The joke around the area was that he had fifty sets of those coveralls and changed into a fresh one as soon as a fleck of dirt or sweat appeared on the one he had been wearing. No one who knew him made jokes about him not working hard, for he worked as hard as anyone. He just managed to stay clean while doing it.

"How did all of you get into town?" Wally asked.

I pointed to where our vehicles had stopped and told him, "We drove in last night. That far, anyway. The ash was starting to give us troubles. Cars wouldn't run." My voice trailed off as I couldn't think of anything else to say.

Wally gestured at the highway that ran past town and said, "I've been watching all night. Nothing is moving on that highway. Nothing. We all know that's not a major artery or anything, but when have you ever seen it completely empty?"

"We're cut off then, aren't we?" Mister Glass asked, adjusting his glasses as he stepped out into the yard.

"It looks like it." Wally gestured around and said, "No phones, no electricity, and the vehicles aren't going anywhere. I got a generator at my house, but it's starting to sputter. And I don't think it's short on gas."

I asked, "Do we know if there's anyone else left in town? Anyone alive, I mean?"

"I think we need to go door-to-door," Sabrina Miller, Wally's sister-in-law, said. She was a slight woman with a hatchet face who always looked like she had just been sucking a sour pickle. First impressions aside, I had always known her to be very friendly.

As everyone seemed to agree to that idea, I heard Aunt Jenny saying to Wally, "Ordinarily, I wouldn't advocate breaking and entering, but I'm thinking that it may be a while before anyone gets to us and, well, we better make an inventory of all available food and water in town."

Wally, who had always been as full of bluster and bravado as anyone I had ever known, wiped his brow like he was sweating, then nodded and said, "We'll make a list of everything we take and what house it was taken from, so we can pay it back someday. Let's bring everything we can find to the post office. We'll store it there and start divvying it up as needed. Blankets and pillows and stuff, too."

"How long are we going to have to wait?" someone, a man's voice, asked.

"No way of knowing," Wally answered. "I gotta figure we'll see some airplanes or helicopters at some point today, making a survey. But if this thing's really wide spread, it may take a while for anyone to get to us. You know they'll hit the bigger towns first. We need to plan on being here for the long haul."

I started to say Claire and I would work our way to the south end of town, but instead snapped my fingers and said, "We need to put some people on a burial detail, Mister Preston. We've got three dead."

"That we know of," someone chimed in. Realizing he had no idea what we meant, I filled Wally in on the Spencers and Annie Meyers.

He shook his head and mumbled something like, "I knew I should have come over and checked on them." He seemed to get his wind, then, and said more forcefully, "I think I saw that Larry

Warshek had his D-4 by his place. That's pretty near the cemetery. Maybe we can fire it up and—and at least get a grave dug. Freddy, you come with me and let's see if we can get it running long enough to dig a grave. Some of you men, you start carrying the bodies up to the cemetery. The rest of you, go with the ladies and start checking house-to-house."

"Wally," I said, as everyone started off in various directions, "I'm going to run up to the ranch and see if we still have any horses."

"We don't have time for personal—" he started to object.

"I need to find out, Mister Preston. And, well, some horses might come in handy until we can get the vehicles up and running."

He looked like he wanted to argue, then nodded and said, "Come right back, OK?"

I took Claire's hand and we started off up the hill. It was a mile to our ranch from the center of town, all of it uphill. Claire and I had been walking and running the distance for all our lives, but never through a cloud of ash. We wanted to run, but soon learned we couldn't—due to both the expected difficulty of breathing and the unexpected slipperiness of the ash beneath our feet. So we tied our makeshift bandanas back on (glad we had pocketed them) and walked as fast as we could. By the time we got to the ranch, we were both worn out and sweating where the bandanas were. This, of course, just made the ash cling even more.

I had always thought the road from Como to our ranch was one of the prettiest in the world, the way it wound through the forests of aspen and pine, Little Baldy brooding over the ranch and the great mountain Silverheels beyond. Even after most of that forest had burned, I still loved the sight of coming home. There had already been some growth after the fires, which had been a promise of things to come that I had enjoyed. Seeing it all covered with a coating of ash, though, was like a nightmare version of its normal winter coating.

We made it to the barn and found eight horses huddled together on the lee side of it, a thin coating of ash on them but not too bad. We opened up the barn and let them in, then set about currying them and washing out their nostrils with damp cloths. I don't think it was my imagination that they were happy to see us. There were more horses scattered about the ranch, which I hoped had been able to find shelter, but I knew I couldn't get to them all for a while. I wanted to, but I knew we were needed back in town.

As if reading my thoughts, Claire said, "Let's don't go back, Josh. There's nothing we can do down there. Let's just take care of the horses and, and wait for Mom and Dad to get back."

I wasn't sure how to reply to that idea, so I said, "I'm going to go check on the house. See if I can get the generator going."

"I'll, um, I'll keep working on the horses," she said.

I was a little surprised. Not that my sister loved the horses, for it was her defining characteristic, but that she was willing to let me out of her sight. Granted, the house wasn't all that far away, but one of the few remaining stands of trees was between the barn and the house.

"I'll be right back," I told her, to which she merely nodded.

I made it over to the house and let myself in. I called out for my parents, hoping against hope, but heard no reply. A quick perusal of the house revealed that it was empty as expected. Our generator was operational, though, owing to the fact that my father had built a shelter for it that was designed to keep the snow off in the winter but allow plenty of air in to keep it running. The microscreens he had used had kept out most of the ash—an innovation he had thought of when we were just worrying about the relatively paltry amount of ash from a forest fire. I turned the generator off and said a prayer of thanks for it as I walked back outside. Claire was walking over from the barn, then, and asked, "Everything ship shape?"

"Perfectly."

"Except empty, right?"

"Yeah."

She seemed hesitant, then said, "I don't mean to abandon everyone else, but, um, you saw what the horses here were like. I think we need to go check on the ones by the north barn. I mean, I bet everyone in town is checking on their dogs and cats and … everything."

I was torn. I wanted to check on our horses, too, but I also wanted to be back in town with the other people. I'm not sure if it were out of a sense of duty or out of some masculine desire to be a leader. I had liked being a leader and a part of me felt like I might lose that if I didn't get back down there. Someone like Freddy or Mister Preston was going to take over and, before you knew it, I would just be another teenager, a kid. Yes, I knew that's what I was, but I was also at that age when I was anxious to be more, and frustrated when I wasn't. Or when I wasn't perceived as an adult.

It occurred to me that Claire was right, though. We had made a commitment to those horses. I nodded in agreement and went back inside the house. Praising the Lord that our gun safe wasn't one of those electronic jobs, I opened it and pulled out a rifle and two pistols. As I handed Claire the one she often used when we'd go shoot targets, a semi-automatic Ruger, she recoiled briefly, asking, "What for?"

"These are ... uncertain times, Claire. People are going to get jumpy if help doesn't come soon. But, well, I'm—I'm also thinking about the horses."

She started to put the pistol back into the safe, but I stayed her hand and said, "You remember about three years ago when that horse fell with Dad on it and he had to shoot it? I don't want to have to do that, either, but you know how slick all this ash has made everything. If one of our horses is out there with a broken leg, well, we need to take care of it."

She looked at the pistol in her hand and whispered, "I'm not sure I could."

"I'm not, either. About me, I mean. But, well, we might just have to. For the same reason we just spent all that time sponging out the noses of the horses here." She was looking down at the gun frightfully, so I gently raised her chin and told her, "I know you, Claire. You'd rather suffer yourself than see one of the horses suffer."

She finally nodded and, reaching into the safe, took out the holster for her gun. Heading over to the stairs to our rooms, she said, "I need to get a belt." I nodded in agreement and followed her up the stairs.

I stopped by the restroom thinking I would brush my teeth dry, but then turned on the tap out of habit and discovered the water was on. In surprise, I turned on the light and found that it worked. Letting out a yelp of excitement as I remembered the solar panels I went into Claire's room to tell her the good news and found her sitting on the floor and crying.

"Claire?" I asked as I dropped to my knees in front of her.

She swatted me away lightly and said through her tears, "So what if the horses are all right? There's no traffic on the highway."

"What?"

"What if they're all dead?"

"The horses?"

"No, stupid! The *people*. What if everyone's dead and all that's left is just us and those few people in town? Maybe the Spencers were right and we'd be better off just killing each other now. Better than watching each other die one by one! We're the youngest people we've seen, Josh. Even if we can survive … to what end? So that ten or twenty years from now we can just sit around and be the last two people on earth?"

I wasn't sure what to say and I was trying to figure out a way to take her gun away from her without a struggle, but I finally just sat down next to her and put my arm around her. She leaned against me and cried.

After a while, she stopped crying, then she wiped her eyes and looked at me. She said, in a cool, measured voice, "We need to check on the horses."

I nodded and got to my feet, then helped her to hers. She hugged me and thanked me and I didn't know how to reply. We were about to leave the room when she asked, "Why is my clock working?"

"Huh?" I replied, before thinking. "Oh, I forgot to tell you. Dad's solar panels are working. And, apparently, the water pump is still pumping out of the well."

"I wonder if we should get up on the roof and dust the ash off of them?"

"Wouldn't be a bad idea, at that."

"Sorry I called you stupid," she said as she wiped her nose with the back of her hand.

"Yeah, I'm going to have to tell on you," I quipped.

She glared at me and, holding up her hand, asked, "Mind if I wipe this on your shirt?" Then she went into the restroom and I could hear her running water in the sink. When she came out, I gathered she had washed not just her hands, but her face as well.

Soon, we were up on the roof of the house, brooms in hand, and sweeping the layer of ash off the collection panels. That done, I stopped and looked to the east, across the valley. I had always been amazed by that view. It was nice from our front porch, but I always loved getting up on the roof. Seemed like it was the equivalent of being another hundred feet in the air.

Claire pointed and said, "Looks like they got that old bulldozer running."

"Still nothing on the highway, though."

"Could we, I mean, do you think we could take some horses and go look for Mom and Dad?"

"Yeah. We should. Maybe we could rig some bandanas for them. The horses, I mean."

She smiled an actual smile at the thought, then said, "C'mon. Let's go check on the north horses."

As we walked the dirt road to the north barn, I couldn't get the picture out of my mind of what we had seen from the roof. The South Park Valley was a moonscape, nothing but gray ash as far as the eyes could see. And apart from that gash I had mentioned earlier, caused apparently by the wind whipping over Boreas Pass and through the Selkirk valley, everything was still under a cloud of ash. The highway—which ran north to Jefferson and south to Fairplay—disappeared into that cloud in either direction. If our Mom and Dad were still out there, I only hoped they had been able to take shelter somewhere in Fairplay, for being out on the highway looked to be a death sentence comparable to what Annie Meyers had faced. Though, it occurred to me, they could have passed the night in the car as Claire and I had passed time in the truck.

Before the fires, the rutted road we walked was a tunnel through thick forest. Now, it was a path through a burned-out wasteland with a little, very little, green grass and aspens starting to come back. Here and there, short pine trees were underneath the ash. I wondered how long they could survive before being choked out? Could a strong wind or some rain clear it out? I couldn't imagine what it might take to save it all, but earth had had volcanos before and survived. And hadn't I read somewhere about apple crops that had actually flourished in volcanic ash?

We found most of the horses, again on the lee side of the north barn. We could think of three that were unaccounted for and hoped they had found some shelter in one of the remaining bits of forest or in some trough in the hills. One horse that was missing, one we called Star on account of the blaze on his face, had a reputation for wandering off so we figured he had done so again. He was also an uncommonly smart horse, so had probably found a nice little spot somewhere. We set about currying the horses and, again, sponging out their nostrils. Like the other horses, they seemed appreciative of the effort, or maybe just happy to see us. I found myself a little thankful for the fires and the other factors that had caused us to sell off much of the herd in years past, for these twenty-two horses we now had care of seemed plenty for Claire and I to deal with. In the days when our ranch had run better than two hundred horses, well … it occurred to me that we would probably just be watching most of them die—or having to kill them ourselves.

"How long's the feed going to last?" Claire asked as we gave them some hay from the barn.

I smiled and motioned for her to follow me outside. "I saw this from the loft," I told her quizzical face. Out beyond the barn, I pointed back towards the Selkirk area.

"Green grass?" she asked in surprise.

"It's like those high winds must have blown the ash off the grass. After we get things settled in town, let's come back and drive the horses up that way."

"What about Mom and Dad?"

"Once we get the horses on good grazing, we can go look for them."

She nodded, then said, "They're dead, you know."

"What?" I asked incredulously.

"I think everyone is. Everyone in these mountains, I mean. Nothing can survive that ash. It's just us and the people in Como." I started to object, but she said, "I imagine there are people out on the plains, and maybe everything east of the Mississippi is just fine. But something tells me that everyone in the Rockies is dead—or dying."

"You can't know that!"

"I can't, but I do." She smiled wanly and told me, "I hope I'm wrong, but somehow I know I'm not."

It was my turn to take her hand and, as we walked back towards the horses, I asked, "You remember Grampa's story about the old lady?"

Claire shook her head and looked at me with interest. I explained, "Grampa Galen told me a story—more than once so I'm surprised he didn't tell you. Anyway, he said when he was little, this really old lady who was some kin of ours came to visit. He said she was a great story teller, always telling him and his sister these stories about far off lands and battles and stuff. But then, one day, he said he was sitting with her down by the pond and she told him a story about our family that she said was true. She told him that one day something terrible was going to happen and our family would be left alone. Almost alone in the world."

"Probably just some crazy old lady's story," Claire laughed.

"That's what Grampa said he thought. But he said the old lady told him that one day, way in the future, a young woman would come and ask for our help, for the Overstreet's help, and if we gave it, it would save the family and the world."

"'The world'?" she asked skeptically.

"Yeah. He said the old lady told him that a day would come when there would be a world war or some kind of natural disaster that would wipe out almost everyone on earth, but that people would survive here and there in little pockets and valleys. She said some people would even move underground. And she told Grampa that one of the places that people survived would be right here and that it would be Overstreets who would survive. He said she had always told all her other stories with a glint in her eye, like they were just stories, but he said she made a point of singling him out and telling him this one story and making him promise that he would pass it on. That one day, if a lady came asking for help, we would be ready to give it. He said he passed the story on to Dad but was never convinced Dad believed it."

"Can you blame him?"

"No. But what if you're right? What if everyone within a thousand miles is dead except for us few here? And what if that lady was right? Maybe she was a prophet, like in the Bible—"

"Prophetess," Claire corrected.

"OK, prophetess. Maybe you are, too. What if she was right, though, and it's up to me and you to keep the Overstreet name alive until that young woman can get here?"

"You know how crazy this sounds?"

"Yes, I do." I smiled and added, "Which is probably why Grampa didn't tell anyone outside the family. I still remember very clearly the day he told Rusty and me, though. We were up at Lake Jefferson, having a picnic with just the three of us, when he told us. Made me and Rusty swear we would never forget the story."

"We're not going to tell anyone in town, are we?" She said it like a question, but I don't think it really was.

"I wasn't planning on talking to anyone about it but you."

She gave my hand a squeeze, then let go of it and, taking up the rifle that we had set just inside the barn, said, "I think our next order of business is to go back to town and see what they've found. Then, I think we ought to get everyone to move up to Selkirk." When I looked at her strangely, she said, "I don't think we can survive in all this ash. And, if anyone does come looking for life from an airplane, that swath of green's going to be easier to spot than a grey dot in the midst of a grey expanse."

"It's up to you, Josh," she said suddenly.

"What's that?"

"Saving the world. If I get married and have kids, they'll have my husband's last name. If there are going to be Overstreets around, it's going to be up to you."

Then she smiled a genuine smile and told me, "And I love you, but I am *not* going to repopulate the world with my brother."

"It would never have occurred to me," I replied with a chuckle. "I guess I better find someone to marry, then."

"Well, you know, when you do, you have to clear her through me."

"I do, do I?"

Chapter Five

> *It is not despair,*
> *for despair is only for those*
> *who see the end beyond all doubt.*
> ~J.R.R. Tolkien

I had been on some dates before, but had never really had a girlfriend. It wasn't for lack of wanting one, but things just never worked out.

For one thing, I lived about sixteen miles from my high school. Guys who lived in town, see, they could walk a girl home or easily go by her house after class. At least, that was one of my primary excuses. Another of my excuses was that neither Fairplay or Como had anywhere good to take a date. No movie theaters, no dance halls that were open to teens, etc. It was a complaint voiced often by those of us who probably wouldn't have had the nerve to ask someone out if there had been more opportunities for entertainment.

When I had asked the fairer sex out on a date, it had usually been to go with a group or to double date over to Breckenridge. There, one could ice skate or hit the shops or take advantage of any number of activities. It was fun, and I never had a date complain, but as I looked back on those days from our ash-covered world, I realized that I had let the event substitute for me. I wasn't taking a girl out and getting to know her, converse with her, or anything. We made light conversation on the highway from Fairplay to Breck, and then we skated or biked or did whatever activity we had gone for. It was fun, but it kept me from knowing anything about *them*. Maybe another advantage was that it kept me from revealing anything about myself.

See, I had this idea in my mind that what girls wanted was a guy who *did things*. I had played on the football team, but I was just an offensive lineman and not very good at that—owing to being the smallest lineman on the team. I had tried the other sports and while I could enjoy baseball or softball, again, I wasn't very good. Just good enough to not be an embarrassment, but never good enough to be noticed (hence my only hope of playing college ball had been as a walk-on). Academically, I was in the top half of the class, but—again—not high enough that anyone noticed or particularly gifted at any one subject. I had qualified for college, but it wasn't like anyone was throwing scholarships my way.

I was six foot tall, medium of build, with brownish hair. I'd never known anyone to recoil from me, but I hadn't known any girls to swoon over me, either. I could tell a joke pretty well and, owing to my reading, could write fairly well when I had to, but these didn't seem to be the sort of things that the girls noticed.

The reality is that I was probably too self-absorbed to be attractive. I wanted a girlfriend who would come out to the ranch and ride horses with me. I wanted to ride in places like the Selkirk or over Boreas Pass and tell the girl all I knew about Hamilton and Peabody and the old mining and ranching days. I always heard about how every girl loved to ride horses ... but I wasn't meeting every girl. Only Lysette wanted to go riding with me and it took a long time for me to realize that she really liked my horses and would rather I just stop talking. It took me so long to realize that because I was so wrapped up in my stories that it never occurred to me to ask her—or any other girl—about her story. What did she enjoy? Did she have a story—either one she had lived through or had read somewhere? I never asked and, so, I never found out.

It finally dawned on me—too little, too late, it seemed at the time—that girls might like a guy who noticed *them* more than a guy who only wanted to be noticed.

It was coming on early evening by the time we walked back down to town, our thinking being that we didn't want to risk the horses on the slick ash just yet. And, in fact, we didn't have to go all the way into town as the cemetery was about halfway between our ranch and town, maybe a little towards the town side of the halfway mark. We found everyone from the night before, as well as those we had seen in town with Wally, and a few more people who had been discovered by the searchers. A large grave had been dug and they were in the process of putting a dozen bodies into it. I noticed we weren't the only people who were armed, though we had left the rifle back at the ranch.

Yes, a dozen.

In searching the houses of town (of which there weren't all that many), they had found nine people dead. Seven of them were from a single family and it appeared to those who found them that the father and mother had executed the five children—ages 13 to 4—then turned the guns on themselves. We had known them as the Turners and they had always been a little strange—even in school the kids had kept away from others for the most part—but no one could imagine something like this. If they subscribed to any particular religious belief, none of us knew about it.

The other two bodies belonged to elderly people. Mrs. Kline, they said, appeared to have just died in her sleep, though it was a strange coincidence if it happened when it did. Mrs. Ortiz was known to be on oxygen and it was thought that the power outage was what had killed her. It was Aunt Jenny who had found the elderly Hispanic woman and she said Mrs. Ortiz's hand had been at her chest like maybe she had been having a heart attack when she died. None of us were doctors or coroners, though, so it was all just speculation.

The additional people in the gathering of the living belonged the Marquez family: father, mother and three children, ages 17, 15, and 12. Their seventeen year old, Oscar, and I had known each other since we were in elementary school and while not close friends, had always been friendly. Alexa, their daughter, was fifteen and came over quickly to hug Claire. They had never been close that I knew of, but the four of us had been riding the school bus from Como to Fairplay for a long time and had become almost something like cousins. Their 12 year old was a boy named Jesse who had Asperger's, or high-functioning autism. He was a whiz at all things academic, but had always been very awkward socially. Oscar always looked out after him, though, and even managed to get Jesse to participate in sports now and then. Jesse came over and shook my hand when Oscar did, but didn't say anything.

I looked around and realized we five were the only "kids" present. There was no one else in the town of Como who had kids, though there were often kids or teenagers in town owing to the people who had weekend homes there. None of them seemed to have been in town that weekend. Most everyone else who lived in Como was a grandparent, or childless.

Sideling up next to Oscar as the last of the bodies was lowered into the grave, I asked, "Where were you guys when this hit?"

"Coming back from Fairplay," he replied. "Car conked out just the other side of Red Hill. We tried to get it going again and would make it a few yards, then it stopped for good. Stayed in it all night, then, when the sun came up, we hoofed it. Just got into town a little bit ago and saw everyone going from house to house."

"Did you, um, did you see my parents?" I asked in a whisper.

"No. Were they in Fairplay?"

"Supposed to be."

In reply, Oscar subtly crossed himself. I wasn't Catholic, but appreciated the gesture and kind of wished for one of my own. I felt a little guilty that I hadn't been praying for my parents. Had been avoiding thinking about them, in fact. I said a prayer for them in my mind at that moment. And Rusty.

I had thought even less about my older brother than I had about my parents, and maybe for the same reason: avoidance. Rusty and I always got along about as well as Mom and Claire, and for less reason. Aside from the aforementioned games of catch, Rusty and I just tended to rub each other the wrong way and we never knew why. When I wanted to ride horses, he wanted to read. When I wanted to read, he wanted to ride. If he had a hankering for a pizza, I had one for burgers. But, many days of the year (before he went off to college, anyway) before the sun went down we'd get out in front of the house and play catch—with a baseball, a football or Frisbee. Claire had a good arm, and she and I would play catch now and then, and sometimes Dad would join us, but it hadn't been the same since Rusty went off to college. Using a terminology I once heard in a science class, I think those games of catch were the "expressive component" for Rusty and I to apologize for the fights of the day.

How was he doing? Had the ash cloud really spread that far? Was Claire right? She had mentioned Mom and Dad specifically but she hadn't mentioned Rusty at all. That was surprising when it occurred to me because I may have been closest to her but Rusty was her hero. If she were down, or had been picked on, or whatever, she always went to Rusty. Some of my battles with Rusty may have been jealousy over how she idolized him, though I never would have said it, even to myself.

And suddenly I was wondering if I would ever see him again. He was supposed to be getting ready for his fifth/senior year of college and I hoped he was OK, but I had serious doubts about anyone being able to get to **us** any time soon. Maybe I would see him some day.

So it was with genuine tears that I began helping shovel dirt on our recently departed. Almost everyone else was crying, too, and I wondered if they were crying over the people in the grave or over everyone else they might have lost? For myself, I was sorry about the people in the grave, but probably not enough to cry. My tears were for my mother and father, my brother, and everyone else I knew who I suddenly thought I would never see again in this life. As soon as we had the grave filled in, I went hastily and stood by Claire. I put my arm around her and she put her head on my shoulder and, suddenly, I was as anxious about the idea of her being out of my sight as she had been when I got out of the truck the night before.

Had that really been less than twenty-four hours before? I looked at my watch, realized it still wasn't functioning, then glanced ineffectually at the sky. It **was** close to twenty-six hours since the wall of ash had hit, so I was guessing it about a day since I had tried to get to the water bottles. In my mind and in my body, it seemed like it had to have been several days, if not weeks.

Wally Preston said a few words about the deceased and read the 23rd Psalm from a Bible he said his grandfather had given him. Then Danica Frowley surprised us (surprised me, anyway, though I don't know why) by using her very good singing voice to lead us in singing "Amazing Grace." Claire had always possessed the best voice in our family and sang out with abandon during what I knew was one of her favorite hymns. The rest of us sang along but I wager I wasn't the only one thinking a duet between Claire and Danica would sound better than the rest of us put together.

After a prayer, we all started to walk away, then it was clear we didn't know where to go. Bringing Claire with me, I went over to the one person who seemed most likely to be our leader, if not necessarily the most qualified. "Mister Preston," I said as we drew near.

He turned and said, "I think you can call me Wally, Josh. Way I hear it, you took charge up there at Selkirk yesterday."

"Not really," I replied, shuffling my feet though I was trying not to. Then, looking him in the eye, I said, "But I wanted to talk to you about that, sort of. Claire and I were at our north barn and it looks like the winds have blown down Boreas Pass and swept the ash out of that valley. You can see green and everything. I was thinking maybe we all ought to find any tents or whatever and move up there. Maybe even start dragging whatever we can from town and building some shelters up there. Get out of this ash."

Wally seemed friendly rather than condescending when he replied, "You make it sound like this is permanent. I'm sure this will all blow over soon. We'll be seeing search planes any day now and—"

Danica, who I hadn't realized was standing nearby, said, "I'm with Josh on this. I think we're in for a bad way for a long time and, well, even the valley up there may not be a solution but it seems a better place to start than here."

Wally didn't seem to like the intrusion and told her, "You're welcome to do whatever you want, Miss Frowley, but I am staying here. We have our houses, it's near the highway—"

Lester Marquez spoke up and said, "Mind if my family and I come with you, Josh? If I can get my RV up the road there, we can live in that until we can get a more permanent shelter put up."

"People, people," Wally said, drawing more people into the conversation than previously had been, "There's no need to do this. Our best bet is to stay together."

Mister Marquez looked Wally sternly in the face and said, "We won't be that far away. Send for us if you need us." Then, he turned to Oscar and Jesse and said, "Boys, let's see if we can get the RV going."

"If not," I told him, "Maybe we can hook it up to my horses."

Mister Marquez clapped me on the back and said, smiling, "I'm getting a laugh just picturing that, but that might be the way to go." Then, to his wife Elana, he said, "Let's gather our things and try to get going in the morning."

Alexa chimed in, "Let me and Jesse get everything we can from the garden."

"Especially the seeds," Jesse said, surprising us partly because he so rarely spoke up on his own. "We ought to plant a new garden, so we'll have vegetables." His father rubbed Jesse's head proudly, then they started off towards their house.

"Mister Preston, I'm not trying to start a revolution. I just— that valley just looks to me like the best place to be right now."

Wally merely nodded then left without speaking.

Claire turned to Danica and asked, "Do you need somewhere to sleep tonight? We've got a couple bedrooms or a couch you can use."

"That would be great," she replied. She cast a glance toward the south and said, "I wonder if my house is covered in ash?"

"Where'd you live?" Claire asked in a friendly manner.

"Just west of Fairplay, on Highway 9." She smiled unconvincingly and told us, "For once in my life, I'm glad I live alone. Glad I'm not having to worry that someone—or some pet—is out there in the ash." She didn't seem glad when she said it.

I started off towards town, leading Claire to say, "Um, Josh, home is this way."

"I'm going to see if I can get the truck running," I told her. She nodded and caught up with me, Danica walking along behind.

Three vehicles were still where we had left them, though Mister Glass's van was only about a hundred yards further on than where I had last seen it. I popped the hood on the truck, knocked all the ash I could from the air filter, and closed everything up. I started to go to Danica's car but she said, "Leave it. I can come back for it another—wait. I do have a change of clothes in there. Might as well take those with me."

It took us a while, but we finally got the truck back up to the ranch. Once there, I wondered why we had gone to all the trouble as I didn't think we'd be using the truck much for a long time. Not only was there the issue of the ash, there was the matter of gas. We had a tank at the ranch that we used to keep all our ranch vehicles running, but it was due for a fill-up on Monday that I doubted would come. There might still be a hundred gallons in the tank, but how long would that last? No, I was figuring we were a horse and foot operation for the foreseeable future.

As we made our way into our house, Claire commented, "I hope you weren't offended about us showing up at the funeral with guns."

Danica reached into a pocket of her cargo pants and produced a compact, .45 caliber Colt. After displaying it for a moment, she explained as she returned it to the pocket, "I am a single woman who is frequently the last person out of a bank in a rural area. I am a great believer in self-preservation."

"Miss Frowley," Claire opened, only to be interrupted.

"Call me Danica."

"Danica," Claire amended. "Do you think you were right about what you said? About this being a volcano—the ash, I mean?"

"It seems like it to me."

Claire bit her lip for a moment, then asked, "Could we really be the only people left alive?"

Danica paused, then replied in as cheerful a voice as she could muster, "If we survived, I bet other people did, too. It may just be a long time before we can make contact with any other groups. On the other hand, we just don't know. It could be that most everyone in Fairplay is fine and worrying about us." She paused, then added, "But right now, I think we better plan like we're all that's left. I like that gardening idea those kids had."

Danica said she would prefer to sleep on the couch than in one of the bedrooms. We hadn't said anything, but maybe she sensed that we were still thinking of those rooms as belonging to Rusty and our parents. The funny thing was, and I realized it even at the time, if we had known without a doubt that our family members were alive and well, we wouldn't have had the least bit of trouble with sharing their rooms. The uncertainty made us protective of those rooms, I think, for I noticed that Claire seemed relieved when Danica elected for the couch.

In the hall upstairs, Claire stopped me and said, "Is there any chance this is all a dream and we're going to wake up in a world with no more ash than that produced by a boring old forest fire?"

"That's a thought to sleep well to." She hugged me tentatively, but I returned it strongly and then she held tightly to me. We stood like that for quite a while before she kissed me on the cheek and then let go to walk to her bedroom. It occurred to me that she had never kissed me on the cheek before, that I remembered. Then it occurred to me that I wished I had returned the favor, but she was already in her room.

"There were a couple houses in Como that had solar panels, I noticed," Danica said as we ate breakfast. "Yours seems to work well, and didn't someone say that Mister Glass was a retired electrician? As long as we have sunlight, those are going to be a great boon, but we may need to plan for a future that doesn't include any electricity."

"Why?" Claire asked, beating me to it.

"If the ash cloud moves back over us, we may not be able to count on solar power. There's also the matter of maintenance. Maybe things will work for years, but if there's anything I know about mechanical things it's that they will eventually break down. Our manufacturing capabilities are almost nil."

"People came to these mountains without much," I pointed out.

"But Como was a rail town, and before the train got here they were packing things in on mules and with wagons. This area has never really been self-sustaining."

"The Utes and Cheyenne lived up here for a long time," I mentioned.

"And that may be who we have to pattern ourselves after," Danica replied. "We may be in for a pretty minimalist existence for quite a while. Leave the modern world behind. Even if we can keep the solar panels going, we don't have an endless supply of lightbulbs."

I gestured with my fork as I said, "But we don't have to become primitive ourselves. We have books and Bibles and stuff like that. We don't have to become a bunch of people in loin cloths sitting around a fire and banging on rocks."

"You're right, of course," Danica agreed. "But we don't have to read very far into those books to see that man can quickly become a very uncivilized animal. If things get worse, and we're scrabbling for every amount of food … "

"One day at a time," Claire injected, trying to sound cheerful.

"You're right," Danica nodded with a relieved smile. "'Sufficient for the day is its own trouble,' as the Good Book says."

"That's one of those verses I always hate to 'amen'," Claire quipped.

It turned out that Danica Frowley was a passable horsewoman, so we set her up on one of the horses from the south barn and, with Claire and I each mounted on another, took the eight horses there to join the others at the north barn. The space would be too tight to keep them all inside, but Claire and I felt the best thing for both us and the horses would be to have them all together. When we got to the north barn, we were excited to find that Star had returned, as had a younger pony we called Lazy. That only left one horse unaccounted for, an older buckskin we called Buckie. We figured she was just back in the woods somewhere and would eventually find her way back.

As we had finished the last of the milk at breakfast, I was really wishing for a milk cow. A few people in the area had cows, I knew, so I wondered if any of them might be milkers and if any of them were still alive.

And accessible. They might be alive but if we couldn't get to them, they would be no more good to us than any other dream. I realized that one of the things we needed to do was start taking an inventory of what we had. Whether we put everything in common with the other survivors in Como or just started bartering with our supplies, it would help to know what we had (and what we didn't).

It was my plan to eventually go back to the south barn and transport all the hay—and anything else we might need—to the north barn. I had, in fact, many plans, and as we slowly rode the horses down the path to the north barn, I began to try and work through them in my mind. My original thought that we move to the green grass of the Selkirk was tempered by the thought that our house had electricity and running water. So, I wondered, should we live in the house and just run the horses on the green grass of the Selkirk (and run any cattle we could find there as well), or should we try and move our whole lives to the Selkirk? I didn't know enough about building a house, but I figured I could learn and I was betting that Mister Glass could show us how to move the solar panels and install them in a new place. Back to the first hand of my argument, though, was the question of "Why move at all?" The house was at the edge of the ash cloud (which I was sure would still be moveable) and the distance between the house and the Selkirk was less than two miles, and only about a mile to where the green grass started. Buried within this idea was the idea that that house was *my house*. It was where I had grown up and where my stuff was contained. There was a certain romance about starting over, building a frontier cabin, living like my ancestors. But I still wanted my stuff, even some of the useless bits.

I was also wondering how feasible it would be to take a couple horses or the pickup and try to get into Fairplay to find Mom and Dad. A part of me said Claire's intuition was right and they had perished in the ash. Oddly, it was that part of me that didn't want to go to Fairplay for, as long as I avoided going, I could always dream that they were still alive there. If I went, besides running the very real risk of not being able to make it there, I might find incontrovertible evidence of their deaths.

On another hand to that argument was the idea that maybe they were alive and their only hope was if I came to get them. Could I make it at all? I had serious doubts about being able to get the pickup—or any other vehicle, for that matter—through the ash. Horses? Could I keep a horse breathing any better than I could a car? I would need to pack in a considerable amount of water just to keep the horses alive, and then we'd have to come back. It seemed like a fool's errand, but I couldn't see how I could avoid it. They were my parents, after all. I knew then that I was going, I just didn't know yet when.

At the barn, twenty-four of our twenty-five horses accounted for, I pointed out the green grass of Boreas Pass to Danica, who commented, "That's so strange. The wind must come off the ridge there just right to keep the ash blown away. No telling if it will last, but I agree that it's our best bet right now." She took a step closer, then pointed, "I was working with all of you a couple weekends ago and I remember there was a flat place off on the north side of that cut over there. A lot of sediment had settled in there and we were remarking about how quickly the grass was growing there. I'm thinking that might be a good spot to start a garden, if it gets as much sunlight as I remember. Government helicopters might arrive at any moment and offer to take us to somewhere safe, or we might be here for a while. If there's any chance at all of us having to winter here, we need to get some vegetables growing as soon as possible."

"You ever garden?" I asked.

"A little," she replied with a shrug. "My mother *always* had a garden. I hated working it, but now I wish I had paid more attention. I think I can figure out the basics, though. We're going to need to figure out how to get water to it, though. If that stream is still running, we're golden. But if it's been clogged up by the ash, then we're going to need to carry it from somewhere."

"We have a well and a pump or the ranch," Claire told her. "And we've got that big fiberglass tank on a trailer that we use for getting water to the horses. I bet we could figure out a way to pull it with horses."

Danica smiled at her and said, "That's the kind of thinking we need. I'm trying not to be pessimistic here. I think we're going to be in for a rough time of it, but it may not be as hopeless as I think it is in some moments."

"Where does your Mom live?" Claire asked her softly.

"I grew up in El Paso. Never knew my father. He was just a name on my birth certificate. My mother died while I was off at college. Heart attack at forty-three. I used to wonder if I'd make it past forty-three." She made a gesture to encompass all our surroundings and added, "Now, making it *to* forty-three seems a lot less certain."

It was Claire who broke the silence by saying, "What say we saddle up some horses and head over to Danica's garden spot? Time to start planning for the future, right?"

"Right," Danica and I said in unison, which gave us a bit of a much-needed chuckle.

We saddled up three fresh horses and filled some canteens from the pump beside the barn and mounted up. As we set out, Danica commented, "It just dawns on me that, if we are the last people left on earth, then I'm the last black person. I've been used to being one of the 'onlies', but I never thought I'd be *the only*, you know?"

"Surely there are other people in the world," Claire commented.

"Probably," Danica agreed. "Very likely, in fact. And if the volcano really was somewhere in the Pacific northwest, then Africa might be the least-affected portion of the planet, in which case black people might suddenly be dominant—at least by numbers. Still, right here, it just gives me pause to think I might never see another person like me." She laughed, looked a bit embarrassed, and added, "I know we're not supposed to notice skin color anymore, but we do. Maybe not as bad as it used to be, but I think it'll always be there—here. Just kind of makes me think."

"You're not that old, Miss—Danica. You could have children, and they would be, well, half black, right?"

Trying to make light of the subject, Danica smiled as she said, "You do bring up a good point, Claire, though maybe not the point you were thinking of. If we are either the last people on earth, or just trapped here in this little pocket—possibly for years—

without seeing anyone else, should we, um, reproduce? Do we have a duty, even, just to keep the human race alive?"

"You make us sound like an endangered species," Claire responded, trying to make it sound like she were joking, too.

"We may be, Claire." We rode on a bit before she added, "I read a book when I was in school about this futuristic society where something like this had happened, though their problem may have been a war. Anyway, for the propagation of the species, they started matching up males and females like you would do with cows and bulls. It seemed silly and fantastic at the time but, well, you're right, Claire: I am still in my child-bearing years. Do I have a responsibility to reproduce? Or do I still have the luxury to try to find a man to fall in love with?"

"What about morality?" I asked, trying to think of a better way to ask, but rather enjoying the nature of the conversation. I think it was because I felt like a grown-up, conversing over weighty things. "Do things like marriage and faithfulness still apply to the equation or is it just about reproduction?"

"That's a good question," Danica responded. "But maybe not germane. Let's say that, for the propagation of the species, I 'get together'," she made quote marks with her fingers, "With one of the men who are left here. We only get together with each other. We produce one or more children and remain faithful to each other. Wouldn't that fit the imprimaturs of morality? So I don't have anything to worry about from God on the transaction, but, well, I don't want to be a cow. I have nothing against producing children, but I still want it to be with a husband I love. I'm one hundred percent against if someone were to suggest all of us females in our child-bearing years start having sex with the men just to get pregnant. No way. But, is it immoral for me to hamper the continuance of the human race because I don't find any of the men here appealing?"

"Wow," I replied with a chuckle. "That's a much bigger question than I had in mind!"

We were interrupted from our roundtable discussion by Claire, who said, "Is that smoke?" while pointing off toward the northeast.

We all pulled up and looked in the direction of Mount Volsh, the only mountain in the area whose forests had remained mostly unscathed during the fires—or, at least, less-scathed. Some of its lower regions seemed to be in the area that had been blown free of ash and, rising from the trees, there did appear to be a darkened wisp. "Isn't that where the Mondragon house is?" I asked, though I knew the answer.

"Think maybe one of them was here for the weekend?" Claire asked.

"Let's go check," I suggested, turning my horse in that direction.

"Who are the Mondragons?" Danica asked as she followed us.

"One of the oldest families in the valley. Came here almost the same time as the first member of the Overstreet family that settled here—more than two centuries ago. They sold most of their land to my great-grandfather, but kept a little bit with a house on it. Mostly just come up here on weekends, like a lot of other people in the valley. I think they live at Longmont the rest of the time."

Claire smiled playfully and said, "I remember how you used to have a crush on their daughter. What was her name?"

I thought about pretending I didn't know what she was talking about, but answered, "Lysette." At a rather piercing gaze from Danica, I explained, "She was a couple years older than me. Friendly, but she was never the least bit interested in me. Claire's right, though: on weekends that Lysette was in the area, I always managed to find a lot more work to do on this portion of the ranch than usual. She liked riding horses, so I could always get her to go on picnics and stuff with me so long as we went a-horseback. Took me a long time to admit to myself that the only interest she had in me was in horseback riding. I mean, she was never rude and it's not like she played me, really. She just liked horses."

"So," Danica asked with a laugh, "What if the propagation of the species required you to get together with Lysette?"

I'm sure I turned red as a beet as Claire replied for me, "I doubt that he would object to the idea in theory." Then she smiled at me and added, "But I know my brother and, like you, he'd still like to have a woman who loved him back."

"And you?" Danica asked. Then, "Sorry. None of my business."

Claire shrugged and told us, "I've always figured I would get married someday. Have kids. That was supposed to be way down the road, though, after college and my first million," she chuckled. "Never gave it much thought, but I suppose I would much prefer it be from love rather than duty."

"I thought you teenagers were supposed to be hormone-crazed lunatics," Danica chided.

"Well, maybe," I replied with a laugh. "I like to think that, when it comes down to it, my mind will overrule my hormones."

Chapter Six

Ash on an old man's sleeve
Is all the ash the burnt roses leave.
Dust in the air suspended
Marks the place where a story ended.
Dust inbreathed was a house—
The wall, the wainscot and the mouse
The death of hope and despair,
This is the death of air.
~Thomas Eliot

Back in the days of the gold rush, the valley where sat our fledgling town had been "home" to as many as twenty thousand people. Gold mines had lined the mountains and, two and three centuries on, one could still see some remnants of the work that had gone on there. In the valley below our town, where our little valley or rift opened out into the wider South Park Valley, there were still piles of tailings, dropped there by the mines in centuries past and never moved because, well, what would anyone do with them?

From what I had read, most of the mines would shut down over the winter because it was just too expensive to try and keep the miners alive in the cold, let alone try to move gold or equipment through frozen tundra. So the miners would head down to Canon City or Denver and live off their summer wages for as long as they could. By spring, they would be broke and no matter how much they might hate mining, it was an easy job to procure and back they came. They lived in tiny shacks and did back-breaking work and, I'm guessing, dreamed of making enough money to go do something else. Some of them probably did. According to the stories I had read, though, the only people who made money during the gold and silver rush days were the store keepers who sold goods to the miners. Some of them had become millionaires and founded empires that produced billionaires.

When fall would come, and the snow would begin to pile up on the peaks, most of the mining would shut down. The railroad would try to keep the line running over Boreas Pass for as long as they could, but there were several stories about the loss of life and equipment as the result of trying too hard to make one more run. They even tried building a man-made tunnel over the top of the divide that would, they hoped, enable them to run the train a couple more weeks in the fall and start up again two weeks earlier in the spring. It turned out to be more expensive than it was worth … and in the spring they discovered a family of mountain lions had move in. I think they tore the tunnel down and used the wood elsewhere.

Then the snow would pile up and everything would shut down, except for a few desultory operations here and there. In some cases, no one knew anyone had stayed behind to work the mine until their dead body was found frozen in the mountain the next spring.

When spring came, the snows would melt and the water would flow down and form the Tarryall, a bubbling, gurgling stream of fresh, mountain water along whose banks I had spent many hours of my childhood. I wasn't much on fishing, but I used to like to float boats down the stream. In my teen years, Rusty and I had built a sluice after a pattern we had found in an old book and tried our hand at washing for gold. We found some flakes now and then and, had we cashed them in, it might have almost been enough to pay for the wood we had bought to make the sluice. I still have the little pouch of gold dust we panned, it's only value now in the memories of Rusty it conjures up.

Fording the stream we called the Tarryall required going out of our way a little and using one of the bridges along the road from Boreas Pass. I took this as a good sign: the stream was still flowing. It was cloudy from the ash, but at least it was water. As long as it flowed, I figured we had a chance of surviving.

There had been a time when the Tarryall was one of the most prospected streams in America, with no less than three towns in less than a mile's length built along its edge and thousands of miners pulling ore out of the surrounding mountains. The house we were heading to might have one day been on the edge of Peabody, a mining town that existed only in the history books for, even before the fires, all evidence of it had been gone for over a hundred years. Many was the time I had ridden my horse over the lands where

Peabody and Hamilton had once sat, where thousands of men had plied their trade and businesses had sprung up—everything from the expected saloons to, in Hamilton, an opera house that had attracted the top names of its day. As I had ridden over those old townsites, I had been amazed that they were completely gone. It occurred to me that morning, riding with my sister and Danica, that all the towns I had grown up with might be gone, too.

We rode up close to the house, tucked in among the aspens and pines as it was, and I called out, "Hello the house!" When the ladies looked at me with puzzlement, I told them, "Seemed like a good idea in case they're as paranoid and armed as we are."

"Good point," Claire said with a nod.

As we rode closer, the front door opened and a tall, thin man close to my age stepped out. He looked nervous, but asked, "Who are you?" The sun was in his eyes, causing him to squint. He had short-cropped blonde hair and glasses in the latest fad style.

Suddenly, a figure appeared behind him and asked, "Josh? Claire?"

"Lysette?" my sister and I asked in unison as we got off our horses.

Lysette came forward and hugged Claire and I, then turned to the blonde man and said, "Steve, this is Josh and Claire Overstreet. We've known each other since … when? Before we even went to school, right?" As Claire and I nodded, Lysette told us, "This is my husband, Steve Carrier." We all shook hands and Steve seemed taken aback by the whole situation. I gathered he was shocked to find they weren't the last two people left in the world.

I almost wouldn't have recognized Lysette. She had cut her long, dark hair and she had put on probably thirty pounds since the last time I had seen her. I figured out why the instant I heard a baby crying from inside the house. As Lysette darted in, I introduced, "Steve, this is Danica Frowley, our, um, banker." It occurred to me as I said it that the bank she ran was probably buried under ash and who knew whether it's assets were valid currency anymore or not?

As they shook hands, Danica told him, "*Was* a banker. Now, I think I'm just a refugee like everyone else."

Lysette reappeared then, holding a cute little baby girl (based on the pink) who looked to me to be about three or four months old. Lysette held her proudly and said, "This is Angela."

"Named for your grandmother, right?" Claire asked, taking the baby as girls are so often wont to do.

"Both our grandmothers, actually, but I'm impressed you remembered that. When would you have ever met my grandmother?" Then, as if realizing the situation we were all in, Lysette asked, "What's going on?"

I gestured and said, "Danica thinks it was a volcano, somewhere off to the west. This morning, we were on our way to scout out the old Selkirk campground. The wind seems to have blown the ash off that part of the valley, so we're thinking we'll see if we can find a place up there to start a garden, maybe put up some houses."

Steve objected, as if talking to children, "You make it sound like this is the end of the world and we're going to be stuck here like people from some old TV show. Surely the government will send out rescuers any time now."

"Maybe," I replied, not liking the man (and telling myself it wasn't because of jealousy), "But if this thing really did come from the west coast, and if it blanketed several states like we're thinking, it could be a long time before anyone gets to us. We're just trying to be prepared."

"Well, I think you're getting all worked up over nothing," Steve told us, though it was mostly directed at me. "We'll probably be helicoptered out of here this afternoon."

I started to reply, but Claire interrupted with, "That would be great. But right now, we're just trying to see what our options are."

Lysette injected, "We came up here expecting to spend a couple weeks, so we brought a lot of food with us. We'll be happy to share—"

"Let's not—" Steve started to object.

"These are our neighbors, and our friends," Lysette said, in a calming voice. Then, she smiled (which actually made her look like the Lysette I remembered) and added, "Let's let them go about

75

their business for now, Steve. If the rescuers come today or tomorrow, we'll all have a laugh at our panic."

I wasn't really thrilled with the way she put that, but nodded in agreement and got back up on my horse. Danica followed suit and Claire did as well after handing back the baby and commenting on how pretty the little girl was. I was about to ride away, then turned and asked, "You remember that stash of fireworks your little brother always kept back in the old mine?"

"Yeah," Lysette replied, confused.

"Check and see if those are still there. If you need anything, send one up and if we see it we'll come."

"We'll be fine," Steve told us in no uncertain terms.

"Just in case," I replied, as conciliatorily as I could manage.

"It's a good idea," Lysette replied, which Steve eventually nodded to.

When we were out of hearing range, Danica commented, "Well, that was awkward."

"He could be right, you know," I pointed out. "We could get rescued this afternoon."

"He wasn't any more convinced of that than you are. He's just one of those husbands who's jealous of every guy who looks at his wife," Danica told us. I looked at her to see if she were joking, but she didn't appear to be.

Just then, we felt a tremble in the earth. It was less pronounced than the one we had felt on Saturday, but it lasted longer. Just when we were about to ask each other when it would stop, it did. It was followed a few moments later by another tremor, of less strength but longer lasting. "Wonder what that means?" I asked, to receive shrugs from both ladies.

No more than twenty minutes later, we were riding into the green cutting Danica had suggested for the garden when the lighting changed. We looked up to see another wall of ash coming towards us. One of the ladies screamed and I imagine something unpleasant escaped my lips. Grabbing the reins and signaling for the ladies to do so as well, I led us over to the shelter of a rock wall. Pulling a ground tarp from my saddle bags—and thanking the Lord it was there!—I directed them to huddle with me against the rock face. The horses instinctually turned away from the blowing wind and we put the tarp over our heads just as the wall of ash hit.

The sound was deafening and there was nothing to be seen in the complete darkness, but it rolled over us quicker than the ash cloud had on Saturday. It was probably no more than fifteen minutes, though in the middle it seemed like the rest of our lives. As soon as it passed on, we were up and sponging out the noses of the horses.

"Another volcano or the same one?" I asked, not really expecting an answer.

Danica, seeing what we were doing and following suit with the horse she had been riding, replied, "No way of telling. Sure didn't last as long as on Saturday, so I'm thinking this was either a smaller volcano or just some sort of aftershock. I think I've read that those things sometimes go on for days after a major eruption."

The wind was still blowing pretty good, making us all glad we had worn jackets. It was Claire who pointed out, "Look. This little valley still has clear skies. And everything around, maybe it's my imagination, but everything else looks even darker to me."

"I think you're right," I commented. "For now, this is still the best spot."

"I don't know how long we can count on that," Danica injected morosely, "But I say we try to make the best of it. This is the best spot right now. If things change, we roll with the change."

"How soon do you think the Marquez family will get here?" Claire asked.

"Depends on whether they can get that RV running and keep it running," I answered. I looked around and said, "I say we dig out those old tents and set them up near those trees over there. They seem to be pretty sturdy and they would block the wind fairly well. I like the idea of sleeping in my own bed, but I'm thinking we're going to need a presence here, to watch over the horses and the garden. And, well, some place we can duck into if more of those walls of ash come our way."

"Makes sense to me," Danica agreed.

"When do we go look for Mom and Dad?" Claire asked, out of the blue it seemed to me.

I wanted to reply, but it took me a while before I was able to say, "We gotta figure out if we can. Can we even make it—"

"Josh, we gotta try. You know they would come looking for us."

"I also know they wouldn't want us risking our lives for them," I argued. Then amended, "But you're right. Let's get you and Danica settled in, tents set up and all, and get the horses over here. Then I'll go—"

"We'll go," Claire corrected. "I'm going along," she said, matter-of-factly. "Think we can get going by first light tomorrow?"

It took me by surprise, but I answered, "Yeah. First light."

At Danica's insistence, we set her up a tent near the barn. She said she would much rather stay there until we got back, than alone in the wide open meadow or even our house. The corral would make it easier to watch over the horses and she said she felt less exposed there. Plus, I think she liked the company of the horses better than the idea of being completely alone. Oscar had come by and told us it was probably going to take his family at least another day and maybe two before they could make it up to the meadow. This had further convinced Danica to stay near the barn. So, we set her up with a tent and some bedding—including the mattress off Rusty's bed—all the food from our house, and all the other items we (or she) could think of her needing. She even borrowed a couple books from our shelves and a lantern to read them by.

Claire hugged her nervously as the dawn broke and said, "Take care of my horses. Our horses."

"I will. And don't worry: you'll be back and taking care of them in no time."

"I hope so," Claire said, before mounting.

We set out with a string of six horses. On two we rode, on two we carried some gear and as much water as we thought they could handle, and the other two were along so we could trade out as we expected it to be an arduous trip for the horses. We weren't expecting a vacation for ourselves, either.

As we headed from the ranch into Como, Claire suddenly said, "You know what seems wrong with this week, Josh?"

"Everything?" I replied with a chuckle.

"Well, yeah. But I was thinking: today's Tuesday. Can you ever remember us having a Sunday without church? Even when we were snowed in and couldn't go anywhere, Mom and Dad would hold church for us in the living room. We should have done something like that."

"We went to a funeral on Sunday."

"I'm serious, Josh!"

"So am I, mostly. But you're right. This coming Sunday, let's have church. Even if it's just us two."

"And let's start praying together," she suggested, though it seemed stronger than a suggestion. I was a little surprised because Claire had always been the least-interested in spiritual matters of anyone in the family. Or, I thought, maybe it was just that it was usually Mom who prompted us to go to church so, of course, Claire always came up with a reason not to.

So I finally replied, "I think that's a good idea."

"You think he's up there? God, I mean. After something like this, you think maybe he just turned his back on us? People were always saying we were no better than Sodom and Gomorrah. Maybe this was his judgment."

I had no idea how to reply to that. I considered myself a Christian and I had always attended church—even went on my own a few times when my parents were out of town—so my first response was to rebel against what she said. At least, about the idea that God might not be up there or listening anymore. It went against everything I had ever believed to even think that. On the other hand, I couldn't completely discount her judgment hypothesis. We lived in a pretty wicked world, but was it any more wicked than the world had always been?

Such thoughts led me to thinking about the Book of Revelation. I was no scholar, but I had read it once, after hearing a guy on the TV say some things I didn't agree with about it. I had gone and read the book and come to disagree with the man on TV even more, but I could kind of see where he got what he said. I was convinced he was twisting Scripture for his own ends. Anyhow, I hadn't memorized the book or anything, but I remembered there being a passage in there about the sky being darkened by smoke from the abyss. That sure seemed like what we were seeing, but I wasn't confident that that was the only interpretation of the passage. I told myself that when I got back to the ranch, I ought to look that passage up. It suddenly occurred to me that I ought to carry a Bible in my saddlebags, but decided against going back for one then. I'd get one as soon as I got home, for we had several in the house.

I had advocated at first that we take the back way, which would save a few miles, and bypass Como. Claire had rightly pointed out, though, that if Mom and Dad were to try to get to us the most logical way to do so was by the highway as it was the much better road. The back way was a string of dirt roads and sometimes just pathways and, even in good conditions, usually took at least twice as long as the highway route. Then, Claire clinched it by quoting from Tolkien and my favorite book by saying, "Short cuts make long delays."

We found Como to be a town of some bustle as people were trying to figure out who had what and what could be shared. Several people were out and starting to till up garden space, a process that involved a lot of rock removal. Those rocks just below the surface had been one of the reasons no one in Como—at least, in my memory—had much gone in for gardening. It was interesting to see what desperation would do for people.

We discovered that a few more people had been added to the town's population. There were two families from across the highway who had made it into town as they had seen the shaft of sunlight that cut through the gash in the cloud. They had brought horses and several people and were trying to set up in a couple of the abandoned (we presumed) houses. There were also two single men who had come in separately from off the Elkhorn. One told a story of how he had lost his cattle, his dogs and his wife (in that order) and wasn't hesitant at meeting us to say that Claire and I were on a fool's errand if we thought we could make it into Fairplay. I didn't like the man and I didn't like how he looked at Claire, so I just kept us moving, ignoring his bluster as it receded behind me.

"He could be right," Claire said when we were out of ear shot. "This could be a fool's errand—or a suicide mission."

"You don't want to turn back, do you?" I asked. I was asking myself if I did. And, I wondered if I were hoping she would want to turn back so I could turn around and claim that it wasn't my idea.

"Do you?" she asked.

"Yes. And no."

She managed a smile and told me, "My thoughts exactly."

By the edge of Como, near the pile of rocks that had been a railroad roundhouse a couple centuries before, we had to put on our bandanas, as well as the ones we had fashioned for the horses. They weren't thrilled with the idea, but they all trusted Claire—more than they trusted me, it seemed—and put up with it. Whether they realized why we were doing that to them I rather doubted, but they did seem to breathe easier.

We took it slow. By the highway, the distance from Como to Fairplay was only fourteen miles, but I thought we'd be doing very well to make it in a single day. Not only did the trek up Red Hill Pass scare me, I just wasn't sure if we could exist in all that ash. The sky wasn't as thick with it as it had been two days before, but it was still a horrifying mess. And the horses seemed to have their footing, but it was tentative at times. We had picked six of our best and both Claire and I trusted them to find the best way. Normally, that would have just been the highway, but those weren't normal times.

So we would plod on for half an hour, then get off for a few minutes, long enough to check the horses' noses and mouths, then remount and ride on. At the base of Red Hill, we switched saddles to fresh horses and started up. All my life, and for at least a hundred years before that, there had been a rock at the base of Red Hill Pass, just off the north end of the road. It wouldn't have been an especially noticeable rock except that a long time ago someone had painted it to look like a cow. It didn't look at all like a cow if you were coming at it from Como, but if you were heading down the Pass—especially in a car going the speed limit—it could almost pass for a cow at a quick glance. A very stationary, solitary cow, but something like a cow. The local joke had always been to call it "The Petrified Cow" and we had a lot of stories we told visitors about how it had gotten that way (frozen in the winter, baked in the summer, etc.). No one was dumb enough to believe our stories, or even think it a cow if they gave it a second look.

It really did something to me, though, to see that the petrified cow was buried in ash. I could see a lump beneath the ash where it lay, but to not be able to see it was an experience that shook me—much more than similar trips when I couldn't see it for snow. I had to give all my attention to going up the Pass, but my mind kept going back to that stupid rock. Like it not being there meant my world really was changed. Irrevocably.

The highway department, and the railroad more than a century before, had made the path up Red Hill Pass more than passable. It was steep, and occasionally gave some trouble to the cars of flatlanders that weren't acclimated to the altitude, but for us locals it was just something you drove over without thinking. There I was, though, prodding my horse to make the climb, with her all the while trying to balk. I didn't know if it were the steepness or just the feel of the ash on the asphalt, but my horses didn't want to make that climb at first, and neither did the other five. Claire was able to get her horse to take the lead, though, and with that trail blazed the rest of the horses were willing to follow. I rode the drag and had some appreciation for what Mister Glass had gone through on Saturday night (Sunday morning). And, under ordinary conditions, the road wouldn't have been scary for me as it was three lanes wide and with a healthy shoulder to either side. Still, as the ash getting kicked up by the horses in front of me reduced the visibility further and further, I found myself hugging the right-hand wall of the mountain much more than was necessary. Sure, there was a dangerous drop-off to the left of the road, but that road was a good twenty-five feet wide, and maybe more! Once the fear of that drop-off was in my mind, though, I couldn't shake it.

It was noon (I think, couldn't really tell by the sun!) when we got to the top of Red Hill Pass. We unburdened all the horses and let them have a breather, and ourselves as well. There was a place at the top of the pass where the road cut through the top of the mountain and, in that cutting, we found a little respite. We washed out the horses' mouths and noses, took a drink and a little food ourselves, then just let the horses hang their heads for a bit. They hadn't complained, and they weren't lathered up or anything like that, but I could tell the horses were no more thrilled about the journey than we were.

The landscape from Como to Red Hill was, in my opinion, some of the prettiest in the world. Not that I had been many places, but I had seen pictures and I would have put our view up against any other vista in the world. That day, though, it had just been a gray, formless landscape through which the cutting of the highway was barely visible, beneath a gray, lifeless sky through which the sun couldn't quite break through. At first, Claire's bright orange western shirt and blue jeans had been a welcome sight to break up the gray, but now they were the same color as everything else. My clothes were the same. We had brushed the majority of the ash off the horses, so they were at least something brown in the sea of gray, but I knew they would be gray again before we reached the southern base of the Pass.

We had sat down in the cutting for a little while before Claire, acting restless, had gotten up and walked to the south end of the cut. Normally, one could see Fairplay from there, which I had purposely avoided. When I heard her gasp, though, I jumped to my feet and went to join her.

If the South Park Valley north of Red Hill Pass had been a moonscape, the valley to the south lacked even that definition. The ash looked to be even deeper, the ridges and runs less defined, and the sky even darker and flatter. Not only that, but while we could see bumps in the terrain where Fairplay was supposed to be, we could see no movement. Granted: it was a few miles away and the visibility wasn't good, but I had expected to see a yellow bulldozer plowing the road or someone like us on horseback. There was nothing moving. Even the clouds of ash just hung there oppressively.

Claire's hands had been to her mouth this whole time, but now she lowered them and asked, "Do we go on?"

I wanted to say no, that we should just turn around, but what I came out with was, "Let's get to the bottom of the pass. Maybe it's not as bad as it looks."

She nodded and stepped over to where her saddle lay on the ground. Picking up the blanket and shaking it out as best she could, she laid it across the back of Scout, and then patted him as if apologizing for what she was asking of him. I found myself doing the same thing as I saddled Sluicebox, the youngest of the horses on the trip but, to my thinking, the steadiest of them all. Even as a colt, Sluicebox had been more sure-footed than the average horse. Maybe to make up for the stupid name he had been stuck with.

We loaded up the pack horses with the water, gave each horse a fresh sip, then I held all six while Claire fitted their bandanas back on. She kissed each horse in turn, and whispered something to each, then we mounted up. I was able to lead off that time, though, and was glad of it because I knew Sluicebox would not only be sure-footed himself, he would find the best way down for the others.

The road was again wide as it went down the south side of the Pass, but the steep drop-off was to the right this time, so we stayed to the left. Sluicebox didn't have to hug the wall, though, and I let him have his head.

As we neared the bottom of the Pass and discovered that the ash was as deep as we had feared—almost up to the bellies of the horses even on the highway—we discovered a new problem. With all the ash, and perhaps with all the trees being covered as well, it became hard to breath. We stopped and sponged out the horses' mouths and noses, and gave them drinks, but it was no help. They were breathing laboriously, and so were we. We tried to go on, but made it only a few yards before it was clear that we were walking into a death trap.

I finally told Claire, "If we make it into Fairplay, it's going to have to be without the horses."

She nodded and said, "But we've got to get them back to the top of the Pass first. At least they could breathe up there."

I nodded and we turned around. The horses were still having trouble breathing, but they seemed happy about the idea of going back. We took it slowly and it was late afternoon by the time we again achieved the top of Red Hill Pass. Even though the altitude was greater, the air was better on the north side of the Pass and the horses seemed grateful. They were breathing easier.

As we rubbed them down, I looked over and saw that Claire was crying. I stopped what I was doing and came over, asking, "What is it?"

"They're all dead, Josh. Or they're dying. Everyone in Fairplay that we know is gone. Mom and Dad probably choked to death two days ago and—and ... " She put her head against the horse she was brushing and cried. I touched her back tentatively, watching the ash fly up as I did, and could think of no honest argument. After a bit, she raised up her head and said, "Maybe it's not like this everywhere. The same winds that have protected our little space and ruined Fairplay, they've probably protected and ruined other places. Denver may be just fine while the Springs are toast—or vice versa. Or maybe everything in the world is gone but our little valley. How do we go on?"

"Do you mean into Fairplay, or just in general?"

"We can't go into Fairplay, Josh. On that score, we have to head back to Como, if we want to save the horses—and ourselves. But how do we go on at all?"

"Let's um, let's see if we can get down at least to that old road that goes off to the west. Might be able to get out of the elements a bit there and, well, spend the night." Claire nodded and went back to work on her horse. When we had given them all a breather, we started down the Pass and just made the cut-off I had described before dark. We knocked some ash off a stand of grass that had been somewhat protected by a blow-down, picketed the horses there, then rolled out our sleeping bags. Laying there, so close we could hear each other breathe, I reached out and touched my sister and said, "We ought to have a prayer." She didn't say anything, but took my hand and held on tightly. I don't remember what I said in prayer that night, something about God watching over our parents and Rusty or even welcoming them home, and then we both drifted off. Mine was a fitful sleep but when I woke up some time later, I realized Claire was still holding my hand. That made me feel better and I actually slept better after that.

Chapter Seven

The time is now near at hand which must probably determine whether Americans are to be freemen or slaves; whether they are to have any property they can call their own; whether their houses and farms are to be pillaged and destroyed.
~George Washington

We awoke to a day at least as gray as the one we had left, and it seemed even more so. With heavy hearts, we saddled two of the horses and distributed everything we had among the other four. We each took a sip of water but, wisely or no, we didn't feel like eating and just set off.

"Fairplay's just another coal mine, now," Claire commented as we rode towards Como.

"Hmm?" I asked, the comment seeming to have come from nowhere—and made no sense (to me).

"I remember reading a book about Como during the old mining days. I think you were the one who turned me on to it. Anyway, I remember reading about the coal mines that were east of town. I remember reading that in one of the mines, I think it was called The King Coal but that might have been another mine in the area, they had a collapse and something like ninety-seven workers were buried. They never dug them out because it would have cost too much trouble and, because, I think their official statement was something about how they were only Chinamen to begin with. I used to have nightmares about us riding our horses over that portion of the valley and those dead workers coming to the surface like zombies in an old movie, maybe because they had just been left like that."

When she didn't seem to be about to say anything else, I asked, "What's that got to do with Fairplay?"

"We—you and I—just decided to let the dead lay where they fell."

"We didn't have another choice."

"But what if it's like that in Buena Vista and Salida and Hartsel and even Denver? Doesn't it make you—I don't know. Doesn't it give you the creeps?"

"Yeah." After a bit I added, "But I don't know what to do about it other than go on living."

Entering Como just after mid-day, we came across Mister Glass and found that some more people had come in just in the last twenty-four hours. Two of them were an elderly couple who had been trapped in their RV east of town but had finally managed to walk in, and the rest were part of a group of hikers who had been trapped in a bus about halfway to Jefferson. They had been walking since Saturday and were barely alive when they got to town. There were three of them and they said the rest of their party—six people, led by the tour guide—had headed off toward the northeast, thinking hope lay in that direction, and hadn't been seen since.

A surprising amount of food had been found and brought to the old Mercantile building. Much of it belonged to the owners of the Como Hotel, but other dried foods had been found stored in some of the various weekend homes around town. Wally Preston had formed a committee of five people who were tasked with doling out the food in as equitable a manner as possible. In addition, some tomato and spinach seeds had been found in one of the houses and most of these had already been planted in the gardens about town. It would be inaccurate to say that the mood about town was hopeful, but maybe it wasn't quite so glum as when we had left.

The belligerent cuss who had berated us about leaving saw us and came up to rag us about our lack of success. Before I could even respond, someone who had been standing near him hit him in the head with a well-thrown rock and he fell to the ground. I jumped off my horse and went over to him, finding him writhing and moaning, as blood gushed from a cut on his scalp. As I ripped his shirt and tried to fashion a bandage of it, someone shouted, "Let him bleed to death! We don't need anyone like him around here, anyway."

Others ignored the voice and came to my and his aid. Eventually, we got him calmed down enough to wrap his head with the makeshift bandage. The cut itself didn't seem to be all that bad, but I wondered if he might have a concussion. I couldn't remember how you were supposed to tell, but he was taken away and led to the house where he was staying before I could pursue the idea. I had no idea who threw the rock or shouted for the jerk's death, but I found myself more afraid of them than of the jerk. He had just been a nuisance, stressed like we all were by the events of late, and maybe the same could be said of whoever threw the insult, but whoever threw that rock was upset enough at events to resort to violence.

The Marquez family, we learned, had already headed up to the valley, leaving early that morning. We were anxious to get up there and check on the horses and Miss Frowley, but opted to go to our house, first. Maybe we were hoping our parents would have somehow made it there. There was only a little "new" ash on the road—probably having blown there—so the trip from Como to the ranch only took a few minutes, like it would have under normal conditions. After we rubbed the horses down and picketed them on the grass that had once been our front lawn, Claire and I went in and showered and changed clothes. Once that was done and we were standing in our kitchen, I broached, "Is this fair? We've got a house with running water and electricity and everything while people in town are trying to figure out what to burn."

"I was afraid you'd have that thought, too," she replied. "I tell myself that it's probably not going to last, and if it breaks neither you or I are going to know how to fix it—plumbing or electricity. Or is that just an excuse? Are we being selfish or is it reasonable to try and hold on to this as long as we can?"

I tried to think of an answer, and actually thought of several—from both sides of the fence—before replying, "I wish I knew." After a bit, I added, "I wish this house were closer to the north barn."

"Why?"

I rinsed off my dishes, set them to dry, then said, "Like you got a feeling about our parents, I get a feeling that our survival hinges on living closer to Boreas Pass. I don't see how this place here could become untenable like Fairplay without Selkirk facing the same fate, but I just think it will."

"People move houses," she told me. "Even in the old days. I've read stories about how they would up and move one of these gold towns around here to another spot. Not just the tents, but the houses, too. They'd jack them up and put them on skids or wheels or something and move them. Or, they would take them down and, board by board, move them and reassemble them somewhere. That might be our best option, anyway. Tie into that well by the north barn, set the solar panels to catch maximum sun."

"I think you're on to something, Sis."

"Of course I am. Everyone knows I'm the smart one, now that Rusty's go—" It had started as a joke, but then she realized what she was saying and rushed over to me. Throwing her arms around me she bawled like she hadn't since all this happened. Oh, she had cried—and I had, too—but this was bawling, her whole body shaking with the sobs. I held her close and let her cry and rather thought I should join her but, for whatever reason, at that moment in time, no tears came to my eyes.

In the morning we found Danica currying the horses. She smiled when she saw us, then asked with something like worry, "Back so soon?"

"We, um, we couldn't make it to Fairplay," I told her.

"It's like the whole valley is dead," Claire explained. As we added our string of six back into the herd, we told her about our little adventure.

"I guess we can drive the horses out onto the grass," I said, looking toward that splotch of green on the lower reaches of Boreas Pass. It was so unreal, it looked like something someone had created on a computer, casting part of the photo in black and white and the rest in color.

"The Marquez family got there yesterday. I showed them where I picked out for my garden and they picked out a spot not too far from there. We were going to start plowing today. Or hoeing, anyway." As she patted one of the horses on the rump to, apparently, signal it that she was done, she told us, "Another couple came out from Como and settled near the Marquez family. Ryerson, I think their name is. Middle-aged couple, in their mid-forties I'd guess. Said they just recently moved to Como. He was going to start teaching school in Fairplay this fall and she was going to raise the family."

"They have kids?" Claire asked with interest.

"Couple pre-teens, they said. I haven't seen them, yet. Said the kids were helping pack stuff up at the house in Como."

"What are they living in?"

"Pop-up trailer."

"Oh yeah, I know who that is," I suddenly realized. I hadn't seen them, but I had noticed the trailer when it pulled into town a couple weeks ago. "I think they were going to renovate the old Curtis place. Probably would be easier to start over than rebuild that place. My father looked into buying it and said it needed a lot of work."

"They seem like nice people," Danica commented.

"How'd they get the trailer up here?" Claire asked.

"Pulled it with one of those little Australian cars. They were moving slow, but it wasn't having the sputtering problem all the rest of us were having."

I didn't know much about foreign cars, but I had a sudden urge to see under their hood. Danica interrupted that thought by saying, "Oh, and we got a single woman. Her husband was in Kansas when it happened. I told her she could live with me until we got her a place of her own." In a lowered voice, as if we weren't the only people around, she added, "Her name's Julia Croft and she's expecting."

"Oh wow," Claire muttered.

As we started gathering the horses for the drive, Danica commented, "I'm sorry to hear about your parents. I mean, I guess they could still be there, holding out somewhere."

"Thinking that seems worse," Claire told her.

"I'm sorry. I didn't mean for it to."

As Claire swung bareback onto one of the younger ponies, nothing more than a homemade hackamore as a bridle, she began to tell Danica about our plan to dismantle some or all of our house and move it down to the well by the barn. As she gave Danica way more details than we had discussed—including many I hadn't even thought of—I realized Claire had given the matter a lot of thought. I also realized, for the umpteenth time in the last few days, that my baby sister was a grown woman. In her face and in her body, she could have still passed for an adolescent at first glance (though she was tall, almost five-ten), in her mind and thinking she was a woman, and growing more mature by the moment. Whatever world we built for ourselves, I was glad to have Claire in it; not just because she was my sister, but because I realized she would be an asset.

We went to get the other horses and drive them onto the good grass, and were surprised to find all of them accounted for. The lone missing horse had returned. Her name was Buckie and she looked bedraggled and was covered with ash, but she was there. We rubbed her down and made sure she had plenty of water and, generally, fawned over her. When it came time to drive the horses, we were going to let her stay behind and rest but she wouldn't be parted from her fellows. She was wobbly and slower than the others, but we kept her close and got them all to the green grass by mid-afternoon.

The Marquez family was already hard at work tilling the soil where their garden would be, so Claire and I set to work with Danica on one for the three of us. The Ryersons, Seth and LuAnne, started work on a plot near ours. The single woman, Julia, went to work on Danica's garden and started making plans for her own. If she was pregnant like Danica said, she wasn't showing, yet. Our reasons for having the gardens all close together like that were many: we could share in the work while still having our separate gardens, we could take turns guarding each other's plots (in case there were any wild animals that had survived the ash), and Mister Marquez had a plan for diverting water from the Tarryall that would be more manageable if all of us had our gardens rowed up like that.

One of the issues was seeds, but it turned out that the Ryersons and the Marquezs both had a lot of vegetables with them, so we began drying the seeds from them. At that thought, Claire went back to the ranch house and fetched all of our vegetables, even the ones I had tossed in the trash that morning, thinking they had gone bad. With some hard work and some blessing from above, we thought we might have a possible start on some gardens.

That evening, the eleven of us sat around a small fire and talked of the future. "Claire and I have been talking," I said, "And we're thinking we'd like to dismantle our house—or a portion of it—and rebuild closer to here. We've got a well over by the north barn and it still seems to be flowing pretty good."

"I have been thinking similar thoughts," Lester told us. "If the August storms come this year—who knows if such things have been thrown off kilter—we'll want some sort of shelter then. Our RVs and tents will be enough. What we want for the winter, though, is something more substantial."

"What about a long house, like the pilgrims built at Plymouth Rock?" Danica asked. "Something all of us could fit in? We've got plenty of logs we could use, though some of them are a bit charred."

Seth Ryerson spoke up, "I think a common building might be something we'll want eventually, but I think we would be better off building five small but separate structures. Or four, if you would prefer to stay with the Overstreets. Or six, if you and Ms. Croft would prefer separate domiciles."

"I'll stay wherever there's a bed," Danica chuckled. "But I'm curious. You sound like you have a reason for being against the common house idea."

He hesitated, then explained (sounding like the teacher he was), "Common living quarters have rarely worked well for anyone other than an authoritarian society. Even the pilgrims didn't start to flourish until every man and woman had some incentive to build for themselves and their families. Then, the group itself got stronger." He shrugged and added, "I'm a history teacher."

Elana Marquez spoke up, saying, "Winter can come early in these mountains, or it may not come at all. But if it does, and if we get the heavy rains in August, we might only have a couple months to really prepare. I say we figure out a work schedule and allot time for gardening and time for building. *And*, I say we build seven buildings."

"Seven?" several of us asked at once.

"Seven," she said. She was a stout, kindly, Latina woman who had always appeared to me to be very meek and mild, but I was seeing that she could make her wishes known when she wanted. She elaborated, "I agree with Mister Ryerson here. It's not just a matter of property, which I believe in, but of space. We're going to be working hard, side-by-side to survive. We need a place—or places—where we can withdraw now and then. But, I think we need a building that we can all use. This first winter, assuming no one comes to rescue us—and I for one don't think they will—let's just build small cabins that are big enough to sleep in. Have a stove for heat, of course. But we're going to be dealing with privies here, so we won't even have restrooms. Anyway, these next few weeks, we may only have the time to build the minimum. But let's build a common building that will have a full kitchen and a space where we can eat together when we want—"

"And play games!" Jesse injected.

"Or have a dance," his older sister, Alexa, offered.

"And church," Claire added with an excited nod.

Everyone seemed to like the general idea, though I was pretty sure I saw a grimace on the face of Julia Croft at the mention of church. Maybe Elana saw it, too, for she quickly continued, "Then, next spring we can all start adding onto our houses as we see fit. Right now, though, I think our first thought needs to be all about survival."

"You know," Oscar Marquez injected, "If we build our houses over there, on the south side of the greensward, we'd only be a couple hundred yards from the Overstreet's pump, and we'd still be where, for the time being, anyway, the sun is shining. And we could start gardens on both sides of the valley and see if one side is better than the other." I saw in him the same longing I was feeling to be counted as one of the adults. I felt like I was already there, since I was the oldest member of my family and most of this was taking place on my—or our—land. But I also got the impression that he was talking the way he was to impress someone. Who? I wondered. At the time, I figured it was his parents.

I didn't think about the Oscar question any longer, for it came to me to offer, "There are working solar panels on top of our house, as well as storage batteries in the basement. I think Claire and I can loan those to the common house for as long as they are needed. Right, Sis?"

"Sounds good to me," she replied. "And like you were saying: I bet Mister Glass could come show us how to hook them up."

We slept back at our house that night, but in the morning Claire set to work with the gardeners while myself, Oscar and Seth fired up the Overstreet family chainsaws and started cutting logs for seven buildings. There were plenty of dead trees around, the trick was to find the ones where the wood was still useable. Then, we would cut them down and use the horses to drag the logs into place. We also set to work finding then smoothing out the best places (we thought) for the buildings. Lest anyone think the work was divided between the sexes on a sexist basis … I can only say that we all volunteered for the job we got.

It was just the second day of this building when I had stopped to take a drink of water and my eye went to a particular spot over on the back of Little Baldy, just below the hogback that connected it to Silverheels. Claire caught my eye and asked, "What are you looking at?"

I turned to her and said, "Just thinking of building a log home and started thinking about how to notch the ends and all and, well, I thought of Uncle Chip. Remember that log cabin he had up there? Thing never leaked, always held the heat in in winter, and it survived the fires."

"I thought about that, but it's covered in ash now."

"What about Uncle Chip?"

She looked in the direction of his cabin, then told me, "He's been in Oregon for a month, visiting his grandchildren."

"Supposed to be. You know him, though. He comes back from one of those trips and it's a week before he drops by to tell us he's back. Always says he didn't want to bother anyone."

"You think he might have come back?"

"I'm thinking even if he didn't, it might not be a bad idea to go take a look at that cabin of his, if we can get to it. He built it the old-fashioned way, you know, the way we're going to have to build. We might learn something just from seeing how he did it."

Claire looked back towards where Uncle Chip's cabin was and said, "You know, that stand of trees we were looking at this morning—the ones you and Lester were saying looked good for building—they wouldn't be more than a quarter mile from his cabin. If we can make it to that stand of trees, we ought to be able to make it to his cabin."

"That doesn't necessarily follow," I chuckled, "But I'm willing to give it a try. I'm especially curious to see how he built the rafters. I remember that he did it with pegs instead of nails and I'd like to see how he did that."

Shortly thereafter, I mentioned the conversation to Lester and he and Oscar, as well as Seth Ryerson, were anxious to see the cabin and see if we could learn from it. Up to that point, we were all sold on the *idea* of log homes, but none of us had ever actually built one. And the ones we had seen built—in Como or wherever else— had been kits put together by professionals. We were suddenly all keen to see how it had been done, or, at least, to try and learn from one that was already assembled. More than one of us remarked that we wished Uncle Chip were around to instruct us.

The next morning, we made our way up to the stand of trees where we thought we could get a good supply of logs for our homes. I realized the irony even as I was thinking it: a week before a stand of burned trees was depressing, now a stand of burned trees that were still intact was a blessing. We got to the trees and found that more of them were alive than we had found anywhere else, which cheered us all. We began to cut down the dead ones, and say prayers for the living ones.

Once we had marked the ones to be cut down, myself, Lester and Seth set out to go to Uncle Chip's cabin. This left Oscar and Claire to run the chainsaws until we could get back. I was a little concerned about that at first, but Claire assured me she could teach him how to use one.

It wasn't as far as I had thought to Uncle Chip's cabin from the forest glade, and with bandanas over our faces, we made it in pretty short order. I was pointing out the features of the cabin, and what we ought to look at more closely, as we walked up the driveway. And then I noticed that my uncle's truck was in the carport and sprinted up to the porch. Banging on the door, I called out, "Uncle Chip!" Opening the door, I pushed inside, calling his name.

But there was no one in the cabin. Why his truck would be in the driveway and him not at home I couldn't figure, and it took a good bit of the wind from my sails. I had never really cared for Uncle Chip—him being a strange, surly old man to my mind—but it was hard to suddenly realize another member of my family was gone. I shook myself of the thoughts and, with the guys caught up to me, we started trying to learn what we could from Chip Cespedes' cabin. It would have been nice to have had his personal expertise—despite how he might have delivered it—but we had to satisfy ourselves by just looking closely at his work. I think we learned a little.

Over the next few weeks, we all worked on the gardens and everyone worked on the houses, though myself, Claire and Seth proved to be the most skilled with the chainsaw. Jesse, who didn't say much, was turning into quite a gardener, and everyone was starting to show skills—in most cases, skills they didn't know ahead of time they possessed. Gradually, the walls began to go up and, when the late August rains hit, we even had some semblance of roofs on them, though there was considerable leakage. The rains were welcomed, though, for not only did they allow us to catch some fresh water, they settled much of the ash in the sky. The downside was that they tended to make the ash on the ground even slicker than it had been before and, some days, once it started raining it didn't pay to walk anywhere no matter how restless one might be. Once the rainy season ended, we set to work in earnest on the roofs and were able to get all seven buildings in the dry.

The cabin Claire and I built for ourselves was just ten foot by twelve foot, with sturdy walls and some windows we had taken from our house. In my "spare time", I often went back up to the house and worked at getting the other windows out, for use in our future home. As the days went by, we robbed more and more from that house, and would one day take all the wiring we could get to out of it. Claire and I talked about restoring it one day, but I think we both knew that was becoming less and less likely with everything we carried to our new house. Even the stuff we weren't taking with us, we were giving away or storing with the plan of one day taking it to the new house. It was hard in some ways, but—at least for me—it helped me to make a clean break with the past.

In the mean time, back at our new community, Claire and I held a church service the first Sunday morning. Danica and the Marquez family came, as did the Ryerson family. Julia Croft, while invited, politely declined. We sang a few songs, Claire had found some grape juice in the house which we used for Communion, and then I read the first chapter of the book of Acts (as it seemed like a good place to start a new community). Afterward, we all ate together and invited Julia to join us for that, but she declined that, too. She ate all other meals with us, though, and was as hard-working as anyone we had.

We didn't have a lot of contact with the people in Como, but there was a little. Wally and a couple other men came out one day in August to see how we were coming along, and told us of the doings in Como. Several gardens were going good, they said, and everything was running smooth except that they had had to build a jail to keep Charles in—Charles being the guy who had been clunked in the head with a rock the day Claire and I came through. It seems he had gotten hold of some alcohol and had been trying to pick fights, so they had thrown him in jail. The length of his sentence or who had served as peace officer hadn't been mentioned. Nor did they mention what building served as the jail, for we had never had one in Como in my lifetime, the nearest jail being in Fairplay.

We saw Lysette and her husband occasionally, but they seemed to be mostly keeping to themselves. I did notice that Lysette had started a little garden by their back door, but I never saw her husband working it. Then again, I told myself, it wasn't like I went by there all that often.

Inside our little cabin, I had built a wall of planks between my bed and Claire's. It didn't stop the sound or anything, but it gave us each a bit of privacy. Still, we talked each other to sleep on more than one night. I rather expected to hear Claire crying on some nights, especially as tired as we were, but I never did. I assumed we were both, if not over our loss, coming to terms with it.

Claire was riding Darling one afternoon in early September, just giving the horse some exercise, when the mare must have stepped wrong on a stone or something, for she went down on a fore knee, throwing a surprised Claire off. I had been nearby in the garden when it happened and saw the whole thing. Dropping my hoe, I ran to my sister, hoping she wasn't injured.

Claire, though, had gone into a roll and came up with remarkable quickness. By the time I got over there, she was kneeling by Darling, who was on her side and trying to get up but unable to. "Calm down, Darling," Claire was trying to tell the horse, but the horse was crazy with pain and fear.

Claire looked up at me and pronounced, with anguish, "I think her leg is broken." As I stepped closer, the diagnosis was clearly correct.

"I'll, um, hand me your gun." Mine was over by the garden. I usually carried it with me everywhere, but had yet to fire it, even in practice for we hated to waste ammunition.

Claire stood up and said, "No. Darling has always been my horse. It'll, um, hurt less coming from—she'll understand if I do it." I merely nodded, unsure of what to say. Claire patted the horse gently and said some more comforting words, words that seemed to calm the frightened horse a bit, for she stopped thrashing as much. Then she stood, took out her gun and said, choking back tears, "I'm so sorry, girl. Please forgive me." Her hand trembled a bit, so she brought up the other hand and, steadying the gun, pulled the trigger. One shot was all it took. Claire dropped the gun then and fell to her knees, sobbing.

I knelt beside her and, putting my hand on her back, said, "You did what you had to do."

"I know. And something might have happened even if we'd never had the volcano or the fires or any of the other things that have happened. But the horses, Dad loved the horses. We all did, but having to—this was like killing Dad." She turned and hugged me, saying, "I sometimes wish I had gone to Fairplay with them."

"Yeah, me, too," I replied, surprising myself, for I had tried to not admit such things even in my own mind.

A crowd had gathered then, though they were keeping a respectful distance. Julia Croft had seen Claire fall and the others had started our way as soon as they heard the gunshot. As Claire gathered up her gun and we stood up, Lester Marquez said uncomfortably, "I almost hate to bring this up but, um, horse meat, it—well, we could use some fresh meat. We haven't seen a deer or an elk in days and—"

It was Claire who said, "You're right. She—she shouldn't be wasted."

Lester then offered, "Let me and Oscar take care of her for you. You don't need to watch."

"I'll help," Seth Ryerson told us.

I led Claire over to the garden and set her to work with me, for which she seemed appreciative. We made small, and even stupid, talk as we got rid of the weeds that had sprung up since the last rain. Jesse came over and showed us how we could do a better job. He was abrupt and, in other circumstances I could see where he would have been extremely annoying, but we had all come to realize that when it came to gardening, the kid knew his stuff. His mother told me one day in a low voice, as we stood just the two of us and watched him work, "I know this is going to sound terrible, considering what everyone has lost, but I can't help thanking God for what he has done for Jesse. I would read about autistic children who were good at computers or engines or something but Jesse, he never showed interest in anything for more than five minutes. But he loves this gardening stuff."

"He may save us all," I had told her, to receive an appreciative smile.

"Have you talked to Julia?" Claire asked as we were in our cabin, getting ready for bed.

"Just to say 'hello'," I replied. "Why?"

"Oh, I don't know. Maybe more than any of us here, my heart really goes out to her, being alone like that."

"Danica's alone."

"Yeah, but, well … Danica was alone before. Julia's only been married a little over a year. They came up here so her husband could teach school—like Mister Ryerson. Then, a couple days before the ash cloud, her husband—his name is Dwight but sometimes she calls him D.J.—went with his brother from Denver to go get a car from someone in Kansas. I guess they had bought it on-line or something. He was supposed to be back late that Sunday night." Claire came around the partition, dressed in a flannel nightgown—for the nights could get pretty cool, the skin of her thin legs showing beneath the flannel—and said, "You and I, we're about ninety-nine percent certain what happened to Mom and Dad. We don't know about Rusty, and I think about him a lot, but to lose your *husband* like that. I mean, maybe things are fine in Kansas or maybe he died getting back. If he's alive, he's got to be worrying about her, wondering if she's alive and if he can ever find her. It's," she chewed her lip a moment, then finished, "It's almost a comfort knowing Mom and Dad are dead, you know? Does that sound terrible?"

"I think I get what you mean. On the other hand, I kind of like the idea that Rusty's OK out there. That even if we never see him again in this life, he's getting to live a life, meet a girl, get married, all that."

"Well, yeah, but he's our brother. If D.J. is still alive out there somewhere, he may never be able to marry again because he's always going to wonder about the wife and child that might be up here."

"Maybe not," I offered. When Claire looked at me in surprise, sitting at the foot of my bed, I told her, "If all of the mountains are covered in ash, they may have no reason to suspect there is anyone alive up here. We've seen no search planes or anything. If he's out there, odds are he's grieving for his dead wife and baby and, maybe someday, he'll remarry."

Claire stood up, wiped her eyes, then said in a slightly accusing tone, "That's even worse. Julia's got to know that." She went back to her side and turned out the light, saying, "Good night."

"I didn't mean to make things worse," I told her. When she didn't say anything in return, I offered, "Good night. Love you, Sis."

"Love you," she replied in muted tones.

It was the next day that myself, Seth and Mister Glass were trying to hook the solar panels into the batteries for the common house, or The Kitchen as we called it. According to Mister Glass, in town they had consolidated all the solar panels they could find on the old Mercantile building, where they had been able to fire up (cold up?) the refrigeration units. Mister Glass was also telling us how they had had to throw Charlie in jail again when Claire came running up, saying, "Josh, someone's coming!"

"From town?" I asked, wondering if it were our parents for her to be as excited as she was.

"No. From over the pass."

We all stopped what we were doing and looked up, to see that she was right. At least seven figures were coming over Boreas Pass, though they were still a long way off and it was hard to determine whether they were male or female, though at least three of the figures looked to be no more than children.

"Anyone coming from that direction's bound to have come far," I commented. Then, to Claire, I said, "Come on." I swung aboard a nearby horse, she did the same, and we coaxed a couple to follow along with us.

We got up to the figures and a bedraggled lot they were. Three adults, a man and two women, a couple boys who might be near my own age, and two children walking—a blonde-haired girl who might be twelve or thirteen, another girl so alike I took her to be a sister, except with darker hair, and a child of no more than five: a boy, I thought, but his hair was so long and his appearance so grubby it was hard to say for sure. The blonde-haired girl was carrying what I thought was a baby-doll at first, but soon proved to be an actual baby. So there were actually nine in the party.

"Praise God," said the oldest-looking of the women, a gray-haired woman of probably sixty-odd whose clothes were ill-fitting like they belonged to a much heavier woman. "Some of us thought we heard a gunshot yesterday and the others were saying we were crazy but we were about to die and, and praise God! You're real!"

Claire and I got quickly off our horses and offered rides to the newcomers. None of them weighed much, so we weren't worried about doubling up on the horses' backs. Claire offered to carry the baby and the little girl reluctantly allowed the baby out of her arms. "What's her name?" Claire asked.

"He's a boy," the girl said in that exasperated voice young girls are so good at. "And his name is Bobby. I'm Adaline," she added, as if she realized how rude the previous words might have sounded and trying to apologize. "And I don't want to ri—I'd rather walk," she said, as she looked nervously at the horses.

"Pleased to meet you Adaline." Claire said, ignoring the girl's truculent tone. I was impressed, for Claire had gone through her own period of turning every statement into an insult to the other person's intelligence. "I'm Claire and this is my brother, Josh. You look like you need to ride or we'll have to carry you like Little Bobby here." Adaline barely nodded my way, then climbed nervously aboard a horse, behind a woman in her forties with brown hair and sunken cheeks who I took to be her mother. Adaline held on to her mother with a look of fright and winced every time the horse moved.

They introduced themselves and they proved to be the Isaacsons, grandmother, son and daughter-in-law, three kids and three cousins. It was to take me many days to figure out which were the kids and which were the cousins, so I won't even try to line it out at this point in the narrative. They had been vacationing in Breckenridge and staying at a condo above the Blue River Reservoir when the ash cloud had hit. The house where they were staying had been in a tiny pocket much like our larger pocket and for two months, they had survived by breaking into nearby houses to find food. The father and one of the older boys had even made it into Breckenridge once and looted the grocery store for all they could carry, but the air had been going bad there as it had in Fairplay and they had barely made it out alive. I was to learn later that another man had gone on the foray with them and not survived the trip. A month and a half after the ash cloud had swept over everything, one member of the party had happened to catch a glimpse of the sun through the hole in the clouds we called our own and they had set out to try and get to a place with sunlight and, they hoped, better air. Until they heard Claire's gunshot, they were thinking they were the only people left alive in the world.

"Does anyone still live in the Blue River valley?" Danica asked, as the Isaacson family told their tale that evening.

"Maybe," the father, Evan, answered. "When we went to the grocery store, it was pretty picked over. And my brother, he swore he saw someone moving around down the street. Neither myself nor my son saw anyone, but my brother swore he did. But that air down there … I look back and I'm surprised any of us are alive, especially my son and me. It was like breathing sulphur."

"We've experienced the like," Claire told him. She was playing with little Bobby while Alexa and the little blonde girl Adaline looked on and offered helpful suggestions concerning baby care. Most of the rest of the Issacson clan was asleep on the floor of the common kitchen while we had what my uncles would have called a confab around the fire. It was a cool September evening, but not cold yet, though those of us who were from the mountains could tell we didn't have many warm days left.

The Isaacsons picked out a section for their garden—in the row with the rest of the gardens, because of the need for water—and set to work. And work it was. As mentioned earlier, these were the *Rocky* Mountains (emphasis added, but I can't take credit for it). When most people from outside the mountains think of them being called that, they think of the giant boulders they saw in the canyons as they drove up from Denver or Colorado Springs. Those are there, but what most people don't know until they've dealt with it first hand is that the ground is peppered with rocks from the grass down, from little pebbles to rocks bigger than your foot to those giant boulders.

So what had to be done for one of our garden plots was not just to plow some furrows and then plant. First, and we had all done this on our plots and took a hand in helping the Isaacsons with theirs (knowing they might not get to do any actual planting until the spring), one broke up the top layer of soil, like you'd do with a garden anywhere else. But then, you went over it on your hands and knees, picking up all the rocks you had loosed and tossing them aside. Then, like it used to say on shampoo bottles, repeat … and repeat. The reality was that you could no more get rid of *all* the rocks than you could sprout wings and fly, but it was necessary to get rid of as many as possible.

Then, once the top soil was relieved of most of its rocks, it wasn't bad soil—as could be attested to by the fact that our South Park Valley had been known for a couple centuries as some of the best natural hayfields in North America. However, it had never been widely planted for vegetables or the like because of the rocks and short growing season. So we realized that what made for pretty good garden soil was to take the wheel barrows or wagons and get loads of the ash and spread that on the garden. Sadly, we had enough ash readily available to keep our gardens covered for eons.

As to the wagons, we had one that belonged to the ranch. It was just an old buckboard that had belonged to our ranch for time out of mind and only got used maybe two or three times a year— once for the Burro Races parade in Fairplay every year, then maybe a time or two when we would have the kids from church or school out for a hay ride. The running joke was that it had belonged to my great-grandfather and, even though every board, bolt and piece of metal had been replaced at least once, it was still the same wagon. Lester, Oscar and I had reinforced the bottom of it and done some work on the suspension, and since then it had been remarkably useful.

The next morning, Seth and I were out working in the gardens early when one of the teenage Isaacson boys came over. He reached into the pockets of his jacket and pulled something out, saying, "When we looted that grocery store, I saw these and grabbed

up all I could. Pop didn't think we'd ever get to use them but, here."
And he handed us packets of seeds: tomatoes, corn and lettuce.

"Wow," Seth and I said in unison.

It was Seth who said, "We gotta show this to Jesse. It's probably too late to plant any of them this year, but he'll know."

"Is Jesse the little boy?" the teenager asked, surprised.

"Yeah, but he knows gardening," Seth replied.

We were actually meeting with some success with our summer garden. Lettuce and cabbage had come up, as well as some tomatoes. If the freezes would hold off at least a couple more weeks, we looked to have some good squash and even a few pumpkins. We had some stalks of corn, but so far I was doubtful of their providing enough ears for us to actually eat. As Jesse had pointed out on more than one occasion, though: our main goal on the corn was to produce enough kernels to be used as seed for the next year. I remembered back in school how Jesse had been stuck in the "special" class, where he was expected to meet low expectations and, maybe, someday, get a fast food job. I was looking at our gardens and thinking that, if our little community survived, it would one day be named Jesseville, or something like that.

The truth was, from what we had heard from Mister Glass, our little community had already come to be known by the people in Como as Overstreet. It seemed to me that it could have just as easily been called Ryerson, Marquez or Frowley, but I was secretly proud as well. I wondered if Claire would get married one day and make the fellow take her last name. I thought about suggesting it when the time came.

Who would she marry, though? At the beginning of our ordeal, Oscar had seemed to be paying her special attention, but he hadn't seemed to be focused on her anymore. They were friendly, but then, they had been for years. The two of them had been in the same classes for the last eleven years and we had all ridden the school bus together, so there was no reason why they wouldn't be comfortable with each other. On the other hand, they had never shown any interest in each other before. Oscar was about the same height as Claire, or close to five-ten. He was solidly built, though not heavy. He had a darker complexion than either Claire or I, and dark brown hair and darker brown eyes. I had never heard if girls thought him attractive, but neither had I any indication that he was ugly. Of late, he had certainly proven to be a hard worker. It occurred to me to hope that last sentence could be applied to me, as well. And then, I realized that the sentence before probably applied to me, too.

I had been out on a few dates in high school, but not many. And now, it was looking like I would never get another chance. Not only was there not anywhere to take a girl for a date, there weren't girls to take on dates. Miss Frowley? I had been talking quite a bit with her and we had found that we both shared an interest in the history of our little valley, but we had nothing else in common. She was pretty, and she was single, but I couldn't get past one little thing. Call me silly, but I couldn't get past her age. Not to mention that I never had any indication that she thought of me as anything other than a friend. The only way I could see myself ever getting a date, let alone married, would be if some other miracle family drifted in after being trapped in a pocket somewhere else. A miracle family with a teenage girl. My prayers got real specific on the matter for quite a while.

October came and went without a heavy freeze, so we were able to have a pretty good harvest for our first autumn. Belts were going to be tight that winter, but we felt like we had learned enough that, if we could make it through the winter, the next summer would actually see some progress.

This optimism was tempered by several factors. For one, the autumn winds had brought a change to the cloud cover above us. There no longer seemed to be quite as much ash hanging in the air, but neither was there a clear spot directly over our heads. Our solar panels were struggling on some days, and this, of course, made us worry about our crops. They came through, as said, but we wondered whether there could be a new crop the next spring if we couldn't see the sun.

Our optimism was also tempered by the shortening days of fall. I had always enjoyed fall in the past, but we didn't have the brilliant colors of the aspens like I had grown up with. I also missed—and I think the others did as well—the days of spending a fall evening inside, with the family, watching the TV or playing games. We had a few games in the common kitchen, and they helped while away some hours, but we were all becoming acutely aware of just how addicted we had been to television, recorded music, and endless electrical lights. We had lighting in the kitchen, but we tried to be somewhat sparing of it just because we had a finite supply of bulbs. Tad Isaacson, the oldest teenager of that clan, had an idea of going back over Boreas Pass to a large hotel that had been under construction above the town of Breckenridge and appropriating (which sounded better than stealing) all of the light bulbs that could be carried. He and I spent many an hour— sometimes joined by his cousin Jonathan—planning a Breckenridge excursion. Besides light bulbs, we were thinking about blankets, mattresses, and anything else that had been left behind by civilization.

We occasionally had visitors from Como, but the two communities kept separate for the most part, though I never knew the reasons why. For my part, I liked our green grass (while we had it), but my main excuse for not going very far afield was that there was so much work to be done. Lysette and Steve Carrier had actually come over and joined us for church a couple times, and Lysette was getting to know LuAnne Ryerson and Julia Croft pretty well, so we came to think of them as a part of our community though they were still set apart. The Carrier baby was of a similar age to Bobby Isaacson, and could often be seen being watched over by the two Isaacson girls, Adaline and Samantha. Mister Glass came often, for he seemed to be a man who genuinely enjoyed working as an electrician and was just happy to have things to do. I think he also liked our company but felt some sort of loyalty to the Como crowd, so he still called that community home.

We were all surprised when, one day in late October, a man came from Como pulling a hand cart laden down with goods of some kind. As he got closer, I got apprehensive as I realized it was Charles, but I tried not to let him see it in me as he drew closer. When he was about ten yards away from where myself, Lester, Tad and Seth were standing causally but defensively, he looked at me and asked, "You're Overstreet, right?"

"That's me," I replied, more than a little confused.

He jerked a thumb toward the cart he was hauling and said, "I come to see if you'd let me set up my tent with you folks. I can't take that Como crowd no more."

"Um," I said as I took a step closer, "We're a free country—other than what we've already staked out for gardens or personal property but, well, you have, um, something of a reputation."

He wasn't as heavy as when we had seen him before—but then none of us were carrying any extra weight anymore. He was still pretty disheveled, a sparse beard covering his cheeks and his hair looking long and greasy. He was silent a moment, then said, "I admit I was wrong to talk to you that day you and your sister went looking for your folks. Wrong to talk the way I did, I mean. I lost my wife to that ash cloud, and Lord only knows if my kids are still alive or not. They were in Oklahoma when it hit. So I had no call to disparage anyone who went looking for family. Maybe I was mad because I knew I couldn't go looking myself." He paused, then said, "And you probably heard I was the reason Como's got a jail. I admit: I got liquored-up one night. Everything just seemed so hopeless. Still, I didn't—everything that goes wrong in Como from now on, it's going to be laid at Charles Levinson's door. I'm asking you to let me move in with you folks. I'll help with the gardening, I'll build for you, you just name it."

The other men looked to me, which both surprised and annoyed me a little, so I replied, "Everything to the south side of the road belongs to my family. To the north side of the road, you can see where everyone has staked out gardens. Other than those boundaries, I can't legally or morally stop you from setting up a camp."

He rushed forward and took my hand, saying, "Thanks. I'll fit right in and do my share of the work. More than my share! You'll see: I'm a nice guy once you get to know me."

He lived out of a tent while he built a sort of dug-out downhill from the gardens. He was true to his word and pitched in with any kind of work we did, and worked hard in the process. He often took his meals with the Isaacson family and provided fresh meat for all of us with a series of traps he was running. I was afraid he might trap out the valley, but when I talked to him about it he claimed to have a system for when and where he ran his traps that would keep the animal population thinned but healthy. According to him, there were more animals crowding into our little valley than we could support, so it was something like kindness to them to thin their numbers. When he said it, it made sense, though I hadn't seen much evidence of varmints, let alone excess ones, so I remained skeptical. On Sundays, he joined us for church and even seemed to know the songs. He didn't bathe much, that we could tell, but he did take to shaving before church.

I still didn't like the way he looked at Claire. They were just quick little glances and, to be honest, the other single men had noticed Claire as well for she was becoming more shapely as her seventeenth year progressed. Most of them would blush if they knew I had caught them glancing at her, but Charles Levinson's glances would last longer than the others'. He'd give me a sheepish look, as if embarrassed about being caught looking, but then he'd look again. So far as I knew, he had never said anything to her other than, "Pass the lettuce, please," but I still didn't like him. I told myself it was just a latent prejudice, lingering from our first encounter. I told myself about all the work he had done since arriving. Still, I couldn't get past the idea that I just didn't *like* him.

Of an evening, after work and before the sun went down, we often played a game of baseball—or a game like baseball—out in the meadow. My family had always kept lots of gloves, bats and balls around and it seemed the Marquez family was the same. Some days everyone, from Mrs. Isaacson the matriarch down to their five year old, David, would be out there playing what amounted to slow-pitch with a hard ball. Oscar and Tad were often the pitchers and, when someone who could actually hit—like myself or Charles—came up to bat, they might try to throw some overhand pitches by us. I was a decent hitter, but Charles was a beast at the plate. He couldn't run, though, so even when he knocked one seemingly into the next county, he often had to stop at second base to catch his breath and give his legs a break.

Poor Claire. Claire could catch anything that came anywhere near her. She had a good arm—"didn't throw like a girl" was the comment frequently made. But she couldn't hit to save her life. I'm pretty sure Tad and Oscar were even trying to hit her bat, but she almost never made contact. And then she would get frustrated and, somehow, get worse. And she would get mad at the pitchers if they tried to walk her. The blonde-haired Isaacson girl, Adaline, was proving to be quite a hitter for her size, which at first was no more than five foot tall and probably less than eighty pounds. They said she had never played before—and it showed in her throwing and catching ability—but she was one of those people who just seemed to have a perfect natural swing and an incredible eye for the ball. Her brother was even starting to throw overhand to her as well. Soon, she was not only hitting, but was learning how to speed up or slow down her swing and place the ball. She just couldn't catch for anything.

On a cold but dry day in early November, the sky looked clear to the west, so Tad and his cousin Jonathan suggested they finally try and make a lightbulb run. I agreed to go with them, as did Charles, which rather surprised us. I wasn't crazy about him going, but I liked that idea better than leaving him behind with my sister. So the four of us saddled up, taking a fifth horse along that was carrying two crates packed with dried grass in which we hoped to store light bulbs and a sixth horse that was hooked up to Charles' handcart. We were on the trail by eight in the morning, and were looking into the Blue River Valley well before noon. The Boreas Pass road had been hard hit by the years and would have been very hard to navigate in a car—maybe impossible—but it wasn't really a problem for something no wider than a horse.

I could hardly believe what I saw when we looked at the Blue River. I had always loved that view, any time of the year. In the fall, there were always the changing colors. In spring, the promise of growth. In summer, the mountains were covered in green and wildflowers and the sky was a pearlescent blue. In the winter, the ski runs cut artistic patterns into the trees.

That day? Another gray moonscape like we had seen around Fairplay. I could see the lines of the ski area in the gray across the valley, but it was like looking at some sort of weird, relief, pencil drawing of Ski Breck. The town below was just a gray, jumbled mass of indistinct shapes. Charles let slip a cuss word when he saw it and I couldn't argue his feelings.

"Everybody just die down there?" Charles asked incredulously. Then, "What else could they do? Just like when my wife died. She just choked to death and I couldn't stop it. Then, I half-hoped I'd die, too."

There didn't seem to be anything else to say, so we began making our way down the pass road and into town. We didn't have to go far before we started coming to houses. It was Jonathan who asked, "Why don't we just start here and start gathering lightbulbs or anything else we can use? What's that hotel going to have that these places don't?"

"And none of it's ours, anyway," Tad reasoned. "We're either stealing from a single-family residence or a corporation, but if it's stealing from one it's stealing from the other."

"They're right, Overstreet," Charles said. "It's like the old maritime salvage laws: finders keepers."

"I agree," I said to their surprise. I wasn't sure why they were surprised. I had come on the venture, hadn't I?

So we broke into the first house we came to and started taking every light bulb we could find. There was no sign of life in the house, nor any dead bodies, so I guessed it was someone's vacation home and not a residence. That made me feel a little better about "appropriating" everything. Still, there was a notepad by the fridge so I wrote a note to the owners in case they ever came back, telling them where their stuff had been taken to. The other men thought I was silly, but it became our practice after that. No one ever called us on any of the notes.

We were gathering the last of the lightbulbs when we heard Tad give out with a shriek of triumph. The rest of us followed the sound into the garage and found Tad gesturing proudly to a wall of shelves. "Oh my Lord," someone mumbled, in what I gathered was a prayer of praise. The rest of us echoed him in one way or another.

For, there on the wall, were dozens of gallon cans of beans, pickled beets, and other vegetables. There were even some cases of fruit cups. Charles smiled at me as he clapped Tad on the back and said excitedly, "This beats finding a whole lightbulb factory, don't it?"

"You know what we need to do?" I replied as I nodded in agreement. "We're going to need to build a bigger wagon."

"Oh, we can get all this on my cart," Charles assured us.

"But these other houses along here, they might have more stuff like this," I told them. "Might be that a lot of people stock up for the one weekend a month they come up here. And we might ought to try to get another run in before winter hits."

Before making another trip, we decided to check the next few houses just to see if they contained anything worth coming back for. None of them had quite a cache of food as the first house, but they all contained bedding, blankets, bulbs ... and two of them had bodies in them. They were months dead and desiccated, but we found the remains of three people in one of the houses and five in the other. They looked to me to have suffocated, just based on their positions, but we had no way of knowing for sure. The air was bad even that high up in the valley, but not as bad as I imagined it to be down in the town proper. It occurred to me that we now knew we had access to all the bulbs, electrical wiring and even solar panels we were very likely to need. The only drawbacks were going to be transportation and the grisly discoveries we might make. We covered the dead bodies with blankets from their houses, but decided not to bury them at that time. Whether we would ever come back and do so I rather doubted.

We got back to our little encampment shortly after dark and, as we had predicted, the canned foods were met with much more joy than the light bulbs or the blankets we had piled on top of the cart. We started making plans for another trip and, suddenly, no one was wondering how we would keep warm for the winter. Adaline and Alexa, who were becoming quite good friends it seemed, both asked if there were clothes in those houses but I had to admit that none of us men had even thought to look. I had peered into some closets myself, but had only been looking for durables. I thought I might have seen some wearables, but I couldn't have even said which house they were in. I told them I would try to grab some clothes on the next trip, thinking in my mind that we'd need soft goods to pack between the breakables, anyway.

"You know," I said as we gathered for an evening meal together, "We ought to let the people in Como in on this."

"They don't need it," Charles told us. "They've been scouring every house from the Elkhorn to Red Hill. They got bulbs, Romex, you name it. Lots of canned goods, too."

"Still, seems like we ought to share," Claire injected.

"Let's get what *we* need, first," Charles said. It was said politely, and everyone seemed to agree with him. Everyone but Claire and I, anyway. She gave me a look that I took to mean she was with me, but said nothing. We had never discussed Charles, but I had gotten the feeling that that was partly because neither of us wanted to talk about him at all.

Chapter Eight

Beauty provoketh thieves sooner than gold.
~Shakespeare

We had been talking about having a Thanksgiving Day celebration before we found/appropriated/absconded with all the stuff from the houses in Breckenridge, then suddenly we had plenty to celebrate with. Food wise, we knew we had still better be somewhat conservative, but we were suddenly reveling in having plenty of blankets, lightbulbs and even—after a second trip into town—mattresses to go around.

Still, we began the day with a prayer and moment of silence for all that had been lost, then we set to cooking up the "feast" that was planned. Compared to how we had been eating, it *was* a feast, but it might not have looked like one if it had been put before that many people a year before. Still, we all enjoyed it and even Julia Croft took part in our moment of going around the common room (it was rather cool outside) and saying what they were thankful for. When Lester Marquez and Danica Frowley led us in prayers of Thanksgiving, everyone bowed their heads and I even heard Julia say "amen" with us. She had never come to one of our church services, but she often joined us for meals afterward and didn't mind if we continued whatever conversation might have been started during the service. Lysette and Steve joined us as well, with people taking turns holding their baby and the Isaacson's baby. Steve didn't really seem excited to be there, but he was friendlier than I had known him to be up to that time. Though they had joined us now and then for church or one thing or another, I had always gotten the impression that it was at Lysette's instigation.

With names like Isaacson and Levinson, I had been a little surprised that they had joined us for the church services, thinking they might be Jewish. Charles said his family had been Southern Baptists for as long as anyone could remember and Thelia Isaacson, the matriarch of the family, told me that while there might be some Jewish blood in their family way back somewhere, it was so far back no one could even say for sure it existed. As for church affiliation, it sounded like none of the family had ever set foot in a church for anything but weddings or funerals and probably checked "Other" on the religious preference section of the census forms. Still, they seemed to like the fellowship of our church get-togethers and came every Sunday. Adaline and her cousin Samantha, who was just six months younger, both enjoyed the singing and had gotten Claire to teach them all the songs. In fact, on that Thanksgiving day, a quartet consisting of Adaline, Samantha, Claire and Danica treated us all to a concert of several songs—some religious, some secular—that was applauded by all. At Steve's encouragement, Lysette even joined them for a couple well-known songs and proved to have a better voice than I had ever realized. Several people asked why Thelia and her daughter-in-law Inez didn't join the choir but both women laughed at the suggestion.

After lunch and the choir concert, we went outside and played touch football. Everyone but the babies participated some, though after a while it was just a game of five on five. Myself, Charles, Claire, Danica and Tad took on Lester, Jonathan, Steve, Oscar and Adaline. My chauvinistic tendencies started to roil at my getting stuck with "two girls" until I learned that Danica was faster than anyone else out there—a fact I hadn't really seen in our baseball games because she so rarely got a hit. Until the other team started just stationing someone twenty yards down field to cover the long ball, my team's strategy was for three of us to block while whoever was playing quarterback threw it as far as they could and let Danica run under it and catch it for a touchdown. We were ahead by three touchdowns before the other team caught on and started defending against our bombs. After that, our strategy still boiled down to, "Find a way to give Danica the ball." Danica, who I had never really known in her professional capacity but had seen around town in her well-tailored outfits, and who had been nothing but helpful on anything we did around the valley, was proving when it came to football to be both athletic and extremely competitive—one might even say "hyper-competitive". I was especially glad she was on my team.

Adaline, bless her heart, was to football what Claire was to hitting in baseball. The poor girl couldn't catch a bus and was too chicken to block. Eventually, I think they started just sending her on pass routes to get her out of the way. Tad, her brother, had an easy interception at one point which he tried to tip into her arms but she still dropped it. She kept trying, though, which I had to admire.

I also realized that afternoon that Oscar still had a thing for my sister by the deferential way he treated her. I think she realized it, too, and couldn't decide whether to be angry for being patronized or flattered by the attention. Flattery seemed to mostly win out. The two did more jawboning than the rest of us, which I'm pretty sure drew everyone's attention as much as it had mine. When we finally stopped for supper—a light supper as we had all filled up pretty well at lunch—Oscar and Claire sat beside each other. They didn't seem to say much, or what they did say was in low voices. I think they thought no one was noticing but the reality was *everyone* was noticing.

I think it brought a smile to most faces, too. I know it did mine and I thought I caught the Marquez adults looking on with approval. The only people who didn't seem pleased were Tad and Jonathan, who saw in Claire the only eligible woman available. I smirked to myself that at least they had someone to dream about. I didn't even have that!

When supper wound down, some people drifted off to their own cabins or dugouts, but most of the younger set stayed in The Kitchen (for so we still called the common building, even though most of its square footage was open space). We had been playing the aforementioned checkers and someone had devised some chess pieces, which had occupied several evenings pretty well. There was also a deck of cards, though it was getting some bent-up after the months of play. We had been excited, though—not at canned vegetable level, but excitement nonetheless—to find some games in one of the houses we had "visited". There had been a couple kids' games, which the little ones enjoyed—and even most of us older individuals had enjoyed playing them—plus some of the old standards like dominoes, Monopoly, and various card games.

We were debating which game or games to play, when Jesse tugged at my sleeve and asked in his quiet voice, "Josh, would you play me in this?"

I looked to see that he was holding a faded and beat-up box which appeared to be as much tape as cardboard anymore. On the lid was a picture of a baseball player and the legend "Strat-O-Matic Baseball." I didn't turn him down, but I did say, "I've never even heard of that game, Jesse. Where'd you get it?"

"I found it in the house with the dead people—"

"You weren't supposed to go in there," I told him.

"I was looking for seeds. And the bodies were covered up. Anyway, I found this in their closet. I've read the rules and I think I can teach you how to play."

I kind of wanted to play something with the group, but it was the first overture Jesse had ever made to me that didn't involve gardening and I felt honored. So, I smiled and said, "Sure. Let's see if we can figure it out."

Half an hour later, I would have said—and did tell all in the room—that it was the most complicated game I had ever heard of. Fifteen minutes after that it suddenly clicked for me, and by the hour mark I was actually enjoying the game. There were cards representing Major League Baseball players of the distant past, charts, dice and score sheets. We each picked a line-up from the cards, rolled the dice at the appropriate time, and checked the charts. Soon, we were learning the intricacies of whether or not to have the infield in or not, when to call for a steal, and how to put on a hit-and-run play. I understood baseball better than Jesse, but he picked up on the game mechanics more quickly and, so, our first game was pretty evenly matched. The second game, I beat him handily, but in the third game—once we learned the game we could play a full nine innings in less than half an hour—Jesse's team mounted a comeback in the ninth and won it on a walk-off homerun.

Part of the fun was that, by halfway through the second game, many of the other people in the room were watching our game. Some were cheering for my team, some for Jesse's, and some were just cheering (or razzing) as the mood took them. By the end of that third game, several other people had picked up the mechanics of the game and were not only offering unwanted advice, they were planning how they would play it once they got a chance. Jesse mentioned that there was a whole box of players and soon he and

119

Jonathan Isaacson were mapping out a season that, they said, would take us all the way through the winter. I wasn't sure I needed *that* much Strat-O-Matic, but their enthusiasm was contagious. We finally decided we would start out with a tournament and then go from there. Even Adaline and Samantha wanted to play, so it looked like we would have at least an eight team tournament, and if we opened it up to the adults—the *other* adults, I emphasized—maybe larger.

It was then that I realized I was the oldest person in the room. Sure, Claire, Oscar and Tad were just a year younger, and Jonathan close behind them, but I was officially an adult. At least, I was by the standards of a world that no longer existed. As I withdrew a little and watched everyone talk about the tournament, or get involved in another game of some sort, I wasn't sure which world I belonged to. Was I an adult, or was I one of the kids? I also wasn't sure which world I wanted to be a part of. The adults of our group, while I had come to respect most of them—with different levels of respect, I admit—were seeming to me to be awfully beaten down. Not just from the hard work, but from all that we had lost. The younger set, though, they were like most younger people and had a resilience about them I admired. They probably missed their toys and video games and other such things, but they were suddenly really enthused about a cardboard baseball tournament. And, it occurred to me, while they might miss how things used to be, they had all been excited for our little Thanksgiving celebration and had even made decorations out of pine cones and such, whereas the adults seemed to have approached it as just another day or even as a day to be dreaded because it was hard to be thankful amidst so much loss.

Maybe my choice wasn't between being an adult or being a child, and maybe it wasn't a choice between surviving or thriving, but it seemed that way. And I wanted to thrive. I also remembered, as I had so often, that I was enjoying this new world. It was hard, and I missed much, but I also felt like I was becoming a man in it. I looked down at my arms and saw that I wasn't bulked up, and probably never would be, but I had put on some muscle that hadn't been there the year before. I felt like I was a man and hoped that, even when the other adults were around. I was considered one of the adults.

"What are you smiling at?" Adaline asked, shaking me from my reverie, in part because I hadn't noticed her moving over beside me.

"Oh, just enjoying Thanksgiving," I replied, which did have some truth in it. I looked at her green eyes in her youthful face and didn't think I could explain what I was really thinking. She was one of the children, maybe older than the youngest, but still a child to my mind. She and her cousin Samantha had made one of the desserts, though, but I wasn't sure which one. Still, I said, "You're a good cook."

"It has been nice, hasn't it? The holiday, I mean," she commented, as if the idea had just come to her by surprise. Then, almost out of the blue it seemed to me, she asked, "Do you think we'll ever get to leave this place?"

"Where would you like to go?"

She thought a moment, then said, "Home. I miss my dog."

"You had a dog back in Phoenix?"

She nodded and, looking more youthful than ever, said, "Painter. He's a chocolate lab and when he was a puppy he had these spots all over him. They say when I first saw him I said he looked like someone had spilled paint on him, so we called him Painter." She laughed genuinely, an awkward laugh like so many girls of that age can have, and added, "He was so dumb! He'd eat anything. But he was really sweet and, well, maybe I'm glad he didn't come on the trip with us. He might not have made it."

"Where is he now?"

"Some friends of ours who live outside of town were going to watch him. They have a lab, too, and the two of them play together really well. I used to think it was a shame we'd had Painter fixed because I always thought he and Riley—that's the other dog's name—I always thought they'd have cute puppies. Dumb as rocks, but cute," she added with another laugh. Then, "You ever have a dog?"

"We did. Several, in fact. Our last one died last spring. He was a blue hela and pretty old. When he died, my mother said she couldn't stand the idea of burying another pet, so we didn't get one. If I know her, though, one of these days she would have seen someone giving away puppies and she would have taken one. My Mom loved dogs, but she hated losing them."

"Sounds like my mother," Adaline told me. "I wonder if there are any dogs left anywhere."

"Surely there are somewhere."

In a more subdued voice, she asked, "I heard my parents talking and they said we might be the only people left alive in the world. You think that's true?"

"I honestly have no way of knowing," I told her, trying not to contradict her parents too forcefully. "I like to think someone's still alive out there, though."

"So they'll come rescue us?"

"Mmm, partly," I replied with a shrug. "Mainly, I just like to think that humanity will go on and I'm not sure if we can carry the torch all by ourselves."

Someone invited us over for a game of cards then, so we went and thoughts of dogs and life before quickly dissipated in the frantic moment of "spoons".

Winter came shortly after that. We'd had a little bit of snow, but it had usually been gone by mid-afternoon. Snow came the week after Thanksgiving, and it stayed. Then it was followed by more snow. And still more.

On the one hand, I was grateful. I thought white was better to look at than gray (though I had been known to get tired of white in winters past). Snow meant the world, the planet itself, was still operating like it should. On the other hand, though, snow was always something of a hardship back when we had well-insulated houses and four-wheel-drive vehicles and nearby stores stocked with food. When that first big snow hit, I think we all knew we were in for it. We began eating more sparingly, though trying to eat enough to keep our strength up. We couldn't do much outside, but everyone took turns with the horses just for something to do, even though they all acknowledged that the horses belonged to Claire and I first.

And we had school. It started because Elana Marquez and Thelia Isaacson thought their youngsters needed to continue their educations. When they realized Seth Ryerson was a teacher by training and trade, they enlisted him to teach their kids. Seth was a good teacher, possessing patience with kids that I really admired for I had so little myself. They worked out a system of pay that seemed equitable for them all—trading on future crops and/or assets—but I think Seth was as happy to have something to do as he was about any promise of pay. Claire and the two oldest Isaacson boys balked at the idea at first, but then Oscar talked them into creating a "senior class" wherein Mister Ryerson was going to teach them college prep courses. It might have done me some good to sit in on those, but I told myself I was too busy with the horses. The reality was that I was too busy being *out* of school as I had graduated in May. Like all the adults, though, I took a turn now and again helping Seth with the little kids, and didn't mind as it cemented me as "one of the adults".

We didn't hear much from Como during the month of December. Mister Glass came out once via snow-mobile but he couldn't get it started and had to walk back. Several people tinkered with the snow mobile after that, but we never could get any life out of it. If he hadn't ridden it over, we wouldn't have believed it ever ran at all. He seemed surprised that Charles was still with us, but didn't say anything about it after his initial looks. He also seemed surprised that we had a school and offered to come back in the spring and help with some practical science classes, especially anything that had to do with electricity. Seth sounded interested in the idea and they started making plans. I was thinking I would like to get in on that class myself, now that we had a virtually unlimited supply of copper wiring, light bulbs, and other electrical items.

Thelia Isaacson asked Mister Glass if they had a school going in Como, but he said the few children they had were being homeschooled. "If they're getting anything at all," he added under his breath.

The weather turned colder a couple days after Mister Glass left and we all restricted our movements to the absolute minimum. We had built a shelter onto the side of the barn that allowed most of the horses to find some cover, but still, they liked to get out in the pasture. So Claire and I would check on them every day, make sure they were fed, and chip through the ice on their water troughs when needed, taking them walking when we could. Others came and helped us now and then, but mostly kept to either their own cabins or The Kitchen, with limited time traveling in between. Charles only came over once a day, usually for the noon meal, though he did show up one day with a deer he had shot. I still worried about us chasing what little game we had away, but the fresh meat put most of those thoughts out of my mind. We could see puffs of smoke rising from the chimney of Lysette and Steve's house, but they didn't venture our way during those coldest days. And no one could blame them. Charles did take a haunch of the deer down to them and said they were very thankful.

I still didn't like the looks he gave Claire, but he rarely ever said anything to her and was otherwise respectful of her and everyone else. He even came over and played games with us once in a while, though he always laughed and said he couldn't grasp the rules of anything harder than checkers. He was a good checker player, though, and not too bad at dominoes though he always brushed his rare wins aside as mere luck. I had such a negative opinion of him that I kept thinking he was setting us up for a bet, at which time he would prove to be a better player and win whatever we were betting, but he never did. I didn't think it had anything to do with us not betting anything.

As we neared Christmas, we started making plans for another feast of sorts. It might not have been more food than we usually ate, but it was going to have more sugar and we were going to dole out some cans of soft drink we had found. There was talk of presents, and we all thought we were being pretty sly with our gifts. Everyone but the two babies agreed to participate in the exchange, including Lysette and Steve. We finally wound up drawing names so that everyone was guaranteed to give at least one gift and receive at least one.

We awoke Christmas morning to a sunny day, if very cold. Before we could even make our trips to the privy, I handed Claire a gift I had wrapped in some Christmas paper I had appropriated from one of the houses we … shopped at. She looked at it in surprise and asked, "Did you draw my name?"

"No, but you're my sister," I told her.

She hugged me, then darted back to her side of the cabin and came back with a similarly wrapped present in hand. Smiling, she offered it and said, "I guess we think a lot alike."

I motioned for her to open hers, which she did, to reveal a carved frame with a picture of the whole family in it. The picture had been taken the previous summer, while Rusty was home from college, but I had carved the frame myself. I thought it was some of my best work—and it should've been, considering how long I had been working on it.

She put her hand over her mouth, then said, "It's beautiful, Josh." She hugged me again, then took the picture and frame over to her bedside and put it there. She sat on her bed and looked at it for a moment, then looked over at me and asked, "Do you think Rusty's still alive?"

"I hope so," I replied, coming and sitting beside her. I rarely came on her side of the cabin and it felt a little odd. It also felt right. I patted her hand and added, "I like to think Rusty's still going to college, or maybe at this time of the year he's gone home for Christmas with some girl he's going to marry. Or maybe he's helping with the search and rescue efforts and has plans to come look for us."

"You think if he's out there he wouldn't have already come for us?" she challenged, though I got the feeling she hadn't really wanted the moment to go that way.

"It's been six months and we haven't seen or heard a single aircraft go over. No vehicles have come from outside the valley since the Marquez family crossed Red Hill Pass. If there's anyone still alive out there—and I gotta think there is somewhere— whoever's out there is either scrabbling for their existence like we are, or they've written off this whole section of the map."

"I'm sorry," she told me, wiping her eyes. "This is supposed to be Christmas. The joy of the birth of the Son of God. The new birth offered all of us."

"Yeah, but the holiday has always been about family, too. Hard not to think about our family today." I hugged her, kissed her on the cheek, then said, "I better open my present, huh?" She nodded, so I picked it up from where I had set it beside me on the bed and opened it up. I found a nice photo of my whole family in an antique silver frame.

"I've done some work for Thelia and she insisted on paying me. She gave me that frame, so I went back to the house one day and picked out that picture." She reached over to the picture I had given her, then held it next to the one she had given me. "We really need to start thinking independently one of these days," she told me with a chuckle.

"But why? We're the smartest people we know, right?"

We had some pictures of our family already. Most of them we had boxed up and stored in the basement of the old house. Many of those, though, were family pictures from one and two centuries before. They held some interest, and I didn't want to lose them if I could help it, but Claire and I had both remarked that the sad reality of picture taking in the last few decades was that if you didn't have ready access to electricity and a monitor, you couldn't see them. There were voluminous pictures of our family of five available, but electricity was at a premium and printer ink non-existent, so the few photos we actually had in print were quite precious to us.

We heated up some water and cleaned up (I had gotten quite good at taking sponge baths, but one of my first projects of the spring was to build a bath house onto our little cabin and bring over one of the tubs from our old house, even if it meant heating water on the stove to get a warm bath in it). It was becoming enough of a priority that Claire and I were both thinking of starting on the next semi-clear day rather than waiting for spring.

It was still pretty early in the morning, by our old standards, anyway, when we headed out of our little cabin and over to The Kitchen. There, we found Thelia, Adaline and Julia already at work on the food, while Tad and Lester finished setting up the tables and chairs. Soon, other people were filing in and, while it made for a crowded space, everyone seemed happy to be there. Even Julia Croft was wishing people "Merry Christmas". Not that she had balked at any mention of it before, but she made it politely clear that she did not share the faith the rest of us claimed.

We were pleasantly surprised when Mister Glass showed up just before lunch, bringing some bread he had baked himself. He said some individual families in Como were celebrating Christmas, but it had always seemed like a family holiday to him so he had decided at the last minute to take us up on the invitation we had extended earlier in the month. The bread made me think his decision wasn't as last minute as he professed, but then he told us that he had a bread machine and that it didn't use much power.

As we all gathered around the tables, which took up most of the room, it was Charles (cleaner and more groomed than we had ever seen him) who said, "Our little community being called Overstreet, I think it'd be fittin' if Josh or Claire led us all in a Christmas prayer."

There were several assents, even from Julia, so I looked at my sister and found her gesturing that I should take the honor. I hesitated, then said, "Let's all join hands with the people to our right and left." I had meant that we just do that at each table, but the people at the ends of the tables had managed to take the hand of someone from another table so that we wound up with a long, snaky, human chain of hands around the room. Even the babies were included, and didn't seem to mind too much. I cleared my throat, then said something like, "Dear Lord, we have a lot to thank you for. And, I think I speak for everyone here, when I say we have a lot we'd like to ask you. A lot has changed since last Christmas, and I wish I knew why. And we all have family members and friends we can't account for, so, um, we just ask that you look after them. I thank you for this group of people, and all this food you have provided and, on this day especially, I thank you for giving us your son. It's in his name we pray, Amen." There were several "amens" uttered after that and I happened to see as my eyes opened that the Marquez family were crossing themselves. It made me smile, for I had seen them doing it so often after group prayers that I had been tempted to take it up myself. They always worshiped with us on Sunday, and would make the occasional reference to something Catholic, but on the whole, we just all seemed to be

Christians together with no denominational barriers. If I were looking at it through stained-glasses, I didn't mind and didn't want to change.

We enjoyed a good meal and some good conversation, though I didn't talk much, being happy to listen. Mister Glass and Danica got into a discussion about whether our current system of bartering were sustainable and when or if we might switch to some sort of money system. The Isaacson clan was discussing with Charles their respective heritages, going back several generations it sounded like. The kids were having kids' conversations (mostly about the presents). The teenage boys were playing up to Claire while Alexa, Samantha and Adaline tried to play up to the teenage boys. Steve and Lysette were taking a small hand in the conversation at the Isaacson table and the Ryersons were participating in the monetary discussion. Julia was sitting near Lysette and, I imagined, talking about motherly things.

I smiled, for this was my town. It didn't matter whether it kept my name or not, it was my town. I had had a hand in the building of every structure and had worked and played beside every person in that room. I thought back to trying to get a tarp over the Ryerson's RV when a sudden rain came up after a limb had punched a hole in their pop-out. I thought about the books I had discussed with Lester Marquez and Danica Frowley, who were both avaricious readers. I preferred articles, mostly about ranching, but they were introducing me to some of the great novelists, like Lewis and Dostoyevsky. I thought of our games—both of the table top variety and out in the meadow with a baseball or football—and how much fun we had with them; bonding, I think was the word I was looking for.

It wasn't perfect, I knew. I still missed my parents, and my older brother. We thought we had enough food to last until spring, but it might be a near thing. Hard work and cold weather (and ash and all) made for short tempers some days, bringing some shouting matches but no one had come to blows. We had plenty of blankets and our cabins were snug, but some days you just had to go outside and there was no way in the world to stay completely warm. And while snow had covered the ash, we all knew that meant the snow was going to melt and the resulting mud might be a catastrophe as bad as the ash cloud itself.

It wasn't perfect but, at that moment in time, it was about as close as it could be in my mind.

We were just finishing up with dessert—the cake Adaline and Samantha had made—when Claire leaned over and told me, "I'm going to stretch my legs. Go check on the horses. Scout's been favoring that right foreleg, you know."

"Want any help?"

"No, I just need to walk off that cake. I'll be back in five," she said as she patted my shoulder then left.

I'm not sure how many minutes it was later, but I was thinking it was about ten and I hadn't seen her come back in. Many people were up and milling around as we tried to rearrange the room for the present exchange, but it was hard to say who was where. I was pretty sure Claire wasn't in there, though. I looked for Oscar and realized he was putting a folding table away. Then, it occurred to me that someone was missing. I made another quick scan of the room and realized Charles wasn't in it.

Now, there were plenty of reasonable explanations for that, I told myself. He could have gone back to his dugout to get his present, or maybe he'd gone to the loo. I also told myself that if anyone else had been absent I wouldn't have given it a second thought. I tried to tell myself I was just being prejudice and that he had been a hard worker and good citizen over the last few months. But my mind was also recalling all those moments when I had caught him casting a glance Claire's way and I found myself lunging for my coat, which hung by the door.

Someone asked me what was up, but I didn't answer and, just as I opened the door, we all heard a scream from the direction of the barn. I ran as fast as I could over the snow and ice, putting on my coat as I went. In the barn, I found Claire with a torn blouse, a bloody lip, and Charles holding her against a wall as he tried to put one hand over her mouth and pawed at her with the other. Claire, meanwhile, was digging her fingernails into his cheek and drawing blood.

I tackled him with all the force I could muster in my six-foot, 180 pound frame. It sent us rolling, but away from Claire, which was my primary goal. When we stopped rolling, I realized I was astraddle him and began to wail on his head with both fists. I don't know how many blows I landed, or how long we were like that, before the Isaacson men and Mister Glass pulled me off of him. Charles's face was a bruised and bloody mess and he was moaning softly, but I had no more pity for him than a wolf I had once shot who had been trying to attack one of our dogs. The thought occurred to me and I realized I did kind of regret shooting the wolf. I didn't regret pounding on Charles Levinson and would have gone back to work on him if they had let me go.

Finally, I had the presence of mind to turn to Claire and found her sitting on a bench, being tended by Thelia and Julia. Over the din of noise and the blood pumping in my ears, I heard Julia asking, "Did he, did he violate—"

"He was trying, but no," I heard Claire respond. I slumped in the arms of the men holding me, praising God for that little bit of news.

Lester Marquez was there then and said to Oscar, "Let's get him over to his dugout."

"What are you going to do with him?" a voice, female, asked.

"Make sure his injuries aren't life-threatening, then keep him under guard until we can have a trial."

"A trial?" another voice asked.

"We need to do something," Lester said as he and Oscar helped Charles to wobbly feet, "Before we become animals."

"Looks like he already became one," Tad said, gesturing with contempt at Charles.

"He's right," I said, adrenaline leaving my body and rendering me shaky. I sat down on the ground and said, "My actions need to be judged as well as his."

"His are clear—" Thelia opined.

"We need to be sure," I pronounced. I looked to my sister and said, "I'm sorry, Sis. I don't doubt you—"

"I know," she replied. I could see she wasn't crying. She was mad, and it wasn't at me. I realized then that if Claire had had access to her gun, Charles would be sporting a hole the size of a .45 caliber bullet, maybe several.

After Charles was safely out of the barn, Claire turned to Danica, who was nearby, and said, "Danni, would you come help me clean up a bit?" She gestured at the hand that was holding her blouse up and said, "I need a fresh shirt."

"You probably ought to lie down—" Danica started to tell her.

"No, no, I'm all right," Claire assured her, and us. "I just want to clean up and then, um, let's get to those presents. I know the kids are anxious."

"We can wait—" said several voices at once.

"No need." She looked at me and gave what I thought of as a forced but reserved smile as she said, "My big brother took care of everything. Besides, we've got a Christmas play to put on."

I thought I was over the wobblies by that time, so I got up and came over to her, offering my hand. "I'll walk you back to the cabin, Sis. Danni, if you'd come with us?"

"Absolutely," she replied.

Together we tried to help Claire, but she was determined to walk under her own power, which she did. In fact, I would say she was walking forcefully. Danica and I were more trying to keep up with her than helping her in any way.

In our cabin, Claire told me, "Josh, would you, um, watch the door while I change?"

"Sure," I replied, reaching for the handle.

"From the inside," she quickly requested. "Don't get— please don't get out of my sight."

"Sure." So I stood and faced the door ... this was not, as I have mentioned, a big cabin. As a consequence, I was standing about six inches from the door as I faced it. It occurred to me that if someone were to suddenly come in, they would smash my nose. Still, it was what she wanted and I desperately wanted to help.

It was only a few moments later that she was tapping me on the shoulder then turning me around and saying, "Let me look at those hands, Josh."

"I don't think any of that blood is mine," I commented as she took a wet rag and began to bathe my hands. Danica was behind her, sitting in one of our old wooden chairs from the ranch house, apparently trying to decide whether Claire's blouse could be saved or not.

I looked at Claire's face and she looked OK, except that her bottom lip was swollen and a bruise was forming that went from the bottom left of her mouth, along her jaw. I couldn't see a cut, so whatever blood had been on her face before must have come from him biting her lip, I guessed. She was intently washing my hands but not meeting my eye.

I extricated my left hand from her ministrations and gently lifted her chin, asking, "Are you all right?"

Her tongue went to her lip, then she looked back down at my hands and said, "I'm fine. Heart's just beating fast, that's all."

"What happened?" I asked.

Though I hadn't made her meet my eyes, she looked into mine and said, "It was noth—"

"Claire," I started to scold.

She breathed deeply through her nose, a clear sign she didn't want to say anything, then relented and said, "I went out to check the horses, like I said. I think Scout saved my life. I mean, you did, but Scout did first. Well, what I mean is, I was petting Scout on the neck when his ears pricked. That put me on alert and I spun around just in time to see Charles there. If it hadn't been for Scout, he would have snuck right up on me. As it was, I was at least aware that he was there. Then he lunged for me and that's when my blouse tore. I tried to scramble away from him but—but he got hold of my belt. When he started tearing at my belt, like he was trying to rip it and my pants off all at once, that's when I screamed. Then he hit me and things got kind of fuzzy. Next thing I know, you're on top of him and beating him like a bongo drum."

She suddenly threw her arms around me and whispered, "I have the greatest big brother in the world!" Then, still holding tightly to me, she buried her face against my shoulder and muttered, "Thank you Jesus!" several times.

Just then, Danica was squeezing past us toward the door and saying, "Why don't I go join the others and tell them—what should I tell them?"

"That I'm OK and we'll be along in a few," Claire replied, looking at Danica with a smile and moist eyes. "And, um, thanks, Danni."

When Danica had left, Claire suddenly said, "I need to sit down," and practically pulled me down on top of her. I just barely caught the corner of the bed then gently nudged her over so I would have a place to sit. She patted her thighs and said, "Praise God for blue jeans and leather belts, huh?"

"Yeah."

"I am never wearing a dress again."

"You almost never wear a dress anyway, Claire."

She stuck her tongue out at me, then winced, "Ow. I must've bit my tongue when he hit me."

"Maybe that's where the blood came from," I commented, though I hadn't really meant to say it out loud.

"How do you bandage a tongue?" she asked, a smile in her eyes. Then, she smiled wider and told me, "I really do have the best brother in the world. I'll never be able to thank you enough."

"I'm just glad I was there—and that I caught him off-guard. Under ordinary circumstances, well, he's got some weight on me."

"Maybe, but you had righteousness and family protection on your side." She bowed her head and said aloud, "Dear God, thank you for Josh."

"And thank you for Claire," I added. "And thank you for taking care of her."

"What do you think they'll do to Charles?" she asked, in a very calm voice.

"I don't know. Don't really want to think about him. What say we just go celebrate Christmas with everyone?"

She practically jumped to her feet as she agreed, "Excellent idea, Big Brother."

Even though I had suggested it, I asked, "Are you sure you're up to it?"

"Thanks to you, all I got was a torn shirt and a little bruise. I felt worse when I had to shoot Darling." She offered her hand, saying, "Come on. Let's go to the party."

It didn't really click with me at the time that she was maybe just a little too ebullient. I just assumed she was telling me the truth and the attack hadn't hurt her all that bad. Physically, she had come out with only the one minor hurt, and some bruises on her back where he had shoved her against the barn wall. I wouldn't know until later how much more painful and long-lasting emotional pain can be.

Everyone welcomed us back into the party, showing special care for Claire, who made it clear she didn't really want any special care. It seemed like everyone there, maybe even the babies, came by at least once to say how brave I had been and how Charles had deserved every blow he got. I asked what they were doing with him and Lester told me he was out like a light but that someone would go over there about every half hour and check on him. According to the men who went, Charles alternately cussed them for keeping him tied up and cried like a baby saying he was sorry and begging to be turned loose. Sometimes he did both on the same visit, but eventually he just fell asleep, they said.

In the kitchen, the chairs had been rowed up so that we were all facing the north wall and a Christmas play was put on, starring Alexa, Adaline, Claire, Jesse and all of the Isaacson children. It was a mixture of songs and skits (and even one attempt at what may have been a dance by Adaline) and loosely told the Christmas story from the Bible. The singing was pretty good, the acting was pretty bad, but we all enjoyed watching it. Even Julia Croft was in it, briefly. I think we expected her—with her rapidly expanding form—to maybe play Mary, but she was just an extra in a scene that needed more bodies. Claire didn't have a large part, but everyone admired her fortitude for tackling it at all.

After the skits, we arranged the chairs in a large circle and began with the presents. Everyone had drawn a name, except Mister

Glass, but when he heard the plan he had gone over to his pack and pulled out an item and hastily wrapped it in a (clean) napkin. We discovered through elimination that Thelia had drawn Charles' name and Charles must have drawn Jesse's, so Mister Glass gave his present to Jesse and received a gift from Thelia. Both gifts worked out fine as Mister Glass received a packet of razors and Jesse got a carved, wooden chess set. Mister Glass told me later he had planned on just giving the chess set to our collection but had hoped it was a good gift for a boy like Jesse. I told him honestly that I could think of no better, for Jesse was becoming quite a chess master—besides already being our chief gardener and go-to rule guy where Strat-O-Matic was concerned.

For myself, I had drawn Seth's name and presented him with a leather belt on which I had tooled most of his name. When he looked at it questioningly, I explained that tooling a belt took longer than I thought and I would be happy to put the "TH" on his name as soon as Christmas was over. As the recipient, I got a nice, greyish-blue knitted scarf from Adaline. She seemed pleased when I told her it would be just the thing to wear when I had to check on the horses or work outside in those winter months. Claire received a brooch from Julia that I didn't think looked like it would go with anything Claire had ever worn, but she thanked Julia for it warmly, anyway. Claire had finagled behind the scenes to get Oscar's name and had given him a scarf much like the one I got, though in brighter colors. We all sang some Christmas songs after that, nibbled on some of the leftovers from lunch, then eventually wound up setting the tables back up and playing various games around the room.

It wasn't all that late, but I could tell later that Claire was flagging and offered to her quietly, so only she could hear, "Would you like for me to walk you home?"

"Shows, does it?" she asked with a laugh. Then, standing up, she said, "Thanks everyone for—for everything. I think I am ready to rest, though." Several of the ladies hugged her, as did Oscar, then she put on her coat and took my hand. "You can come back and play some more, if you like," she told me as we went out into the cold and windy night.

"I think I'm ready to just settle down. Danni loaned me a book I only got a couple pages into, so I think I'll read on that."

"You really don't have to babysit me," she said as we entered our little home.

"I know. I'm kind of partied out."

"One favor, though."

"Anything," I replied.

She looked rather sheepish, then asked, "I just realized I should have stopped by the, the you-know-what. Would you walk me over there and, and stand outside?"

I thought about making some crack about that being better than standing inside, but had better judgment and assured her, "Sure." Once we were back at the cabin, I told her to lock the door while I made a quick trip to the loo. She seemed hesitant, but then I heard the bar being put in place. I remembered then that our reason for the bar had been to keep the wind from blowing the door open. We'd never really considered the idea of some person breaking in.

When I got back and knocked and told her who I was, she quickly opened the door. She was still wearing her coat, which she took off then kissed me on the cheek, saying, "Thank you. And, um, I would really appreciate it if you would just stay here and read or whatever."

"I honestly don't want to do anything else," I told her.

She smiled and said, "You get on your side of the wall and I'll get in my bed and I'll sleep like a baby just knowing you're there. Stay up as long as you like."

It was a half hour or more later, as I sat in bed in my long-handles and a thick robe, reading the book Danica had loaned me ("The Parish Papers" by George MacDonald), when Claire poked her head around the corner and said, "I can't sleep, Josh. Could I, um, could I come cuddle up to you?"

"Sure," I replied. I scooted over, closer to the wall/partition that bifurcated our cabin, and patted the bed beside me. She was wearing the jeans from earlier and a sweatshirt and socks and, climbing under the covers, cuddled up next to me with her head on her own pillow, which she had brought with her. "Since when do you sleep with jeans?" I asked.

136

"From now on," she replied. "You just go ahead and read. I'll be all right."

"Really?" I didn't want to question her, but then, I doubted what she was saying.

"Just be here, all right. I'll, um, I'll be able to talk about it tomorrow maybe." She lay on her side, her back up against me as I lay on my back, and was soon breathing steadily in sleep. I read for a while, then realized the day had made me pretty tired as well and, turning off the light, fell asleep. I couldn't remember ever sleeping in the same bed as my sister—truck cabs didn't count—and thought it was weird but was soon too asleep to think about it more.

She woke me with her screaming some time later. I asked her what was wrong (maybe not in the nicest voice possible, I'm sorry to say) but she just told me she had been having a dream. Then she thanked me and climbed out of bed. I soon heard her getting into her own bed and no other sound was made until morning.

When I woke up, I found that she was sitting up in her bed, reading the book I had been reading the night before. It surprised me, mostly because Claire had never been a fan of fiction. She smiled and said, "You looked like you could use the sleep and I didn't want to leave the cabin without you so," she gestured with the book, "This is pretty interesting. The wording is hard to follow at times, though."

"It was written in the eighteen hundreds," I told her, rubbing my eyes. "You're welcome to read it anytime you like."

"Thanks. Let me know when you're ready to head to The Kitchen. Take your time, but I'm starving."

We had just sat down to some biscuits and gravy, with coffee to drink, when Lester Marquez and Evan Isaacson sat down with us. They asked how Claire was doing, then Lester said, "We've been talking, and we think this idea of a trial is the right thing to do." It took me a minute to remember what they were talking about, then I nodded and he continued, "None of us is a qualified judge, though, and there's no way we can come up with a jury of twelve adults."

Evan interrupted, "So what I suggested we do is put the names of everyone eighteen and over in a hat and draw out three of them. Those three people will be a tribunal, like they have in the military."

"What do you think?" Evan asked.

I looked at Claire, who looked at me as if to say I could do the answering. "That sounds good to me, I guess. I don't think my name should be in the hat, though, since I'm one of the … what? Plaintiffs? At any rate, I'm her brother so I wouldn't think it would be proper for me to be a judge. Who else does that leave?"

"Us, our wives, Miss Frowley, Tad is eighteen now, and so is Oscar. And the Ryersons. Steve and Lysette, if they'll participate. Julia Croft, of course. And my mother," Evan answered.

"Should we make a rule about not having more than two members of a single family in the tribunal?" Claire asked. "I mean, ideally, you wouldn't even want two, but that might be hard in our community."

"Let's get all the adults together and decide," Lester said, then got up as if to go do just that. Evan seemed confused for a moment, then followed.

"You sure you're up to this?" I asked.

"I'd like to get it over with," she replied.

Lester and Seth presented the plan to Charles later that morning. I was a little surprised that Seth went along, thinking he might be prone to take a more academic approach (whatever that might mean) to the situation. He seemed to think our plan was a good one, though, and actually volunteered to go along with Lester. They came back saying Charles had been skeptical but resigned. After receiving Claire's permission, it was agreed to have the trial that afternoon. That really surprised me, but no one could think of any preparations we could do as no one even had access to a law book. Evan Isaacson pointed out that we had the Bible and most everyone, even Seth, seemed to think that was as good a resource to start with as any.

So, after lunch on a bitingly cold day, the adults drew lots and the tribunal fell to Thelia Isaacson, Seth Ryerson, and Elana

Marquez. Only Elana seemed hesitant, but she said she had put her name in knowing it was a possibility. It was agreed that the tribunal must come to a complete agreement—all three parties voting together—and that any deliberations they undertook would only be divulged later if all three agreed to do so.

At three in the afternoon, Charles Levinson was escorted into The Kitchen. He wasn't tied up, as it was deemed such a sight might prejudice the judges. He was as clean and as subdued as I had ever seen him, but he refused to meet either my or my sister's eyes. He looked at everyone else imploringly, though, but I don't think he was getting much sympathy from anyone. Not even for the voluminous bruising on his round face.

The children (Alexa, Adaline, Samantha, Jesse and those younger) were over in the Isaacson house with all the games while Jonathan had elected to stay with the adults and watch the proceedings. Oscar and Tad were adults by then, Tad seeming disappointed his name hadn't been drawn from the hat.

Thelia, Seth and Elana sat down at a table facing the rest of us while Charles sat on the front row along with Claire and I. There was space in between us, but I also made sure I was sitting between Charles and my sister. Someone had found an American flag, which was hung on the wall behind the judges.

When we were all seated, Thelia slapped the table and said, "This, the first court of … our town, is now in session." She told me later that she had been about to call the town Overstreet, but didn't think that would be proper since the plaintiffs were Overstreets. I understood her reasoning and didn't mind too much as we had never officially named the town *anything*. "Miss Claire Overstreet, do you have a charge you would like to make before this court?"

"I do," Claire replied, after swallowing hard.

Thelia motioned and Evan came over to stand before Claire, a Bible in his hands. He motioned for Claire to stand up, which she did, then for her to put her hand on the Bible. "Do you, Claire," he asked, as if trying to recall memorized words, "Do you promise to tell the truth, the whole truth and nothing but the truth, so help you God?"

"I do," she answered confidently. It was then it registered on me that Claire, who almost never wore any make-up other than a little blush and—once in a great while, eye liner—had covered up the bruise on her face with make-up and a little bit of lip stick. I was both surprised and impressed. (Partly surprised to find out that Claire even *owned* lipstick!)

As Evan retreated to his seat, Elana said, "Would you bring your charges, please?"

"I charge Mister Charles Levinson with attempted sexual assault."

"I did not—" Charles blurted out.

"You'll get your chance," Thelia told him, pounding the table. "Now, Miss Overstreet, would you give us the details of this alleged attack?"

Claire took a deep breath, then said, "I had gone out to the barn to check on the horses after lunch yesterday. I was petting Scout, when I saw his ears prick up. I knew Scout sensed something, so I turned around. Mister Levinson was right there and he grabbed for me. When I jerked away, my blouse tore in his hands. Then he slapped me and knocked me against the barn wall. Then he grabbed at my pants and started pulling at them. That was when I screamed. Then he lunged for me and was trying to silence me when Josh rushed into the barn and pulled Mister Levinson off of me." She stood there for a moment longer, then nodded and sat down.

Seth spoke up, then, asking, "Mister Charles Levinson, would you like to give your account of the events?"

"I sure would," he replied earnestly.

Evan came over to him and, holding out the Bible, said, "Put your right hand on the Bible and repeat after me—"

"No sir."

"Excuse me?" Evan asked, shaken.

Charles pointed at the book and said, "It says right in there not to make vows, not by God in heaven or by the earth. I ain't going to compound everything by making the man upstairs mad at me. You either take my yes as yes and my no as no or forget it."

Evan looked at the judges in confusion. The three of them leaned in together, whispered for a bit, then Thelia motioned towards Charles and said, "If that is your wish, Charles. Go ahead and tell us what happened."

"It's true that I followed Claire, Miss Overstreet, out to the barn. She's a wonderful young woman and quite attractive, as I'm sure every man here will agree." He was saying all this in a far more charming voice and demeanor than I had ever known him to possess. He smiled and continued, "I was just going to talk to her and, well, plight my troth, as they used to say. And yes, I did sneak up behind her. Just being funny, you know? We all do that now and again, make each other jump, right? Only she screamed for some reason and lunged backwards. Looked to me like she had tripped and was falling, so I tried to catch her but all I caught was shirt. It tore, and then I was trying to help her to her feet when Josh there—he couldn't have known what was going on and I don't blame him for trying to protect his sister—he lunges at me and, before I can explain what's really going on, he starts pounding on me. Like I say: I don't blame him. He was just protecting his sister. He just didn't know what had really happened." He sat down, then popped back up and said, "That's all I gotta say," then sack back down.

"Does anyone else have anything they would like to add to these proceedings?" Seth asked.

I raised my hand, so Evan came over and swore me in. As I stood there, I said, "Your honors, when I heard Claire scream, I rushed into the barn. What I saw was Charles, Mister Levinson, holding my sister to the wall with one hand and his other hand over her mouth. She was scratching at his face and her blouse was torn, so I knew immediately what was happening. Yes, I did tackle Mister Levinson at that point and proceed to beat on him with my fists."

It was Elana who asked, "Did you actually see Ch—Mister Levinson tear your sister's shirt or try to remove her pants?"

"No, ma'am. Not exactly. He seemed to be pulling at her pants when I got there, but he wasn't making any progress. But if it happened the way he said, why does my sister look like she's been smashed in the mouth? And why was he holding his hand over her mouth?"

"I wasn't!" Charles objected.

Thelia banged her hand on the table, then asked, "Does anyone else know anything that might impact these proceedings? Notice that I said '*know* anything.' We have no need for hearsay."

Danica Frowley raised her hand, so I sat down. Evan swore her in, then she said, "When I got to the barn, Josh—Mister Overstreet was already beating on Mister Levinson and some of the men were trying to pull them apart. I, along with you, Judge Thelia, went to Claire's aid. I can testify that her face was bloody, but I can also tell you that, when I helped her change into clean clothes later, she had bruises on her upper arms consistent with someone having grabbed her there."

Seth looked at Claire and asked, "Are those bruises still visible?"

"Yes, sir," she replied. She took off her sweatshirt, underneath which she was wearing a tank top. The bruises on her arms were plain to see by all in the room.

"How do we know she hasn't had those for days?" Charles objected.

Seth looked at him and asked, "Would you be willing to hold your hands up to the bruises and let us compare them for size?"

"I would not," Charles replied, sinking lower in his chair.

"Miss Overstreet, do you contend that you received those bruises from Charles Levinson?"

"Honestly, sir, I can't tell you when I got them. I assume it was when he shoved me against the wall, but I cannot clearly remember him grabbing me right here specifically. I can tell you, though, that I didn't have these bruises yesterday morning."

"Does anyone else have any evidence they would like to bring?" Seth asked, looking over the crowd.

Oscar raised his hand, to everyone's surprise, and after being sworn in said, "I have caught Mister Levinson staring at Claire many ti—"

"Wait," Thelia interrupted. "You may have, but it doesn't have any bearing on this case."

"But he—" Oscar tried to continue.

"A man looking at a woman may or may not indicate anything other than that he finds her attractive," Elana told her son. "We cannot let such discussion sway our minds here. Does anyone have any other *real* evidence to submit?" Oscar glared at his mother as he sat down, then crossed his arms defiantly. When no one else spoke up, Thelia said to the other two, "Then I guess we should adjourn somewhere and discuss the case."

The three of them stood up and decided on their way out that they would go over to the barn to discuss their verdict. It seemed like a cold place to me, but I didn't think it was my place to speak up.

"So we just wait?" someone asked.

"For how long?" Charles blurted out, though I got the impression he hadn't meant to say anything.

"You got somewhere to go?" Ted asked him insolently.

"You've all got me tried and convicted, so I'm ready to just get out of here."

"You think we'd let you go?" Jonathan, feeling his oats, asked in much the same tone as his cousin had used.

Evan Isaacson stood up then and said, "Boys. There's no good can come of this. Let's just play games or something." Then, he looked at Charles and asked, "Would you rather us escort you back to your house?"

"If I leave here, you're all just going to talk about me behind my back. I think I'll stay." With that, he faced forward and acted for all the world like the rest of us weren't in the room. Evan and some others got a card game going but Claire and I just sat and talked to Danica.

Claire nudged the dark-skinned woman conspiratorially and said, "I wonder why Mister Glass keeps coming over here?"

"I don't know what you're talking about," Danica responded, but it seemed clear that she did.

I didn't, and said so. "I think Mister Howard Glass," Claire chided, "Has his eye on a certain lady banker."

"We're just friends," Danica replied uncomfortably.

"You know," Claire told me, as if Danica weren't right there, "It turns out Mister Glass isn't as old as we've always thought. Everyone always talked about him being retired, so I thought he was sixty-something—because of his gray hair. But it turns out he retired from the military and isn't all that old."

I had finally caught up to the conversation and was able to get past the idea of Mister Glass being younger than we always thought just because I was intrigued by Claire's overall premise. "Now that you mention it, he has been coming over here often. I thought it was just because Como is boring."

"Well, I'm sure that's part of it," Claire told me. "But notice who he always sits by when he joins us for meals."

"He doesn't—" Danica started to object but was interrupted by the opening of The Kitchen door and the return of the judges. "That didn't take long," she mumbled, echoed by several over people in the room.

The judges took their seats and bade everyone else to do the same. The card players put their cards down and looked respectfully to the front of the room. Evan sensed that the judges were looking at him, so he rose and asked, "Your honors, have you reached a verdict?"

"We have," they replied in eerie unison. Evan sat down and motioned that they should elaborate. The two ladies looked at Seth, who cleared his throat then said, "We, the tribunal of this court, do find Mister Charles Levinson, guilty on one account of attempted sexual assault."

Charles didn't say anything, but I noticed his features get hard as Seth continued, "Now we come to the sentencing phase. If these were normal times, a court would sentence you to five years, at least, behind bars—"

"You can't do that!" Charles blurted out.

"No, we can't," Seth told us all.

"Nor do we want to," Thelia injected. Embarrassed, she motioned for Seth to continue.

He said, "Therefore, it is the ruling of this court that you be banished from this valley. You have two days to pack up your things and then you will move. We are setting a boundary of five miles from this spot. If we see you any closer than that, we will take whatever measures needed to capture you and then we will hold you captive in your dugout for no less than one year. During that year, we would provide you with the absolute minimum of food and no more freedom than to go to the privy and back. If that seems unacceptable to you, then move beyond the five mile range and live in freedom."

Seth turned to the crowd and asked, "Does this seem fair to all of you?"

Most everyone assented and someone commented, "More than fair. He's lucky Claire didn't shoot him."

Seth had brought a hammer from the barn, which he pounded once on the table as he said, "Two days from right now, Mister Levinson." He looked at the clock on the wall and said, "If you are within the five mile range at 4:57 on Thursday afternoon, we will incarcerate you for one year. Do you understand?"

"You can't do this to—"

"We already have," Seth pronounced. I had always thought him a somewhat mousy school teacher, but he had all the authority of a judge at that moment.

At that, Evan and the other men of our community stood up and surrounded Charles. As they escorted him out, he alternately threatened and pleaded. He was careful to never look at Claire, though, and mentioned only me by name. My heart beat faster but I remained as stoic as I could.

When Charles was outside and the door shut behind him, Seth said to Claire and I, "Two hundred years ago, in these very mountains, they would have hung him. I hope you understand that we just didn't think we had the authority to do that."

"I understand," Claire responded before I could. "And thank you."

"I think he's just a coward," Seth said to me, "But it might do to keep your gun handy, Josh."

"Um, yeah."

That evening, we just sat around and played games, but the proverbial elephant was in the room. We made it through the evening without so much as nodding at his trunk, though. Myself, Jesse and the two Isaacson boys had a mini-Strat tournament, which

I won behind the stellar pitching of someone named Mike Scott. For our "official season" we were still using the Hall of Fame players, but sometimes it was fun to dig into the box and pull out an old-timey team, which gave you some stars and some ... others, as they were actual teams, made up not just of All-Stars but of regular Joes as well. The box contained several dozen teams, so we were years away from exhausting all the possible combinations.

I was focused enough on the games that I wasn't paying much attention where I should have, so it took Julia Croft leaning over surreptitiously—something not easily done with her expanding form—and whispering, "I think Claire is about worn out. Want me to walk her to your cabin?"

Embarrassed, I looked over and saw that Claire was definitely flagging, so I said I was ready to head to bed and asked Claire if she'd like to go to the cabin with me. She quickly said yes, then said she'd be happy to stay longer if I wanted to. I assured her I was ready to go to bed and she gladly began putting her coat on. I cast a look at Julia and mouthed "Thank you" to which she replied with a nod and a smile. Every now and then, I was surprised when it occurred to me that Julia was actually a very attractive woman. Don't know why I didn't think that at other times, but maybe it was just because of the pregnancy. I know women talk about other women "glowing" during pregnancy, but guys don't always see the same thing. She wasn't ugly when pregnant, but I had a hard time looking past that swollen belly and her filled face.

It was a fiercesomely cold night so Claire and I darted as fast as we could across the space between the kitchen and our cabin. I checked the inside of the cabin to make sure no one was there, then she followed closely behind and shut the door, quickly barring it.

"I think I'm going to sleep like a log tonight, Big Brother," she told me as she kicked off her shoes and climbed into bed.

"Dressed?" I asked, curious.

"For now. Maybe not forever."

I nodded and started for my side, then came over to hers and asked, "Could I pray with you, Sis?"

"I would like that," she told me with a smile, holding out her hand to me. I took it and knelt on the floor beside her bed. I prayed for her and thanked God for protecting her and prayed that she would have a peaceful night's sleep. When I had said "Amen", she brought my head down and kissed me on the forehead. "I love you, Big Brother."

"I love you, too, Sis."

She held on to my hand, then, and asked with faltering voice, "Would you, um, could you … Would you mind just staying here for a little while? Tell me a story about you and Rusty. Tell me about that time you went and stayed in the dorm with him."

"It wasn't that interesting."

"I know. Just tell me something, please."

I thought back, then smiled and asked, "Did I ever tell you about the time Rusty and I decided to take that old snowmobile—you remember? The one we used to call the Rocket? Did I ever tell you about the time Rusty and I decided to take it over Boreas Pass and into Breckenridge?"

"No!" she asked with interest. "Was that the one that Dad always said you could trail by finding all the pieces that had fallen off of it?"

"Yeah, that's the one. Well, Rusty had this idea—this was back when he was just fifteen and I was eleven, so he couldn't legally drive us anywhere. Anyhow, Mom and Dad were off somewhere—and I guess you were with them—and Rusty said we could take the Rocket to Breckenridge and be home before you got back."

"And you believed him?" she asked with a laugh.

"Hey, he was my big brother," I answered, a similar laugh in my voice. "And he was Rusty!"

I lunged out of my bed when Claire called out and rushed to her side. I was fully expecting to find Charles in the cabin, but we were still alone and the door was still barred. I knelt beside her and in the vague light of the moon reflecting through the window and off the snow, I saw that she was still asleep—or appeared to be. I gently brushed the hair from her forehead and whispered, "It's all right, Claire. You're safe and I'm here."

She started crying then and said, still not opening her eyes, "Mom? Where's Mom?" I wasn't sure how to answer that, but then her eyes came open, wide as in fright. She looked at me and asked, "Josh? Josh are you here?"

"Right here, Sis."

She reached out and touched my face, then said, "I was dreaming that Mom was being attacked and I wanted to help her and—and I couldn't. Did I cry out?"

"Yeah, but it's OK. It was just a dream."

"But Mom's still gone," she replied. She started crying then and I guessed it was more about her being attacked than about our parents being gone. I know their deaths still weighed on us both, but I was pretty sure this particular crying jag was sparked by Claire's own, fresh trauma. I just held her hand and let her cry and occasionally told her I was there with her. I woke up later, still kneeling beside her bed and holding her hand. I gently put her hand under the covers and quietly went to my side of the cabin, realizing when I did so that falling asleep while kneeling is hard on the knees, and the back, and the neck. I wasn't long in my bed before I was sound asleep, though.

Chapter Nine

An exile's life is no life.
~Leonidas of Tarentum

Charles Levinson loaded up his hand cart first thing in the morning and took off, cussing us all in the sunny but cold morning. None of us seemed sad to see him go. Myself, Tad and Jonathan mounted up and made sure he continued going long past Steve and Lysette's place. Steve came out on the porch with a rifle in his hand, making sure Charles knew he wasn't welcome to settle anywhere around there.

I wondered where he could go. There wasn't a perpetual ash cloud in the sky anymore, so it was conceivable that life might be livable in more places once spring came. We had allowed him to take a generous supply of dried fruit and, with his traps, he might make out all right. I told myself that, as a Christian, I ought to care for a fellow human being, but that day I was just glad he was going the opposite direction from where my sister was.

She hadn't been in favor of me leaving her, even though I would be in sight for the whole ride, but Danica assured us both she would keep close tabs on Claire until I got back.

Claire slept much better that night, as far as I could tell. I never heard her, anyway, and she said she had a nightmare-free night. I know she had a couple more nightmares in the ensuing weeks, but for the most part she seemed successful at putting it all behind her. She never talked about Charles Levinson, but neither did anyone else. One time, when we were all eating together, I heard someone wonder how he was making out but someone else expressed the sentiment that they didn't care and there were several assents.

New Year's Day was bitterly cold, and whether there were new snow falling or it was just snow and ash being blown off the mountains we couldn't tell, but it was hard to see and miserable for breathing outside. We really "learned the ropes" then,

It had been Oscar Marquez who had first suggested the ropes, having read about the idea in some book when he was younger. We attached ropes to each of the buildings, including the barn, and—on days like that when visibility was almost nil—you could make your way from one building to another by walking slowly and holding on to the rope. Every building had a rope that ran directly to The Kitchen—which was in the center of our compound—and our cabin also had a rope leading to the barn. We got the horses out and worked them some on days when we could, but there were some days when all we could do was go check on them. Every house also had a rope to the nearest privy, of course.

New Year's Day, we gathered in The Kitchen and ate lunch together and spent the afternoon playing games. I played a couple card games and even lost a Strat game to Adaline—this wouldn't have been a big deal to me, but it apparently was to her. We also came to the decision that each household should have some food stored in their individual abode in the event a day or days were to come when it just wasn't safe to make it to The Kitchen. So we carefully doled out some supplies from The Closet (a room we had built onto The Kitchen) and hoped that we wouldn't have a day where we *had* to use them.

Oscar had seemed nervous all day, like he wanted to tell me something, but wasn't sure how. In the mid-afternoon, when I said I was going to go check on the horses, Oscar volunteered to go with me. I told him I would appreciate the company and, truthfully, we had all said on more than one occasion that day that no one should go out alone, except to the privy. Even then, when the little girls went, we encouraged them to take someone with them—not for fear of Charles or bears, but fear of falling on the ice.

So we held onto the ropes and, unable to see a thing, made our way to my cabin, and then from there to the barn. Inside the barn, it seemed pretty toasty, which with the absence of wind and all the body heat from the horses, was probably the nicest place to be that day. We started rubbing them down and checking them over and making sure they had enough of everything. A thin layer of ice had formed on one of the troughs, so I chipped that away. Still, Oscar remained silent while I occasionally caught him moving his mouth as if working out a speech.

I was just about to give up on hearing it when he stood up straight, drew extra air into his lungs, and blurted out, "Josh, I would like your permission to court Claire."

I was surprised, mainly because I had kind of figured that had been going on for quite some time. Still, I replied with a bit of a chuckle, "Seems to me she's the one you ought to be asking."

"I want to do things the right way. It used to be that the man always asked the girl's father or the eldest male of her family. I was thinking about it and it occurred to me that it would be a good idea here because, well, if you have anything against the idea, I'd rather know now. Us all living in such close quarters and all."

I thought for a moment, leaning against a horse we called Gluepot (as a joke, she was actually the fastest, most nimble horse we had). Finally, I got my words together and said, "Oscar, I appreciate you coming to me like this. But I'm serious when I say the decision is with Claire. I've known you for, what? Twelve years now? And while I never until recently thought you two had any interest in each other, there is nothing in your character to give me pause. So, I guess what I'm saying is that you have my permission, but I will back whatever Claire's decision is in the matter."

He exhaled, making me wonder if he had been holding it in this whole time, and said with a relieved smile, "Thank you, Josh." He offered his hand, which I took, then said, "If she will consent to letting me court her, and maybe someday marry her, I promise I will always treat her honorably."

"I can't ask for anything more than that, Oscar."

That night, as we changed for bed on our respective sides of the cabin, Claire asked, "I know Oscar talked to you today. What do you think of the idea?"

"Of him talking to me at all or what we talked about?"

"Oh, you know what I mean," she scolded.

"It's like I told him: it's what you think that matters."

"But what do you think of us? Of me and Oscar? Do you think it's a good idea?"

I thought a moment before replying, "I've got nothing against it, if that's what you mean."

"Are you decent?" she asked. When I said I was, she came around to my side, dressed in a flannel nightgown, but with jeans underneath. They were different jeans, but still jeans. She glanced down and said, "Baby steps." Then, sitting in the chair on my side while I sat on my bed, she told me, "I've always dreamed of getting married, having children, all that. But I was going to go to college first, maybe start a job. Be in my twenties at least. I guess … I guess I don't want to be so locked in on a defunct plan that I miss an opportunity."

"Do you love him?"

"I think so. I mean, there are three eligible guys here that aren't my brother—four if you count Jesse—and Oscar's the only one I'm interested in."

I thought long and hard before saying, "That's not a ringing endorsement. You know, we could still be rescued at any time and maybe east of the Mississippi they're still having colleges and people are working jobs from factories to white collar stuff. If that suddenly happened, would you want to be married to him then?"

She looked guilty as she said, "I don't know. I mean, if I commit to marriage, I believe it should be for life. And if it's life here, then Oscar's a great guy."

"But part of you still wonders if there are other options out there?" She merely nodded guiltily. I reached out and put my hand gently on her knees, then waited for her to make eye contact with me. When she did, I said, "Claire, you're the smartest person I know. That doesn't really come into this decision, though. What I mean to say is, well, you are seventeen years old, about to turn eighteen. You are an adult and you have more wisdom than any adult I know, or have known. Oscar asked me for permission to court you and I gave my permission, contingent on how you felt about the matter. The more I think about it, I think courting is a great idea. You're not promising to marry him, you're just setting aside some time to get to know each other. Tell him what you've just told me. Don't be in a hurry. Maybe a year from now we'll have a wedding on New Year's. Maybe it'll be five years from now. Or, maybe you'll court and get to know each other and decide all you were meant to be was friends. Just go into this honestly and pray about it and trust that God will show you what to do."

"It sounds so simple when you say it that way."

"Maybe it is. But we want it to be like in the stories, where the two people know from the moment they meet that they're going to be soul mates or whatever. And then, real life throws us a completely different scenario and we're confused because it's not like we wanted. Maybe we should stop wanting things to be the way they aren't and just accept things for how they are."

"Oh, who's being the wise one, now?" She arose, gave me a hug, then said, "Good night, Big Brother."

"Good night, Little Sister."

We had something of a break for a few days. The sun came out and the wind let up and while it wasn't tremendously warm, by comparison it seemed like summer. We rode the horses and hooked up a sled (for both functionality and fun) and started making plans as if spring were just a few days away.

It wasn't.

In the second full week of January, we were reminded just what winter could be like. Fresh snow fell, to mix with the existing snow and ash, the wind blew and reduced all visibility, and we huddled in our cabins and only went outside when we absolutely had to. Adaline came over to our cabin one day and played cards with Claire and I. After cards, we discussed books and how life was before and I was struck by the wild swings one encounters when talking to an adolescent or teen girl. One moment she was sounding very grown-up and sophisticated, the next saying something or doing something like a child. The awkwardness, the overdone laugh, it reminded me of Claire just a few years before. Then we both walked her home later as neither of us wanted the other to have to come back alone. We had been amazed when Adaline showed up at all, but she was a thirteen year old girl now, used to living in the city and constantly going to friends' houses, and our little community was proving to be quite confining to her. Add on to that the fact that she and Alexa had had a falling out over something recently (which would soon be cleared up, we were sure) and ours had been the most logical cabin to come to when I learned that her cousin Sam had taken Alexa's side in the argument.

As we got back to the cabin, we decided to make our way to the barn and check on the horses. Once in there, Claire asked, "I'm not all that far from Adaline, am I?"

"Mmm? What?" I responded.

"Oh, I remember being twelve and thirteen. So convinced I wanted to be a woman, and still wanting to comb out my doll's hair. And your body's telling you one moment that you're maturing, then another you can't control the hormones and cry over the stupidest things."

"You weren't like that," I countered.

She slapped me playfully on the shoulder and laughed, "Hello! You didn't even want to be seen getting on the same school bus as me back then. And, looking back, I can't really blame you. I didn't want to be around myself sometimes."

Becoming thoughtful, I asked, "If we could have that world back all of a sudden, what do you think you would least take for granted?"

"Indoor plumbing comes to mind," she replied with a chuckle as she chipped ice from one of the troughs. "But really, I couldn't narrow it down to one thing. Plumbing, heat, the ability to leave this valley. Mom and Dad. What about you?"

"All those." I laughed and added, "Eligible girls."

She came over to me and hugged me, saying, "To be honest, one of the things that keeps me from wanting to fall in love with Oscar is I—I hate to leave you behind."

I leaned back to get a look at her face and asked, "Seriously?" When she nodded, I said, "Claire, that's ridiculous. If you get a chance for happiness with Oscar or even someone else, don't pass up on it because of me. There may yet be someone out there for me."

"I pray for that."

"Thanks. You know, God has carried us so far. He can even produce a wife for me if that's the plan."

She let go of me and went back to her work. It was several minutes later, as she stirred the hay and I curried one of the horses, that she asked, "Do you think God's really there?"

"Yeah. You don't?"

"I—I don't know," she told me, still working. "I love the songs and I really enjoy our church services. And some days I really do think he's there and he's carried us through this. And that day you saved me from—from Charles, I was sure God had sent you. But sometimes, I think of all we've lost and I see that gray landscape in the distance and, well, I just wonder. We're not even to the middle of January, you know."

"What's that got to do with it?"

"February's always been the worst month around here. I just don't know if we can make it through."

She wasn't saying anything I hadn't thought, but there was something scary about having it out in the open like that. I had it in my mind that, if we could get to spring, we could start seeing some green again and we could plant and ride the horses. I envisioned us going into Breckenridge and gathering all we could there and—with a whole summer of planting and harvesting—I thought we'd be better set for the next winter. Still, right then, as I could hear the high winds buffeting the barn, I was wondering if we would make it to spring, let alone beyond.

I finally answered the original question when I told her, "I think I believe God is still there. And I admit that part of it probably is because I *want* to believe. I want to believe our folks are with him and that the few of us between here and Como aren't the only people left in the world."

"I think about that aunt we were talking about when this first happened. Remember?" she asked, to which I nodded. "I think about what she told Grampa and the obvious conclusion is that she was crazy, or had dementia. But what if she were telling the truth? If she was, well, then that means you're going to get married and have kids."

"How do you figure that?" I asked with a laugh.

"My kids won't be named Overstreet."

"That occurred to me once, too. We may not be the only Overstreets either, though. We got some cousins over at Leadville— or we did."

"It's you. I'm just sure it is," she told me.

"You're sure about that but not about God?" I asked, trying to make it sound like a good-natured joke, but rather regretting having said it before it was all the way out of my mouth.

She actually smiled in return and quipped, "Maybe I'm not as far past thirteen as we thought. Maybe I'm just an emotional, hormone-crazed adolescent."

Julia Croft went into labor during the last day of January. The other mothers in our group offered their assistance as we didn't have any medical personnel. Ahead of time, I would have guessed someone like Thelia Isaacson or Elana Marquez to be the most help, but it turned out that Lysette came over and—from all I heard— made a very capable mid-wife. Even Steve came over, not just to watch his own child but to keep Julia and Lysette company during the ordeal. For months, Julia had been telling us that she was prepared to deliver the baby herself. I had always gotten the impression that she was psyching herself up for it—I knew I would have to, if it were me. Seth Ryerson said he had delivered one of his own children—due to a freak snow storm that had prevented them from getting to the hospital—but on the day Julia really went into labor, he had a cough and didn't want to get anyone sick. I don't know why I was surprised, but I was when I heard that Adaline had assisted Lysette and done a very good job.

Dwight James Croft II was born on February 1. He was a healthy—8 pounds two ounces—boy with a fully developed set of lungs and looked, to me, like he had been squeezed in a vice, the way his head was so pointy and his face so red. (Can you tell these are the comments of an eighteen year old boy?) Everyone who saw him pronounced him a miracle and congratulated Julia for how well she had done. And, like the pioneer parents of our ancestors, she was up and walking around soon.

Seth's cough kept getting worse, so I mounted up and rode into Como to get Wally. He wasn't a doctor—we didn't think we had one—but he was an E.M.T and knew more about medicine than anyone else we could think of. When I got to Como, though, he was not easy to find as they were as shuttered up as we were. Finally, I found him in the little house that had always sat behind his home. Turned out the little cabin was more solidly built and easier to heat than the bigger house.

"You know, we got a doctor," Wally told me.

"We do?"

"Yeah. Came in last fall. He retired and was living about halfway to Hartsel when the ash hit. Managed to get him and his wife and daughter here. He's living in the Spencers' old house." He hesitated, then said, "I'll go with you and introduce you."

At the Spencers' old house, we were greeted by a middle-aged woman with iron-gray hair and a somewhat simple demeanor. She looked at me suspiciously, but recognized Wally and let us inside. As we stamped our feet, a tall, thin man of Asian cast with only a fringe of white hair left on his head came from the direction of the kitchen. Wally said, "Hal, this is Josh Overstreet. He's the leader of that group up the canyon and—well, you tell 'im, Josh."

I shook the doctor's hand, then said, "I'm not really the leader, but—never mind. Our school teacher's sick. Got a cough that just won't go away and it's driven him to bed."

"You have a school?" Doctor Hal Pormon asked in surprised. Then, "You can tell me about that later. How will we get to this settlement of yours?"

"I brought an extra horse," I told him. "Can you ride?"

His face actually lit up as he asked, "An actual horse? Young man, you just made my day."

His wife and daughter didn't seem to be as thrilled about his journey as he was, but he assured them he would be back and I promised to escort him back myself as soon as I could. Bundled up, we set out on what was a cold but, mercifully, windless day. He wore one of those big, furry, hats, like I always associated with Russia, though other countries wore them, too.

As we crossed the cold, white expanse, the doctor asked, "Do you really have a school?"

"Yes sir," I replied. "Just about ten kids, from little ones to some seniors in high school. I graduated last May, myself. From regular school, in Fairplay, I mean."

"That's fine. I mean, about both the school and your graduation. There are more than a dozen people of school age in Como and we are doing nothing for them. I think one family homeschools, and I applaud them for it, but the other children, I don't know if they are getting any instruction. My limited contact with them makes me think they are not." Then, "So, tell me about your town, Mister Overstreet. I have met Mister Glass and he speaks highly of it, like it's some sort of Shang-Ri-La compared to Como."

"It's hardly that, sir. And winter's tough on us. But we've got a good group of people and I think that, if we can make it to spring, we'll really get things going. We had some pretty good gardens last summer and those were just started after the ash cloud. With a whole summer, I think we can do pretty well. And we've all got plans for expanding our houses, most of which are just cabins right now, little more than shacks."

"Why not live in one of the houses in Como? Plenty sit empty."

"The grass was greener, Sir," I told him with a smile he couldn't see because of the scarf Adaline had given me, which I was wearing. "We have a good well, plus water from the Tarryall. And, well, my sister and I wanted to be near our horses and there just wasn't a good place to keep them near Como."

Shortly, we arrived at our little community and I could tell it didn't look like Shang-Ri-La to the good doctor. Just a handful of small log cabins, covered with snow, around a central building that wasn't much bigger and with a barn nearby. The sun being out, Claire and some of the others were out walking the horses, just to keep them limber. Smoke trailed from every chimney. "Not a bad little place," was all he said about the view.

I led him over to the Ryerson's cabin and then took the horses over to the barn. Adaline had seen us coming, apparently, and came over to help me rub down the horses. She always acted like she was afraid of them, but she was getting better. We still hadn't gotten her to ride one after that first trip into town off the

Pass, but she was making herself get used to being around them, which I admired.

We were in the kitchen later, drinking some tea to warm up (I had always hated tea, but it was something we could make and it helped a bit on cold days) when Julia came in with the baby. At least, I assumed it was the baby. She had him pretty heavily bundled up and could well have been a sack of potatoes.

"Josh," she asked, "I was just by the Ryerson's cabin and the doctor asked if we have any onions?"

"I don't—" I started to reply.

I was interrupted by Adaline saying, "I know where there are some wild onions. Would they work?"

"Wild onions?" Julia and I asked in unison. Other people in the room may have joined us. I was the one who completed, "In this weather?"

Adaline, suddenly nervous because of all the attention, said, "You know those boulders over past the gardens, where Alexa and Samantha and I go to pl—hang out now and then? The wind has kept the snow from piling up there and they get warm from the sun on the rocks. I picked a plant from there once and my mom said it was wild onion. There's more over there."

I turned to Inez and asked, "You're sure it was onion?"

"Yeah. I even had Addy pick some for me and I've added some to soups," Inez replied.

I reached for my coat and handed Adaline hers. As we put them on, I said, "Let's go ask the doc if wild onions will work. If so, show me where to pick them."

Inez started putting on her coat, then, saying, "I better come along. If you don't know what you're doing, you can pick a lot of useless greens." Julia, who hadn't taken off her coat or put down the baby, stayed in The Kitchen. It was still deathly cold outside, but the sun was shining brightly off the snow so it improved our moods after the last few weeks of gray and cloudy white.

In the Ryerson's cabin, I was surprised at how wan Seth looked. He smiled at me though, and extended a hand, which I shook. He coughed, then said, "I just can't shake this cough. Thanks for getting the Doc here."

"No problem," I told him. "Now, we're apparently going to go get you the makings for an onion sandwich, for some reason."

The doctor, who looked more grim than he had on the ride, said, "I'm actually hoping to make an onion poultice. A year ago, I would have just given Mister Ryerson here a shot and a couple pills and he'd be back terrorizing the school kids in a couple days. We are a little short on those medicines, as you may have guessed, so I need to go back to the remedies our forefathers used."

"Do they have to be big onions?" Inez asked. "My daughter knows where to get some wild onions."

"In this weather?" the doctor asked, surprised. Then, shrugging, he added, "Never mind. You just go get me some onions. I do not believe their pedigree will make any difference."

LuAnne Ryerson and the two kids thanked us and the three of us set out.

Adaline led us over to the rocks beyond the garden and, at first, seemed to panic when she didn't see wild onions, or much of anything growing for that matter. But then, she perked up and made her way quickly to some boulders about a hundred yards east of where we had started. There, she let out a happy sound that wasn't quite a word and pointed her mother and I to the spot where there really were some green things growing. I realized quickly that the spot was shielded from much of the wind by the boulders, plus it received the morning sun—on the days we got any. That morning, I bet they had practically been baked by the sun. Inez showed us what to pick and we harvested, it seemed to me, quite a few onions, especially for the time of year. Most especially because I had been walking or riding by the plant all my life and never realized what it was. I wondered what else might grow in those mountains, once summer was back, that was edible?

When we brought the onions back, Doctor Pormon mixed them with some other ingredients we had around and, I was to hear from LuAnne, put them on Seth's chest, along with a hot towel, in what he called an onion poultice. According to him, it was how they treated pneumonia back before all the modern drugs. I wondered if it worked back then, because it didn't work for Seth. He succumbed and died on February 21, the coldest day we had seen that year, so cold we didn't even have a thermometer that would register it. The mercury, or whatever was at the bottom of our thermometers, just appeared to have run and hid.

We all took it really hard, his widow LuAnne and the kids hardest of all, of course. For my part, it just didn't seem real. I had gotten to know him over time, though not as well as I suddenly wished I had. Just "surface" friendship such as is often common among men. We had played ball together, sat together at meals, and worked side-by-side in the gardens and in the school. When he was gone, I suddenly realized I didn't really know *him*. I didn't know why he might have left his previous teaching position or why he had chosen to live in Como when he first arrived in the valley instead of at Fairplay where his job was going to be. I knew he and LuAnne had met while attending college in Longmont years before, but I didn't know why she was the girl for him above all others. I had all these questions I wanted to ask of him and, suddenly, no way to ask them. When I cried at the funeral, I think I was crying tears of anger at myself, more than anything.

It came to me, as we wrapped his body and placed it in a snow bank, planning to come back and bury him in the ground once that ground had thawed, that I didn't know anything about anyone I was living with. Here we were, less than two dozen people—a couple score more living in Como—and we might be the last people left alive on earth and I had never bothered to get to know any of them. I had just walked blithely through life, and through disaster, with focus on no one but myself. Dwight Croft, after all, was only five years older than me when the disaster hit, his (presumed) widow only three years older. I was living my life like I somehow thought I had been given a special dispensation from God that it would never end. Like I wasn't living in a land covered in ash, cut off from any other life (if such life existed), facing near starvation. A person watching me would have thought I was on vacation.

People around me looked to me for leadership. Maybe it had started because we were on my land (or, mine and my sister's land), but I had increased it because everything we did, I was the first to take a hand. Gardening, hunting, going to Breckenridge, going after the doctor. If they thought I was doing it all because I cared, though, how could I tell them that I had done it all because I thought it was fun? That I was glad I didn't have to leave the ranch and go to college. That I wasn't feeling hemmed in by the ash but rather enjoying carving what I thought of as our friendly little empire out of this corner of the world. As I stood there by our makeshift grave, listening to Evan Isaacson read Psalm 23, I realized I was walking through the valley of the shadow of death unafraid not because I was leaning on God but because I was so completely self-centered that I didn't think about anything at all.

It was all brought home to me in an instant—far less time than it has taken you to read these last few paragraphs, in fact—that I could die. I could be the one being packed in snow, or dirt. What struck me wasn't the age old question of "Will anyone notice?" because I knew Claire would. No, what came to me was that if God really had spared me from the ash, it was to *be*. Not necessarily to be something, as in something big like a doctor or the savior of these people, but to move beyond self-centered existence and *live*. For him, for other people. To not take days for granted. I would look back later, maybe, and see in myself just another teenager, but in the middle of it I didn't like what I saw in myself. I felt like I was the embodiment of the Dostoevsky comment that, "Man is sometimes extraordinarily, passionately, in love with suffering" in that, through all this death and mayhem, I was secretly enjoying myself.

I remembered a friend of mine from high school named Carver. Jimmy Carver. One weekend, he went to a party even though he was under age for drinking and got toasted. Rolled his car on the way home, spent a week in the hospital, and had everyone telling him he had been given a second chance at life. Six weeks later, he was busted again for drunk driving and had his license taken away. I remembered thinking at the time that he was a moron. There he was, given a second chance, and he had gone out and blown it. Beside the snowy grave, I realized I was little different. I wanted to be different but, at that moment, I also wanted to be warm.

After the short service, we all went back to The Kitchen. We were numb, but the cold was only part of the reason. We had considered Charles an elephant in the room at the trial, but that was nothing to the elephant of a widow and her children. We took turns trying to be supportive of the kids and everyone gave LuAnne a hug, but we all felt inadequate to the task. Probably because we were. We couldn't replace her husband. We could do a lot for the kids, but we couldn't be their father. The sun broke through late in the afternoon, lighting everything up and actually raising the temperature up to where we could record it, but it did nothing for our mood. I don't think its stretching things to say that we were all lower that moment than even on the night of the ash cloud. Then, we hadn't known what was coming—even if it seemed fearful. Here, we had something concrete to fear and it was chilling us all far more than the cold outside.

Julia came to our church service that first Sunday after Seth died. Just walked in, the baby bundled up in blankets, and sat down without saying a word other than greeting. I welcomed her to the service, but didn't want to make her uncomfortable, so I didn't dwell on it. I got the impression other people felt that way, too. Every Sunday after that, she was in service with the rest of us though she never spoke up and, if she sang along with us, it was very softly.

We would lose two more people before the weather warmed up. Elana Marquez died of an apparent heart attack the first week in March. If she had been having any pains before that, she never told anyone. Her family took it hard, of course, but Lester and Alexa seemed to be the worst off. Oscar threw himself into his work, and it was never easy to tell what Jesse thought about anything, but Lester and Alexa wore their mourning on their sleeves more evident than when people used to wear black arm bands. We all cut them some slack, but it was tough going. Adaline and Alexa had another falling out over it, but they eventually patched it up when the next death came our way.

It was later that same month, early in the morning, that Claire and I had gone over to the Tarryall to see if we could chip through the ice to get at the fresh water beneath. With some work I had made it, but it was rapidly freezing back over even as I scooped water out. Claire mentioned that whatever we carried in our buckets would have to thaw before we could drink it. We had been at the stream for no more than thirty minutes—and probably more like twenty—when we started back. The snow was blowing, if not actually falling, so visibility was limited, but I thought I saw something lying on the path between the Isaacson house and their privy. I almost didn't see it –and Claire hadn't seen it—and I almost kept on walking, thinking it was just snow piling on something they had set outside (which makes no sense, but I was in a hurry to get home). Still, I called for Claire to stop over the noise of the wind and stepped over there to see what it was.

I dropped my bucket of frozen water as soon as I realized it was Samantha, the brown-haired twelve year old niece of Evan and Inez Isaacson. "Sam!" I called as I dropped to my knees beside her. She didn't seem to be breathing and there was a patch of red on the path beneath her head. I momentarily debated about whether to move her or not, but figured the cold couldn't be good for anything that might be afflicting her, so I picked her up and carried her to their house. Claire was still holding her buckets and kicked at the door with her feet, shouting, "Let us in!" and it was opened by Inez.

"Hold your—oh my!" she exclaimed, then directed me to put Samantha on the nearby couch. Dropping to her knees by the girl, Inez asked, "Where was she?"

"About halfway between here and the loo. Looked like she might have slipped on the ice."

"She only stepped out two minutes ago," Inez was saying as other members of the family came into the room.

"I was coming back from the stream," I said, though quickly realized no one was paying any attention to me. Adaline came into the room then and rushed to Samantha's side, imploring her cousin to wake up. They had to pull her away so that Inez could tend to the injured girl.

Two days later, Claire and I were barely up and around when a knock came at our door. I made sure Claire was dressed, then opened the door, to find Adaline standing there. She was in jeans and a sweater, but not a coat, and didn't appear to be cold. "Get in here before you freeze!" I said, hustling her inside and realizing I was saying something my father would have said. It was all I could do to keep from asking, "Where's your coat?"

So Claire asked, "Where's your coat, girl?"

"I just, um," Adaline stammered, though not from the cold, it appeared, "I—I just wanted you to know that Sam died in the night.

"Oh my," Claire said, coming over quickly and pulling the little blonde girl into a hug. "I'm so sorry, Addy." I thought of her as little, but at that time she was probably five-two or even five-three, and still growing.

"She never woke up. Since you found her, I mean. She never woke up and we couldn't feed her or get her to take any water or anything. Pop said she had a fever, but Doc Pormon said there wasn't anything we could do about it other than what we were already doing. Do you think anything we did was worth the effort?"

Claire cast me a glance as if I should be the one to answer and I tried to return the sentiment. She and Adaline were sitting on a love seat we had brought over from the ranch house, so I took a chair that was nearby. All I could think to say was, "You and Samantha were pretty close, huh?"

"Not until we got here." Adaline wiped her eyes, then said, "We both lived in Phoenix, and we saw each other all the time, but we never had a thing in common other than blood. I never got to know her because I guess I never thought I had to. And now she's— I'll never get the chance." She leaned her head up against Claire and cried silently. The expression on her face made her look even younger than her thirteen years.

"Does your family know you've come over here?" I asked, suddenly thinking how worried they would be if Adaline had just wandered out without telling anyone. They might be out scouring the countryside.

"Yeah. I told them I was coming to see you two and tell you the news." She sat up, then, and said, "I probably better let you get about your day, huh?"

"Not at all," Claire told her. "You're welcome to hang out here as long as you like. 'Sides, it's kind of fun to have another woman around the house."

Thinking I should pitch in, I offered, "Yeah. Claire needs someone to talk to and, well, I'm a guy and we're all morons."

"Claire's lucky to have a brother like you," Adaline told me.

"Yes, I am," Claire agreed, giving me a wink. "But you've got a couple pretty good brothers, too."

"I guess. I mean, they are. You just," she looked at me, then didn't say anything else for a while. When she did, it was just to tell us about a time when she and Samantha had snuck out of the house in Phoenix—where they had been having a sleepover—and had tried to go to a late movie, only to have the theater owner call the police on them, who then contacted their parents. I got the impression from the story that Adaline and Samantha had been closer than we had been led to believe earlier.

Adaline wound up spending most of the day with us, even helping us in the barn—though staying away from the horses, still. She even talked me into playing her in Strat-O-Matic, less from a love of the game and mostly from a desire to not go back to the cabin where Samantha had died.

Losing Samantha was the most shocking of all three deaths, at least to me. Maybe just because she was so young. It's not like the others were so old as to be at the end of their life, but they had at least had a chance to live some of it. Samantha was just a girl, a little girl to my mind, and it seemed so unfair. All of the Isaacsons took it hard, of course, but I had become pretty good friends with Jonathan and losing his sister put him in a kind of a numb funk for at least a month. I couldn't blame him, as that left him all alone to watch over David. Oh, he had his cousins and his grandmother, but Samantha and David had been the last members of his immediate family. We all tried to give him some time, and he eventually became his old self, but I remember him telling me once—a couple months after Samantha's death—that he expected he would carry her death with him for the rest of his life. "She came through so much, like the rest of us, to just die from a fall on the ice," he had said. "It just seems like a bad joke."

I was sitting in the kitchen with Evan Isaacson and Lester Marquez, everyone else apparently grieving in their own way in their own cabins a few days after the funerals, and asking in what I hoped was a jovial manner, "So, Evan, how is it that there's such a huge gap between Adaline and Bobby? Eleven years isn't it?"

Evan smiled and said, in a low voice, "You might say he's an 'oops baby'." After a chuckle from all of us, he added, "In a way, that's not true, though. We actually started trying for a third child about a year after Adaline was born. Inez was only thirty-five then, and we hadn't had any trouble getting the first two, but something was different, I guess. After a couple years, we went to the doctor and he told us it was me. That I wasn't, well, you know. So we figured two was all we were going to get and were happy with that. Ten years later, surprise!"

"If he didn't look just like you," Lester teased, "I'd tell you to go get a DNA test."

I was making some similar comment, about how little Bobby looked like a carbon copy of Evan when Julia Croft came in, her baby wrapped warmly in blankets. After settling him down on the floor near us, she stood up stiffly, formally, and said, "Gentlemen, I would like to apply for the job of school teacher."

I think I spoke for all three of us when I asked, "What?" Personally, I was surprised not just by the abruptness of the request, but that I would be addressed with it at all. I wasn't *that* much of an adult!

She took a breath, as if preparing something she had memorized, then said, "Teaching meant the world to my husband. And I was an education major myself, though I hadn't yet completed all my classes. Still, I sat in here for many of Seth's courses and helped him when I could, I know where the students are in their studies, and I would like to take over in—in Seth's place."

We were all stunned into silence, but finally, Lester said, "Julia, I don't doubt that you could do it. I don't think any of us doubt you. But, well, are you sure you're up to it?"

"Like I say, I almost had my degree and—"

"No," Lester interrupted in a gentle tone. "I don't think any of us doubt that. What I mean is, and fellas, correct me if you think I'm wrong, I'm just wondering if you're, um, emotionally ready. Well, that's not exactly how I mean it. I just mean, with all you've been through—new baby and all." I nodded along, and I think Evan did, too.

"Sirs," she addressed us, or the two men, anyway, "I don't know anything about gardening, but I'm willing to learn. Josh, I don't even like horses. But if I have to just keep sitting in that cabin, and knowing there are kids here who need teaching … well, I'm asking this, maybe it's for the wrong reasons, but I admit I am asking this partially for *my own* emotional state and well-being." I think Lester was about to reply when she added, "And I want to do this for Junior. It's important to me that he have a school one day."

Lester looked at me, I looked at Evan, and Evan looked back at Lester, then we went around the triangle a few more times with mixtures of looks, shrugs and eyebrow raising. Finally, I stepped out of the silence and said, "Julia, if you want to tackle the teaching job, we'll support you all we can." I looked at the other men and added, "Just promise us this: if it's ever too much, or you need our help in any way, you'll tell us right away."

"Agreed," she replied, exhaling her breath as if relieved. I wondered if she really thought we would turn her down? And on what basis? And had I really been part of the decision, or just the other two men, who were not only older but had kids in the school? I liked responsibility, but I wasn't used to it.

Chapter Ten

To own a bit of ground,
to scratch it with a hoe,
to plant seeds,
and watch the renewal of life—
this is the commonest delight of the race,
the most satisfactory thing a man can do.
~Charles Dudley Warner

As the snow began to melt in patches, we worked to clear off our gardens and start planting. Jesse had been able to do some research in some books procured in Breckenridge and found a few plants that might grow early, even at our altitude. He had also picked up a book about things that already grew in our area that were supposedly edible and/or medicinal and we were all on the lookout for them. Adaline, after her success with the wild onions, considered herself an expert at finding rare plants and, truthfully, she did seem to have a gift for it. I also began to plan another expedition into Breckenridge. Boreas Pass was still covered in snow, but I had hopes that maybe the air down in the Blue River valley would finally be breathable and we could … forage. I never could get it completely out of my mind that we were stealing, no matter how many euphemisms or justifications I came up with.

Claire volunteered to come with me, and I didn't think it was fear of letting me out of her sight so much as she just wanted to get out of our little valley. She and Oscar were growing closer and she often spoke of a future with him, though no official announcement had been made. I was envious of their relationship, but still didn't see that I could do anything about it.

I had a daydream, though. Over on the other side of the Blue River valley, where the ski area used to be, there were some giant hotels. I had a daydream that, even now, there was a family living in one of those hotels, eating all the food, scavenging stuff like us, who had a daughter somewhere between the ages of 16 and 21.

I didn't say I had a lot of hope. I knew it was just a daydream.

Still, I had been trying to make good on my resolve by Seth's grave—recalled to me by the other two funerals and now in the fore of my mind as we finally buried them in dirt—to try and get to know the people around me. I still played the games, but rather than *just* playing the game or sitting at the same meal table with someone, I endeavored to get to know them. I asked questions and I listened to answers. I was finding them interesting for the most part, but I was disturbed that—almost to a man or woman—there was an undercurrent of fatalism in them all. They were looking forward to planting and foraging, but I got the impression that everyone approached every moment just waiting for another shoe to drop. Some figured another ash cloud would sweep through, or the winds would change and bury us under the old ashes. But even those who didn't seem to worry about that seemed to have it in mind that if we didn't die this year, it would be next year.

And no one spoke of rescue anymore. It had been almost nine months, after all, and we hadn't so much as seen a vapor trail in the sky. We heard from Como periodically—and more regularly as things began to thaw out—and they told us that no one had seen anyone on the highway other than those few people who had straggled in before winter hit, like the doctor and his family and a half-dozen others who had crawled in. There was a story one day of several Como residents seeing a repeating flash of light coming from far to the east. Convinced it was Morse code, three men had set out to go see who might be there. It turned out to be a mirror that had been hung on a porch as part of a wind-chime. No one had seen it previously, they guessed, because the sun had never been at the right angle until that day. The house was long empty. Another man determined to walk into Fairplay by the back trail and was never seen again. And we never did hear what happened to the Roxon brothers.

It was the first week of April when we finally decided to mount the expedition to Breckenridge. There was still much snow on the pass, but I reasoned that it would be easier to cross the snow and ice than the mud and ash once things started thawing out. We were also getting dangerously low on just about everything, so I deemed it time to go while we still had the strength to go. We only had enough snow shoes for four people (not having figured out how to make our own, yet), so we were limited to a caravan of four people. Tad and Jonathan joined on the expedition. Oscar would have gone, but Lester broke his leg in late March and it fell to Oscar to take care of the family—and his father. So he kissed Claire good-bye, which drew them both some good-natured ribbing, and we three guys promised to bring her back safely.

We started out early in the morning, before it was even light, and made the summit by noon. It was hard going on the west side, owing to the afternoon sun each day already having made that side of the road a slick mess. We made it to the first of the houses— long since looted (by us)—and slept inside it. We had brought our own sleeping bags so the beds were quite comfortable (the mattresses too big for us to have carried over the pass). The next morning, we were up early and started into town.

It still looked terrible, but not as bad as the last time we had been there. The sun hit the east side of the valley every afternoon and had melted much of the snow away. The snow, as it melted, had made a morass of the mud, which made for miserable travel. On the other hand, we could see places where grass was starting to poke through. Even a few pine trees had weathered the ash and storms and were starting to spring to life and I saw a few tiny aspens here and there. I pointed them out to the others and said, "Nature's caretakers there. If this whole mountain doesn't slide downhill with the mud, and if they can get some steady sunlight and just enough moisture, the aspens will retake this hillside. Then will come the pine trees. One day, it might all look like it used to."

"I remember Dad telling us about the aspens after the fire," Claire related as we walked, carefully making our way down the road to houses we hadn't foraged in the previous fall. "He said the aspens will come up and grow really fast. They stabilize the soil and provide cover so the ground plants can grow. But then, the pine trees start to grow. They grow for years and years in the shade of the aspens until, one day, they overshadow the aspens. Then, the aspens start dying off because the pine trees have taken over. Dad said it was the way things were supposed to be, that God had designed it all because the pine tree was a sturdier tree and, long term, would take better care of the mountain. Still, it always made me kind of sad for the aspens. They were like nannies who had raised the children, but then the children just ignored them, then killed them." She laughed and shook her head, saying, "Silly way to think, huh?"

Tad and Jonathan both said she wasn't being silly, but they still had crushes on her and wouldn't have disparaged her if she had credited the whole eco-system to intelligent fungi from Mars. Tad was the athletic one of the two and, I thought, probably got girls' attention—when there were girls around to give attention. Dark, curly hair, winning smile, all that. Jonathan was a skinny teen and had a prominent Adam's apple and overbite. He wore glasses and tried really hard to tell jokes but had no timing whatsoever. He was very smart—often helping Julia not just with the younger kids but with the older ones as well—and I heard he had already been on the radar of several colleges even when a sophomore in high school. I considered them both friends but had the annoying feeling we were going to grow to be three single old men, dreaming about the women who had populated the world when we were young. Jonathan was only seventeen, though, so maybe—I thought—he could marry Alexa one day. I didn't know that they had any interest in one another, but I thought one day that might not make much of a difference if hormones had anything to say about it.

We found the remains of an old hotel or condominium of some sort that was almost covered up with flowing ash. Still, we made our way inside via a window that I gathered had once opened up well above ground but by then was almost at ground level. The place had a closed-in, fetid smell, but we came to a vending machine and that gave us some hope. I was just about to break the glass—for there were lots of nutritionally dense foods in there (trail mix, candy bars with nuts)—when Jonathan stopped me and pointed. There was a sign about a restaurant.

We followed the signs and came to a large dining area full of people. Once Claire had stopped screaming and the rest of us could get our nerve up, we went past the dead bodies—all huddled together as the end came—and into the kitchen. There were a few more dead bodies in there, looking to me like they had died choking. Was it the ash cloud? Or had a gas pipe ruptured? The place didn't smell good, but I didn't think I was smelling gas. There was rotting food out on the counters and knives and other utensils were on the floor near the hands of the dead, as if they had died while preparing the meals. Whatever had killed them, it had done so pretty suddenly.

"That ash cloud hit here during supper," Jonathan commented. "We survived where we were, but these people choked to death while they were eating, or getting the food ready."

Tad swore and I couldn't disagree with him. Claire asked, "How did we survive? We were just in a pick-up truck cab."

Jonathan answered what may have been a rhetorical question, "It seems to me that the ash came through not in a solid wall as it appeared, but in varying densities. We couldn't see it with the naked eye, but in this one spot, they got hit with a really thick cloud. Other places, less so. But it seems to have been the luck of the draw."

Tad, never liking to be shown up by his cousin, injected, "When we went to raid that grocery store, it had already been picked over. But the town seemed empty, except maybe for one other person we thought we might have seen. So maybe some people survived for a while, even days, while others were knocked out right away."

"I hope it doesn't sound cruel if I say I hope Mom and Dad were in one of the places where it happened quickly," Claire commented. I nodded in agreement.

We made our way over to what looked like the pantry. A man in an actual chef's outfit was slumped against the door of it, so we had to move him out of the way. His body was dry and flabby at the same time and I had this picture in my mind of it falling apart as we pushed on it. Thankfully, it didn't. So we opened the pantry door and found another jackpot. There were canned goods galore and boxes of powders, everything from cake mixes to gravy. Even some tinned meats, which made me wonder how they fitted into the fare of what appeared to have been a high-class and high-dollar place.

As the other three started trying to figure out how much they each could carry, I went in search of something, though I didn't know what at first. I soon found it, though, and came back, saying, "Guys—and Sis—I have an idea. I found an eight-foot plastic table, you know: like the kind we've got back in The Kitchen. The top's pretty slick, right? What if we turn it upside down and attach some ropes to it then use it like a sled? I think four of us could pull more weight that way than the four of us can carry out of here separately."

"It's worth a try," Tad agreed. "And if it's too hard, we carry what we can and cache the rest somewhere that we can come back to."

We carried the table out onto the road and turned it upside down. We had brought rope, which we tied on to the table legs in a way that we hoped would make it easy to pull. Then, we went back into the hotel, mostly able to ignore the grisly visage in the dining room, and carried out armfuls of food. We wrapped our cargo in sheets procured from the hotel or condo or whatever it was and made the "package" on our sled as secure as possible. We experimented with pulling it and, when we had it as loaded as we thought we could get it and still move it, we tied off the load and set out.

It was hard work and we didn't make it very far before night fell. We laid our sleeping bags very close together, lit a fire, and made sure there was plenty of firewood close at hand to feed into it. We slept fitfully that night and awoke long before the sun was up. We were cold and miserable and grumpy, but decided we'd rather get going than just sit there. Besides, the path was visible by star and moonlight, so we weren't worried about getting lost.

By the time the sun was up, we had made it a pretty good distance. We took turns, having two people pulling the table-sled while two people pushed and, by noon, we were within sight of the summit. The problem then, was that as the sun came out it made the snow on top slushy. While the table was working fairly well as a sled, we were having a hard time getting much purchase with our feet. We were growing more miserable all the time and making each other as irritated as we could. Several hours and many shouting matches later, we seemed to only be about a hundred yards closer to the summit than we had been at noon. Finally, we agreed to stop where we were and back track a few hundred yards to where we had seen some blowdowns and get firewood, leaving our makeshift sled parked, within sight of the summit. I'd like to say the fire warmed our spirits, but if it did, it wasn't by much. Thankfully, we were too exhausted to do anything about how angry we were when we all went to sleep. I had even shouted at Claire a time or two, something I would have sworn before the trip that nothing could ever make me do.

Judging by the stars, I think we only slept about three hours, and then we were all awake. We made ourselves some hot chocolate (we had had the sense to grab some packs of it before tying the rest in with the foodstuffs) and that lightened our mood a little bit. A chocolate candy bar apiece helped, too. I might have been on the verge of nineteen, and the others close behind, but we were still kids in more ways than any of us would have admitted. Finally, we decided to push on and found that the weather was colder than we thought for the path to the summit had frozen back over. Wearing snow shoes, we actually made better time in the middle of the night than we had all the previous day as it made the path slicker and, thus, easier to push our sled on. I was a little worried about us all getting frostbite, but I was more excited about the time we were making.

At the summit, we took a breather and watched the sun come up. We soon started out again, hoping to get some distance before the snow could start thawing out again. After the winter we had been through—and felt like we were still in at that moment—I thought it was ironic that I was actually wanting the sun to not melt the snow. I said as much to the others and I think they appreciated the levity as their grumbling was less than it had been.

Three hours later and we were stuck in the slush again. Before our grumbling and sniping could get out of hand, I suggested, "Let's leave it here." At their gasps (and outright rebellious words) I pointed and said, "Look, there's our valley. If you stare really hard, I think you can even see smoke coming from a chimney. Let's go down and get some horses and that old sledge, the one with the really wide runners. Maybe even enlist some other people to come help us."

An hour later, maybe less, we encountered a group of our friends. They were on horseback and coming up the Boreas Pass road to meet us. Apparently, they had seen us struggling in the early morning light and had decided to come and meet us halfway. They had even brought the sledge with the wide runners! By evening, we had the load off the mountain and into our little town. Needless to say, our fellow townspeople were excited by the haul! I got several hugs just for the chocolate alone.

"Josh?" Claire called softly from her side of the cabin as we lay in our separate beds that night. "I don't think I can ever get the sight of those people in that restaurant out of my mind."

"I know what you mean," I replied.

After a bit, she added, "Breck was a small town, relatively speaking. Still, what if all the hotels in town are like that, and the restaurants? And Frisco and Dillon and—and what if Denver's like that? Or what if only half of Denver is like that, would that somehow be worse?"

"Worse?"

"Yeah. Which would be worse: everyone wiped out at once, or half the population suddenly having to bury the other half?"

"Can I choose none of the above?" I asked, trying to add some levity to a conversation I wasn't enjoying.

"Do you—do you think the restaurant Mom and Dad went to eat in is like that? On the bright side, those people didn't appear to have suffered for long. Not even long enough to make for the door. If Mom and Dad did die in the ash cloud, I hope it was quick like that."

"Yeah," I mumbled, liking the conversation even less.

Suddenly (for I hadn't even heard her get up), Claire was on my side of the cabin and saying, "I want to go back to Breckenridge. Or Fairplay. Or Denver." She sat down on the foot of my bed and asked, "Do you ever have the feeling that if we don't get out of this little valley you'll explode?"

"Not really, no."

She was wearing a flannel nightgown but I happened to see that she was wearing denim shorts beneath it. She never mentioned the attack, and I hadn't heard her having any nightmares in more than a month, but the shorts told me she still wasn't over the ordeal entirely. But then, I had no idea what a reasonable expectation was for when she would get over it. Maybe never entirely. After all, I wouldn't really expect her to forget it. I was shaken from such thoughts by her saying, "I love you, and I think I am falling in love with Oscar and, well, this really is a good group of people. I've got nothing against anyone here but, well ... I feel hemmed in." She smiled and said, "What I really hated most about our trip was the sleeping bags. I hate being cooped up like that. I hate being cooped up like this. I want to get on one of the horses and at least ride to Jefferson. And I think the worst part of it all, what's really driving me crazy, is knowing that I can't. We don't even know if we can go further into Breckenridge. What if we really are stuck here for life? I can't guarantee that I won't go crazy."

I wanted so badly to have the perfect words to say to her, something that would cheer her up or take away her anxiety. I didn't. And I couldn't really identify with her anxiety. I might have nightmares about the bodies in that restaurant, but I would wake up and be comforted that we were still in our little valley. Things weren't perfect. We had lost three members of our community—four if you counted Charles Levinson—but it was still our community, or *my* community, anyway. I loved that it had fallen to me to go get the food, and that I had pulled it off successfully. I was enjoying helping Julia out with the teaching now and then, and I was really glad I had started to get to know people.

I figured our community would grow. In my mind, I saw us having children, and then them having children of their own. I saw us taking back the countryside from the ash, a little bit at a time, and building larger homes and better gardens and doing some trading with Como. And I figured there had to be other pockets where life had survived and one day, maybe years away but one day, we would trade with those towns and find that they had preserved books we hadn't or could bring back some technology we had lost. Claire was looking into the future and still seeing the ash cloud while I was seeing blue sky.

Maybe she was too pessimistic and I was too optimistic. Maybe there was a future but it wasn't as bright as I made it out to be. Still, I told myself, I'd rather be the optimist. Some days it might not be as practical, but it *was* more cheerful.

She patted my foot and said, "I wouldn't have made it this far without you, Josh. Thanks."

"You're a lot stronger than you give yourself credit for," I told her truthfully. "A lot stronger than I ever knew you were."

"I've never really needed to be strong," she replied, as if the idea had just come to her. "I've always been the baby of the family, and the little girl. No one's ever really expected anything of me."

"That's not true—"

"It is," she contradicted. "But I do like what we just did, and that when I volunteered no one objected, 'She's just a girl.' I guess I'll just take one day at a time, huh?"

"You know, you're as much of a reason why this place is called Overstreet as I am."

"I doubt that, but thanks for saying it."

On my nineteenth birthday, May 4th, Claire baked me a cake (using one of the cake mixes we had liberated from the restaurant) and even frosted it. Everyone sang "Happy Birthday" to me and several people presented me with presents, mostly books. Adaline had knitted something for me that, right out of the box, I couldn't tell what it was. Turned out it was the start of a sweater but she hadn't gotten very far. She said by winter it would match the scarf.

After the party, which also doubled as our lunch that day, Steve and Lysette took me aside. I was surprised that they would, then more surprised at the reason. We were outside, enjoying a sunny day as we sat on a bench near the gardens, when Steve finally explained the reason for the confab. "Josh, I was wondering if you would sell us a plot over here and let us build close to the rest of you."

"You don't need to buy from me—"

"It's your land, Josh. Well, yours and Claire's. We want to move over here closer, but I want it to be … legal isn't really the word. Call it pride, but I want a piece of land that's ours, free and clear."

I thought a moment, then replied, "OK. We don't really have use for money anymore, so maybe we can do it like the old Homesteader's Act: you prove up on the land and it's yours. You leave and it reverts back to Claire and me. Sound good?"

"I still want to find a way of paying you for it," Steve insisted. "Maybe by working it off in some way. You're always talking about building on to your cabin; maybe I can help with that."

"Can I ask what brought this on?"

They looked at each other and Lysette seemed to prod him with a look, so he told me, "Some of it was just this winter. We felt awfully isolated from the rest of you guys. But then, well, a couple weeks ago I saw that Charles Levinson trying to steal something from our shed. I don't know what, and I ran him off. Maybe he was just sleeping in the shed. I don't know. I like that little house, but suddenly I had this picture in my mind of him or someone else going after Lysette or Angela and, well, I just felt too far away. If it was just me, maybe I'd stay, but I don't trust that man and I pictured him doing me in and attacking Lysette. Plus, this past winter, if there had been something wrong with one of us, there would have been no way to send for help." He smiled and added, "I'm a city-boy at heart and I'm ready to move back to town."

After that conversation got around, the other families (and Danica) decided they wanted a similar agreement. So we drew up some contracts and everyone signed them and I had no idea what to do with them from there as the concept of it being "my land" or even "our land" in terms of Claire and myself had long gone out my mental window. Still, everyone seemed happy with the arrangement and began making plans for how they were going to build, plant, etc. Jesse and Mister Glass even began working out a plan for a municipal sewer system that seemed impossible to me, but they were undaunted.

Claire seemed on edge about it at first but when I asked her about it, it turned out she didn't care whether people owned "our land" or not. What had rattled her was the idea that Charles Levinson was still nearby. No one else claimed to have seen him— we even asked the people in Como—but we had no reason to doubt Steve, either. Everyone renewed their vigilance, at least for a while.

We found out that Como had lost several people over the winter, too. When word got to them about Steve's proposal, we wound up selling two more town sites in Overstreet, one to Freddy Wilson and his wife, and another to a family named Lewis that had five kids (three girls but all under dating age, darn it!). I was a little surprised at first that Howard Glass didn't want to buy one of our town sites, but then I found out he didn't need to as he was marrying Danica Frowley. This news surprised exactly no one, in spite of what I said in my previous sentence, as we had all been expecting it to come at some time. We were all happy about it as Mister Glass had seemed like one of us for quite a while—and we were excited to get an electrician.

I half expected that the announcement of Danica's coming nuptials might spark Claire and Oscar to follow suit, but if Oscar had such an idea, Claire didn't. Claire and Danica had gotten very close over the previous ten-plus months—Danica almost becoming a surrogate mom to Claire in many ways—so I wouldn't have been surprised if Claire had followed her in this. I think Claire was genuinely fond of Oscar, perhaps even falling in love with him, but I think she was also still holding out hope that there was life outside our little valley. Specifically, life for her outside the valley.

Having gotten to know Danica pretty well—maybe better than I knew anyone except Claire—I couldn't help but wonder if Danica were really in love with Howard. He was a nice guy, and they seemed to genuinely get along, but I wondered if she were marrying him out of something like … I started to write "desperation", but that wasn't it. Like I say: they clearly enjoyed each other's company. He was about fifteen years her senior, but it wasn't like he had one foot in the grave or anything. He was widowed, but that seemed to be safely in the past, owing not just to time but what had happened in between. It occurred to me that maybe I was putting too much stock in the "happily ever after" stories. I thought back to my parents and, while I always knew they loved each other, it wasn't an "ushy-gushy" love. It was a stable, committed love. I reasoned that maybe that's what Danica and Howard had.

One day when Howard was helping me in the garden that belonged to myself, Claire and Danica (and, soon, him) he chuckled and said, "It's kind of funny, huh?"

"What's that?" I asked, not really paying attention and hoping he hadn't said something before to lead up to this moment.

"Well, here's Danni, this beautiful, successful young woman. And back when there are millions of guys in the world to choose from, she can't find one. How is it that, now, she's found me?"

"Hand of God?" I asked rather absently.

"Must be. You believe in God, Josh?"

"Yeah," I replied, finally paying attention. "Do you?"

"I didn't, before all this happened. Weird, huh? Back when everything was going great, well, it wasn't that I didn't believe in God, I just didn't have a lot of use for him. Figured I'd stay out of his way and he'd stay out of mine. But then, that night when we were all up here huddled in our vehicles wondering if it was the end of the world, I found myself praying."

When he was silent for a while, I prompted, "Praying for what?"

"You know, I wasn't sure. You'd think, in a situation like that, I would have been praying for deliverance, or death without pain. But really, I think I just kept asking God, 'Are you there?'"

"What do you think the answer was?"

He shrugged, pulled some weeds and added them to a little pile of weeds which would eventually be carried to the compost pile, then told me, "I think the answer was 'yes,' but I couldn't tell you why I think that. I didn't hear a voice from heaven, and life's sure been hard since then, but somehow, I know He's there. I've enjoyed coming to church with you folks over here, and I'm really looking forward to being a part of that. Part of your whole community over here."

"Como's got an actual church building. Anyone actually use it?"

"Now and again," he replied with another shrug. "There's a few people that get together at the doc's place and worship every Sunday. I joined them a few times. Good folks. Something about what you've got going here just … I don't know. Speaks to me or something."

"Probably 'cause you get to sit by your girlfriend," I chided.

He blushed and replied, "There's something in what you say."

As I had feared, the problem of spring and early summer was that the snow melted and the rains came and they washed all that ash off the mountains. We worked hard on and in our gardens, often having everyone who could wield a hoe, shovel or whatever out there, trying to build spreader dams that would funnel the muddy ash off our gardens. A little wouldn't have been bad, and might have even helped, but this was a struggle to, seemingly, keep the entire mountain from engulfing our gardens and homes.

On the bright side, the gardens were coming in good. And as the ash got carried down into the lower reaches of the valley and out onto the flat lands beyond Como, more and more grass sprung up. This allowed for more room for our horses to roam and forage (and we had three new foals which were doing well). There was also grass out there in the valley on which some cows were to be seen mulling about. We weren't sure where they came from, but the people of Como took great pride in them and hoped to be able to produce beef in a year or two as there was one big old bull who had apparently been watching over the heifers in the proceeding months. Where he had kept them we never knew for sure, but by the end of summer there was the start of a good herd out there on the grass—a couple calves, and more three and four year old stuff that had been hiding who knew where?

The wedding was in early June and we had it out in the meadow, attended by everyone the bride and groom knew to be alive in the world as the entire population of Como had come over. There were rumors that one other person still existed in the world, but other than that day in the spring when Steve saw him, no one had seen Charles Levinson for sure. Of course, anything that went missing in Como was blamed on him.

We expected Boreas Pass to be at its best by early July, so we started making plans to make another foraging trip into Breckenridge. It was our plan to take some wagons and horses and go get everything we could carry away. The people of Como only had three horses among them, but they had some wagons and were willing to send able bodies, so we had it proposed as a joint venture, with the loot being shared equally. I was still a little hesitant about what we called our enterprise, until in a conversation with Julia she pointed out to me that it had long been a law of the sea that the right of salvage came to whoever found the goods once a ship was abandoned. We weren't at sea and we weren't plundering old ships, but the law seemed like it ought to be the same to me.

Helping with the school, I had come to be pretty good friends with Julia Croft. She was about seven inches shorter than my six foot, had long brown hair and smooth skin with just enough of an olive cast to it to make me think there was some middle eastern blood in her background. I had asked her about that once and she said the coloring came from her father but where he got it from she didn't know. She had dark brown eyes and a ready smile and, once she had lost all the baby weight, I thought, had a very attractive figure. Her little boy had sandy blonde hair he had gotten from his father, she said. I wondered if that made it harder, seeing her husband so clearly in the baby, or if that were a comfort. I asked her about it one time and she said she couldn't really see any of D.J. Sr. in Jr. other than that both had a quick temper. I remembered how people were always saying Rusty and I both looked just like our father and my mother responding that we didn't.

Other than the wedding, the highlight of my June may have been that I made it into the World Series of the Strat-O-Matic tournament Jesse had put together that started way back in the winter. Through cold nights and rainy ones, we had played a season of eighty games per team, the teams drawn at random from the box. I had fielded the 1986 Houston Astros and Jesse had fielded the 2027 St. Louis Cardinals. In all, we had had ten people playing, with teams from the 1914 Chicago Cubs to the 2036 Texas Rangers.

Why there were no teams more recent than those Rangers we always wondered but had no way of finding out. On the night of the World Series, we decided to play the full best of seven series as we had the game down to the point that we could generally play 9 innings in under a half an hour. We had kind of figured some of the other participants might watch some of the games, but it turned out that most of our town came to the Series. What had started just as Jesse's family wanting to support him had grown into a full-on baseball party, complete with food and drinks and—this really surprised me—a little wagering on the games. It was all in good fun, but some extra garden work or turns at cleaning the privy were up for grabs.

I started Mike Scott in game one and he mowed through the Cardinals with no problem. I had trouble scoring runs, too, though, and only managed to eek out a 2-0 win. I ran Nolan Ryan out there for Game 2 (we had actually heard that name even in our century) and was quickly up two games to none. Jesse rearranged his line-up for Game 3 and came from behind to beat me in the 9th. I won Game 4 and it seemed like it was all over because I could start Ryan again in Game 5. We had a pitcher's duel going, though, and Jesse won it 3-2 in the 12th inning. I think we were all hoping for a deciding Game 7, just for drama's sake, but the dice were all rolling my way and my team won Game 6, 8-1 with someone named Bob Knepper almost throwing a no-hitter for eight innings. The one run Jesse got came in the 9th inning, off my closer. Most of the crowd had stayed for the whole time, occasionally cheering certain "plays" but mainly just reveling in a chance to have a party. It was our first party since the wedding and the release seemed to do us good.

Ours was not a perfect community. We had our squabbles. Someone thought they were doing more work in the gardens than someone else, and another person levied the charge that some people weren't doing their part in the community kitchen now that so many of the houses had kitchens of their own and so forth. We mostly put such differences aside for Sunday church, but even then there was the occasional squabble about whether to sing more or less or whose turn it was to preach or whether what had been preached ran counter to Scripture or not. Sometimes, one party

184

wouldn't speak to another party for a day or two, but we all lived so close that couldn't be sustained for long and got worked out—sometimes with the help of a mediator but usually just between the parties concerned.

On the Fourth of July, we invited the people from Como over and had a big get-together. We challenged them to a game of baseball (and they won, which was really annoying because it was our field and we were so much younger and, in short, so much more overconfident). Before the game, we sang the Star Spangled Banner, and Evan Isaacson led a benediction, then we had a picnic and, on the whole, had a really good time. One of the men from Como—Sturgis, was his name, though I never knew whether that were his first or last name—had a plan for packing down the ash on the road between Overstreet and Como and making it almost like a paved road. The wherefores and whithertos were argued for quite a while and, by the time the day ended, it didn't look like work on the road would start before the next summer, if at all. Still, as with the idea of bringing us a sewer line, I was fascinated by the concept and was sure that, if we lingered long enough in the valley, we would figure such things out.

Late in the afternoon, the ballgame played and most people just milling around or showing the gardens to the people of Como, I stopped by where Claire sat with Oscar and a few other people and said, "I'm thinking of walking up to the old house. You want to come?"

Claire shook her head, so I looked to the rest of the crowd and asked, "Anyone else want to join me?"

Julia surprised me by saying, "I could use a walk." Then, "Adaline, would you watch Jr. for me?"

Adaline seemed hesitant about the offer, which surprised me as she practically raised the younger members of the Isaacson family, but finally said, "Um, yes ma'am."

"We're not in school, Adaline. Call me Julia out here."

"Yes ma'am," Adaline responded, to get a laugh she wasn't expecting. She turned red with embarrassment, as 13 year old girls are wont to do.

As we walked up the path to my old house, I asked, "You ever seen the old place?"

"Just from a distance." Then, as if she needed to re-explain herself, said, "I just kind of wanted a walk."

"You play a good third base," I told her.

"I played softball all through school," she said with pride. "A couple colleges tried to recruit me, but I knew I wasn't at that level."

"You seemed good enough to me."

"Thanks," she said with a laugh, though I hadn't intended it as a joke. She patted me on the arm and that sent a strange thrill through me. "Really, there were a lot of factors. I was good in high school, but not great. I knew college would be a whole new level of competition. I also knew that to compete at the college level, I would have to devote a lot of time to it and I was going to need a job—not to mention keeping my grades up. Then, I got to college and would occasionally play a game with one of the club teams and I realized that I had lost any joy for the sport back when I *had* to play it. When I could just go out there and play, on my own terms, like today, I liked that."

"You obviously know the sport. You ought to play in one of our Strat-O-Matic tournaments."

"I tried a game of that, remember? I'll play blackjack or an occasional round of 'Monopoly', but what you guys see in Strat-O-Matic I don't get. Too complicated for me." Before I could rebut the point, she said, "Reminds me of these games my brothers used to play. They called them strategy games and they would have like a million little pieces and roll twenty dice. They knew the back story for every one of the pieces and, well," she looked at me and smiled as she said, "They loved it. Had friends over just about every week and it was good, clean fun I guess you'd say. They tried to teach me, but that's just not how my mind works."

"You have a beautiful mind," I objected.

"Why, thank you," she said with a curtsey. "There are things I know well and things I do well. Those games were one of the things that my mind was not made for." She looked at me again and said, "You have a good mind, too, Josh. I admire the reading you do. It's too bad you couldn't have gone to college."

"You had brothers?" I asked, the compliments making me uncomfortable (mainly because I wanted to keep hearing them and knew I probably shouldn't).

"Three. All younger than me, though the oldest was only two years younger than me."

"Any sisters?"

"I did. She was born with a hole in her heart. Lots of surgeries, then died when she was eight. I was eighteen then and off—off at college. I threw myself into school to avoid the grief."

"I'm sorry," I commented.

"It's the kind of thing that happens in life," she replied quietly. Then, perking back up, said, "But I like to think that my brothers are still alive, back in Indiana. Wondering where I am, not even knowing they have a nephew, but still alive."

"Yeah. I like to think my brother is still out there somewhere, too."

As we neared the house, she said, "You know, if that ash cloud came from the Yellowstone volcano … we could be the only people left alive in North America. People have been warning that it might blow for two hundred years and—I'm sorry. I hope your brother's still alive and I hope mine are, too. I just—"

When she trailed off and didn't say anything more as we stepped up on my old porch, I told her, "I know. I wonder what happened, and I'd love to know, even if it means that everyone else is dead. Still, I like the possibility that maybe they're not. That maybe we're just locked here and most of the world is all right but they can't get to us for some reason."

"You think there's anyone else out there?" she asked me. She was standing on the porch and I wasn't, so our eyes were almost level, hers just a little higher than mine, in fact. "Really. What do you really think?"

I smiled and looked away, knowing it was going to sound crazy, but told her, "My grandfather told me about a relative of his he had met when he was little. He said she was a crazy old lady named Marianne who was a cousin or aunt of *his* grandfather.

Anyway, she told my grandfather that one day something like this was going to happen but that one day further on, someone was going to come from the outside needing help and there would be Overstreets here to give it. Crazy, huh?"

She looked at me like she thought I was joking, then asked seriously, "You believe him? That he really met such a person? Or had an aunt who said that, I mean?"

"She may have been crazy, but I believe my grandfather actually met her, if that's what you're asking."

She just smiled and said, "That's … wild. I hope it comes true." She looked around at the house and asked, "What happened to all the windows?"

"I've been taking them out. I want to use them in my new house, and in Claire's. Some of them I already have."

"Why not just move up here?" she asked, then looked around and said, "The ash is still pretty thick here, isn't it? That is so strange. But look!" she said excitedly, hopping off the porch and kneeling by the old well, "Grass!" She got down on all fours and blew the ash away from the little tuft of grass. She looked up at me and smiled, saying, "One day, maybe next year or the year after that, maybe there will be a whole yard here again."

"There was never much of one," I commented with a chuckle. "But oh, Mom tried. Used to threaten Rusty and I with a broom if we even got close to stepping on it.

"I bet you miss your parents, huh?"

"Yeah. Some days, it's worse than others. I bet you can identify, huh?" I regretted it as soon as I said it.

She stood up and went over to the house. Looking in, she said, "Sometimes, I'll feel like he's right there. A couple times, when I've gone into our cabin, as I turn the light on, I'll swear I see him standing there, out of the corner of my eye. Then I turn to look and it's just an empty cabin. Or I'll think of something that happened in the past and I'll turn and be halfway through asking, 'You remember that time when—' only to realize he's not there. Some days, I still can't believe he's gone."

She turned to me, then, and asked earnestly, "Can I tell you something, Josh? In complete confidence?"

"Um, sure," I replied, having never heard anyone use that phrase in real life.

"Sometimes, and sometimes it's just moments, but I realize that I haven't thought about him in hours, even days. Like I've moved on. And I feel so guilty. I know I can't bring him back, and sometimes it's like part of my brain is OK with that. Do you think that's cold? Heartless?"

"I think it's normal. Though normal is probably something different for everyone," I added with a chuckle. "If you never cared, I'd think that was weird. Or, if you did nothing but cry, I'd be worried about that, too."

"The day Seth Ryerson died—we weren't that close, but he was a teacher like D.J. and it was like my own husband died. I knelt there after we had put him in the actual grave and told Seth's dead body that I would always love D.J. and I *knew* I would never move on. Maybe that was just emotion talking, but I feel guilty that here I am, not four months later and I do feel guilty to be moving on at all. Sometimes, I feel like I should be like one of those widows in the old books, the ones who wear black crepe for the rest of their lives. I'm a *widow*. That's supposed to be an old lady, right? I mean, I know it's not really. Young wives have lost their husbands for time immemorial. Especially soldiers' wives I guess I *may be* a widow, and sometimes I do want to wear black. But other times, I just feel like a normal twenty-three year old and—normal being a relative term," she ended with a chuckle. I was trying to think of a meaningful response when she said, "Thanks for letting me say all that. I think I just needed to get it out there, to say it out loud." I was suddenly glad I hadn't thought of anything to say to interrupt— I mean "comfort"—her.

The house had been undisturbed, which was comforting on the level that I had been afraid I might see evidence of Charles Levinson staying there. It was unsettling, though, because I had rather hoped to see the signs of a pack-rat or some other sort of varmint. The idea that all the varmints were exterminated was unsettling.

I had moved the furniture we hadn't taken with us away from the windows, and had tried to seal the holes where the

189

windows used to be with old tarps, blankets, or anything that would work that we didn't need. I hoped to eventually split the rest of the furniture between my house and the one I hoped to build for Claire someday, but we were still heavily involved in just staying alive and the little bit of a kitchenette I had built onto our cabin would have to be enough for the time being.

Suddenly, Julia was lunging at one particular piece of furniture and asking, "You have a rocking chair?" She sat down in it and said excitedly, "Pardon me if this is rude of me to ask, but could I borrow this—for my cabin, I mean? You can't imagine how many nights I've rocked Junior to sleep and wished for a real rocking chair. D.J. was going to build me one, he said, but he was horrible with wood-working." She surprised me by adding with a laugh, "You should've seen these shelves he built me. I loved him, and he could do a lot of things, but woodworking was not one of them."

I suddenly felt bad that I hadn't offered the chair to her sooner, or to one of the other families with babies to rock. I told her, "I'll get the wagon and have it at your place tonight."

"No hurry—"

"I'm going to Breckenridge tomorrow. I'd like to think of you sitting in that chair, rocking Junior." I motioned to encompass the house and asked, "See anything else you like?"

"I'd feel guilty taking anything else." She winked and added, "But I'll think about it."

Chapter Eleven

Do not do an immoral thing for moral reasons.
~Thomas Hardy

We set out for Breckenridge early on the morning of July 5th. In our group were two wagons and eight adults, including Claire and Danica. Danica came along because she was still a newlywed and her husband was coming along, she said. Claire came along because, well, she was Claire and when she decided to go we all knew better than to talk her out of it. Not that we had a reason to, but most everyone accepted that Claire was a strong-willed person when her mind was made up. Oscar was on the trip, too, but their relationship had not progressed, as far as I knew. Inez Isaacson had volunteered to take care of the horses, to which Adaline had offered to help.

The Boreas Pass road was bumpy, but dry so we made good time and actually were pulling into the edge of Breckenridge by just after noon. We made our way to the hotel, figuring to start there with the rest of the canned food in the pantry. We had warned everyone about the bodies, but there were still several gasps—which were regretted because the smell was worse now that summer was there. Even those of us who had been there before found the sight a hard one to take. The bodies were a little more desiccated, the lips pulled back a little further from the teeth. Still, it occurred to me to be most disturbed by the fact that, once again, no varmints seemed to have disturbed the dead.

We went into the kitchen, and then to the pantry. I glanced at the dead cook, then opened the pantry door and an exclamation of surprise escaped my lips. Everyone jumped and it was Tad who leaned forward and asked the question that was on my mind, "Where's all the food?"

Several people said versions of, "What?" so I elaborated and Claire, Tad and Jonathan corroborated, "There was a lot more food in here when we left. Big cans of lima beans which we left because I hate them and—"

"Someone came and got it," Claire completed for me.

"My money's on Charles Levinson," someone said.

I realized that was the most logical conclusion. Charles hadn't been with us when we had raided this pantry before, but he had been with us when we had gone to the houses up the street, so approaching this hotel would have been the next logical stop. The thing that stuck in my mind, though, was that those cans that had remained behind had been *big* cans. Like gallon cans of lima beans and artichoke hearts (which made my skin crawl just thinking about them). I could see a hungry man carrying off one can of each, but would a man carry off several of each?

"OK, so we hit the next few houses," I said, as I turned from the pantry. There were mumbles, but no one had any argument and everyone was ready to get out of Hotel Death.

We checked the next few houses and it looked like they had already been picked over. We found some more dead bodies, but no signs of recent life. And honestly, we couldn't tell whether the pantries had been picked over by some looter (like us) or just hadn't been stocked recently by whoever had owned the house. We were much further into town when we hit on a garage that had several cases of sports drinks stored in it. It was coming on toward evening, then, so we loaded up the drinks and then picketed the horses. Most of the people elected to stay in that house—or one of the nearby ones—just because of the beds but I had spotted a nice, outdoor daybed type thing and drug it over to the deck near the horses. Claire found a chaise lounge and set it up near me. Some people were surprised that she didn't sleep inside with Oscar, except for the people who knew her. I didn't know how Oscar felt about chastity, but I knew how Claire thought on the matter and was proud of her for it. If Oscar objected, it was in private and elsewhere he supported her, which I admired. We all gave Howard and Danica a hard time about them being on their honeymoon but they shut us up by not denying the accusation.

In the morning, we decided to split up into twos and explore the town, then come back together at noon and take the wagon wherever stuff was found, rather than dragging it everywhere. So, we unhitched the horses and those of us who didn't mind riding bareback got a chance to do so. Claire rode bareback as well as she rode with a saddle, but it always took me some getting used to.

I was surprised when Claire opted to go with me instead of Oscar. Once we were out of earshot of the others—and making our way down a gray track between what were once really fancy houses—I asked, "Everything all right between you and Oscar?"

"Yeah. Why do you ask?"

"You're riding with me instead of him."

She was silent for a while, then said, "He keeps asking me to marry him. And maybe one day I will. I kind of think I will. I do think a lot of him. But … I'm just seventeen, Josh. I know I'll be eighteen any day now and I also know women used to get married way younger than that. I just don't know that I'm ready for it."

"There's no need to hurry, Sis. You just take your time and, when it's right, I'll bet you know."

Claire smiled at me coyly and asked, "I bet you wish she were here instead of me, huh?"

"Huh? Who?"

"Oh come on," she chided, riding close enough to backhand me lightly on the arm. "You know who I'm talking about."

"No I don't!" I replied sincerely.

"Really?" She reined in her horse and asked, "Seriously? You mean, you and Julia aren't an … an item?"

"What? Julia? Me?" articulation failed me. "Whatever gave you that idea?"

"The way you're always hanging out together, the way she's always touching you. You seriously haven't noticed?"

"She's just friendly," I objected.

"No, she's not. I mean, she's friendly enough, but she doesn't treat anyone else that way." When I didn't say anything, she blushed and said, "I thought you—like when she went to the old house with you. I figured it was so you two could be alone."

"We just talked about the house, and the past," I defended, while thinking I had nothing to defend.

"Do you think she's pretty?"

"Well, um, yeah," I replied. "But she's still in love with Dwight—that's her husband's name," I countered, even though I was wondering from the conversation the day before just how accurate that statement was.

"I saw you holding Junior, yesterday—"

"Everybody holds Junior," I replied quickly.

"I know, I'm just saying … I don't know what I'm saying. If something does happen, though, you two make a cute couple."

"I'll, um … OK." Finally, I had a reprieve and said, "Let's check that restaurant up ahead."

The air was thick in the valley, and we breathed in the ash stirred up by our walking horses, but it was breathable. And, like in the yard of our old house, here and there I even saw a sprig of grass. A couple of the aspen trees were starting to have a few green leaves and some of the evergreens seemed to still have life in them. Still, it was a gray, dead, town over all.

The door to the restaurant was unlocked, so we walked in, leaving our horses tied up out front like we were in some old western. There were no bodies, but the detritus all over the place made us think the place had been abandoned in a hurry. We made our way into the kitchen and I happened to notice that the large, metal door of the walk-in freezer was just barely opened. I peeked in, then shut it the rest of the way. "What?" Claire asked at the look on my face.

"When the storm hit, they must have hustled everyone into the freezer, thinking it would be the sturdiest place. They left the door open a crack for air and—and died in there."

Claire put her hand over her mouth, then shook her head and said, "Let's see if they have a pantry, like that other place."

They did and we were able to carry several cans of food out to the front of the building. There was another restaurant two doors down. We found the kitchen full of dead bodies but were able to carry many cans of food from the pantry out the back door. That done, I suggested we mount up and go get the wagons as we discovered how everyone else did.

"I'm telling you," Claire said, "We piled more food than this out here. And we stacked it neatly."

194

"So someone came along and grabbed some of it," Lester Marquez opined. "Whoever it is, they probably need it as bad as us, they just don't have a wagon."

"Aren't you curious, though?" she asked him, as well as the rest of us.

"Sure," Lester replied. "But it seems like it's someone who doesn't want to be seen. If you want, we can leave them a note telling them where we are and, if they're friendly, to come on."

"I don't like that idea," Evan Isaacson stated. "What if they're people we don't want?"

"I don't think we can make that call without knowing them," Lester countered. "Besides, even if there's something we don't like about them, wouldn't it be better to meet them on our turf, where we've got numbers?"

"Who's to say they're bad?" Danica injected. "They may just be fearful. If they didn't carry off this whole pile, then it's probably just one or two people. They may not have seen another human being for eleven months. Even the most well-bred human might be skittish after all that."

"I say we leave them a note," I volunteered. "But not exactly like Lester said. Let's just tell them who we are, but not where we came from. Let's say we'll be back in a month and meet them at that hotel on the mountain, or some other spot."

We debated the idea for a while, but eventually I think it was curiosity that won out and we decided to leave some notes about town in prominent places. We also left some cans of food with each note, to (hopefully) show our good will. When we started back up the pass, we had two wagons full of canned goods, some other items like tooth paste and soap, and a lot of grisly mental images. I was relieved that I was starting to become inured to them, but a little worried, too.

We spent a second night in town, then set out early the next morning to go home. The pull up the pass was harder with the fully loaded wagons, but we eventually made it to the top by late afternoon. We pushed on and, as it was summer, we had plenty of light to make it back. We finally pulled into Overstreet just after nine at night, tired but glad to be home. The people of our town had seen us coming down the road and many of them had come out to greet us. We had built a larger community storage shed next to the community kitchen and everyone who came out helped us unload our wagon and put the goods in storage. The people from Como continued on, arriving there after dark if they went the rest of the way without stopping. Word got out about the idea that someone might be alive in Breckenridge and, to paraphrase Mark Twain, the rumors were around the town before the truth even had its pants on.

By the time we had everything unloaded, I was worn out and ready to head to bed. Claire apparently had a second wind or something and elected to stay up with Oscar and some of the others for a while. I was just glad she was willing to stay up. I loved my sister and didn't begrudge taking care of her, but all through the winter and spring it had started to get on my nerves the way she had to know where I was at all times. I understood it, but it was still confining. I had said as much to her during a moment of irritation—probably at the end of a long day, if I remember correctly—and had hurt her feelings. I wasn't happy with the way it came out, or that I hurt her feelings, but if some good came of it, it was that we had finally talked about things: our anxieties vague and specific, and what we meant to each other. I was quickly asleep on that night after our latest raid, but I did hear her come in some time later.

It was morning, as we were taking turns in the newly inaugurated bath tub—complete with a solar water-heater invented by Howard Glass (who was now the most popular man in town because of it)—I asked her, "How was your date last night?"

I was in my bedroom and she in the tub, but she could hear me just fine and replied, "We broke up."

"No, come on. Seriously, what did you do after I went to bed?"

"Just what I said. And I only came into the cabin maybe fifteen minutes after you."

In my mind, I had been asleep for quite some time before I heard her come in, so even though it wasn't the most important part of what she had said, I asked, "Seriously? I thought you were up hours later than me."

"Nope. Just long enough to break up with Oscar."

"But why? Why break up with him?"

She didn't answer at first, and then I heard her getting out of the tub. Shortly, she was standing by the partition that divided our halves of the cabin, dressed in a robe, and saying, "He wants to get married now, or, at least, before summer's over. I'm not ready for that. He laid down an ultimatum, so I took him up on it—just not the way he was hoping."

"Well, I'm sorry, Sis. Are you OK?"

She didn't seem to just be "putting on a brave face" as she replied, "It's for the best. Remember when Rusty broke up with that red-haired girl? I remember being really sorry for him but he said it was better to have it happen then than later, when they were more serious or even married. I understand what he meant."

Trying to lighten the moment, I recalled dreamily, "Ah, the red-head. I remember at the time I was hoping she'd decide if she couldn't have Rusty she'd go for his younger brother."

"You thought she was cute?" Claire asked in surprise.

"Are you kidding? She was a knock-out!"

"Huh. I never thought she was that pretty."

I had long contended, and would have it confirmed for me many times in my life, that what women thought made for an attractive female and what men thought made for an attractive female were not always the same. I did remember the red-head's name (Angelique) and I still remembered very well the way she had looked. At the time, I thought Rusty was insane for letting a girl who looked like that get away, but I eventually gained enough maturity to understand why he had. Even then, though, if she had made a play for me, she wouldn't have had to play very hard.

"Well, anyway, I'm sorry, Sis."

"Don't be," she dismissed with a wave as she walked back to her side of the cabin.

Our gardens were going good that summer and some people attributed that to all the ash. Many people recalled stories from the Pacific northwest about apple crops improving in the years after a volcanic eruption. I quipped that, all in all, I could think of better ways to raise a garden than under an ash cloud. We were in good enough spirits that the joke was well-received.

It had been more than eleven months and we hadn't felt any more rumblings in the ground since those initial ones in the first couple weeks. People of our community speculated often whether any more were coming, but we had nothing on which to base our (un)educated guesses.

The kids had been a little disappointed that we didn't let them take summer off from school. At least, they said they were, but I think they would have been more disappointed if they hadn't had it to occupy their time. And the "summer hours" were much less than in the rest of the year. Just enough that Julia wouldn't have to start over with them in the fall, or such was her plan.

Julia was pretty good with the kids. Maybe not as gifted as Seth had been, but she knew what she was doing and, as the months went on, had gotten better. She might have lacked his passion for the work, but she equaled or excelled him in knowledge. Most of us adults took turns helping her, but as the school term had progressed it was becoming clear that some people were better helpers than others. Some were willing but didn't have the drive, while others were not particularly willing (and gladly traded school-helping duties for extra gardening duties or taking care of something else that needed doing around town.) We graduated Claire, Tad and Oscar at the end of July and had a big party for them. Even managed to find some cardboard and make the sort of silly hats one expects a graduate to wear. The diplomas they got, hand-lettered by Julia, said they were graduates of Overstreet High.

There was much that needed doing. Besides working on everyone's houses—and trading off there, as well, for some people had one skill and some another—there were the gardens and the horses. In some ways, we lived in a commune, but as time had gone on we all began to barter for each other's services. The vehicles were chancy at best, and rarely worth the effort to keep them running for very long at a time (besides the fact that we were running out of gasoline), so our horses were in great demand. Claire and I worked out a system of renting out the horses—for work of many kinds—which was paid back to us with some other service.

For instance, a team of our horses was used to drag logs down out of the forest (burned logs, like before) for the expansion of the Isaacson's house, for which Evan and family paid us by doing most of the work on the bathroom addition to mine and Claire's house. I had gotten pretty good at roofing, and was nimble enough to crawl around on the joists that I helped with several of the roofs and was paid back in various ways. Claire, besides being the best person for working with the horses (even when our horses were loaned out, it often took one of us to get them to cooperate), had proved to be a pretty good seamstress (a fact that surprised even her, for she had almost failed Home Ec) and was often called on to make curtains for one house or another or even mend clothing. She tried her hand at making some new clothing out of material we had procured, but her early efforts were … early efforts. I'll leave it at that.

   With all the work going on, July was a busy month and the thirty days we had set for ourselves passed quickly. Soon, we were gearing up for one more trip over to Breckenridge. We were going to take both wagons again, but this time we were going to look not only for canned foods at Breck residences, we were going to see if we could come across things like shovels, rakes and other tools that might be handy. I was also thinking some additional snowshoes and maybe even cross-country skis would serve us well in the coming winter. We talked about possibly making one more trip in September, but the Rocky Mountain weather at that time of the year made setting such plans in stone an iffy proposition.

   "I wish I were going with you," Julia told me on the night before we were scheduled to leave. We were outside her cabin while Junior crawled around before us. It occurred to me that, a year before, Julia probably would have recoiled at the idea of a baby that age playing in the dirt, but we were all a lot less dirt-phobic than we had been. We had been able to put plank floors in the houses over the summer—often made of planks from houses we had torn down in Como or buildings from our old ranch—but we were still not up to the status of smooth, clean floors we had all been accustomed to so recently.

"Why is that?" I asked, mostly watching Junior for it was my turn to jump up and bring him back if he started to edge too far away. He wasn't crawling, yet, but he had learned how to scoot and could get off his blanket before you knew what had hit you.

"Oh, I always loved Breckenridge. Dwight and I honeymooned there. It was on that trip, in fact, that we heard about Fairplay. We started sending resumes to every school district in the area and they were the first one to hire us. Dwight, I mean, I hadn't graduated, yet. Then, we discovered I was pregnant and my plans for going back to college were getting put on the back burner."

"You would hardly recognize it," I told her. "Even the mountains don't look the same. And some of it's, well, pretty grisly."

"I know. And I shudder to think about it, especially the way Tad and Jonathan like to describe the dead bodies in such detail," she added with a demonstrative shake. "Still, I've never been confined to an area this small for this long. I guess I'd like to see something else, even if it is pretty bleak."

"You could come with us. We've got two women along already."

"I know, but I can't leave Junior. Maybe by next summer we can go over there and even take him with us. Or make one of those trips some people have mentioned to see if there's anything left of Buena Vista or Bailey."

"I think those would be too much even for a one year old."

"Maybe. Probably." She stood up and, looking east across the valley, its green grass dotted with a few cows and horses, "But I do dream about getting out of here some days."

"You and Claire should form a club. She always says the same thing."

Julia looked back at me with those dark eyes and asked, "Are she and Oscar a thing again?"

"Who can tell?" I replied with a laugh. Acting as if I were calculating something, I said, "Hmm, this being a Monday, but tomorrow being an odd day of the month … yeah, they might be back together."

She laughed and patted me playfully on the shoulder. It was something she did often, and I had noticed that Claire was right: she only did it to me. It sent a thrill through me every time, but I was never sure what it meant. Sometimes, I wasn't sure what I *wanted* it to mean.

Julia Croft was a pretty woman, with—I thought—a figure that was just short of incredible, curves in all the right places. She was only three years older than me, and she seemed to like my company. I *knew* I liked hers. On the other hand, she had been to college and almost graduated. She had already been married—hadn't been a widow all that long, in fact. And she had a kid. He was a great little kid and I had even once been able to swallow my own bile and change his diaper in an emergency, but he was still a kid.

Now maybe, I told myself, if she didn't have a kid and if she weren't a recent widow, I would "make a move". We had gone on walks together, sometimes with Junior and sometimes without, but we hadn't even held hands unless it was something like me holding hers to help her cross the Tarryall or climb up the side of a mountain. Still, I told myself, I could deal with the age and education differences—they didn't seem like that much—and all else being absent I could ask her out on a date or, at a moment like that beside her cabin, just pull her into my arms and kiss her. The reality was probably that I wouldn't have had the nerve to do such things even if the conditions had been right, so it was nice to have the wrong conditions to blame my reticence on.

As the sun set behind us, I stood up and came to stand beside her, watching the sun rays still striking the far eastern hills. "Well, I better be heading to bed. We're wanting to get an early start in the morning." It was coming up on that time of year where afternoon showers could hit every day, though none of them had come so far.

To my surprise and delight, she put an arm around me and, without looking at me, said, "You be careful. I expect you to be back here in time for church on Sunday."

I put my arm around her, liking the feeling more than I wanted to admit to myself. I tried to think of something to say to take my mind off what it was thinking, but what came out was, "Why did you not come to church before? Did—did Dwight not like church?"

"Dwight loved church. It was me who refused to go."

I looked at her in surprise, my mind momentarily leaving the thought of having a woman in my grasp, and challenged, "Really?"

"Oh yeah. Dwight grew up in church, a Presbyterian. He sang in the choir and went to youth conferences and preached and everything. He loved church. Used to try to get me to go to church every Sunday."

"So, why did you not want to?"

"This is too nice of a moment for me to go into that," she replied. She looked up at me and smiled, saying, "I promise: I'll tell you when you get back. To answer another question, one that was probably coming, I started coming to church after Junior was born because ... because ... I told myself that it was because I wanted him to know what was beyond, beyond death. But the reality was that I woke up that first Sunday morning of his life and I had never felt so lonely in all my life. I went just to be with all of you and, well, I realized that as long as I kept going, no one ever asked about it." She quickly added, "I do like it. I do. And I've learned a lot. For one thing, I've learned it's not what I thought it was."

"What did you think it was? Or is that part of the later discussion?"

"Later," she replied, a wan smile on her face. She looked back east and said, "Right now, I just love the look of the sun when the last rays illuminate the far ridge there. Like it's a promise that, if I watch that spot, I'll see the glory of a new day in just a few hours."

"That's a cool way of putting it," I complimented. She squeezed me lightly with the arm that was around me and I was in hog heaven, all thoughts of suns and Sundays and everything else gone.

I turned to her and her face was looking up into mine. The sunset was perfect, the moment was perfect, and she was beautiful. I put my other arm around her and I kissed her.

I had had a couple kisses before in my life. More if you count those silly "spin the bottle" games from junior high. Even then, I could probably count my total number of kisses on both hands—with fingers left over. I just mean that I had kissed a girl before.

That one was different. This, I told myself, was not a silly school kid thing, but a real kiss. A kiss of a grown woman. A kiss from a grown woman. And boy did she feel like a woman in my arms! And she kissed like a grown woman (whatever that means! It's what I was thinking at the time, if I was thinking at all, which I rather doubt).

Suddenly, she was breaking it off and saying, "I'm sorry."

"No, it's my fault—" I said, though not sure what I or we were apologizing for.

She backed up a step and put her hand to her mouth, then said, "I'm not—you are a very good friend and I care deeply about you but, this—I'm … I'm not ready. I'm not."

Then, I figured I did know and was sorry for pushing things, and for thinking the thoughts I had been thinking just minutes before when I had wished for a moment like that. I told her sincerely, "I'm sorry. I didn't—I didn't mean to mess anything up."

"I know what you mean," she replied, which was good, because I didn't. That hadn't been what I had meant to say. "Standing here, arm in arm, that was great. Talking to you—not just now but every time we've had a conversation—I appreciate it more than I can tell you. But this," she gestured at her mouth, "I can't. Not yet. Maybe not … not yet. I hope you won't be mad at me."

"Not at all." I picked up Junior and handed him to her, then gestured roughly in the direction of my cabin and said, "I should probably go get a good night's sleep. Lot's going on tomorrow."

"Yeah. You do that. And, um, take good care of yourself, right?" She reached out like she was going to touch me as she so often had, but then her hand stopped before touching me. I reached up my hand, not sure what my intentions were, and we wound up grasping hands for just a moment. She smiled at me, then let go and said, "Good night. Thanks for a wonderful evening."

"It was my pleasure." We kind of nodded awkwardly and she went inside her cabin and I went to mine, pretty certain I wouldn't be sleepy ever again.

It *was* quite a while before I fell asleep.

She had come out to see us off, but so had most of the rest of the town, as well as a good-sized delegation from Como. I think she shook my hand, but then so did a lot of other people. On the trip over the pass, all I could think about was her kiss, and how she had felt in my arms. I asked myself what I was really feeling. Was it something real, something lasting, or just the hormonal thoughts of a nineteen year old boy who gets to hold a girl close for a moment? Was it a moment that might be repeated, grow into hours and days and years, even? Or was it just a moment, not to be repeated or at least never recaptured? The trouble with asking such questions at such a time is that they are unanswerable.

I had lain awake for quite a while the night before, reliving the kiss, asking what it meant, rehashing every interaction with Julia for the past four months. I remembered every moment, every one of those touches. I thought of how she looked in dresses, jeans and, especially, shorts. I thought of her shape, her hair, her lips, her eyes. I was lucky my horse was paying attention to the rough road because I sure wasn't.

"Earth to Josh," came the voice from beside me. I turned, surprised, to find that Danica had ridden up beside me and had been trying to get my attention.

"Mmm? What?"

She just smiled and said, "You looked like you were a million miles away." She looked around at the bleak landscape and added, "I'm sorry to interrupt. A million miles away is where we'd all like to be."

"Oh, just thinking ... thoughts."

"That's a good thing to do with them," she chided with a laugh. "Care to talk about them? These thoughts of yours?"

I looked around and while no one was riding especially close to us, I still felt they could hear us so I replied, "You know, I think I would but, maybe another time. Somewhere where we're surrounded by fewer ears."

"Lemme guess," she said, softly but it seemed to me like she was shouting, "You're thinking about a girl."

I think the way my skin looked instantly sunburned probably answered her question. We were a small community no matter how you sliced it, so I was glad she dropped the subject as it wouldn't have taken her long to guess who I was thinking of. Still, it occurred to me that she would be a good one to talk to, as I already trusted her wisdom in other matters and her ability to view things from a female perspective would be invaluable.

Trying to keep the subject off of me, though, I asked, "What about you? You went from being alone in the outside world to getting married here. Was it—was it just ... circumstances?"

The fact that I could ask the question at all probably tells both what a good friendship I had with her and what an understanding lady she was. She thought for a moment, then said, "I can't deny that circumstances played into it. But they weren't everything. See, when I was working seventy hours at the bank, I told myself I would slow down one day, meet the right fella, all that. I probably never would have, though. Until I retired," she added with a rueful chuckle. "Then, I would have looked around and seen that I was surrounded by old people."

"You think you would have ever noticed Howard?" I asked.

"I ask myself that. The truth is that I probably wouldn't have. And he probably wouldn't have noticed me, either. This," she said, gesturing at the surrounding ash, "Just changed everything. I realized I didn't want to spend the rest of whatever life I have alone. It's not like I settled on Howard, though. Like I looked up and said, 'Oh well, better him than nothing.' It's more that I finally got over myself and started realizing that he was the kind of man I had always wanted."

"How's that?"

"He listens when I talk. He's funny. If he thinks I'm wrong about something, he tells me, but he does so in a respectful manner. He treats me like a lady."

"Even though you can outrun him?"

She laughed and replied, "As far as we know, I am now the fastest human being on earth. Seriously, though, I like that he lets me be me, but he pushes me to be more than I've been. And I push him, too."

"Really? I don't doubt you, Danni, but I'm suddenly realizing that every relationship I've ever had with a girl was based about ninety-nine percent on hormones. You make me—watching you and Howard together, too—you guys make me want to be more. To find more with a girl—a woman—than I've ever looked for before."

She looked thoughtful for a moment, then told me, "I have never enjoyed receiving unsolicited advice, but I'm going to pretend you solicited this." She smiled at me then continued, "Relationships, even great ones, often start by being just dropped in our laps. We suddenly meet someone and, before we know it, it has grown into something else, something bigger. And I'm not just talking about romance. You and I have known each other for years—since I first came to the bank, in fact. But it's only been relatively recently that we became friends. You could truthfully say we were just dropped together. But we've been dropped together with a lot of people and, while there's no one in our little group I can't stand, I think I can also truthfully say that you have become one of my best friends. We didn't set out to do that, but it happened because we found that we had some similar interests." She took a breath, smiled again, and told me, "All of that is my long-winded way of building up to the advice: the woman you eventually fall in love with—and I'll say right now she's going to be a very lucky woman—you may fall just as an accident, but love—true love—must be pursued."

I think I knew what she meant, but I valued her opinion enough—and had become comfortable enough with her—that I asked, "What do you mean? Like bringing her flowers and going on walks?"

"That may well be part of it. Some girls don't like flowers though." She paused as we rode on for a few minutes, then explained, "I mean that, well, I think back to some of my previous relationships. The ones that didn't go anywhere. We had that initial click, but never pursued anything other than that." I guess she could tell by the look on my face that I was still confused, so she recalled, "I met this one man not long after I moved here—to Fairplay, anyway. About my age, we went to the same church, and somehow we found that we both liked skiing. It was winter, so we went over to Breck on our days off for at least a month. When we talked, we often talked about skiing. We got along fine, but then after a month—and he was thinking things were, um, ready to 'go to the next level' as he put it. I told myself I wasn't ready for *that*, but that it might be in the future, so I began to try and move our conversations from skiing to other topics. From the simple like favorite song to the more deep like faith and children. I began to realize that—and he realized it, too, maybe even before me—that we had none of that stuff in common. In some areas, some pretty important areas, we were diametrically opposed. We broke up in a fight over, would you believe it, politics.

"What I'm saying in all this, though, is that, well, let's say you begin to ... feel something for one of the young women in our town. That's natural, and good. But when I say that true love needs to be pursued, I mean you need to have some long conversations about things and really find out what she believes. And it might be the first time *you* find out what you believe on some of these things. To pursue love, though, means even more than that. It's actually something you taught me."

"Me?" I asked with surprise.

"Yes. I've gone to church on and off all my life, know quite a bit of the Bible and a lot about it. Back in a world with census forms, I would have checked the box that said, 'Christian.' When you and Claire suggested we have a church service, I thought that was a good idea. Thought it would be good for the mental health of our community, you might say. And I figured I would be good at it—"

"You are. You're our leader—"

"Not really. I may be becoming one. But what I really know, I have learned from you. Because in you, Josh, I have seen someone who doesn't just read the Bible, but lives it. You're not perfect, but you're trying. You are the first person I have met since my grandmother who seemed to be passionately pursuing God."

"And you're saying I should pursue a woman like that?"

She shrugged and replied, "Maybe not exactly. But I'm also saying … back before all this ash, back in Fairplay, I went to church most Sundays. Sung the songs. Occasionally even taught a Sunday school class if they needed me to. But I was really just going because my grandmother had instilled in me that I *should* go. I didn't have any kind of relationship with our father or our savior—no more than you have with your waiter who brings you what you want when you want it. I didn't take it seriously, just casually showed up when it was convenient to me. I don't think you will, but when you meet the young woman you want to pursue, *pursue* her. Don't just casually let things drift. You mentioned the flowers and the walks. Well, I've seen too many couples—been part of one myself once—who started out that way, but then once they became an 'item', they just settled into a routine. It might have even contained flowers. But they got so used to each other that they stopped pursuing."

"Does Howard pursue you?"

"Oh, wonderfully so," she told me with a warm smile. "He listens when I talk and he asks questions. He doesn't bring me flowers because he knows I don't care for that, but," she looked around and then said in a low voice, "He draws me these little pictures and brings them to me."

"Pictures of what?"

"The baseball game, or a piece of mining equipment he spotted over on the mountain. A simple sketch of a columbine. Or a quick sketch he did of me when I didn't realize he was looking—or maybe it's just from memory. He knows he's caught me, but he never stops pursuing."

"That's really cool," I commented. "And Danni, thanks."

The road into Breckenridge wasn't too bad, for Boreas Pass, I mean. It began life a couple centuries before or more as the bed for a railroad that transported gold from Breckenridge into Como, where the cars could then be linked up with the line that ran into

Denver. After the railroad closed down, it became a dirt road for summer tourists who wanted to drive a high mountain pass. Even back in the days when it was ostensibly maintained, it was ever a rough road for it was eleven thousand feet up in the extremely rocky Rocky Mountains. A little bit of moisture would erode the dirt between the rocks and make the road worse. Add in a layer of ash, which made some spots better and some worse, and the trip could be an arduous one.

We made it into Breckenridge by mid-afternoon, a longer trip than what we had expected, which led to several discussions about how we were going to have to do some work on the road the next summer if we wanted to continue making the trip into Breck. Within that discussion was the question of how much longer such trips would be profitable. We might continue to find canned goods for years, and there were other things to be scavenged like copper wiring and wood—even entire houses if someone wanted to dismantle them, move them, then reassemble them. On the one hand, there might be things that could sustain us in Breck for decades—maybe we could even move over there if the grass continued to come up in the ash and the Blue River continued to flow. On that ever-present other hand, though, was the fact that we were all still living under a cloud of fear: fear of another volcano, fear of another ash cloud, fear that some little something might shift and destroy our whole eco-system and way of life. Even the less Bible-read among us were starting to live by James' warning not to plan too far ahead.

We got to our first marker and it was clear someone had been there. The same was true of the second and third markers. No message had been left at any of them, though. The next day would be the thirtieth day—the day on which we promised to return—so we elected to find places to sleep for the night and see what or who we might meet the next day. I think we were all anxious—in the truest sense of the word. Some anticipation, some dread, no real facts. Like the month before, I chose to sleep near the horses and Claire chose to sleep near me.

I was in a sort of chaise lounge that was very comfortable, but like the night before, my mind wouldn't let me sleep. I didn't think I was fidgeting, but Claire asked, "Something on your mind?"

"Little bit of everything," I replied. Then, "Someone's here."

"What?" she asked, sitting up.

"No, not *right here*. I mean, someone's alive in Breckenridge. Odds are, they're people just like us but, well, what if it's like in those old dramas? What they used to call 'movies.' Used to see them late at night on-line. You know: civilization's gone except for zombies or people with shotguns."

"If they were like that, wouldn't they have picked us off one by one the last time we were here, when we were all separated?"

"I know. They're probably just folks like us, scrabbling to survive, maybe thinking they were the last people on earth then here we come. We've got horses and guns and, well, we might look like invaders."

"There's another thought," she brought up. "What if they are just like us and want to come back to Overstreet with us? Just how many people can our little swath of green sustain?"

"I read once that, during the gold boom days, Como had ten thousand people. And there were another ten thousand spread across Hamilton, Peabody and the rest of the gold camps in our valley. So, at that time, the valley was supporting twenty grand. There's not even a hundred of us."

"But they were also bringing in food by rail. And I don't think the valley could have sustained that many men indefinitely."

"So much is unpredictable," I commented. "If we can keep pushing back the ash, or if the grass keeps overtaking it, I think we'll be OK. And Jesse found a book somewhere about hydroponics. If he can get that going, we might one day have fresh vegetables even in winter. That reminds me: didn't there used to be a bookstore in town? If we could find that, might find some books that would be helpful."

"I don't know about that. It was mostly fiction. Might be entertaining, but I don't know how valuable," she told me.

It was a while later that she said, "I watch the sky a lot. Always hoping I'll see some sign of an airplane. A vapor trail or something. I never do. We may not be the last people left alive in the world, but for all practical purposes. we might as well be." She suddenly sat back up again (I could see shapes in the moonlight, besides hearing the creak of her daybed) and asked, "When Oscar and I get married, will you give me away?"

"It's 'when' is it?" I asked with what I hoped would be received as a good-natured chuckle.

"Probably," she replied in a scolding voice. "Will you?"

"I would be honored."

"And what about you?"

"What about me?" I asked.

"When will you get married?"

"I don't see much evidence that it's even on the horizon," I replied with a chuckle.

"Oh, you will, one day. Maybe sooner than you think."

"That sounds like a plot," I replied. I saw her lay down then and the conversation stopped. I was awake for a while longer, thinking of the Breck strangers, of women in general and Julia Croft in particular.

The next morning, we went to the spot where we had placed the first of our notices. It was in the middle of what had once been a city park; the dog park, to be exact, and seemed like a nice, open space. (I hadn't been the only person envisioning a movie ambush.)

We were standing around or sitting on the wagons for perhaps half an hour before the question of "How long do we wait" was asked in earnest. We spent the next fifteen minutes debating the answer before Claire said in a whisper that shushed us all, "I just saw something. Over by the old school."

"OK," I said, taking the lead, "Everyone just look relaxed and friendly. Until or unless we learn differently, let's just assume whoever this is, is just like us. Stranded by the ash cloud and thinking they're the last people on earth."

Then, we all saw him. A stocky, black man came cautiously around the old school building, something in his arms that was either a rifle or a big stick. He wasn't pointing it at us, but he did have it at the ready. He was walking slowly and cautiously. I decided to take the initiative and cover some of the ground between us with equally measured steps. I expected to hear Claire object, but then realized she was right beside me. I smiled as I wondered why I had anticipated anything else.

The man hesitated when he saw that two of us were coming to meet him, but then he continued on. As we drew close to each other, I saw that he was a couple inches shorter than me, but outweighed me a good bit. He had no fat on him—none of us did, anymore—but he looked like one of those guys who is just built more solidly than the rest. He wore clean clothes and new-looking shoes and the rifle was well cared-for.

When he stopped, we did, too, about ten feet away from him. I opened, "I'm Josh Overstreet and we come from just over Boreas Pass, near Como." It crossed my mind to say, "We come in peace" but I had the good sense not to.

"Where's that?" he asked, not suspiciously but curiously. I pointed in the direction of the pass and he said, "Name's Hutch. Billy Hutchison, but everyone calls me Hutch. I'm from Kansas City."

"Really?" Claire and I asked in unison.

"Well, I was. Got here with my family for a vacation. 'Bout five minutes after we had set foot in our hotel room, the ground shook. Half hour after that, the world came to an end."

"Are you all alone? I'm Claire Overstreet, by the way, his sister."

"A few of us left. Were you the ones—I saw a campfire up on the mountain about two months ago. Was that you?"

"It was," I answered. "We had no idea anyone was still alive in this whole valley until we saw that someone had gotten the rest of the food out of that hotel pantry."

"Was that the hotel you were in?" Claire asked.

He shook his head and said, "We were on the other side of the valley, up by the ski area."

I motioned for the rest of our group to come over and, when they did, said, "Guys—and gals—this is Hutch. He found our messages."

"Ya'll got ten of you left over there?" he asked.

"Over fifty, actually, if you count the people of Como," I replied.

He whistled and said, "Far as I knew, there was just five of us left in the whole world." I thought the whistle had been just a sign of his being impressed, but it must have been a signal, for four other people appeared from different places around the park. There was a teenage girl (!) who looked like she might be Hutch's daughter, and three people of Asian cast—two women and a man. All were armed and walked cautiously over.

"I'd really like to hear your story," I told Hutch. A couple of my people agreed, so we all made our way over to a pavilion wherein were some dusty (or ashy) picnic tables. There were some introductions and handshakes all around as we walked, then more when we had sat down. I noticed that my ten sat together as did Hutch's five.

I offered Hutch a sip of my bottled water, but he smiled and produced a bottle of his own, then started, "Like I say, we'd just barely got to town when that quake hit. Me, my daughter Shaniqua, and my—" he choked a moment, "And my wife and sons. When that thing shook us—well, we were in a room that was on the back side of the hotel, barely any view of the mountains, but we were figuring we'd be out biking and hiking and, never mind. That quake, it shifted the doors on our room and made the ground slide up against the window. We were trapped. We were pounding on the door to get out, but then we thought smoke was coming in under the door so we thought the place was on fire. When I realized it was ash, I got my family to roll up the bedding and put it against the door to keep the ash out.

"We stayed like that for two days. Taking sips of water from the toilet tank after we'd drunk the complementary water in the room. Finally, I decided we were going to have to break the door down and try to get out. Figured we were either going to die in the room or in the hall, so why not see if there was a way out, right?" He choked up again, then just motioned for his daughter to continue.

She hesitated, then said, "We've been scrounging for existence ever since. Mama and my brothers they—they didn't make the winter." She was a pretty young woman, a striking woman. As tall as me and with that kind of perfect skin and grace of movement that the talent agencies used to look for. Still, there was a hard edge to her face that offset much of her good looks as she said, "We buried them when the ground thawed enough to do so."

"We understand," I replied, several other people nodding.

The Asian man spoke up, saying, "I'm Ron Sukagara. This is my wife Dawn, and her mother Sandra. Our story is much the same. We lost my father-in-law in the winter." The only thing that surprised me about his statement was that the mother only looked maybe a year older than the wife. I would have put them both in their mid-twenties, reminding me once again that I was lousy at guessing ages. "We met Hutch and his family last fall, before the worst of winter hit."

"Were there more people at that time, or just you," I counted in my head, "Nine?"

"There were three more. An elderly couple and a middle-aged man," Ron Sukagara told us. "The old couple didn't make it through the winter, though they tried and worked hard."

"And the man?" Claire asked.

"Took off in November. Said he was going to see if anyone still lived in Dillon or Frisco. We never saw him again," Ron told us.

Dawn asked, "Do you know if—if there's anyone beyond our two valleys?"

"We don't," Claire answered her. "Haven't even seen a plane or anything."

"How did you people live?" Hutch asked then. So I related the story of how Overstreet came to be and how Como still existed. They asked a few questions, but mostly just listened.

"Do you—is all your food from scrounging?" someone in my group asked, I think it was Howard Glass.

"Mostly. We've been turning the old solarium on one of the restaurants into a kind of green house. Thought it might help us through the winter," Hutch told us.

"We ought to do that," Danica commented. "Plenty of windows around." She looked at our new acquaintances and quickly amended, "Though I guess we better stop helping ourselves to their amenities."

"Ain't ours," Hutch replied. "Ain't anybody's." For the most part, he spoke very properly, like someone who had taken speech training as a newscaster or something, but then he would slip in a phrase that made me wonder. And then I would wonder which was his natural voice and which was feigned … and whether there were an easy explanation like that.

"In the old west, there was such a thing as squatter's rights," Ron objected. "I think this is our valley."

"The question is," I ventured, hoping to calm what looked to be a building argument, "Do you want to stay? Our valley isn't infinite, but I think we can stand five new people. 'Specially if they're willing to work."

"We do nothing but work," Ron objected.

Hutch smiled and said, "It'd be kind of nice to be working and not just struggling to survive."

"There's a lot of that," I told him.

"Yeah, but I heard your story. You've had the time to play a little ball and start a church. Look, we're all wondering if we're on borrowed time. Is the next quake or ash cloud's going to kill us all? But you people, you've got a—a culture going over there." He looked at his daughter and asked, "What do you say, Niqua?"

His daughter replied without hesitation, "I think if I never see this valley again I won't miss it a bit."

"We will go, too," Sandra, the mother-in-law, pronounced.

I stood up and said to Hutch, "I'd sure like to see that green house you're building. Would love to see you help us build one over on our side."

"Just need some glass and wood," he replied.

"What'd you do for a living, Hutch? Before, I mean," I asked. He struck me as the kind of a guy who was probably a handy man, or a mechanic, or worked with his hands, or did the news.

"Contract lawyer," he replied. "You don't have a court over there, do you?"

"Praise God, no," I replied with a laugh.

I remembered our tribunal later and told him all about it. He seemed impressed with how it had been handled, as well as the verdict. "I admire you for not killing him," he told me. "Don't know that I respect the law *that* much. If he'd gone after my wife, or Niqua … " He left it hanging there, but didn't need to say more.

We made the trip back over the pass carrying five new people, their stuff, and a goodly supply of canned goods and what not that the former residents of Breck had pointed us to. All the way back, we made plans for making Breck runs every day that the weather permitted to get supplies for greenhouses (and continued to wonder why we hadn't come up with that idea on our own). The Sukagara family was polite but quiet, but I got to visit quite a bit with Hutch and Niqua. He proved to be one of those people who probably would have been affable and talkative on the Titanic, while his daughter remained silent. She answered direct questions, but only approached talkative when with Claire or Danica. I wondered if she had always been that way, or just since the disaster—which could affect anyone.

The people of our valley were surprised that we brought people back with us, and some of them weren't too thrilled with the idea, but most of them began to warm up to Hutch as soon as I let him explain his plan for building greenhouses, Jesse especially. (The plan had quickly become one of building at least two greenhouses, one in Overstreet and one in Como.) When it came to where the newcomers would sleep, Hutch and his daughter elected to stay in Overstreet and start building a cabin there, while the Sukagara family went on to Como and occupied one of the empty houses there. Ron made several of the trips with us back to Breck for glass and supplies, but generally tended to hang out with the Como people. For the short term, Hutch and Niqua moved into Charles Levinson's old dugout, which we had been using as a sort of corn crib. Within a week, we had a passable cabin built for them and, by fall, it was as snug as anyone else's place in town.

Julia had hugged me when we got back. It was just a quick hug, such as anyone might give a returning friend, but I liked it. I also noticed she didn't give anyone else a similar hug. Then, I was embarrassed for noticing that.

I was rubbing down the horses when Julia came in later, Junior on her hip. "Is it true you're going to be going back often? To Breckenridge, I mean?"

"Yeah. We're going to need a lot of glass and that stuff's heavy. Not sure how much we can transport at one time."

"I really want to come with you on at least one of these trips. Surely Alexa or Adaline could watch Junior for one night."

"I bet so. It is kind of nice to get out of the valley." I stopped currying and told her, "But there's nothing like when you round that bend up on the pass and you see our green grass here. It's … unreal. Like being in a drama where they go from black and white to color. I love seeing our home. And, um, the people. One of 'em, anyway," I said while, I'm sure, blushing from head to toe.

"I was glad to see you come back. I mean, I'm glad everyone's back, but I was especially glad to see you come back. Safely, I mean." She took a step closer and, looking me in the face, said, "I think some dark little corner of my mind has told me to expect everyone I care about to—to go away. Go away and not come back. I'm glad you came back, Josh."

"I, um, I thought about you, Julia. A lot."

"Oh really?" she asked with a smile. I had been embarrassed to say it, but I think she was getting some entertainment from seeing me squirm. "And what did you think?"

"I didn't know what to think," I told her honestly enough. "I thought about you, how you look, things we've done together … that kiss."

"About that … "

When she didn't say anything, just looked nervously away, I said, "I'm sorry if I shouldn't have brought it up."

"No, it's not—I've thought about it, too. And," she looked back at me and said, "I'm really conflicted, Josh. I want that moment back. I want it back so I can keep it from happening again and I want it back so I can kiss you again. I want this moment back so I could just shut up and I want to throw myself at you and—and I want to never hold another guy other than D.J. again!" What she said wasn't loud, but it was definitely said with emphasis.

She handed me Junior, apparently so she could wave her arms as she said, "It's like I've got a million voices in my head telling me a million different things and they're all clamoring for primacy and they all make sense and they're all moronic. One voice is telling me we may not make it through another winter so live now and another is telling me it's too soon and still other voices are telling me one thing and then another. And one really loud voice right now is saying, 'Shut up, Julia! Don't pour out your heart like this, not to anyone, and especially not to—to a guy you might care about.' I don't know if that's the voice that's telling me Dwight is still alive out there and I'm not a widow or if it's the voice that's saying, 'He's dead, Julia, grieve and move on.' I do care about you, but maybe … and another voice is saying, 'It's Josh. He's your friend and you can talk to him and he'll understand.' Do you?" she asked suddenly.

"More than you'd believe," I replied with a chuckle.

Adaline showed up just then, knocking on the door to the barn and asking, "May I come in or is this private?"

"Come on in, Adaline," Julia answered for us. She asked the skinny, blonde-haired adolescent, who seemed to be growing at a rate of about an inch a month, "You finish reading that book I gave you?"

"Almost," Adaline replied. "I like the story, but they talk funny. Makes it hard to follow sometimes."

Julia explained to me, "I have her reading those George MacDonald books you loaned me. I hope it's all right that I passed them on."

As I nodded, Adaline asked me excitedly, "You've read them?" Then, "I like the ones about the preacher and his family, but that one about the prince that has to go under the mountain and fight the trolls. That was just *weird*!"

"That's what I thought," I told her.

"Now now, children," Julia chastised in a teacherly voice. "You're supposed to be struck by the symbolism."

"There was no symbolism," I countered. "It was just weird." This got a snort of a chuckle out of Adaline, who then looked embarrassed for having made that sound.

We were interrupted by Tad Isaacson bursting in, then whispering, "Guys, come check this out!" We gave each other puzzled looks, then stepped outside, quietly, following his lead.

Once outside the barn he pointed to a small swath of green grass on the far side of our valley. We looked, but it did nothing to alleviate our confusion. Then, he handed me his father's binoculars and said, "Take a look at those black things."

Without the binoculars, I had thought they were just some cattle, or maybe even a few of our horses. I knew Lester had said he would take some of them for a bit of a workout while we were gone. Once I saw what they were, though, I smiled and handed the binoculars to Adaline, who was standing beside me. "Look," I said, excitedly and unnecessarily.

"Deer?" she asked as she zeroed in on them.

"Elk," Tad and I said in unison.

"Is that good?" Adaline asked.

"It's fantastic," I told her. When she looked at me doubtfully as she passed the binoculars on to Julia, I explained, "It means these mountains aren't as dead as we thought. Those elk have been living back in the hills somewhere. Means there's probably people living back in there somewhere, just like in Breckenridge."

"They're so pretty," Julia commented. Soon, a crowd of other people had gathered. At first, they had gathered to see what we were looking at, but as they had seen, they had become excited, too.

"Nothing better than elk meat," someone commented, to quickly add, "Not that we want to kill these, of course. Be nice if we could build up a herd of them, though. They'd be hardier in the winter than the cattle."

Chapter Twelve

Men willingly believe what they wish.
~Julius Caesar

With the sort of myopic, self-centered angst that only a teenage boy can generate, I began to lament my situation. No, not the part of the situation that would seem to merit lamentation: loss of parents, ash-covered world, end of civilization as we know it. No, I found myself lamenting the fact that my dream had come true and we had found a lovely, teenage girl living in a hotel in Breckenridge and I couldn't "make a move on her" because I was kinda-sorta with someone else.

But then, was I? I had no idea, but it's the kind of thing a teenage male can obsess about endlessly, and I did.

I went on a lot of walks with Julia, sometimes just the two of us (and Junior), though sometimes we were accompanied by other people. Our hand-holding was only on those occasions when I was helping her across a stream or to climb, and while we hugged now and then, it was probably just platonic. At least, I think it was for her. I wanted it to be more, but had no idea how to get there. And then, in moments of rare self-honesty, I wondered if I did want things to go any further. Not that there were movies to go to or other events like that, but we really didn't have very much in common. Didn't even like the same kinds of music and while we both liked to read, our tastes were very different there, too. And, sometimes, I got the feeling that she thought I was younger than I was. She treated me that way, on occasion: as if I were some little boy, instead of a man barely three years her junior. Still, she was pretty and she was my friend and I think any man put in that situation develops feelings for the woman and I certainly did. Realizing what you're feeling is no more than hormonal rarely makes those feelings go away.

Toward the end of August, she elected to make one of the trips to Breckenridge with me, leaving Junior to stay with Claire, who said she'd had all of Breck she needed for a while. Oscar was on the trip, but I had lost track of whether that said anything about his relationship with my sister. Some days they acted like they would like to elope right away, and other days they seemed to have no interest in each other. I never really saw rancor, but if it were love it was not an all-consuming passion.

Julia and I were alone on the wagon while Tad and Oscar scouted the road ahead, so I asked, trying to make conversation, "Weren't you going to tell me why you didn't like church?"

"I did say that, didn't I?" she replied, as if she wished she hadn't said it. I just nodded, so she eventually said, "I grew up not going to church. Occasional wedding or funeral, maybe, but that was it. My father, see, he had an almost photographic memory for what he had read and he had read the Bible in, like, three different translations. Always said he knew the Bible better than any preacher, so why go listen? And he was," she hesitated and I was *really* wishing I hadn't brought it up, "Abusive. He always claimed to have a reason, but a messy room warranted a spanking, a word perceived to be back-talk received a slap to the mouth, like that. And he always had a Scripture verse to back up what he said."

She paused, but then started talking as if it were something she had long needed to say as she rapidly related, "The moment I will remember to my dying day, though, was when I got my first period. My father had me face the wall and put my hands on the wall. Then he beat my a-- with a belt while shouting Scriptures about Jezebel and other unfaithful women at me. I look back now and can only be thankful he let me keep my jeans on. I still had huge welts and it was uncomfortable sitting for a few days—"

"Where was your Mom during all this?"

"Standing nearby and crying. To this day, I don't know if she was crying for me or because I'd had a period and she agreed with Dad that it was the first step of a long slide into iniquity. I tried to talk to her about it later, but she just said something about how my father didn't want me sleeping around." She chuckled ruefully and added, "No, I didn't make the connection, either. I got a job cleaning up at a beauty salon after that. My father acted like he was proud of me for the initiative so I never told him the reason was so that I could buy my own pads and tampons and never talk to either of my parents about periods again."

"Did he—did he ever beat you again?"

"Yeah. For coming in late, for going out on a date, that kind of thing. Used to beat my brothers, too. Found out my middle brother, Tim, had had a, um, night emission, and Dad almost killed him. I called the cops on him that time and CPS took us all away. I was seventeen then and went to live with a friend as it's hard to find foster care for someone that old. Went off to college in the fall and—and never saw my parents again. Corresponded with my brothers some, but not much. They let me know when my little sister died—she was still in the care of the state when it happened. They blamed me for breaking up the family by calling the cops. Maybe by now they've forgiven me."

She perked up, then, and added with a smile, "I went to college in Pueblo—because it was so far away and I actually managed to get a scholarship that helped. And loans I have a feeling I'm never going to pay back!" she told me, laughing. "Met Dwight my sophomore year and we just clicked instantly. Got married the summer before my senior year, then moved here. He'd always go to church on Sunday, and I went a couple times, but it was never really my thing and he seemed to accept that. Kind of wish I had gone with him, now." This last part was said without a laugh or smile of any kind.

"I hope our little services don't make you think of your father," I offered meekly.

"Are you kidding?" she snorted derisively. Then, "They do, sometimes. But it's because I'm looking at all you nice people and thinking, 'How is it they read the same book as my father and got such a different meaning from it?'"

"Some people use Scripture as a weapon," I told her. "I mean, I think Paul calls it our sword, but I think that's for fighting evil, not being evil."

"You should have been a preacher, Josh. Maybe you can be ours one day." She smiled then, adding, "You kind of are. You're much better at leading the Bible study than Lester or Evan."

"Not as good as Danni, though, huh?"

"Maybe, just different."

Besides being shook up by her stories of her childhood, I realized something else important. While what she said about

Dwight was just a few words, it was clear that she was still wildly, passionately in love with him. In a rare moment of magnanimity or maturity, it occurred to me that maybe I *didn't* want her to fall in love with me because it could probably never be as deep and moving as what she had with Dwight. Mine, I realized, might be nothing more than puppy love (or hormones, I couldn't discount that idea). I might be satisfied with that, but I didn't want her to settle for me just for the sake of settling.

Still, that voice that was always arguing within me about the other hand, said maybe I shouldn't throw away any possibility as there were so few other ones. Just one, as far as I could tell, to be exact.

We got into Breck by mid-afternoon and were able to load a considerable amount of glass into the wagon, putting blankets and clothing in between, as there was a crew that had gone over the pass the day before and started pulling the glass. Hutch and Ron Sukigara had been part of that team as they both knew the town so well. They had had the foresight to get a lot of tinted glass which, hopefully, would keep the plants from getting too baked on some of our sunnier days.

I slept in my favorite outdoor bed, near the horses, and Julia slept inside the nearby house. I had a vision/fantasy in the night of her being unable to sleep and coming out to join me and, well, you get the idea. As both a Christian and a semi-rational human male, I was rather glad that particular fantasy hadn't come true for I didn't know if I could have handled the temptation it might have presented. I did have the rare good sense not to mention it to Julia later.

Back on the road early the next morning, we had to use four horses on the wagon to be able to make the climb. Even with four, it was slow going and we were still in sight of the Blue River by mid-afternoon. I gestured at the gray-covered town and asked, "What do you think of Breckenridge now?"

"Sad," she replied. "Not just for Breck, though. Is the whole world like this? What kind of life will Junior have?"

I pointed to the side of the road and said, "Look!"

"What?"

"A columbine." When she didn't say anything, I said, "It's the state flower. Or it used to be. Who knows if there's still a Colorado? But Breck looks better now than it did last fall. Maybe not by much, but a little bit. It'll be a while before Junior grows up. Maybe the whole world will look better by then."

"What if it looks worse?"

I thought of a few replies to that, but doubted that any of them merited saying.

We spent the night in sleeping bags on the trail, then got into Overstreet the next day. As we were unloading, Lester Marquez sidled up next to me and said in a low voice, "Steve thinks he saw Charles yesterday."

"Where?"

"By their old house. Steve had gone back there just to check on things and he says it looks like someone's been living there. Said he saw someone darting between those old burned out trees behind the place and thought it looked like Charles."

I wasn't sure what to say to that, so I asked, "What do you think we ought to do? Go after him?"

"Seems like a waste of time to me. We got work here to do. Still, it would pay to be on our guard. He might have mellowed or he might still be nursing that grudge."

One of the most unexpectedly bright spots of that fall was courtesy of Alexa and Adaline. After the success of the Christmas show they had been a part of, they began to find other scripts that they wanted to produce. For Easter Sunday, they had enlisted several people in producing a Passion Play, and for the 4th of July they had written their own patriotic tribute which was amazingly hard to follow. Within that, though, they had discovered that Adaline was a natural comic actress and Alexa was the perfect straight woman. Thus, they began preparing for what came to be known in September as the "AdanAl Friday Night Follies". They had found a book of old comedy routines from the twentieth century which they performed for us, but then they started writing their own material and, for a sixteen and thirteen year-old pair of girls, they were quite talented.

One of their featured ideas was to enlist members of the audience in their skits. Sometimes we would be props, but sometimes they gave us actual lines to read. I got drafted more than once and while it was excruciatingly embarrassing (to me), I took some solace in that it was embarrassing for most everyone else, too. The only person besides the two A's who seemed really good at the acting part was Jonathan, who could deliver serious or funny lines equally well (this was a tremendous surprise, owing to his previously documented inability to tell a joke). As part of these evenings, the two girls encouraged other people to present things as well. At first, it was the ladies who had sung at Christmas, but eventually it was discovered that a couple of the men had good singing voices as well. And Freddy Wilson turned out to be a good story teller—mostly of the humorous kind—and Thelia Isaacson could recite poetry. As the Friday nights went on, more and more people participated—on good weather days even some people from Como would come over to watch—but the scene stealers were always our two teenage girls.

Physically, Alexa was developing first—or faster—with curves that seemed more apparent every time I saw her. With her dark hair and the dark skin of her family, she was going to be what I think they used to call "bewitching". She tended to wear dresses, even when working in the family garden.

Adaline was only growing taller. Though she never got exceedingly tall—stopping at about five-ten when she was 15—for a while there it seemed like she was putting on an inch a day. As my father would have described her, she was "built like a number two pencil". She had long, straight, blonde hair and green eyes and a very winning smile. I'm sure she had her down moments, but I think we all came to secretly expect Adaline to cheer us up no matter what. And where so many people can hear a joke then massacre it in the retelling, Adaline was that rare person who can hear someone tell a joke, then retell it later, except that when she told it, it would be funnier. She usually wore jeans or shorts, rarely dresses, and she had become quite close to Claire since the passing of Samantha, often sitting in our cabin and visiting with her—and trying to draw me into the conversation—until late at night.

We passed the one year anniversary of the end of the world (as we referred to it) with little fanfare, everyone doing what they could to get ready for fall and winter. The greenhouses were built by mid-September and Jesse was helping to oversee the planting in ours. In theory, each family in Overstreet was responsible for a section of the greenhouse and grew what they thought their family would need, but all of us had ceded control of our plots to Jesse and just did what he told us to do. The plants were a testimony to the fact that he knew what he was doing. His hydroponic experiment was still on-going, but with mixed results. Still, I think we all expected him to figure it out. It was just how his mind worked.

As autumn came, we harvested the last of our vegetables from the outdoor gardens and finalized storage plans for the winter. Everyone had their own stores, grown from their own plots, but we also put together a community pantry to help where needed. We also did some bartering there as Claire and I had somehow come up with a bumper crop of carrots so we traded carrots to other families for some of their produce. The suggestion had been made that we put everything in a community store, but we had voted to heed Seth Ryerson's warning. He had taught the kids, and us adults as well, that the Plymouth Rock colony had almost faltered until they gave everyone the incentive of letting them reap the benefits of their own work.

Voting.

That was the other big event that fall, though at the time I wasn't sure I was in favor of it. It was just that someone remarked in October that that November would have been an election year for the United States and Colorado. We joked about casting votes for president, but then the idea seemed to stick on everyone's lips and we began to talk about electing—for starters—a town council and a sheriff. So far, we had been a remarkably peaceful community, most arguments being just the results of frayed tempers and hard work, but there were those who thought we might need to become more organized. What pushed the idea of electing a sheriff to the fore of everyone's mind was when Steve said he had seen Charles

Levinson. It was determined that, rather than just hope for vigilante justice, we would be better off electing a sheriff who would be duly authorized to carry out any punishment should such be required. From there, the idea of a town council gained steam. The talk was that the town council would be charged with planning events for the town, keeping everything neat, marshalling resources when needed, and the like. The real reason for the town council, I was convinced though no one said so out loud, was to make the sheriff responsible to someone. I thought if we had a sheriff he ought to be responsible to the town in general, but people wanted a more structured existence than that.

So, on the Sunday before we were to elect all these officers, it was my turn to lead the Bible study and I brought up the passage where Samuel warns the people of Israel that if they get a king he'll exact taxes, take their sons to fight in wars and etc. I was afraid the sermon/lesson might offend people, and maybe it did. They showed their disapproval by electing me sheriff on the next Tuesday.

When the election results were announced, Julia was the first to congratulate me. She gave me a big hug—the first in a long time, for she had even stopped the playful touches on the arm—and said, "I knew you'd win. You'll be great, Josh."

"But Hutch," who had been the only other name on the ballot, "Actually knows the law."

"And he's going to be a great councilman," Julia told me confidently. "Between the two of you, you'll clean up this town."

"You think it needs it?"

"The privies do stink," she said with a laugh, hugging me again before moving on to congratulate the other winners. I noticed she only shook their hands and wondered if that meant anything. We were still friendly, went on walks together (always with Junior and often with other people), but any spark or hint of romance seemed as dead as the summer weeds in the compost pile. I wasn't sure how I felt about that. Part of me still wanted something to bloom between us, but even I wasn't sure if it were because I really wanted *her* or just because I wanted *someone*.

Also elected to the town council were Evan Isaacson and Danica Glass. There were no pressing civic matters to deal with, so their first order of business was to plan a harvest party for the first week in November. They enlisted so many other people for various duties and responsibilities that we all began to wonder what we had elected *them* for.

One happy gift that Hutch and Niqua brought to the town was that they both could play instruments. So, on the evening of the harvest party, with Japanese lanterns hanging all around and a couple fires to keep us warm, the two of them played music (he on guitar, she on banjo) we could have danced to, if any of us had possessed rhythm. I'm being harsh: *I* possess no rhythm, though many other people had more than their fair share. Still, I was persuaded to dance, or at least stand out on the dance "floor" (a cleared off plot of land near the community kitchen where we sometimes ate outside during good weather) while various women did the actual leading. I think I danced with every female there above the age of ten, including Adaline and Alexa. Oddly, when dancing, it was Alexa who was funny and Adaline who treated each step with the utmost seriousness.

It had been my original plan to just watch the festivities, but first Danica had convinced me to dance with her and then Thelia Isaacson had persuaded me to dance with her. She definitely led and, to keep from repeating that scenario, I began to do the asking. Most just replied politely and we moved as if on purpose, but Adaline seemed unreasonably happy when I asked her to dance. Maybe I had been the first to ask her.

When we were taking a breather later, Adaline asked me, "What would you have been doing if—if things hadn't happened?"

I knew what she meant and replied, "I would be at my sophomore year of college now, trying to figure out how long I had to go before my father would just let me come home and work the ranch. You?"

"I'm fourteen," she replied, in that voice of disdain/angst thirteen year old girls use so well. "Almost. Couple weeks 'til my birthday." Then, as if realizing what she had said might have sounded rude, continued apologetically, "I mean, it's not like I could have gotten a job or anything, yet. I'd be in school and trying out for plays and stuff like that."

"What did you dream?" I asked. "When you grew—when you graduated? What did you want to be?"

I knew she had heard my slip, for she gave me a brief scowl, then said, "I think I would have liked to be a nurse."

"We could use one."

"How can I do that *here*?"

"You know, we've talked about trying to get Doctor Pormon to come over here and give us lessons in first aid. Maybe you could get him to teach you."

"I'm just fourteen."

"Good time to start, then." I leaned closer and whispered conspiratorially, "They elected me sheriff, right? I'm sure not qualified for this job."

"You're the leader of the *whole town*," she stated matter-of-factly. I looked at her with surprise, but she said, "We probably could use a nurse."

"You'd be a good one, I'm sure. You've already helped deliver a baby, right?" I told her sincerely, which elicited a blush. We were interrupted then by a scream and jumped to our feet, like everyone else.

I looked and saw Charles Levinson standing there, across the dance floor, holding his rifle. I got his attention and tried to sound calm as I said, "Hey Charles. What are you doing here?"

"I'm here to kill you, Josh," he replied. He was gaunt and scruffy and I think I could smell him even from twenty feet away. He also looked a little unsteady, so I guessed he might have built up to this moment with some liquid courage. "You drove me away like an animal!" he shouted.

"You behaved like one," a female voice—I don't think it was Claire's—said loudly.

"Shut up!" Charles screamed, looking for the voice.

When he looked back at me, the gun from my waist band (I had started carrying it more regularly since being elected sheriff, more as a badge of office than out of need, I thought) was in my hand. And pointed at him. An indeterminate sound escaped his lips as I said, "Charles, I'm going to have to put you under arrest."

"You don't have a jail!" he shouted back.

"We can clear out your old dugout," I told him. "It's just as you built it."

The barrel of the rifle he was holding came up a smidgen, so I shot him. There might have been a thought in my mind about trying to do like the old shows and shoot the gun out of his hand, but I had spent enough time at the shooting range with my father and brother to know that was a fool's errand. You shoot for the body. And you keep shooting until the other guy can't shoot back.

My first shot took him in the chest and, as he was falling backwards, my second shot went into his chin and out the top of his head. His rifle went off as he was falling, but he didn't even twitch as he hit the ground and lay there like a sack of potatoes. I was just beginning to expect the adrenaline to run out of my system like it always did for the guys in the books, but then I realized his rifle hadn't fired harmlessly into the ground. Out of the corner of my eye, I saw Adaline collapse beside me. At first, I thought she had just fainted, but then I saw the red stain on her abdomen.

"Someone go get Doc Pormon!" I shouted as I fell to my knees beside her. Pushing her coat out of the way, I tore open her blouse near the wound and put my hands over it, trying to hold as much pressure over the wound as I could. I could literally feel each pulse, as her heart pumped blood toward the wound.

"Josh?" she asked, reaching out to me, obviously in shock.

"It's going to be OK, Addy. Just hold on. We'll get you inside and," I said, trying to give her a comforting smile, "And you'll get some experience with that nursing sooner than we thought. You'll hold on, all right?"

"Yes," she said, through clinched teeth. "I'll hold on. Don't let me go, Josh. OK? Don't let me go."

"I won't," I told her as sincerely as I could. As we had danced and as I had been talking to her, I had been thinking of her as something of an equal, one of our grown-up town members, but as I felt her skin beneath my hands and saw the look of agony on her face, she suddenly looked like a little girl to me. "You just keep talking to me," I instructed. As I held my hands to her abdomen, I said a brief prayer for her.

Her mother was saying we ought to carry her inside but her father was saying the best thing for us to do was not to move her but to keep her warm. With that, some of our friends brought one of the fire grates closer, as well as blankets, which they piled over her. Her brother, Tad, was already on one of our fastest horses and riding hell bent for election to Como. Claire, who had more presence of mind than he did under the stress, was following along with an extra horse so the doc would have something to ride back.

"Tell me about nursing school, Addy," I said. "Where would you like to go—if you could go to any college?"

"Where were you going to go to college?" she asked, grimacing at the words and closing her eyes.

"Stay with me, Adaline," I told her. Then, "I was going to go to the University of Northern Colorado. Where would you go?"

"There. I'd go to the University of Northern Colorado."

"Think you'd join the drama club?" I asked.

"Maybe," she replied as her mother put a rolled up coat under her blonde head for a pillow. She forced a smile and said with much effort, "I bet I could do any scene where the girl gets shot really well now, huh?" She clutched at my arm, then, saying, "Oh Josh, this hurts so bad! I don't think I can stand it."

"I know, Adaline. But you've got to, for now." When she closed her eyes again and stopped squirming all of a sudden, I reached out to touch her cheek with one hand and said, "Stay with me, Addy. Stay with me."

She opened her eyes then with an effort and said, "I will. I'll stay with you, Josh."

Her eyes were a piercing green at that moment, a look so stark it would have scared me even if everything else hadn't been going on. Trying to lighten the moment, I said, "Didn't you tell me a few minutes ago you were fourteen? I thought you were thirteen."

"I'll—I'll be fourteen next week—two weeks," she replied.

"What do you want for your party?" I asked her.

She writhed as some wave of pain hit her and cried out. As her mother gently stroked her forehead, she said, "I want another dance. Like this one. But I want every dance to be with you. And I want—I want Hutch and Niqua to play some slow songs."

"Good," I told her with a smile. "Slow is the only kind of dance I can keep up with."

"You dance wonderfully," she told me.

While all this was going on, some of the other people at the party had dragged Charles Levinson off. I was to find out later that they had just caved a bank of rocks over him on Mount Volsh. I hadn't liked the man, and he had been trying to kill me, but I still felt it behooved me to give a fellow human being a marker. So I carved one myself from boards out of his own dugout and put it over his grave a few days later. An ash slide took it out one day and covered the grave and none of us ever bothered to go looking for it or re-mark it.

I kept her talking and, after what seemed like hours but was probably more like thirty minutes, Doctor Pormon was there, riding a lathered-up horse but sitting the saddle expertly. He bounded from the saddle like a much younger man, rushed to Adaline's side, and said, "Let's get this young lady inside. You—Josh, isn't it? Keep your hand on the wound."

Several people participated in carrying Adaline into the community kitchen and laying her on one of the tables there. As I removed my hand, she reached out and grabbed my arm, saying, "Josh, you told me not to leave you so you don't leave me." I looked at her parents, who both motioned that I should stay. So, out of respect for her modesty I stood where she could hold my hand and I could look into her face but wouldn't see anything happening beneath her shoulders.

"Tell me something, Josh," she said, between winces.

"Maybe we ought to let the doctor work—" I started to say, but he nudged me and, when I looked at him, motioned that I should keep her talking. "What do you want to know?"

"Um," she squirmed and it felt like she was about to break the bones in my hand, then asked, "When we're playing Strat-O-Matic, there's an option for having the infield in, right? Why?" She closed her eyes tightly for a moment, then amended, "I mean, in real life. Why would a team bring the infield in?"

I began to explain to her the intricacies of why a manager might call for that and she seemed to be paying attention, when she wasn't gripping my hand like a vice or screaming. The doctor had offered her some alcohol for the pain, but she refused. I wasn't sure whether I admired that choice or not, considering what she was going through.

Finally, after I'm not sure how long, the doctor said, "The bullet is up against her ribs in the back. Let's turn her over." We did and, at her request, I knelt down where she could see my face.

"Why—would you call for a hit and run? What is that in real life?" she asked, through tears of pain.

I had just barely finished explaining it when the doctor told us triumphantly, "There it is!" I heard the "plink" as he dropped the bullet into a metal bowl and then said, "Now, let me clean this brave young woman up and do some stitching." He leaned into her field of vision and said, "I'm such a good stitcher, young lady, that six weeks from now no one will even know where you were shot."

"I was shot?" she asked, surprised, letting us all know just how in shock she had been.

Pretty soon, the doctor was saying, "Let's just let her get some rest." As if on cue, she closed her eyes and started breathing regularly. I gently put her hand on the table and let go, then stood up.

When I stood up, Inez Isaacson threw her arms around me and said, "You saved my daughter's life. I know you did." Evan Isaacson and Adaline's grandmother Thelia were shaking my hands and saying the same thing while Inez still held me tightly. Soon, I had received similar accolades from the rest of the Isaacson clan.

"If Charles hadn't been gunning for me," I objected, "It probably never would have happened."

"That wasn't your fault," Evan told me, to be agreed with by the rest of the family.

"And the way you've stayed with her through all this," Inez told me admiringly. "I just—" she choked up and wiped her eyes, not finishing her sentence.

The doctor encouraged us to go outside, to which I said that I could use some fresh air. Out there, I was surrounded by another crowd of well-wishers and huggers. My insides were shaking like jelly and my brain was a muddle, but there was enough of a nineteen year old boy in me that I took special notice of the hugs from Julia Croft and Niqua Hutchiscn, who most people were starting to call "Nikki". Someone led a cheer for "Our sheriff!" which I appreciated, but what I wanted to appreciate more than anything else was my bed. That seemed in bad form, and I didn't know if I could actually sleep, so I made my way over to one of the fires and sat down. Someone brought me a drink—one of the canned pops we had liberated in Breckenridge—and I sipped it gratefully while listening to people talk about mundane things.

Suddenly, I got the attention of those people who were near me and asked, "What are we doing?" When they looked confused, I said, "We sit in that very kitchen every Sunday and talk about prayer, and now one of our own is clinging to life and we're not praying."

"Um," Claire corrected gently, "We have been. A bunch of us had a prayer circle and were praying the whole time the doctor was operating. Most of Addy's family was in on it with us. They said you would be there but you were keeping her alive."

I didn't know what to say except, "Sorry. I should have known better." Then I leaned forward, head bowed, elbows on knees, and began praying.

It was hard to pray, though I knew I wanted to. When I would close my eyes, suddenly I was there again, holding my hand over her wound and watching her grimace in pain, felling the warm blood pulse against my palm. I had felt pretty helpless then and I was feeling it again. If she died, I didn't know if I could ever recover. I knew her mom had already lost the one niece and I couldn't imagine how she could handle it happening again, especially to her own daughter. So even in my near-delirium, I was probably praying more sincerely than ever before.

But I was also thinking that I had spent all that time touching a young woman's abdomen. It's silly when I look back on it now—I mean, what else was I supposed to do?—but even when it was happening there was a certain … what? Thrill? That sounds coarse, juvenile and corny, but it's probably accurate. I tried my best to hustle those thoughts out of my mind but they kept coming back. And while I hadn't seen anything I wouldn't have seen at a public swimming pool, I had seen more skin than I had since the last time I had *been* to a public pool and that kept popping into my mind. We didn't have any practicing Catholics in town (even the Marquez family rarely crossed themselves anymore), but at that thought I felt like I ought to go to confession.

Some hours later, I had fallen asleep by the fire and was awakened by Evan Isaacson gently shaking me and saying, "Josh? Adaline's asking for you."

I rubbed my eyes and asked, "How's she doing?" As I stood up, I realized not only how stiff I was, but how cold. Someone had been keeping the fire going, and even wrapped a blanket around me, but it was the Rocky Mountains in November.

"Doc says she's going to be fine," Evan answered as we walked into The Kitchen. "He says you holding pressure on the wound like you did probably saved her life."

"I read it somewhere," I replied, still not fully awake.

Inside the kitchen, they had made Adaline as comfortable as possible for someone laying on a table. She held out her hands to me and said with a big smile, "My life-saver!"

"How do you feel?" I asked her as I held her hands gently. She was looking young again, like a little girl.

"Absolutely horrible," she replied with a laugh, then winced. "I gotta stop telling jokes," she mumbled.

"Don't do that. The rest of us won't be able to live."

"Come here," she practically commanded, pulling me closer. She let go of my hands and took hold of my head and brought me closer. She kissed me on the cheek then said, "I can never thank you enough. The doctor says I wouldn't be here if it weren't for you. Oh, and when he comes back I'm going to ask if I can study nursing, like you suggested."

The doctor came in then and told us, "We need to get her to a more comfortable place, like her own bed. *Then* we need to let her get some sleep."

I'm sure it was very painful for her, but we managed to carry her to her cabin and lay her down on her own bed. Before leaving, I knelt down by her bed and said, "If you're up to dancing at your birthday party in a couple weeks, I get the first dance, OK?"

"I wouldn't think of giving it to anyone else," she told me.

"Adaline, we've been praying for you—the whole town has—could I, would it be all right if I prayed for here, now?"

"Oh, please do."

As I walked back to my cabin, exhausted beyond belief, I said another prayer, of thanks for her recovery to that point and prayed it would continue.

I found that Claire was already in her bed. She sat up quickly, startled and asking, "Who's there?"

"Just me, Josh."

"Oh good," she said, laying down and making me think she might not have actually awakened. I got my answer when, in the morning, she said she didn't remember me coming in.

The next morning was cold but sunny, so I bundled up after a quick breakfast and went out to check on the horses. Once satisfied they were OK—and, truthfully, Claire was already with them and she and Oscar were giving them a bit of a workout—I went over to the Isaacson cabin. Knocking gently for fear of waking a sleeping patient, I stood out on their stoop and admired what they had done to the cabin. It was no longer just a cabin, really. It was a *house*. A home. Besides real windows, it had several rooms as well as planter boxes in which they kept flowers and herbs growing in the summer months. And, of course, it had some of Claire's curtains.

Inez opened the door and smiled widely before giving me a hug and practically dragging me inside. "It's our hero!" she announced loudly. I was afraid of another mob hug, but I think the only other person in the cabin was Adaline. I heard a sound come from Adaline's room that sounded gleeful and Inez instructed, "Come back and see how well she's doing."

She led me in to Adaline's room where I found the young woman sitting somewhat propped in bed (not quite sitting up, not really laying down) and her face was shining with a smile. The room had the decorations of a young woman and not, as I might have expected, those of a young girl. She had attached pictures to the walls, mostly landscapes culled from magazines, and she had a bookshelf full of books—the kind she often spoke of reading. I noticed the George MacDonald book there, the one we had sworn contained no symbolism, and smiled at the memory. She was white as her sheets, but she had never had much melanin to begin with, always looking like the one Swedish member of the family. She held out her hands to me as she had done the previous night and said, "Pardon if I don't get up right away."

I couldn't help myself and gave her a gentle hug, making sure not to squeeze too hard or jostle her. She returned the hug fiercely and, for a moment, I didn't think she was going to let go. When I finally could get some breathing room, I asked, "How's the bravest girl I know?"

She smiled and asked, "Brave? How brave do you have to be to be standing in the wrong spot?"

"Oh, but the way you held on last night! I was afraid we'd … afraid we'd lose you."

"Hey, you told me not to leave and I always do what the sheriff tells me," she replied with a chuckle. Then, with a more serious expression on her face but an odd twinkle in her eye, asked, "Did the bullet really go all the way through me?"

"Um, sort of. I mean, it went in through the front and the doctor had to take it out from the back."

She put her hand to where the wound was and said, "So if he hadn't stitched it up I would have had a pierced belly. Just think: I could have worn this massive ring. Maybe even hung my purse on it." At my dismayed look, she chided, "I'm joking, Josh!"

"See, that's the Adaline I need around here," I told her, finally catching up on the joke. Pulling up a chair—where various family members had probably spent the night—I told her, "After the doctor had finished working on you last night, you said something like you didn't know you had been shot. If it's too disturbing to remember, we can move on, but I'm curious: what *do* you remember?"

She pursed her lips to one side and looked toward the window, then said, "You know, I don't remember it very well. I remember you and I talking, then that awful man showed up. I have a vague recollection of falling, though I honestly don't remember being shot as being painful or anything. Then … hmm, my next memories are just a few jumbles. Laying outside while you pressed on my tummy, then being in The Kitchen—is that real? Was the operation on one of The Kitchen tables?" I nodded so she continued, "Then I remember all of you carrying me to here and— did you come by last night?"

"Yeah. You had woken up and asked to see me."

She blushed at that for some reason, then said, "I think I remember that. Not well, but I remember it. I think I just wanted to thank you." She moved her mouth like she was going to say something else, but no sound came out. Finally, she said, "And that was it. Next thing I know, I'm waking up here and the sun's shining and my family's all hovering around me like a newborn and other than the fact that it feels like I have a hot branding iron in my stomach every time I move, I'm doing great. Doc's even been here this morning and says I should get up and walk around the room periodically."

"Really? Already?"

"Yes. He said something about how it might hurt but it would keep me from being so stiff in the long term and how it's good to get the blood flowing and all. He also said something about how walking around helps the body heal or something." She smiled and added, "When I start taking those nursing courses I'm going to have to start paying better attention, huh?" Then, she held out her hands again and said, "Help me up?"

"Are you sure? Shouldn't your mother or someone—"

"I know how to walk, silly," she told me, not in that exasperated teenage voice she was so good at but in a voice that sounded remarkably grown up to me. "And it's not like I'm wearing one of those hospital gowns that opens in the back. Though I guess you saw everything last night—"

"Actually, I was very careful not to see anything except your stomach—and your face."

"You are so great!" she complimented, practically cheering. "Now, let me hold on to you and we'll walk to the living room and back, OK?"

Rather than being alarmed, when she saw us Inez said, "Oh good, you got her up. The doctor said we needed to get her up and walk her around every couple hours during the day, but she has not been a cooperative patient on that score." I saw Adaline scowl at her mother, but the look disappeared quickly. She was occasionally grimacing, or putting one hand to her side (while the other held to my arm) but it seemed to me that she was doing remarkably well for someone who had just been shot less than twenty-four hours before.

As we walked back to her room, Adaline told me, "Doctor says I need to eat" <exaggerated gulp> "liver."

"Maybe the iron is what your system needs."

"If I need metal in my body," she asked as she got gingerly into bed, "Why take the lead out?" Then she smiled at me and said, "Thanks so much for coming over, Sheriff." Then, in a voice that wasn't childlike but with a countenance that was somehow, she asked, "Can you hang out for a while? Just talk?"

"You bet. Want me to explain the infield fly rule now?" I asked with a laugh.

She seemed genuinely confused as she asked, "Where did that come from?"

Chapter Thirteen

*Men are eager to tread underfoot
what they have once too much feared.*
~Lucretius

We were getting things ready for both our Thanksgiving service we hoped to hold in a couple weeks and the rapidly approaching winter (we had already had several snows, though the snow had always melted quickly away) when a delegation from Como approached us. I thought maybe they were going to take us up on our offer to be our guests at Thanksgiving or maybe play in our annual Thanksgiving day football game (providing we could get the ball to hold air), but they were there as "officially concerned citizens of the world" apparently.

They were there because they were concerned about the circumstances under which Charles Levinson had met his doom. Lester Marquez seemed more upset by them than I did as Wally Preston was saying, "Some of our people are just concerned that a man was executed—"

"Wait a minute, Wally," Lester objected. "We have a duly elected sheriff here in Como and Charles barged into our harvest party—*with a rifle*, mind you—pointing it at our sheriff and threatening to kill him."

"Well," Wally replied, somewhat flustered, "Wasn't there a more peaceful solution to—"

"Listen!" Lester demanded. "Charles' finger was on the trigger. If you don't think it was, you go look at that little girl with the bullet hole through her belly. Or ask your doctor that sewed her up! Levinson was about to shoot our sheriff when the sheriff, who had been trying to defuse the situation, shot him. *That*'s the way it was!"

One of the other members of the Como delegation, a tall, thin man with a face like a hawk, said, "We just feel that in the event of a death, there should be an inquiry—"

"This is *our town*," Lester proclaimed. "And we—"

241

"Wait," I said, as calmly as I could. When Lester looked at me in surprise, I said, "We elected a sheriff because we wanted to be a law-abiding town. Maybe it wouldn't hurt to have a commission to look into things like this, make sure we're not becoming a town of vigilantes."

"A commission of who?" Lester demanded, still pretty heated up.

"Maybe people from both towns?" Wally offered.

"The only problem with that is that everyone from our town was at the shooting," I told them. "I mean everyone." I looked around a moment, then said, "Tell you what: I'll let you select the commission from the people of Como if you'll let me bring any witnesses I want and my own lawyer."

Suddenly, Lester seemed appeased. The men from Como were surprised, but agreed, and we agreed to come over on the next day—as no one wanted this to drag through Thanksgiving. I remembered that clause in the old constitution about a person's right to a speedy trial, and I also remembered my father saying how the lawyers had abandoned that promise. I thought to myself that my father would appreciate the speed of our justice in Overstreet.

"As your lawyer," Hutch said as we told him what was going on, "My first advice would have been to turn this whole thing down. I know you're trying to keep everything up and above board, Josh, but where does it stop? This time, we all saw what happened and I'm convinced we can convince them. But what about next time?"

"Huh?" myself, Lester, and a few other asked.

"Let's say me and Steve get into it one day. I don't think we will, but just for the sake of argument, let's say we do. It's a fair fight but one of us is victorious. I'm not talking about a killing, but let's say Steve lands a lucky punch," this was said with a wink to Steve, who had become over time very good friends with Hutch, "And I go down. Maybe I hit my head on a rock and I'm in a coma. Whether I come out of it or not, you—the people of Overstreet— you rule that it was just a fight and a bad break. You don't incarcerate Steve or anything. Or maybe you make him work my garden until I'm better. Fine. But, having opened this can of worms today, what if someone from Como decides they want to jail Steve as a public menace. What then?"

"OK," I conceded, "You make a good point. But I already agreed to this, so maybe we need to establish some sort of agreement for the future."

"That would actually be more in my wheelhouse," Hutch told us with a smile.

Adaline, who I didn't realize was standing nearby, whispered to me, "Wheelhouse?"

"It's another baseball expression." Then, I turned to her and asked happily, "You're up?"

"For a bit. I think I'm tired just from walking over here from our cabin, but I heard about what's going on and—and I want to testify. You saved my life."

"I don't think you ought to be going all the way into Como—" I started to object.

"I can ride in the wagon. I want to be there," she stated in a voice that brooked no argument. "Besides, Doctor Pormon will be right there, right?"

The next morning, almost the whole adult population of Overstreet went over to Como. In spite of her tone of voice of the previous day, Adaline's parents vetoed the idea of her going along. She wasn't too happy with me for siding with her parents, but she eventually succumbed because, I think, she decided she was too weak to fight us. She did carefully write out a deposition of what had happened and asked her mother to read it to the court. A courtroom of sorts had been set up in the old Catholic church and it looked to me like the entire population of Como was there. They had more people than I expected, and some I didn't recognize. They even had a few children, perhaps a dozen.

When we got inside, we learned that they had gone with our idea of a tribunal. Wally was on it, as well as Aunt Jenny and a man I didn't know but was introduced as Luther Faris. An American flag had been hung up behind them and a sheet had been hung in front of the statue of Mary, for some reason. Once we were all inside, Wally banged an actual gavel on the table and called the meeting to order. Then he said, "We the people of the South Park Valley have called for this inquiry to look into the shooting death of one Charles Levinson by Josh Overstreet, in the town of Overstreet five days ago. We will listen to all who would like to have input in these proceedings."

"Your honors," Hutch said, standing up and reaching for the buttons of a suitcoat he wasn't wearing (we had all dressed for warmth, not formality), "As Mister Overstreet's attorney, I would like to have it stipulated that my client has willingly presented himself for this hearing and is under no legal obligation to do so."

"He shot a man!" Luther Faris injected.

"Pursuant to his duties as the rightfully elected sheriff of Overstreet, your honors," Hutch asserted.

"But everybody knows Levinson tried to attack Overstreet's sister and—" Faris argued, to be silenced by the gavel.

"These are just the matters we want to address," Wally told everyone when he had their attention. It had been a little windy as we all rode over to Como, and in that old building we could hear it kicking up fiercely, the old walls and roof creaking under the strain. Then, Wally said, "Mister Overstreet, as both the person this hearing is focused on and the elected sheriff of Overstreet," (this drew some grumbles from the Como crowd), "Would you like to give us your account of what happened first?"

I looked at Hutch, who nodded, so I stood up and said, "My name is Josh Overstreet, and I was elected sheriff of—of our town." Mentioning the name of the town seemed like grandstanding to me. "We were having a harvest party when Charles Levinson showed up with a rifle. He pointed it at me and said he was going to kill me for running him out of town before. I tried to talk him in to surrendering, but he continued with his threats. When he was momentarily distracted, I was able to pull out my gun. When I saw the barrel of his rifle raise, I assumed he meant business and I shot him." I couldn't think of anything to add, so I sat down.

"It was my understanding," Mister Faris said, in a calm voice that seemed mocking to me, "That you shot him twice. Was that necessary?"

I remained seated but answered, "I took a gun safety course with my father, taught by Denny Logan—most of you knew him when he was sheriff of Park County. He taught us safety, but he also taught us that he had told his deputies that, when someone is trying to kill you, you shoot 'til they stop."

"Couldn't you have just shot him in the leg?" Faris asked.

"I wish so, sir. And if we were at a nice, calm, shooting range, I probably could have made that shot. At that moment, though, I was just aiming for the largest target that would stop a dangerous man. My goal was to put two shots into his chest; I just didn't account for the first shot knocking him back like it did."

Faris, speaking to his fellow justices, said, "He admits it!"

Wally looked at Faris uncomfortably, but Aunt Jenny—who had been silent to that point—said in a derisive tone, "We all know he killed him, Luther. We're just here to make sure it was not murder."

Faris started to bluster, so Wally banged his gavel again and said, "Let's hear from anyone else who would like to speak. Anyone?"

As several of my fellow townspeople raised their hands, Faris objected, "They're all his friends! How objective can they be?"

"Luther," Wally told him, "This happened at a party in Overstreet none of us went to. They were all there. Who did you expect to testify?" Before Luther could answer, Wally pointed at Lester Marquez and said, "Lester, why don't you give us your account of what happened?"

Lester stood up and recounted the event as he had seen it. He was followed by several of my friends, who all told the same story. It was Evan Isaacson who first pointed out that Charles's finger must have already been on the trigger for the gun to have gone off like it did. Several people talked at once, some arguing the point and others agreeing with it.

"Your honors," Inez said finally, getting their attention.

"Yes, ma'am?" Wally replied.

Inez stood, somewhat nervously, then said, "My name is Inez Isaacson. It was my daughter who was shot and she asked me to read this," she held up the piece of paper, "To the court."

"Yes ma'am," Wally said with a nod. "Go ahead." I think he was just glad to have something bring a close to the arguing, for the time being, anyway.

Inez cleared her throat and read, "'Members of the court, my name is Adaline Renee Isaacson. I was the one who was accidentally shot. Accidentally in that I don't think he meant to shoot me. He was pointing the gun at Josh. Anyway, when I was shot, Josh forgot all thought of anyone else. He literally used his hands to hold my blood in. And he refused to leave my side until the doctor practically made him leave, after the surgery. I know my testimony may not be evidence as to whether Sheriff Overstreet shot in self-defense or not. I believe he did, in his defense and in defense of all of us who were there that night. I just wanted to write this to testify as to his character, as a character witness.'" Inez paused, as if embarrassed to read the next portion, and as soon as she did I could see why. "'I would also like to say that he's the finest man in this valley and he saved my life.'" She stood there a moment longer, then nodded curtly, folded the paper, and sat down.

Luther Faris didn't interrupt any of the speeches that preceded her, but when Inez had finished speaking, he said, "I am in admiration of your daughter's strength, ma'am, and I appreciate the words she wrote. I also understand her admiration of Mister Overstreet, considering the heroic measures he took to preserve her life. However, Mister Overstreet's actions after the shooting do not mitigate the fact that a life was taken. And may I also add that Mister Levinson was merely reacting to the impinging of his freedoms by the town of Overstreet last winter, when he was thrust out into the cold—"

"Your honors," Hutch spoke up, for the first time in a while, "A lawfully constituted local tribunal—much as what sits before us today—found Mister Levinson guilty of attempted rape and had exiled him from the town—"

"And Mister Overstreet's own sister was the alleged victim," Faris injected.

I wanted to jump up and say something there, but Hutch gently stopped me and said, "That fact is not in argument. One of the people who was on that tribunal is here today. In fact, she has already addressed the court. Several other people who are here today can testify as to what happened in that trial. We can assure you that Mister Levinson was tried, convicted, and treated mercifully. He was given exile, not death or incarceration."

Wally banged his gavel for no readily apparent reason, then said, "This tribunal will now withdraw to deliberate—"

"To what end, your honors?" Hutch asked.

"What?" at least two of the three judges asked in confusion as they stood up.

Hutch remained seated, looking casual but alert, and said, "As I have already pointed out, Mister Overstreet presented himself to this tribunal of his own free will, though he was in no respect legally obligated to do so. I must admit that I cautioned against this because it was never stated what the goal of this tribunal was nor under what authority it was being constituted. We all live in what was once known as Park County, Colorado but, if I may say so your honors, we have no idea whether Colorado still exists, let alone Park County." He stood up, then, and motioned for me to do the same, and said, "While we are somewhat curious as to how you will rule, we are in no way obligated to wait around until you do. Therefore, my client and I will repair to Overstreet and, should you choose to inform us of your verdict, we will take it under advisement."

"You can't leave here!" Faris shouted angrily.

"Mister Faris," Hutch said calmly, "We have presented ourselves and our arguments in good faith and, as I have stated, were under no obligation to do so. If our two communities would like to enter into future agreements as to jurisdiction, extradition and the like, we would entertain such a discussion. Until then, and maybe even after that, what happens in Como is Como business and what happens in Overstreet is Overstreet business. Thank you and good day." He made a motion for me to follow him, at which point the whole Overstreet contingent stood up. There was some grumbling, mostly from Faris, but no one wanted a fight right in the Catholic Church, so we walked out.

Outside, I asked Hutch, "Should we have waited for their verdict?"

Hutch paused, then started for the wagon he had rode in on and said, "I am pretty confident they would have voted in your favor—even if it were only by a two-to-one vote. However, it has been festering in my gut ever since they brought this idea up that we did not need to cede them that kind of authority over us." At the wagons, he said, "We may be the last two communities left alive in the world. Even if we're not, we may not know of any other communities in our lifetimes. It is going to behoove us to work with Como over the years, but we need to establish some ground rules so that *neither side*," he said with emphasis, "Can unilaterally decide something that is not in the other side's best interest. When spring comes, we are probably going to need to work out an agreement on the waters of the Tarryall, for instance. Today, we established our right to negotiate for ourselves in such a fight."

"Was that what this was about?" I asked, as I climbed up into the driver's seat of the wagon. I had already helped Claire up into the seat beside me, so she handed me the reins.

"I don't know about them, but it's what I was about," Hutch answered.

I liked Hutch, and he had been a hard-worker ever since he and his daughter had shown up. She, too, had pitched in wherever needed, especially loving to help Claire with the horses. Still, I think I was afraid that Hutch had some sort of machinations going that I didn't know about and was a little concerned. I realized that part of the problem was that I still thought of Overstreet as "my town" and was reminded that it was Hutch's too. And Niqua's and Tad's and everyone else's. I wanted my town to be my town and so far, I had been satisfied that it had stayed so. On the other hand, I had to admit that other people might want other things for *our* town and while so far none of them had run counter to what I wanted, what if they one day did? Where would I compromise and where would I fight?

I was shaken from my reverie by Claire asking, "What are you waiting for?"

"What? Oh, nothing. Just thinking," I replied, then got the horses going. Then, "Thanks for coming along on this, Sis. It means a lot to me."

"Hey, one of these days people might think of me as an adult, so I better get used to acting like one." She squeezed my arm and added in a voice so low only I could hear it, "Besides, it was my big brother who was on trial. You've always been there for me, when I needed you."

Back at our town, I found Adaline waiting anxiously in The Kitchen so I helped her to her cabin—almost carried her, in fact—as I told her what all had happened. She again expressed the wish that she had been there, but seemed somewhat placated by receiving the details. After tending to the horses, I made my way to the community kitchen. There, coffee or tea were almost always brewing. I hated coffee and wasn't a big fan of tea, but sometimes a warm drink felt pretty good after a cold day in the saddle, or—in this case—on the seat of the wagon. Generally, I enjoyed the feeling of the warmth to my hands more than anything. Once they were warm, the rest of me usually followed.

In The Kitchen, I found Evan Isaacson and Lester Marquez and Hutch already drinking hot drinks and sitting at a table near the pot-bellied stove. I got my drink and came near them, intending just to listen for my mind was awash with myriad thoughts and I didn't think anything I said would be coherent.

Lester was saying, "I keep asking myself: what could we have done differently? I mean, should we have built a jail and kept him in it? I admit: my main reason for voting against that idea was that I didn't want to take a turn watching him."

Evan responded, "You look back at it now, and it seems like all we did was kick the can down the road, then it came back to haunt us."

"But what else could we have *done*?" Lester repeated. "A man like that, who attacks a girl the way he did, they don't stop. He would'a tried again, either on Claire or my daughter, or one of yours." He held up his hands and said defensively, "I know, I know. We all claim to be Christians and we believe in repentance

249

and forgiveness, but you both know as well as I do that there are some people—some kinds of crimes—that don't … go away."

Hutch offered, "In our world before, it's why people convicted of sex crimes went on a registry. They might get out of jail, but there were places they couldn't go—like near a school. I had a cousin that went to jail for rape. While he was in prison, he claimed to have found the Lord. But when he got out of prison, when he went to church he had to have someone chaperone him the whole time. He said that was the way it was going to be the rest of his life."

"You saying that's what we should have done?" Lester asked.

Hutch shook his head and replied, "Not necessarily. I'm just saying that's what they did to my cousin. And he deserved it, by the way." He was thoughtful for a moment, then said, "I wasn't here, so I don't know exactly how I would have reacted. If I had caught him attacking Niqua or my wife, I'd'a probably reacted just like Josh did. If I had been on the tribunal, from all the evidence I've heard, I would've found him guilty. But you know: we can't change the past. The question is: do we want to do something about the future?"

"Like what?" Evan asked, voicing what Lester and I were thinking.

"Do we want to write out our own laws?" Hutch asked. "Our own little Overstreet compact, as it were?"

"We all go to church," Evan suggested. "Why not just use the Bible?"

"Old or New Testament?" Hutch asked. Then he smiled and said, "Sorry, that's the lawyer in me. My grandmother knew the Good Book frontwards and backwards. My wife, she went every Sunday and always took the kids. Me, I'd go when they were serving food. That's neither here nor there. I like that you've included me and Niqua in your community and the church. Still, I think my question's a valid one. For instance, if we say we're going to keep the Ten Commandments, that's pretty easy to enforce. But we sit in this very room on Sunday mornings singing about the 'Wonderful Grace of Jesus', so what if someone gets convicted of, I don't know, lying—bearing false witness? Do we sentence him according to law or according to grace?"

"If we had a crystal ball," Lester opined, "Things would be easier, huh? If we had known this was going to come out this way, we could have just sentenced him to life in his cabin—even if it was a hardship on us. Would've saved his life and Evan's little girl here wouldn't be recuperating from a bullet wound."

"If we'd had a crystal ball," Evan countered, "We could have just told him to keep moving that day he walked up here, asking to live in our town."

"Praise God we don't have a crystal ball, then," Hutch laughed. When we all looked at him, he elaborated, "I can't imagine anyone living in our town being a rapist. But we are all sinners. And those Ten Commandments? We'll each break at least one, maybe all of them but murder. If we had that crystal ball, we'd be kicking Lester out because a year from now he's going to be covetous, and me out because of a lie I tell two months from now and … see what I'm getting at? If we had that crystal ball, we could find reasons to get rid of everyone now and save ourselves trouble for later—and create all new kinds of trouble."

About eight days after that, we had our Thanksgiving festival. I thought the highlight of it was going to be when Adaline showed up, for she had done nothing but rest since the trial. The highlight, though, was when she stood up and went through with the skit she and Alexa had prepared. It was another of their comedy routines, a politically-incorrect interchange between a rather dense pilgrim and an exasperated Indian, which brought laughs from us all.

A couple families from Como, including the Sukigaras, came over to our Thanksgiving feast and brought food to contribute to it. We learned from them that the tribunal had voted to exonerate me. The rumor was that the vote was 2 to 1 in my favor, but Ron Sukigara told us with a knowing wink that the tribunal had been very closed-mouth about who voted what. Ron and Hutch seemed to get along better now that they weren't the only surviving men in a devastated town and I overheard them talking about plans for an intercommunity agreement that would touch on or establish the ideals of jurisdiction, extradition and the like. As sheriff, I found the discussion more interesting than, apparently, everyone else, for it was soon just the two of them talking while I listened.

We tried to play our football game, once Jesse had figured out a way to keep the ball inflated, but it didn't last as long as the previous year because it was just too cold. Besides, somehow Ron Sukigara and Danica Glass had wound up on the same team. Danica could still outrun everyone and suddenly she had someone who could throw seemingly as far as she wanted to run. And, once those on my team started trying to double-team Danica, Ron just started beating us with underneath stuff. It was a shellacking, but I think even the winning team was glad to call it on account of cold. Once we got inside and were warming up, my team was further embarrassed when Danica announced that she had been running for two.

As all the women gathered around her and talked about whatever women discuss in such situations (what little I could hear assured me I didn't want to hear more!), I and the other men congratulated Howard Glass and gave him the ribbing that you would expect.

I was a little envious, as I held Danica in very high esteem. She had been a good friend ever since the disaster and, while she was clearly too old for me back when single, I couldn't deny that she was a very attractive woman. Before her and Howard had started courting, I had wished more than once that the gap in our ages hadn't been so great. I never had gotten around to having that conversation with her about a woman, or women, and suddenly I was wishing I had. I didn't know what I wanted to ask her, though, but I did want some advice. I told myself that any advice concerning women and wooing would be welcome, but I look at my own track record and wonder if I would have been able to listen.

I glanced over then and saw that some people had already moved on from the congratulatory stage of the afternoon and back into their own little worlds. Specifically, Claire and Oscar were sitting in one corner of the community kitchen and laughing about something while Tad Levinson and Niqua Hutchison (he may have been the one who started calling her "Nikki") were having a close conversation in another part of the room. I had seen that relationship coming for days and might have been a little envious that they had found each other if not for the fact that I had found who I was going to marry as well.

I just wasn't sure when I'd get the nerve to tell **her** about it.

It was a good thing the people from Como left mid-afternoon because the wind started blowing a gale at about two in the afternoon (causing the cessation of the football game) and then it began to get even colder. By the time the Como folks left, there was ash coming off the mountains and, by evening, visibility was very low. We could only hope they got back safely as we tried to batten down our own hatches.

The wind was straight out of the north that day and evening, instead of out of the northwest like we had been used to. That northwestern wind was what had kept the ash out of our little valley, but the north wind blew the ash off the Boreas Pass mountains and over our town. Most of the people of Overstreet were gathered in The Kitchen, where a small (emphasis on *small*) dance floor had been set up so that Adaline could have that birthday dance she had been wanting, for her birthday and Thanksgiving fell on the same day that year. The Hutchisons played music and I danced with Adaline—barely, she was about worn out, yet determined to dance at least once—and then some of the others took the floor.

After the party, I made sure everyone made it safely to their houses, then I went to mine. Claire and I took our extra blankets and lined them against the doors to keep the ash out and were guessing other people were doing the same.

Once we were fairly snug and listening to the wind howl outside and hoping our roof stayed on, we realized it wasn't all that late. Claire suggested we play cards so we sat at our table (we had an actual kitchen by then, as well as separate bedrooms, the original part of our cabin having been made into said kitchen and a living room). As we played a game our Dad had taught us when we were little called "Knock-knock", we made small talk. Claire suddenly said, apropos of nothing else that had been said to that point, "Do you still like Oscar?"

"Hmm? What? I never stopped liking Oscar, that I know of," I quipped.

"Well, I'm eighteen now and, well, Oscar and I would like to get married at Christmas."

I wasn't too surprised. I just happened to look up from my cards and saw that Claire looked nervous, so I said, "If you want my blessing, Sis, you've got it."

She smiled, looking quite relieved, and said, "I figured you would be OK with it. Would you still give me away?"

"Hmm," I said, as if thinking it over. "I'm not sure I want to give you away. I mean, not ceremonially. You're my sister."

She laid down a card and knocked on the table, then said, "You know what I mean."

"Yeah," I said after it was revealed she had won the hand. "Like I said before: I would be honored. You're sure, though? I mean, nothing against you marrying Oscar, but you're sure?"

She began to shuffle the cards and then looked me in the eye and said confidently, "Yeah. Yeah I am. I finally realized that, even if we were to get rescued or if we never do, Oscar is who I want to spend my life with."

I could see in her eyes that she was sincere and said, reaching out to take her hand, "That's great, Claire. I'm really happy for you. So, when did he ask you?"

"How do you know I didn't ask him?"

"Is that what you two were talking about over in the corner after the football game?"

She blushed and said, "Yes. And yes, that's when he asked me." Fanning herself with her cards, she said, "I wanted to tell everyone then, but I wanted to talk to you, first. And I didn't want to take away from Danni's moment. Isn't that great—about her and Howard, I mean?"

"Yeah, it is. You know, we're starting to have a lot of little kids around our town. Makes me hopeful for the future, you know." We played along in silence for a bit before I asked, "Oh, what was that about you being eighteen? What does that have to do with it, especially since you've been eighteen since July?"

She laid down a card, picked another up, then said, "Oh, I didn't think you would object to me marrying Oscar, but if you had, I'm eighteen so there's nothing you could do about it."

"Hey, I'm sheriff. Surely I could do *something* about it."

"You try and I'll start a recall petition," she told me with a laugh.

I was still reading a lot—mostly in the evenings while Claire and Oscar visited in the living room. She always insisted that Oscar never enter her bedroom and that the door between the living room and my room be kept open. I appreciated her commitment to chastity—and complimented her more than once—but it did make it kind of hard to read at times. I would eventually get so wrapped up in the book that they could have had a knife fight in the living room and I wouldn't have noticed.

That particular winter, I was determined to read "War and Peace" by Tolstoy. I had always heard about it, and it was referenced in so many other works, that when I discovered that the Marquez family had a copy (that had never even been opened!), I asked if I could borrow it. It was long and sometimes tedious, but I could see why so many people regarded it as one of the greatest literary masterpieces of all-time. I would take a break now and then and read something else for a day or two, but I always came back to it. I was pretty miffed at Tolstoy when he knocked off Prince Andrew—the only truly likable character in the book, in my opinion—but I got over it and finished it, anyway.

I felt an especial affinity with a character who barely even appeared, a young officer in the Russian army of whom Tolstoy said, "There was within him a deep unexpressed conviction that all would be well, but that one must not trust to this and still less speak about it, but must only attend to one's own work. And he did his work, giving his whole strength to the task." That was me. Deep inside, I believed we would come through this ordeal in the ash OK. I think it was a faith in God based on the idea that surely he wouldn't have brought us this far only to kill us off later, but I never felt competent to express the thought to anyone else even as I had become a better leader of our Bible study. I was some heartened when I read that passage, though, and felt like Leo understood me.

Of course, as quoted earlier, I had read that other giant of Russian literature, "Crime and Punishment" by Dostoevsky and loved it. I always wished for someone to talk Russian literature with (now that I considered myself an expert, having read two whole novels' worth!) but the only other person in our valley who had read either book was Darica and she hated both of them.

We weren't sure when the ash got replaced by snow, but the beginning of December found us covered with the fluffy white stuff. The temperature wasn't as cold as it had been around Thanksgiving, but the clouds rolled in and stayed, dumping more than two feet of snow on the valley in less than twenty-four hours. The sun didn't come out for days and more snow kept falling and, by Christmas— when we did get a break in the clouds and some bright sunshine—it shone on a valley buried in snow.

Movement was at a minimum. We had carved paths to each other's houses and to the community kitchen and the barn, but no one was traveling any more than they had to. On that Christmas day, though, we all made our way to the community kitchen and had our annual present exchange. Adaline had somehow managed to get my name again and mentioned that she couldn't finish the sweater before the century changed and so had made me mittens that didn't match the scarf. They were warm, though, so long as I didn't actually want to do anything with my hands. I thanked her profusely and managed to slip her a little gift even though I hadn't drawn her name.

"What's this for?" she asked before opening it.

"Christmas, you doof," I chided.

"But you drew my grandmother's name."

"Yeah, but you're—I just kept thinking about what you said after—after the, um, incident—"

"Me getting *shot*?" she asked pointedly, then laughed at my embarrassment. She opened the box and found a pair of simple earrings, each with a little pearl set in silver. "Wow," she remarked, barely able to get the word out, it seemed. "They're beautiful!" She looked up at me in confusion, then, and asked, "But what does this have to do with me getting shot?"

I smiled and told her, "Well, I originally was going to look for that giant belly ring you had talked about, but these seemed more practical."

She threw her arms around my neck and said, "They're beautiful, Josh." Then, pulling away, she put them in her ears and asked, looking at me earnestly, "How do they look?"

I couldn't imagine that just simple earrings could make such a difference, but she didn't look fourteen at that moment. She was dressed in a nice, Christmas-colored outfit of a scarlet skirt and a blouse of green that made the green of her eyes look like emeralds. Her blonde hair was pulled back from her face with a bow and her smile looked very mature. I finally managed to reply, "Fantastic. They look fantastic."

"I may never take them off," she told me. Then, "Mind if I go show Alexa?"

"Go right ahead."

She moved through the crowd not like someone walking, but like someone dancing. I hadn't seen much of her since her birthday and she appeared to have all her mobility and stamina back. I smiled as I watched her, then walked over to Claire and asked, "You about ready to become Mrs. Marquez?"

She smiled and told me, "Absolutely."

"Well, then, let's round everyone up."

Oscar and Claire moved into her bedroom after the wedding. For the first couple nights, I slept on a spare bed in Howard and Danica's place to give the newlyweds a honeymoon, but after that I went back to my own house. We had built the new rooms on so that the kitchen/living room (the original cabin) was between my bedroom and Claire's, which I think she had planned ahead of time. It allowed them to have the privacy a young married couple needs—as well as allowing me to not have to hear anything that might go in the privacy of their bedroom.

Knowing what was (probably) going on over there made me—as a man in the last months of being a teenager—anxious to bring a woman home as my wife. (Being a teenage male, I was *sure* more of it was going on over there than probably was.) I was more certain than ever who it would be, but I also thought I needed to wait until at least spring to broach the subject—and had serious doubts I would have the nerve even then. In my heart of hearts, I was thinking that if I really prayed and steeled my will I might, just might, have the nerve to bring up the subject some time before I was thirty.

Chapter Fourteen

Yes, I'm in love, I feel it now
And Caelia has undone me;
And yet I swear I can't tell how
The pleasing plague stole on me.
~William Whitehead

We were a little bit better prepared for that second winter, which was good, because it was a whole lot worse. It was hard to say if it were colder, because our thermometers bottomed out at the same point as the year before, but we had a lot more snow. And when we weren't getting new snow, the wind was blowing the snow off the surrounding mountains and making it look like it was snowing. Our days were spent shoveling—off the paths and off our roofs.

One roof collapsed and we lost Freddy Wilson and his wife in one horrible instant. His oldest daughter, who was about eleven, had managed to crawl out and sound an alarm (screaming). We dug her younger sister and brother out alive, but Freddy and his wife were both dead—whether from the freezing cold or being crushed we never knew for sure. We took some comfort in the fact that the expressions on their faces made us think they had never known what hit them. The kids went to live with the Marquez family, as they had known each other in Como for years.

Thelia Isaacson died a couple weeks later, probably from pneumonia but—again—we couldn't be sure because we couldn't even get to Como to get Doctor Pormon. A couple of us tried when she first started coughing, but we couldn't make it more than a couple hundred yards from town. In one of her last lucid moments, she implored us not to try again, saying she didn't want to die with our deaths on her conscience. We were planning one more go at it, though, when the family got word to us that she had passed away. We all mourned her passing, as she had been not just our wisest voice, but grandma to the whole town. Like the winter before, we had to keep the bodies in a snow bank until such time as we could find thawed ground to bury them in. There's something grisly about knowing your friends are temporarily buried nearby that's much more disconcerting than when they're "just in a regular old cemetery." Like the rest of the clan, Adaline took her grandmother's death pretty hard and wasn't her usual jovial self. She liked being around people, though, and took our games very seriously, saying she was determined to create the perfect Strat-O-Matic line-up, one that couldn't be beat.

We were living on pins and needles you might say because, in such weather, it was not uncommon for half the town to have the sniffles at any given moment. With every sniff, and especially with every cough, we worried that we were coming down with pneumonia. Medical thermometers were deployed almost as often as spoons and I think we all heard about it every time someone's temp jumped up a degree. For myself, I got something like the flu and while I was pretty sure I wasn't going to die from pneumonia, when I was kneeling in the snow and throwing up outside (I couldn't bring myself to kneel in the privy), I was about half afraid I *wouldn't* die. I eventually made it through, thanks to some canned soup and rest, but then Claire and Oscar each took a turn with it. The main thing we found to be thankful for was that no more than one of us had it in the house at a time. A few other people in the community got whatever it was—we called it the flu, whether that were the official medical term or not—and thankfully no one died from it, though a few people had come very close. People said I looked like I was going to be one of them during the worst of it, but I never felt that I was close to death myself. Sure didn't want to repeat it, though!

On the plus side, our town was on the verge of growing. Danica and Howard glass were expecting their first child while Steve and Lyssett Carrier were expecting their second. We all gathered in out of the cold in mid-January—again having to use the ropes to find our way—for the wedding of Jonathan Isaacson and Alexa Marquez. It seemed sudden to all of us—and a surprise to those of us who weren't sure they were even a couple—but we all congratulated them. All of us except Adaline, who came to the wedding but sat with her arms crossed and her brows furrowed until it was time to start. She, I gathered after a brief conversation in which she refused to discuss her demeanor, felt betrayed that Alexa was getting married and hadn't told her it was coming until the day before. Adaline served as maid of honor, and managed to look mostly happy during the ceremony, but I could tell she was still put out by it all. (The suddenness of the nuptials would be made evident to all as Alexa's form began to expand over the next few months.)

In the first week of February, something broke several panes of glass in our greenhouse. Whether it were just the wind or an accumulation of snow (we thought we had been pretty fastidious about keeping it swept), we didn't know. We were pretty sure it wasn't man-caused. But the glass did break and took out several of the beds inside the greenhouse, and allowed snow in on much of the rest. We got things patched up as quickly as we could, but at least twenty percent of our plants were wiped out all at once, and many more might have been damaged but we were going to have to wait and see. Jesse nursed the suspect plants like a mother and, in all, we probably lost about ten percent of our remaining crops (though, without Jesse's ministrations, I think it could have been far worse).

Each day, I tried to make it by the houses of anyone who I hadn't seen otherwise (often running into people at our barn or the greenhouse). I don't know if I were doing it out of my responsibilities as sheriff or just because it was my nature—I liked to think nature, but then I remembered that I had had to convince myself to be thoughtful of other people and wondered if duty were the deciding factor. I would stop in and see if anyone needed anything and often found that what one person needed, someone else had. So I might pick up an extra blanket here and take it to there and receive some dried fruit which I would carry to still a third place. On most days, Julia Croft was teaching the kids in the common kitchen—it was used more for school than as a common kitchen anymore—and the school kids always seemed happy to see me. I still helped with lessons now and then—especially with reading—and Julia was appreciative of the help, but something had changed. I honestly don't know if it were me or her, but if there had been a spark of romance there over the summer, it was gone in the winter. I sometimes thought maybe it was just the summer months combined with her grief and maybe even some sort of post-partum thing that led to our kiss for after that, she was friendly but nothing more. Nor could I tell that she had any interest in any of the other single men of our community. We talked, but not in depth. And, after the shooting, she had become more distant. I gathered it had shocked her on some profound level. It had shocked me, too (and everyone else, I figured), but after that it was as if she saw something in me she didn't like. I don't think I would have liked it, either, if I had thought killing were to be a way of life, but I had come to terms with the fact that what I had done had probably saved my own life and, maybe, other lives as well. Adaline, who above all others had reason to hate me for that day, only seemed appreciative.

At the end of February, it had been more than two months since we had heard from anyone in Como and, on a clear but cold day, a couple of us decided to make the trek. I think it was out of curiosity more than anything. So Tad and I bundled up and, rather than try the horses in the drifted snow, we set out on cross-country skis, with snowshoes strapped to our backs just in case. It was just over two miles from our town to Como, so we figured to make it in short order.

It may have been only two miles, but the distance between our two towns seemed greater once we were there. The last two months had been miserable in Overstreet—what with the piled snow and all—but we suddenly discovered that Como—sitting out on bald prairie as it did, had had it much worse. It wouldn't have always been that way. Before the fires, the town would have at least been protected from the west, but that protection had been taken away. So the west winds that we enjoyed because it kept the ash off of us just served to pound Como mercilessly. And the north winds that we had been afraid would tear our roofs off, *had* torn the roofs off in Como.

We picked up our pace and were quickly snapping off our skis and putting on the snow shoes. Beginning a house to house search that reminded me way too much of the night of the ash cloud, we found the houses where we expected there to be people to be empty. Empty of life, anyway. We found dead and frozen bodies in some of them. In some, the roofs were collapsed and the snow had piled up and we couldn't see any sense in digging through the rubble as the collapse had obviously happened some days—maybe even weeks—before.

Tad and I had come into town by the old Boreas Pass road, so one of the last houses we would have gotten to anyway was a stout, large, log home over on the southwest corner of the town. We weren't even going to look there, having given up on finding good news, then the door came open in the log home and a voice asked, "Is anyone there?"

"Aunt Jenny?" I asked, startled and surprised—for different reasons. We made our way over to her and, as she shaded her eyes against the glare of the snow, I said, "It's me, Josh. And Tad. What happened?"

"Oh praise God!" she said, scrambling to us across the snow, so bundled I could only recognize her by her voice. We rushed to her and she practically fell into our arms, saying, "We're at the end, Josh. I was thinking I'd try to get to you guys if I could, but I didn't know if I had the strength."

"'We'?" I asked, trying not to talk louder in my anxiety. "There are others alive?"

"Seven of us," she replied. "We're all in my house. We're almost out of food, and Ron's leg is broken and—" She broke down crying. Of the words she said after that, most were unintelligible, but I did catch, "I've been praying someone would come, but I didn't think anyone would. Praise God you're here!"

As we helped Aunt Jenny back into the house, I turned to Tad and said, "You're the better skier. Get back to Overstreet and help Claire hitch up the sled. I think if you take the path you and I skied over here, the horses can make it."

"Right," he agreed, then set off for where we had left the skis. He called over his shoulder, "Does this make me a deputy?" but kept going without hearing an answer.

Inside the log home, I found it to be little warmer than outside. I looked around at the seven. There was Aunt Jenny, Ron and Dawn Sukigara, and four children, three girls and a boy, all looking to be under the age of eight. They had a fire going in the fireplace, but I couldn't tell what they were burning. Might have been some of the furniture. All seven people had apparently been living in the room with the fireplace and, while they looked up at our entrance, no one moved much. I had some homemade protein bars in my backpack, which I broke into pieces and doled out, followed by water from my canteen. They thanked me weakly and ate hungrily.

"Can anyone here besides Aunt Jenny walk under your own power?" I asked.

"I think everyone can, if we have to, except Ron," Aunt Jenny told me.

"Well, do you have any blankets that aren't already in use?"

"No. We're all wrapped up in them," she told me.

"OK, then. Let's just wait until they're back with the sled and then we'll take you to Overstreet." Then, I said, "Let me go see if I can find you some firewood." I went out and didn't have to look far. There was some buried under a drift next to what used to be Wally Preston's house. I dug out some dry pieces and brought them back. Soon, we had a roaring blaze in the fireplace and everyone's spirits started to lift. "Tell me what happened, Aunt Jenny."

She held her bare hands out toward the fire dreamily, then answered, "Storm hit just before Christmas, then it didn't let up. High winds were knocking roofs off, flattening some places. We had ropes going from house to house like you guys, but we still lost some people in the snow. No one knew it until someone tripped over them. Then, when the winds were at their worst, we all just hunkered down in our own houses, afraid to go out. Gradually, those that were alive made their way here, 'cause we could see that the walls were thick and the pitch of the roof steep. Wally, he set out to go see if he could get help from you guys—must have been a month ago. I'm going to guess he didn't make it."

"Never saw him," I told her ruefully. "Where'd the—how'd the children get here?"

"Ron brought them in. Three of them are sisters and brother—the three dark-haired ones. He said—he said they were in a bad way when he found them," this was said as if there were more to the story, which I guessed to mean she didn't want to discuss it in front of the children. She pointed at the fourth child, a little girl with bright red hair who looked to be about five and was staring intently into the flames, and said, "She just wandered in here on her own. I think she belonged to a family named Carter, but she hasn't said a word in the month she's been here. She's polite, she even helps with the others or with getting food ready—when we had some—but she's never said a word."

"Wow," was all I could think to say in response.

Ron waved me over then and said, in a low voice, "Do you even have a place you can put us up if you take us back to Overstreet?"

"We'll find a place."

Dawn Sukigara, who I had probably only heard speak ten words in the entire time I had known her, said, "Ron and I would like the children with us."

I wasn't sure how they could handle them, as weak as they (the adults) looked, but I saw no point in arguing at that time and said, "Sure. You probably know them best, anyway." I dug around in my pack, thinking there was one more protein bar in there and was happy to find it. It was a little smushed, but still edible. The adults told me to just divide it four ways, which I did and gave one section to each of the children.

I made small talk with everyone and got verbal responses from everyone but the little red-head. She looked at me when I spoke to her, and I thought I saw recognition in her eyes, but she didn't say a word or make a sound. I had seen a pad of paper and a pen, so I grabbed them and came over to the little red-haired girl and asked, "Can you write your name?"

She didn't nod, but took the paper and pen and very laboriously spelled out, "Natasia," ever dotting the eye with a little heart. I said her name and she actually smiled, just barely, and only for a second.

"Why didn't we think of that?" Aunt Jenny mumbled, to get shrugs from the Sukigaras.

"Can you write other things?" I asked in as nice a voice as I could muster. She shook her head and handed me the pad and pen. "That's all right, Natasia. We've got a school in our town, and a really good teacher, so I bet you can be writing all kinds of things in no time." Her response was to start looking at the flames again.

Eventually, we heard the sounds of someone crossing the snow outside. I went to the window and saw Claire pulling up with the sleigh, Oscar beside her, and two men and a woman in back. Tad and Jonathan were on snow skis and had traveled alongside.

In short order, we had all seven people in the back of the sleigh (wheels locked down on a wagon and runners attached) and the three adults who had come from Overstreet were strapping on skis, prepared to ski alongside on the way back. Natasia seemed to panic at the idea that I wouldn't be riding along, so I agreed to ride in the back with her. She snuggled up next to me and gave me something like a smile but still didn't say a word. We told the story of how this had come to be as we rode back to Overstreet and the "patients" seemed to relish getting out of Como. All of them except Natasia told bits of the story and thanked us for rescuing them. We were referred to as the "hand of God" more than once and several prayers of thanks were said on our behalf.

Overstreet didn't have any empty houses, so we set them up in the common kitchen to start with. The Isaacsons offered to let Aunt Jenny stay with them, but the Sukigaras wanted the children with them, so the kitchen was really the only logical spot. We fashioned temporary bedding for them the first night, then went and got beds from Como for them with the sleigh the next day. That two-day window of sunshine was all we got, for it started snowing again the day after that.

Even during the worst of the storms, we had continued to have school. We weren't sure what to do now that someone was living in the school house, but the Sukigaras encouraged us to both keep going and "enroll" the new kids. Truth be told, I think they thought—and I agreed—that the best thing for the kids was something that approached normalcy. So we fed them and schooled them and tried to let them know we cared for them when, inside, I was pretty sure they were all torn up. The new kids acted out at times, but Ron and Dawn were usually able to help them calm down. And, from what I saw, Julia Croft had excellent classroom management skills. The older students, which now included Adaline and the married Alexa, were tasked with helping all the younger students and things went along pretty well, all things considered. I liked being sheriff, but I praised God in every prayer I thought that I wasn't asked to be the teacher.

I stopped by the school at least once each day, to see if they needed anything, and was always greeted warmly—especially by Natasia, who would jump up from her seat and run over to give me a hug. She still had not said a word, but as February turned into March Julia assured me that Natasia was a very bright student. We had no idea how old she was, but Julia guessed her to be close to eight (showing that I was lousy at guessing ages). She could do math and she could write better than we initially thought, but she refused to write anything about herself or tell us her age. Eventually, we stopped asking.

March was as miserable a month as February had been, weather wise. More than one person was heard to remark that— back in the days before the ash cloud—the ski areas would have loved a winter like that one. Heavy snows deep into March, no sun to melt the base, still snowing when April started. For those of us trying to carve out an existence in frontier conditions like that, it had no charm at all. We were managing to stay alive, but it seemed like a constant battle against death. Icy conditions led to two more broken legs, some other broken bones, and just about everyone had to deal with at least one sprain. We also lost one horse, but I almost considered that a blessing for I was surprised we had any that survived. They needed exercise, and we gave them what we could in the barn and out in the stable yard on non-windy days, but they were getting as antsy as any of us.

To keep our sanity, we continued our schedule of Sunday morning church, followed by a meal together in what was a very crowded common building anymore. We also kept up the games, with several of us involved in a Strat-O-Matic tournament Jesse had put together, though these games had to be "floated" among the various houses just to have a place to play them. Anyone who didn't like Strat could usually find a card game or some other board game going on of an evening. We also had the occasional story-telling session or poetry reading (though no one did it as well as Thelia) and Adaline and Alexa continued to write and perform comedic skits—many of which now made reference to marriage. Another way we occupied our time was in planning how we could expand the common building, a pursuit that gained impetus with every day we were stuck in there.

The valley finally started to warm up in April, and then things went almost overnight from ice-covered to mud-covered. It was messy and made things—any things—hard to accomplish, but we were so excited to be outside that we didn't care. Mud slid off the mountains in great, ash covered mounds, but at least for a while we were excited to be shoveling it rather than snow. Even once we started grumbling about it, all it usually took to shut us up was someone mentioning the snowy winter before.

Under Ron's leadership (he was fully healed by then), we fired up the old bulldozer for the last time (we never got it started again) and dug one large grave at the Como cemetery and buried all of the bodies we could find. Wally Preston, it was discovered, had only made it about two hundred yards from town. He appeared to have suffered a broken leg, which we guessed led to his death in the snow. We put up a marker with all the names we knew, though it didn't account for all the bodies in the grave. We had to fill the grave back in with shovels.

On May 4th, the town threw me a big party for my twentieth birthday. I think their need to celebrate the end of winter was as much a factor in the celebration as my having been born. I didn't mind sharing the festivities one bit and even helped with the organizing of it for it had turned into a dance, a feast, a ball game and whatever else people could think of to do. If we had had fireworks, I think those would have been shot off, too.

I got a bunch of presents, got to blow out a candle (we weren't going to waste 20!) on a cake, and play second base in the baseball game. Dawn Sukigara, it turned out, could throw fastpitch and after the "official game" some of us hung around just seeing if we could hit her at all. Ron could, and I fouled off a couple, but mostly we all just looked foolish against her. Adaline even took a turn and proved that her hitting of the previous summer had not been a fluke. And now that she was six inches taller and had developed some coordination (when hitting, still none when fielding) she actually sent a couple of Dawn's pitches flying.

After the ball game, there was a dance, with Hutch and Nikki leading a "band" of kids they had put together and been instructing. I was more than prepared to wait on dancing, but Adaline jumped before me and said, "I owe you a first dance!" She was dressed in a western skirt and matching blouse, with her hair pulled back as it had been on her birthday, except that she looked more than six months older to me. But then, I think everyone who made it through that winter looked more than six months older than they had before.

Adaline was a weird contradiction at that point in time—and maybe had been for a while. One moment she could look very grown-up, and the next she looked like that skinny fourteen-year-old she was in my mind. Personality-wise, she could giggle like an adolescent girl at the most inopportune time, then follow that up immediately with a very wise observation about something. Just when I was thinking she had grown up, she would get upset at the least little thing and run off crying. (Thankfully, she didn't do *that* at the dance, but I had known it to happen before.) That evening, she was mostly on the grown-up end of her spectrum, in both looks and behavior, but she still got the giggles at least once, which I found endearing rather than annoying (though I think she was embarrassed by it when she saw that I had noticed). And she was still quick-witted, leading some people to be a little tentative to speak to her for fear the conversation would show up in one of her skits.

I danced with every woman there, I think, including even Natasia. She still had not said a word, but she smiled when I asked her to dance and tried hard not to step on my feet the whole time. I think I may have stepped on hers once, but she laughed it off. Yes, she made that sound, but no other.

I even danced with Julia Croft. It was awkward and strained and I'm not sure either of us knew why it had to be that way. When the song ended, I was letting go of her hand when she held on to mine and said, "He's out there."

"What? Who?" I looked around, thinking she was talking to me in my capacity as sheriff.

"Dwight. He's still alive. I just know he is. I may never see him again in this life, but—but I will wait for him."

"I understand," I told her. "And, um, thanks for telling me."

"I know it's been awkward between us for a long time, and I know I'm at least partially responsible for that. Maybe mostly. I value your friendship but, well, I love Dwight and—"

"You don't have to explain," I told her, as she appeared to falter for words. "I'm very thankful to be your friend." She hugged me, and then she let go and went to take Junior off someone's hands.

I made my way over to the refreshments and got a cup of cool water. I was standing there, watching the dance and the on-going party, when Lester Marquez sidled up next to me and asked in an exasperated voice, "You ever get the feeling we're just fighting a holding action? And losing?"

"Come again?" I asked, not having really paid attention to the beginning of his question.

He didn't repeat it, just continued, "As far as we know, there's less than fifty people left in the whole world, and every winter we lose more. I don't know how long Howard can keep those solar panels working—even if he is teaching Tad how to be an electrician. Sometimes, I think the lucky ones are the people who died right away, like your parents."

I looked at him in surprise, trying to figure out if I smelled alcohol on him. I didn't, but I wouldn't have been surprised, for this didn't sound like him. "Why do we even bother to go on?" he asked. "You tell me it looked like Doc Pormon and his wife did themselves in after they lost their daughter. Maybe they had it right. Maybe we ought to just end it all now, before it can get worse."

As sheriff, I was wondering if I should take steps, but as his friend I said, "Look over there, Lester. Watch Oscar and Claire dance together. And look at Jonathan and Alexa over at that table. Your kids see a future. It's not the future you had planned, but it's the one they've got. And they're making plans for houses of their own and kids and everything. None of us knows what future we've got, but they're planning for a good one."

"Waste of time," he grumbled, then walked away. I made a mental note to keep an eye on him. I figured he was just in a funk, but I had a fear of him harming himself or someone else.

I made my way over to Oscar and, pulling him aside, said, "I'm worried about your Dad."

"Me, too. I'm thinking the winter was just too long, but he doesn't seem to be coming out of it." He looked over to where his dad was sitting and talking to Jesse about something, then added, "Claire and me, we pray for him every night."

"Best thing we can do," I told him. "I'll keep my eye on him, but you let me know if there's any way I can help."

"Thanks, Brother," Oscar said to me. Claire had long addressed me that way, but it had taken me by surprise when Oscar had started doing it. I was mostly used to it by then, though.

I danced with Claire after that, then just watched for a while and marveled that the Hutchisons still had fingers after all the picking and strumming they had done. Finally, it began to wind down, so I made my way over to where Adaline was watching over Bobby and Junior and asked, bowing formally, "May I have this last dance?"

She hesitated, which surprised me, then asked someone else to watch over the kids and stood up. Extending her hand and putting it in mine, she went with me onto the dance floor. It was a moderately slow dance, which was good because I was the slowest dancer out there—and not in a good way. We didn't speak, just danced, and when it was over I kissed her hand and walked her over to her family. "Evan," I said to her father, "Would you like to patrol the grounds with me?"

"What? Um, sure," he replied. "Addy, could you see that Bobby gets to bed soon?"

"Sure, Pop," she replied, though looking at me strangely.

Once we were out beyond the reaches of the crowd, noisy now as they disassembled the party, I said, "Evan, sir, feel free to pop me one for even asking this, but how old will Adaline have to be before you allow her to be courted?"

He stopped dead in his tracks, looked at me for a moment— a piercing, head-to-foot gaze—then started walking again.

Eventually, when we were almost to the gardens, he said, "I had this dream ever since she was born of her going off to college. She was going to be a nurse or a surgeon or a top-flight business-woman. Now, I don't know if any colleges still exist in the world and there seems to be a better than average chance that none of us will ever leave this valley alive. That might mean next winter, or we might live out a long life right here.

"My brother and I owned a medical records business in Phoenix. Storage, destruction when ordered, that kind of thing. We were doing pretty well. Decided to take the family on a vacation to Colorado. We were looking around for where to go and stumbled onto Breckenridge. I think I might have heard of it during some sporting event on TV. So we pack up both families and our mother and we come to the mountains." He stopped talking for a moment but continued after a bit, "I lost my brother and his wife in the ash cloud, I've lost his daughter and our mother since then. You might say I only have any family left at all because of you, Josh."

He stopped again and, looking off toward the east, where we knew the mountains to be, he said, "I never read my Bible much before we came here. When the ash cloud hit, I kind of figured God had abandoned us. I started coming to your church service, and bringing my family, more for the community than anything. Kind of think there's something to it all now. Sure hope there is, anyway. Started reading that Bible you gave to my family and a couple weeks ago I read this verse in Psalms that said ... wait, it'll come to me. I've never memorized any Scripture, but this one goes, 'Many are the plans in a man's heart, but it is the Lord's purpose that prevails.' Some people might find that depressing, that we're not in charge, but I find it strangely comforting."

He started walking again, so I followed after him. We walked around the gardens, visible more from starlight than from the waxing moon, and he started talking about the garden and then asked some questions about my parents and my growing up. It was wide-ranging and off-topic as far as I could tell, which I figured was his polite way of trying to get me to dismiss the topic entirely. Eventually, we started making our way back across the meadow to our town and still he talked, about everything and nothing. Finally, we arrived at his cabin and he said, "I'm going in for the night. Good night, Josh."

"Uh, good night, Evan," I replied, not just a little disappointed.

He opened the door to his cabin then, as I started to walk away, he said, "Josh?"

"Yes sir?"

"Fifteen." And then he shut the door.

I stood there in stunned silence for a bit, then walked off happily toward the barn.

Chapter Fifteen

Let all thy joys be as the month of May,
And all thy days be as a marriage day:
Let sorrow, sickness, and a troubled mind
Be stranger to thee.
~Francis Quarles

The town charter was finished and submitted for perusal to the town. Only those eighteen and older would be allowed to vote on it, but Julia even had the school kids read over it and make suggestions and ask questions. I don't know that any of their suggestions were taken seriously, though we all did try to figure out a way to make the "free candy" provision come true. By volume, about 99% of what Hutch and Danica submitted was accepted, with just a couple little changes being made as regarded wording here and there. We decided we would vote on the charter on July 4th, just because it seemed like a July 4th kind of thing to do. After deciding that, it so slipped out of our minds that we almost forgot where we had put it when the 4th rolled around.

We expanded the gardens that spring, and did the same for the greenhouse. Over the summer, we built a house for the Sukigaras, and most everyone expanded their house and many people began putting in not just a vegetable garden near the house, but also a few flower gardens. Columbines that came up—whether voluntary or encouraged—were treated like royalty. Many of the cattle had died over the winter, but some had been saved by being in the relatively protected pastureland at the foot of Mt. Volsh, near Steve and Lysette Carrier's old house. So we set about trying to build snow fences down there and other natural breaks within which they might hide. Cattle are not smart animals, so we rather hoped we could train them a bit during the good weather, so that they might find the shelter when the bad weather came.

Lester Marquez seemed to come out of his funk once the days were more sunny and the weather warmer and even got out on the occasional evening and played baseball with us. He didn't have much range anymore, but if the ball came near him he knew how to work a glove. Adaline was almost learning how to catch and—at least as far as average—was the second best hitter out there. Ron Sukigara was easily the best hitter, so it became an unwritten rule that he and his wife were not allowed on the same team.

Ron revealed to me that he and Dawn had tried for years to have a child, had seen many doctors, but had never been able to conceive even though those doctors said there was nothing "wrong" with either of them. We didn't have much in the way of legal proceedings, but when the Sukigaras petitioned the town council for permission to adopt the four children they had been taking care of, it was gladly granted. We made it official on the fourth of July—along with the vote, which passed unanimously—and threw them a big party, deciding we had no idea whether the United States still existed or not. We said a prayer for the country, but put most of the focus on the Sukigara family. Even Natasia seemed excited about the day, though she still didn't say anything.

I asked Ron if it were something to be concerned about, but he just smiled, patted me on the back and said, "Dawn and I were convinced that God was withholding kids from us, but then he gave us four. And I think those kids saved our lives as much as we saved theirs. I have to think Natasia will get her voice at just the right time, just like we got our kids at just the right time." I knew it hadn't all been peaches and cream for them—the kids had lost their birth parents, after all—so I was encouraged just to hear him speak so positively.

When we had a dance that evening, I had my first dance with Adaline as well as my last dance (though I danced with other people in between). At church, I often sat near Adaline and she was known to come over to our house—always when Claire and Oscar were there, a very definite rule set by Evan and agreed to by all—and play games or just sit and talk. She and Claire formed a trio with Danica and they often performed at church or other gatherings. And she still loved doing the skits with Alexa and taking care of her younger brother … most of the time.

We had a good harvest that fall and were able to lay back a goodly supply of food. We had learned much about drying foods and canning and still encouraged everyone to grow and dry and can as much for their own families as they could and only put the excess in the community store. Much barter and trade went on, for services and goods. Jesse Marquez won the World Series of Strat, knocking off Tad Isaacson. Adaline played the whole season and did well, but her perfect team and incredible strategy turned out to be anything but. Fiona Glass was born in July, and Daniel Isaacson was born a couple months later to Jonathan and Alexa, so of course everyone had them betrothed by Thanksgiving.

Thanksgiving Day was cool and sunny, but the wind played havoc with our football game. We still played it, though, and discovered that Adaline had spent the week before the game having her brother throw her pass after pass. No one knew about it, so no one bothered to cover her and she caught her first pass in three years of playing. We were all so shocked she practically walked in for an easy touchdown. She was on my team, so I took the opportunity to give her a hug, even if I were a day early. We had a harvest dance that night and everyone went to bed tired but happy. I was, anyway. I had made it a point to dance with every female there, even though I only wanted to dance with one of them. OK, maybe two, as it was traditional for me to have at least one dance with my sister at these things.

I had just gotten my shoes off when there came a knock on my door. "Come in," I instructed, surprised and curious. Claire and Oscar came in, holding hands and looking sheepish but excited. "What's this about?"

They looked at each other, then Claire turned sideways and said, "I don't know if you've noticed, but, um, we're going to have a baby."

I leapt to my feet and drew her into a hug, then shook Oscar's hand. "How far along are you?" I asked.

"About three months, I think," she replied, smoothing down her shirt. If she was showing at all, I couldn't see it. "You're happy for us, right?" she asked nervously.

"Of course I am, Little Sis! You two are going to be such great parents, I just know it."

"With that in mind," Claire mentioned, nervous again, "Would you mind if, next spring, Oscar and I built a house of our own?"

"You're always welcome here—"

"We know," Oscar said, the first thing he had said since they came in, "But we, well—"

"You want a place of your own. A place to be your own family. I understand." I laughed and added, "But don't build it too far away. Someday, I want my kids playing with your kids in the same yard."

"I know you'll find someone, Josh," Claire said earnestly, like someone who doesn't quite believe what they say.

"I know," I replied, trying to sound wistful. The truth was, I had found someone. I just hadn't told anyone, yet. Well, other than Evan.

Although, after Claire and Oscar repaired to their side of the house, I lay there in bed having second thoughts. Not about my choice, but wondering if she would go along with it. I thought she would, but I kept telling myself I didn't know much about women. Almost nothing, when you came to it. Finally, after probably two hours of tossing and turning, I fell asleep.

I was awake before the dawn and raring to go. So I slipped out and went over to the horse barn. Had them taken care of in short order and then was knocking softly on the Isaacson door a little after seven. Evan answered the door looking sleepy, but I guessed it was feigned as he was already fully dressed. "Good grief, Josh, she wasn't actually born until almost noon."

"I can come back," I told him quickly.

"Who is it, Pop?" Adaline asked from the sink, where she was doing dishes.

"Somebody to see you, I think," he said in a befuddled voice, though he gave me a wink. "Take it outside so you don't wake up the whole house."

Adaline was dressed for the day, though she didn't have shoes on. She put one on while hopping outside, then put her hand on my shoulder for balance as she put on the other. She had reached her full height of five-ten by then (where she would stop, thankfully) and so was almost at eye level with my six foot. She was definitely on the thin side, but over the past year I had started to notice some curves developing where they hadn't existed before. "What are you doing out so early?" she asked casually, still adjusting her shoe.

"Um, taking care of the horses. Why are you up and dressed so early?"

"Oh, I never could sleep in on my birthday." She added with an embarrassed chuckle, "Haven't grown out of it, I guess. Seriously, what brings you over here so early, Sheriff?"

"Um, well, Happy Birthday, first."

"Thank you," she replied, somewhat quizzically.

She had both feet on the ground but her arm still on my shoulder. I couldn't tell you whether it was one of those moments where she looked older or younger. I probably couldn't have told anyone my own name at that moment. I finally took a deep breath, steeled my will, then said, "Adaline, I talked to your father ... half a year ago. Wow, has it been that long? Seems like forever. Anyway, I, um, I asked him how old you would have to be before he would give me permission to court you and—" Her eyes were as wide as quarters and I thought she was going to pass out. I put an arm around her, telling myself it was to steady her, and finally managed to finish, "Now I have come to ask you for your permission to court you."

She had that "deer in the headlights" look on her face for quite a while before asking, "You're serious?"

"Yes. If you would like to think about it—"

"No!" she said forcefully.

"No?" I asked, unbelievably disappointed. Crushed. Ash-cloud disaster level. My countenance sunk.

She reached up a hand and lifted my chin so I was looking her in the eye and said, in the most grown-up voice I had ever heard from her, "No, I do not need to *think* about it. The answer is yes." Then she smiled and, in what I would ever after think of as her "Addy-lescent voice" practically giggled, "This is officially my best birthday ever!" and kissed me on the cheek.

We had had a couple snows in early November, of the kind that come down fiercely then melt off in a hurry. Thanksgiving and Adaline's birthday were pretty clear (if windy) days, but then right after that it started snowing in earnest. It was hard to tell when December started because the snow that came down in late November just didn't stop and there was a period of time in there of maybe forty-eight hours when it was hard to tell whether it were day or night. We got a break in early December of a couple days of sunshine, but the temperature was so cold the snow didn't melt off at all. By Christmas, it would have been a winter wonderland if you were there on a ski vacation but it was just an ice box for those of us living through it.

We were the best prepared we had been, though, with sturdier houses and better insulation and established plans for how to deal with the snow. We got out every day and brushed the snow off our roofs and solar panels and made sure the snow stayed off the greenhouse roof. We shoveled paths between the buildings and even walked the horses along the paths (which, yes, required more shoveling, but of a different kind) and managed to eke out a living during a winter that was every bit as bad as the previous one weather-wise. It was much better, however, in that we didn't lose any people, horses or cattle this time.

I, of course, thought it was the best winter of my life because—for the first time since I "went with" Erin Swinford for two days in seventh grade—I had a girlfriend. We were completely chaste, with the strongest physical contact enjoyed being hand-holding and the occasional hug. I don't know if she had any reticence besides propriety, but I was still cognizant that she was a fifteen year old girl while I was a twenty year old man. I told myself that it wouldn't matter when we were both in our nineties, but at that moment in time physical restraint seemed like the better part of valor.

I longed for the opportunity to take her on an old-fashioned date to a movie house or a play or out to dinner, but we had to relegate ourselves to eating at my house or hers (or sitting next to each other for Sunday meal after church), and no movies. There were plenty of plays, but she wrote and starred in them, so it's hard to say that was a typical date. She occasionally talked me in to being in one of her plays, but often in a very small role because it was discovered that I didn't act as well as she caught baseballs.

Like the winter before, the weather just seemed to drag on and on. Maybe part of it was because I was looking forward to the day when I could take Adaline on a picnic to somewhere other than the horse barn, but it just seemed like the winter would never end. In late February, we had such a long stretch of gray skies that most of our solar-powered batteries ran dry. We read by the lights of candles and fireplaces and kept the old-fashioned clocks in town wound (there were two of them).

Finally, in late March, the weather began to break. We got a couple more snows in April, but they were like the November snows and didn't last long. By my birthday, we were back to shoveling mud but happy to discover that, at least in our little valley, it was mostly mud (no longer consisting principally of ash).

My birthday again became a chance for the town to celebrate more than my birthday, which I didn't mind. We organized games for the kids and kicked off what we called our "outdoor baseball season" and had the requisite dance. Some of the kids Hutch and Nikki had been teaching all winter were getting quite good and we were talking about making a trip into Frisco because there used to be a musical instrument store there. The real reason we were thinking about it was just because we were feeling a little land-locked in our valley, but the music store gave us an excuse to plan. I had actually helped Hutch carve some wind instruments—I mostly just did the rough work while he did the fine, finishing work—but they were only passable at best.

Of course, my first dance was reserved for Adaline, which surprised no one. During my second dance, which was with Julia Croft, she happened to mention, "I think you have made a wonderful choice, Josh."

"About what?" I asked, thinking she was making a joke about me choosing to dance with her.

"Adaline. She is a wonderful young woman."

I'm sure I blushed (for what reason I don't know) as I said, "I sure think so."

"I'm very happy for you," she told me as the dance ended. She added just before letting go of my hand, "Someday, my husband and I will invite you and your wife over for supper. I just know it."

I decided not to wait for the last dance to drag Adaline across the floor again and went and tapped her dad on the shoulder so I could cut in. He handed his daughter off to me and we began to slowly move across the (dirt) floor with steps that roughly approximated a slow dance. "Happy birthday," she whispered to me, for the umpteenth time that day.

"Thank you." Ignoring the music—which didn't necessarily make my dancing worse—I whispered to her, "Adaline, I am twenty-one today. I don't know how much ages ever meant, but they seem to mean even less now. What I'm trying to say, is, well," I had her full attention, yet with full attention she still managed to put her feet in the right places. I swallowed hard, then said, "In six months, you will turn sixteen. In our old world, you might be thinking about prom or a having a quinceañera—"

"A what?" she asked, though I got the impression she would rather not have interrupted me.

"A party some families throw when their daughters turn sixteen—or maybe fifteen. Anyway, things aren't like they used to be. And pardon me if it seems crass that I kind of like the way things are now. It's not perfect in our little town, and I miss some of the old things and having an outside world and—" I took a deep breath, paused in the dancing for a moment, then looked back into her green eyes and said, "I'm saying all this to avoid saying what I want to say. What I want to say is: Adaline Isaacson, will you marry me?"

She grabbed me in a hug and buried her face against my shoulder and I thought maybe she was having a heart attack. If the other dancers or on-lookers wondered what was going on, they had the manners or temerity not to say anything. She finally whispered to me, "What does me turning sixteen have to do with that?"

"I, um, I'm not sure. I just thought your father probably wouldn't let you *get* married before you were sixteen."

"On the frontier, girls got married as early as twelve," she told me, starting us slow dancing again. "Juliet was thirteen, I think."

"And we all know how well that one worked out," I chuckled.

She looked me in the face, for the first time in a while, with a stern countenance, then joined me in the laugh. Still chuckling, she whispered, "If there were another town in the world, we could sneak off and elope."

"Not while you're fifteen, not in Colorado," I pointed out.

"Oh yeah."

"And besides, I still don't know what your answer is."

"You've got to be kidding me," she replied. She suddenly stopped the dance, took a step back from me, signaled for Hutch to stop the music, then said in the voice she usually reserved for her skits, "Sheriff Joshua Caleb Overstreet, yes I will marry you." She seemed to enjoy watching me blush and chided, "You weren't planning on keeping this private, were you?"

"Well, I had kind of thought I would tell Claire before I told everyone else," I replied. Then, I got down on one knee before her and, still holding her hand, said, "I suppose I should make this official and traditional. Adaline Renee Isaacson, will you marry me?"

"Yes, Sheriff, I will," she replied. I rose to my feet and pulled her into a hug and the crowd cheered. We shared our first kiss at that moment and I wished it could have gone on forever. Eventually, we had to breathe and broke it off, to be immediately surrounded by our family and friends congratulating us and wishing us well.

When I could break free of the crowd, I made my way over to where Evan and Inez were standing by the refreshments. Inez hugged me and Evan shook my hand. Before I let go of his hand, I said, "Sir, I want to ask your permission to take your daughter's hand in marriage."

"Well, considering I know my daughter and am pretty confident she has made up her mind so that what I think has little bearing on reality," he replied with a chuckle, "I gladly give my blessing."

"And you, Mrs. Isaacson?"

"Call me Mom," she replied, drawing me into another hug.

Adaline came bounding over there, looking younger than her fifteen years in that moment, and excitedly took my hand. "What do you think, Mom and Pop? Going to let us go through with it?"

"And if we say no?" her father asked in a stern voice.

"I'll just go see the sheriff and the town council and apply for emancipation," she replied in a voice much like his. Then the three of them laughed and her parents pulled her into a hug.

From that moment I went, Adaline in tow, to find my sister. She was in The Kitchen, along with Oscar, fixing up a plate of sandwiches, and smiled when she saw us come in. I suddenly realized I didn't know if she had been out there when the big event happened. When she just looked at us in a sort of puzzled way, I asked, "Um, were you out there just now?"

"I heard some sort of fuss. What happened?" Claire replied innocently.

I'm sure I blushed as I shuffled my feet, but finally I got up the nerve to say, "I had meant to talk to you earlier, but, um, Claire … how would you feel about Adaline being your sister?"

"We're going to adopt her?" Claire asked with a straight face.

I scowled in frustration, then corrected, "I want to marry her."

Claire suddenly burst out with a laugh, then told us, "We were out there when you asked her. I cheered with everyone else, Josh."

"Really?" Adaline asked, her voice sounding young again.

Claire smirked playfully as she asked Adaline, "You don't think everyone noticed that you've had your cap set for him for some time?" As Adaline blushed, Claire turned to me and said,

"The only mystery has been how long it would take you to realize that she was the perfect one for you. Didn't I say so, Honey?"

"Many times," Oscar injected, smiling widely.

"Really?" I took my turn to ask.

Then Claire pulled me into a hug, though her expanding middle got somewhat in the way, and said, "I am so happy for you—for both of you." Then she hugged Adaline and said, "Now, when you two have a little girl someday, you'll name her after me, right?"

"Yeah, sure," Adaline replied. "How do you spell that, again?"

***

We accomplished a lot that summer. We expanded almost every house and built a shop we could all work in, complete with a kiln in which we could bake pottery. We made a few trips into Breckenridge and collected such things as glass, clothing, electrical wiring and anything else we thought we could need one day. We even pulled several solar panels off various buildings there. And in all our trips over there, we never saw another person.

We did see some more wildlife make its way into our valley: elk, deer, marmots and porcupines were all spotted. A couple people thought they saw a brown bear, but no one ever got close enough to make sure. Birds were spotted now and then, though not in the numbers we had once known them. And every time someone spotted a bird, it just made us wish all the more for chicken. None of us had had a chicken or an egg in three years by that point—though we had had some tinned chicken from Breckenridge but it wasn't the same.

The highlight of June was the birth of James Joshua Marquez. He came into the world healthy and shouting and had two of the most doting parents I had ever seen. He was a cute little kid, I had to admit, even though I had rarely noticed kids before that. Claire mentioned once how much she wished our mother could be there to hold him, and a tear came to her eye, but it was just for a moment and then she was back to enjoying her infant son. He was born on a thundering, raining night, the water coming down like sheets. Between the atmospheric conditions, a summer cold being suffered by our town's most experienced midwife Lysette, and little J.J.'s determination to get into the world quickly, it fell to a household visitor to deliver the little guy: Adaline. I boiled water and did everything I could to be helpful without going anywhere near the birth, but both parents assured me afterward that Adaline had been an excellent midwife.

I tried to be a loving uncle, but as far as I could tell, little babies like that didn't do much. Just ate (which I didn't want to see, since he was eating at my sister's buffet) and expelled, which I didn't want anything to do with, either.

The Blue River was flowing that summer, with water coming off the mountains around Breckenridge, so some of us traveled along its banks and made our way to where Lake Dillon and the towns of Frisco and Dillon used to stand. The lake had filled up, but the water was gray, like the mountains that surrounded it. Here and there we could see green plants growing up through the ash, and even some places where grass had spread, but the two once great towns were devoid of people.

Wearing bandanas to keep the dust out of our mouths (though it wasn't as bad as the trip to Fairplay years before, it was still unpleasant) our little group of six—myself, Tad and Evan Levinson, Ron Sukigara, Aunt Jenny (a remarkably good horsewoman and, as had been proved, tougher than any three other people) and Adaline—made our way to the Interstate. For over two hundred years, it had carried people across Colorado at high speed. I remembered reading a diary of one of the early automobile travelers in the Rockies, how they had to stop at Colorado Springs and get their carburetor adjusted before they could go into the higher elevations, and how they had to have it reset when they were returned to the flat lands. Other travelers had written about the hills their cars could make, but only slowly. Then the Interstate had cut from east to west through the Rockies, leveling the pathway enough that even second-rate autos could travel the span at seventy miles an hour.

There it sat, a gray ribbon running through gray-covered mountains. Here and there an automobile-shaped lump could be seen. I wondered if there were anyone in those cars? Or had they maybe sought shelter in one of the nearby buildings, where their bones now rested, awaiting the end of the world? I noticed then that the ash on the Interstate was undisturbed. I guessed no one had been down the highway since the ash cloud had come through.

Standing on a bluff, overlooking the Interstate and the town of Frisco, I felt Adaline's hand slip into mind. I turned and looked at her, only her green eyes visible for she wore a bandana over her face and another over her hair. Such beautiful eyes, though! I said to her what I was thinking, "Some people lived, I bet, but for how long?"

She looked out at the landscape and said, "My aunt Penny died the night of the ash cloud. My uncle, dad's brother, died a couple weeks later. Apparently, he had always had asthma and the ash in the air was just too much. The rest of us, we survived to make it to Overstreet and still we lost Samantha."

Trying to change the subject, at least a little, I asked, "You ever see Frisco before?"

"Maybe." She laughed lightly and, squeezing my hand, said, "I was twelve. I resented being stuck in the car that long with my brothers. I complained about everything. My parents would 'ooh' and 'ahh' about some scenic view and I would just bury my nose further in my book. I was *not* good company."

"I'm glad you grew out of that," I told her, "Because now I think you're great company."

"You know that line about, 'I wouldn't marry you if you were the last girl on earth'? I *am* the last girl on earth. You wouldn't have noticed me if there were competition."

I looked at her and asked, "You don't actually believe that, do you?"

"No. I just feel very blessed to have met you—and that you did notice me." She leaned her head on my shoulder, looking out over the valley, and asked, "So, what were you going to say about this view?"

"We used to come over here and shop some. My Mom liked to shop, but didn't like driving into Denver or the Springs. So we would come over here. Lots of shops, places to eat, and the lake over there would have all these sailboats on it. Cars zipping through here on the Interstate at a hundred miles an hour. Downtown one year, maybe it was Frisco's bicentennial or something, they had all these big posters around of the town's history. Pics from the mining days always caught my attention. Men living in sorry little shacks, muddy streets, all so they could pull gold out of the ground for someone else. Still, I always wished I could travel back in time, just for a few minutes, to see the town when it was like that. Now I kind of get to—except without the hustle and bustle."

"It is weird being the last people on earth," she commented. "I know, I know: we don't know that we are. But for all intents and purposes, we are." Suddenly, she was saying in a louder voice, "Can we just get married now? I don't want to spend another night with that woman that snores like a freight train!"

I wondered where the vehemence had come from, then realized Aunt Jenny had walked up beside us. Hearing what had been said, she retorted, "Me? You realize the only reason he's still going along with this marriage thing is because your bedroom is on the far side of town. He's never heard you sawing logs like a lumber mill in high season."

Aunt Jenny was probably in her mid-fifties, though like Howard Glass, her hair had been iron gray for so long that I think we (by which I mean, me) thought she was older than she was. She had lost a lot of the extra weight she used to carry and was probably just left with muscle, bone and whipcord. When she asked to come along on this excursion, no one dared deny her. Hers was a personality to be reckoned with and had been shown capable of surviving the end of civilization … twice. I was glad to have her come along for two reasons: her wisdom and the fact that it meant Adaline could stay with a woman on the trip. With Evan coming along—not to mention Tad—there had never been any idea that Adaline and I could engage in hanky-panky (we had remained chaste to that point and had vowed to do so 'til the wedding), but it would have been strange to have five guys and only one female together on the trip.

"You know," Jenny said, "Right over there, there was a pharmacy. I wonder how long people lived here in Frisco?"

"You mean, you wonder if they had time to loot the pharmacy or if we can?" I surmised.

"Sure might be worth looking into," she commented. "We were planning on checking into downtown anyway, right?"

So we mounted the horses and, signaling the other three who had been looking mostly at the lake and in the direction of the old Keystone Ski Area, we made our way off the bluff and into town. We wove among stopped cars and discovered the bones of people who had died in the street. Some were still covered in ash but around some the ash had been blown away. I could see the worry in Adaline's eyes as we passed the skeletons—some of which had a little flesh still clinging to them. "The bones are still together," I commented, though I hadn't necessarily meant to say it out loud.

"And that tells us what?" Adaline asked, a bit of an edge to her voice. I guessed she was just being repulsed by all the death around us, though I had seen far worse in Breckenridge. Maybe I was immune to it, or maybe the fact that they were mostly just bones and not flesh made it look like some old amusement park ride.

"It tells us there are no animals around here. Or, there weren't when the people died," I told her.

"Maybe animals ate the flesh and left the bones," she returned, that edge becoming more pronounced in her voice.

"At the risk of being disgusting, if a wolf tears at a body—whether man or cow or whatever—he rips it to shreds. He doesn't rest the bones in proper order."

She started to retort again, then suddenly said, "And these skeletons are intact. Which means if there are wolves or anything back in this valley, they didn't come back until the flesh had already decayed." In that quick way in which she could change moods, she smiled and added, "See how quickly I learn things?"

We made our way to the pharmacy and were able to find the building fairly quickly. The doors were still unlocked and we pushed our way past the mats that had been pushed up against them, presumably to keep the ash out. Other than being covered with a fine layer of ash and dust, the aisles looked to me to be undisturbed.

"This bugs me," Evan commented, blowing the dust off a rack of greeting cards.

"What's that, Pop?" Adaline asked, going over to where he stood and looking at the cards with him.

"Not the cards, honey," he said. "It's this place. I almost wish it were looted."

"But why?"

"Because an unlooted pharmacy tells me everyone in this entire valley is dead. When the power's out and you're scrabbling to live, what do you grab? Food, warm clothes, and—"

"And pharmaceuticals," she completed. She looked around and said, "This is an extension of the valley we were in, Pop. So us and the Hutchisons and the Sukigaras are the only people who made it out of here alive?"

"We sure haven't seen any signs of anyone else."

"How many people lived here?" Adaline asked him. He shrugged, then looked to where Aunt Jenny and I stood nearby.

Aunt Jenny answered, "Actually lived here? Between Breck, Frisco and Dillion, anywhere from sixty thousand to a hundred thousand. Summer weekend? Could have been twice that many again staying here—pretty good crowds of skiers during Christmas and spring break, too."

"And they're all gone," Adaline commented softly.

I made my way to the back counter, still without seeing anyone. I pushed through doors to the back room and found that, as at the hotel in Breckenridge, everyone had taken shelter in the back. I found the dead bodies of seven people, two of whom were wearing lab coats and badges saying they were pharmacists, another in an apron like maybe she had run the checkout stand out front, and four more I took to have been patrons when the ash cloud hit. They were all wearing those little paper masks, I guess hoping it would filter out the ash. Probably not counting on the air disappearing entirely.

"Wish we could have come over here with Doc Pormon," Aunt Jenny said as she pushed past the rolled up mats by the backroom doors. "There's stuff here that would cure just about anything we might catch, but I sure don't know medicine. You?"

I shook my head, wondering if anyone back home knew meds. I picked up a bottle and, reading the label, said, "Whatever this was for, it expired two years ago. This one over here doesn't expire until next month, but doesn't say what it does. Might fight inflammation—"

"Or loosen your bowels," Aunt Jenny said with a rueful chuckle.

"I guess we could at least grab some of the basics, like antacids and stuff. Maybe some of the aspirins might still be good," I suggested.

"Yeah," Aunt Jenny agreed with a nod. She looked around and said, "We might have the means back here to do all kinds of good—"

"Or accidentally poison each other."

She looked at me and nodded. We went back out into the store part of the pharmacy and found the others reaching the same conclusion. Ron was holding up a dusty package and saying, "This would have been great to have two winters ago. Wish I knew what happens to this stuff when it passes it's 'use by' date. Does it become useless? Is it just a government rule but the stuff is still good? Can we risk finding out?"

"I bet the pharmacist has some manuals back there," Adaline suggested. "Would they tell stuff like that?"

Her father replied, "Probably, if we knew how to look everything up. Is it listed by brand name or by the actual medicine name? The question is, how long do we want to hang out in this town to find out? Besides this place giving me the creeps, I remember what it was like breathing this dust every day and I don't think it's healthy."

So we grabbed up some bottles of antacid and some pain killers that hadn't yet expired—or weren't expired by more than a year—lots of bandages, and went back out to the horses. I took a wet sponge and began cleaning out the r nostrils and the other riders followed my lead. As we made our way back to what had once been highway 9, I said, "Do we try some day to make it over the pass and into Georgetown? Or what about the other way and into Vail?"

It was Tad who answered, "I don't see the value either way. No one's been on the road, so those places are probably as dead as here."

"Maybe they're just staying in a valley like ours," Adaline suggested.

I hated to argue with her, so what I said I tried to make it sound friendly. "It's not in man's nature to stay in one place. We have a good valley, and a good life there, yet we six came in search of—of who knows what? Maybe we thought we'd find an even better valley, or other people. Or maybe it's just in our genes to get out and look, to see what's over the next mountain. I think your brother's right: the people of Georgetown and Vail are dead. If they weren't, I think we would have seen their tracks as they did what we have done and came to this valley."

"People in Georgetown would probably be more likely to make their way to Denver than here," Aunt Jenny injected. "The ash and winds came from the west, so they might have just assumed everything west of them was toast, so they would have headed towards Denver. By that same token, if there's anyone left in Vail, and if they started exploring, they would come this way, I'd think."

"Should we leave them a note?" Ron asked, speaking for the first time in a while. "Like you guys left for us in Breck?"

I answered, "I don't plan on coming all the way back here any time soon, maybe ever. Still, it might not hurt to leave a note or some kind of marking in case people ever come by this way. Let them know they aren't alone."

"Do we really want them coming to us, though?" Tad asked. He looked around and offered, "Might be bad people."

"If they're humans, I think we owe it to them and us to try and help," I countered. "Come on. Let's go over to the main intersection. We'll leave some kind of a marker there. If anyone comes on it, they'll at least know they aren't the last people left on earth."

"Who'd come after all this time?" Evan snorted derisively.

"We did, Pop," Adaline told him.

"Good point," he conceded.

That night, after gathering up a sackfull of instruments and strings and reeds from the music store, and leaving a message carved into a board and set at the crossroads, we had camped at the foot of the Boreas Pass road in Breckenridge. The others were asleep, but Adaline and I were still up, huddled next to the fire, as young people in love are wont to do. The day had been warm, but once the heat had dissipated, we had been left with a cool evening and the fire felt good. It was also fun to watch it, sitting there with her head on my shoulder.

I had found the trip back through the Blue River Valley, heading towards Breckenridge, to be much better than the one going towards Frisco. I hadn't seen it at the time, but things had gotten more gray and bleak as we made our way to Frisco, but looking back towards Breckenridge there was actually some green to be seen. Not like the old days, of course, but a green sprig here and there was a welcome sight in a sea of gray. Compared to Frisco, Breck looked like a garden. It made me appreciate our green little valley on the other side of the mountains even more.

Whispering, so as not to wake the others, I asked, "Did I ever tell you about my Aunt Marianne?"

"No," she replied, in a voice that made me think she might have been asleep, or almost there.

"I never met her—she died long before I was born, I'm guessing. Anyway, my grandfather met her. And she—well, you're going to say this is crazy, but she predicted all this."

Adaline stirred slightly and asked, "All what?"

"The end of the world. The ash cloud. Well, she didn't exactly predict it. She just told my grandfather that, one day, something was going to shut off our valley from the rest of the world, and that most people in the world would die. But, she told him that if we stayed together, and kept having kids and all, one day the Overstreet family would save the world."

Adaline raised her head, looked me in the eye, then asked, "How much of this are you making up? Campfire story, right?"

"Wrong. Or, no. I'm not making it up. My grandfather swears—swore—an aunt or cousin of his named Marianne showed up when he was really young and told him that. He said he thought it was crazy, but she made him promise to tell his kids and grandkids. I can still remember the day he told me and Rusty—"

"Rusty's your brother, right?"

293

"Yeah. Wish you could have met him."

"Me, too."

Trying to lighten the moment, I said, "Wish I could have met Marianne, too."

"You think she was telling the truth? You think she really saw the future?"

"Don't know. Kind of hopeful, though." Her hands were on my arm, so I patted them with my other hand and said, "If she could see the future, you might want to think about what that means for you."

She was back to leaning against me and, without even opening her eyes, asked, "And what would that be?"

"If the people who one day save the world are named Overstreet, and I'm the last Overstreet, that means they're your children or grandchildren."

"Praise God for Aunt Marianne, then," she whispered before kissing me on the cheek and, I'm pretty sure, going back to sleep.

In all the trip, we six people had been the only people seen. Hadn't even seen any signs of people. That was true as we went home, too. The sky was wide and blue that day, that beautiful color one only sees in the mountains, but it was still not broken by a vapor trail or even a weather balloon. At least, unlike previous summers, we saw a few birds in the sky. Still no man-made objects, though.

In all, we had been gone a week. The people of Overstreet were happy to see us, and excited about the aspirin, but disappointed that we had seen no signs of human life. There was talk about trying to make the trek over Kenosha Pass and into Bailey—hinting that if we went that far we might as well go on into Denver—but no one was in a hurry to make the trip. Jonathan and Alexa had made it to Red Hill Pass while we were gone—just making a day trip of it— and had reported that no life could be seen where Fairplay had once stood. The air didn't seem dead, like Claire and I had experienced, they said, but they assured all listening that they could see no sign of movement or human occupancy. Someone suggested we take that way and go into the Springs, but there was less enthusiasm for that venture than for the one to Denver and the idea died.

I should probably say it went dormant. We had no good reason to go to Denver or Colorado Springs, but I believed what I had said about human nature and figured, one of these days, we would try it.

For that summer, though, there was too much to be done and I felt a little guilty to not only have missed out on the work, but to have taken so many good workers with me. We had a 4th of July party as usual, complete with eating and dancing, but most of the month was filled with working the gardens, trying to push back on the ash and give ourselves more grazing land, and diverting the Tarryall into holding ponds. The kiln was up and running and Howard and Danica had figured out a way to use fired pots in a water filtration system that we all appreciated. We built on to houses, built new houses for Claire and family and the Sukigaras, and added a second greenhouse. And most evenings, if the rains didn't move in, we got out on the pasture and played baseball. That may sound strange, what with all we were facing, but I think we needed the release more than the exercise. Even those who didn't play would come out and cheer (or razz) the players, bringing drinks and sometimes food and making a picnic of it. In the old days we probably would have spent the evenings watching TV or going to restaurants; I had to figure this was better for our town and probably even better for the individuals.

I got to go on a lot of walks with Adaline, and we spent many an hour just talking, but I did wish for more "dating opportunities" at times. On the whole, though, it was a great summer. Oh, we had a squabble here and there, but from what I had ever seen, ours was one of the most harmonious relationships around. We weren't ignoring problems, we were both just people who enjoyed simple things and didn't enjoy fighting.

As for that, I was sheriff of the most well-behaved town in history. Occasionally, there would be a disagreement of some sort— over land usage, or a division of labor—but most of those could be settled by the parties involved. A few were brought before and adjudicated by the town council. About the only work I ever got to do to that point as sheriff was to occasionally break up a fight between the kids. Lester Marquez got a hold of some alcohol at one point and I escorted him home before he could start a fight with injudicious words slung here and there, but that was about the most policing I had to do.

August saw the rains come in, almost every afternoon. The first couple times it happens, everyone scrambles to the nearest building to keep from getting wet. After a couple weeks in a row of it happening, you just shrug and go on with what you were doing. The rains made everything smell better … except the people. Days of rain tended to make us smell rather dank. Still, everyone else smelled about the same, so you got used to that, too.

On one particularly rainy day, I happened to see Evan and Inez go into the greenhouse, so I suddenly had the idea to go see them. I tromped through the mud, knocked as much of it off outside as I could, then followed them in. They were the only ones in there (for it was kind of a warm, humid place on such days), so I greeted them then said, "Evan, Inez," (I hadn't been able to bring myself to call them Mom and Pop, no matter how many times they told me to), "I would like to speak to you. Would you—and please tell me if you don't like this idea—but, well, November can be so cold and dreary and, well, I guess we could wait until next spring—and I will if you ask me to, but," I took a breath, realizing I was making a muddle of the carefully worked-out speech in my head, "I would like to ask your permission to marry Adaline sooner, before she turns sixteen."

I think it took them longer to follow my words than to think of their response, for Evan looked at his wife, then asked me, "When were you thinking, Josh?"

"Well, part of me was thinking we're not going to be able to play baseball this evening, so I wouldn't mind—no. Sorry. What I was thinking was, um, maybe around September first?"

"Have you spoken to Adaline about this?" Evan asked sternly.

"No sir. I wanted to speak to you two first, since she is a minor."

"A minor who is three inches taller than me," Inez grumbled, though with a twinkle in her eye. Then, she smiled more openly and said, "I happen to know that the idea will not be rejected by our daughter. And while there was once a time when I would have panicked at the thought of my daughter marrying at fifteen, times have changed. I honestly don't think your minds will change in three months and, you know what, Evan? I agree with Josh here: that deep into fall is kind of a depressing time. Let's have the wedding now, when we can still have some flowers and blue skies."

"Now?" Evan replied, surprised (I was, too). "You mean like now?"

"What? No. I mean, I like Josh's idea of September first. I think that would be good—if these rains have ceased, anyway. But you are her father and I'll defer to any wisdom you may have."

"I notice you don't just assume I have some," he replied with a cocked eyebrow. Then he smiled and said, "I see no reason to object. And, well, I remember when we were courting and, well, once a couple sets a date I know that … temptations come their way." He stuck out his hand and said, "You have treated my daughter with incredible honor, Josh, and I am convinced you always will. You have my blessing."

"Thank you, sir," I said as I took his big paw.

I made my sloshing way through the mud and rain to where the young, green-eyed woman who used to fear horses was walking one of the horses around the barn. "Hey Sheriff!" she called out happily when she saw me. "Come to put me in the calaboose?"

"You've been reading those old Clarence Mulford paperbacks again, haven't you?" I teased before kissing her.

"Not so's you notice," she replied in an especially hickish voice. As she turned her eyes back to the horse, she asked, "What brings you over here on this rainy day?"

Now that the moment was there, I found I had lost my tongue again. I finally managed to ask, "What would you say to getting married September first instead of November twenty-seventh?"

She stopped what she was doing and looked at me. Eventually, she asked, "Are you serious? This isn't some weird joke?"

"Do I often play jokes on you?"

"No. But you're not starting, are you?"

"No. And you're not answering the question."

She dropped the reins of the horse, stepped over to me, and looked deep into my eyes, as if trying to see the back of my head. When I flinched and backed up, she asked, "You didn't actually walk all the way over here thinking I would say no, did you?"

I defended, "I thought you wanted to wait until you were sixteen."

She bumped my forehead with the palm of her hand. "Anyone home? Seriously, Josh?" Then she smiled widely and said, "I would have married you when I was twelve. Fifteen was my Pop's idea and sixteen was yours. You don't think it was random chance that's led me to get your name at Christmas every year, do you? Do you realize that, every year, whoever has drawn your name has started thinking immediately of all the chores they wanted me to do for them because they knew I'd do anything to get your name?" In a more serious tone, she amended, "I say twelve, and I've had a crush on you since then, but I think I fell in love the night you literally held my blood in."

"I think of that night a lot. When I was holding my hand over the wound, I was overwhelmed with the thought that I couldn't stand to lose you. I don't know that I was in love with you then, but I think that was the night I began to fall."

She put her arms around me and told me, "I just thought maybe you thought I was too young or something."

"Well, in the world we grew up in, fifteen year olds can't legally get married."

"Do you want to wait until I'm eighteen?"

"Not especially." Then, I held her at arm's length and added, "But honestly? There is something weird about marrying a fifteen year old. When I say it that way, it's weird. Then, when I'm with you, or when I just think about *you*, Adaline, then I can't think of *not* marrying you."

"Remember how we used to worry, 'What will people think?' Well, Josh, we know what everyone in our world thinks. If we don't, we can poll them in five minutes. I think they're all happy with us getting married. I know your sister is not just OK with it but all for it. It's like she's already my sister. But if you think—for their sake or ours—we should wait until November or next year, I will wait." She furrowed her brow and added, "Maybe not happily, but I will wait."

"How's September first for you?"

"Just perfect, Sheriff," she replied in her country voice (she had roughly a million voices, and could slide in and out of them with amazing ease). Her arm around my shoulder, she jumped up, knowing I would catch her. As I held her off the floor, she asked, "But I guess we ought to go clear it with my—wait, you probably asked them first, didn't you?"

"Am I that predictable?"

"Maybe, but mostly, you're that honorable."

The preparations were made and my sister put all of her seamstress skills to work and produced an absolutely stunning dress for Adaline. It was appropriately white and shone like the sun when the light hit it. Alexa served as matron of honor and I tabbed Tad as my best man. As father of the bride, we asked Evan to perform the ceremony and, as far as we knew, everyone in the world came to the wedding.

A big surprise had been given us when Tad approached us a couple days before the wedding. I had asked him to be my best man already, but I had never gotten up the nerve to ask what he actually thought about the union. I got my answer when he came to us and, handing us a small box, said, "I know wedding gifts are usually given at the reception, but I thought you might want this one now. Or be able to use it."

We opened the box together and Adaline gasped as we saw two gold wedding bands inside. She hugged her brother as I asked, "Is this from the gold you panned?"

"I wish." He chuckled as he said, "Turns out, you can't just melt gold down and pour it into a circle. I'm apparently going to need a mold. I'll work on that for my … anyway, these belonged to our grandparents."

Adaline looked at him suspiciously and asked, "Why would you bring Granny and Grampa's rings on our vacation?" It suddenly seemed like a valid question, for three years ago the Isaacson family had left Phoenix for Breckenridge on what was only supposed to be a two week tour.

Tad nodded in agreement that it was a good question, then answered, "Well, back when Mom and Pop started planning the trip, I was looking on-line for things to do in Breck. I ran across this jeweler who advertised that he could take old jewelry and polish it up and set it in crystal. So I snuck these out of the safe and brought them, thinking I'd get the guy to turn it into something I could give Mom and Dad on their next anniversary. Yes, before you ask, baby sister, I asked Pop if this was OK. So, in a way, call it a gift from all three of us—and Bobby. And, well, I guess they were Jon and David's grandparents, too. So anyway, if you don't already have rings, I'd like to give you these."

Adaline hugged him and I shook his hand and I suddenly felt a weight lifting off my shoulders. I had assumed Tad would tell me if he objected, but this seemed like actually getting his blessing and made me feel much more at ease. I mean, as at ease as a guy who's about to get married can feel.

We had set up chairs in the meadow and an arbor of flowers under which I stood and waited for my bride. I couldn't believe how beautiful Adaline looked when she came down the aisle. I had thought Claire was the prettiest bride ever, until I saw Adaline. As she walked toward me, a hand-picked bouquet of flowers in her hand and her hair back in that style I loved so much, I don't think her feet even touched the grass.

I have no earthly idea what Evan said to us. My ears were ringing and my heart was pounding and my mouth was dry. I'm relatively certain I said "I do" at the right time. I could barely hear Adaline say it, though I could see it in her eyes and her smile. When Evan pronounced us husband and wife, he didn't have to prod me to kiss the bride. The crowd cheered, we got congratulations from everyone we knew, and then we went to the reception. I didn't get the first dance with Adaline at that soirée … because she had saved it for her father. But halfway through the dance, he handed her off to me and I had the next several dances with her. We didn't talk, but spent a lot of time looking into each other's eyes.

Eventually, it wound down and I said I would like to take my new bride to my house. Several border-line comments were made, I and Adaline both blushed, but we went to the cabin anyway. Hutch followed along, playing on guitar, and leading what he called a shivaree. Once I had Adaline in the cabin, I bolted the door, and checked the windows as well. We could still hear them singing outside when I pulled Adaline into a hug and said, "Welcome home, Mrs. Overstreet."

"Why thank you, Sheriff," she whispered in return.

Eventually, we became convinced our friends outside had moved on. So I led Adaline into the bedroom and, well, we did what you would expect a newlywed couple to do.

"I think the earth just moved, Josh."

"It did for me."

"No, I'm serious. I think the earth *moved*."

And then I felt it, too. A shaking of the earth just like we had felt years before, only more powerful.

To read more about Josh, Adaline and the rest of the population of Overstreet, or to drop the author a letter (he responds!!), go to www.garisonfitch.com.

And make sure you check out the other Last Valley *novels:*

- *The Last Valley Book 2 – Crazy on the Mountain*
- *The Last Valley Book 3 – Book of Tales*

To learn how the Overstreet family got started, be sure and read the novel "Overstreet".

You can read about the fulfilment of the Overstreet family prophecy in "All the Time in Our World", "Some of the Time" *and* "A Thousand Miles Away".

About the Author

Samuel "Sam" Ben White is a minister, writer, hospice chaplain and cartoonist living in the Texas panhandle. He has published more than two dozen novels on Kindle (most of them are also in paperback). He loves to read and counts Louis L'Amour, CS Lewis and Agatha Christie among his favorite authors. He also enjoys snow skiing, softball, and Mexican food. He is married, has two sons, as well as more pets than he cares to count.

His comic strip "Tuttle's" is read by thousands every day in newspapers across the Texas panhandle, and on-line at tuttles.net. He also writes a blog concerning time travel, writing, ebooks, faith and related topics, which can be found at garisonfitch.com.

Made in the USA
San Bernardino, CA
18 August 2017